SCALP

CARVER PIKE

AUTHOR'S NOTE AND DEDICATION

Nobody hates head lice like parents and teachers, so I'd like to dedicate this one to the parents and school nurses who've had to sit and shampoo – not to mention comb through – a kid's head while he or she whined and cried. To the teachers who've cringed while watching a student scratch his or her head... all while the student in the next seat over is leaning closer to borrow a pencil. Head lice come straight from hell and you're all on that demon-slaying frontline. God bless y'all.

Next, I'd like to thank all the ladies who picked through this book and found all my leftover mistakes and errors. Thank you for helping me clean up my work. Thank you Autumn S., Mary H., Stephanie A., Fran R., Beverly S., and Kaye K. for all your hard work on this book. I couldn't have done it without you.

Thank you Lisa-Lee Tone at Bibliophilia Templum for all the reviews you've done on my books and for spreading the word about my work. You rock.

To Jules for making me believe my happiness matters. For believing in me, for cheering with me on good days, and for helping me through the rough ones. I love you, baby.

To my kids. I miss you guys so damn much, I love you, and I think about you every day. We'll be together again soon. I promise.

To my blended family, thank you for accepting a stranger into your world and treating me like one of your own.

Now, let's let the head itching begin.

1

When Andre Pete put a bullet into a stag, he felt his fist travel along with the slug and reach through the animal's pelt, sizzle past its meat, and grab hold of its heart. Andre was one with his rifle, one with his bullet, and one with the animal. Hunting was religion to him. It cleansed his soul and elevated his psyche. Like a drug shot straight into his system or a drink that was downed so quickly it sank into the bones, taking something's life was on a whole other level. He was a king out here in the woods.

But today, he felt different. The world around him seemed *off*. The forest was too quiet. Since he and his cousin Carl entered the woods, he hadn't heard a sound other than his own boots crunching down on fallen leaves. Even the wind seemed to cease. Its usual whoosh through the trees was barely a calm rattle. The sun was beginning its decline and would plunge them into darkness in a little under a half-hour. Darkness didn't bother him, usually, but Andre couldn't help thinking they should wrap up this trip and head back to the truck.

It's so damn quiet.

Where were the birds? Where were the frogs? Where were the damn woodpeckers?

Andre would have even been fine with the shaking of a copperhead tail trying to convince him it was a rattlesnake. He'd seen plenty of both kinds of snakes. They didn't bother him none, so he tried his best not to bother them. Right now, he wished he heard a hiss. Or a growl of some other animal. Anything to assure him everything was normal. His gut told him something was wrong, and his gut was usually right.

It was right during basic training the night Floyd plucked the tiny razor blade out of his disposable razor and tried to off himself.

It was right the night he came home from Korea to find his buddy's truck in the driveway. Susan had been fucking him for months.

It was right when those three men at the bar kept eyeballing him. They'd jumped him in the parking lot when he'd been too drunk to defend himself. He'd cracked two ribs that night and suffered a concussion.

Now, his gut told him to get out of the woods and go home. He hadn't listened to it any of those other times. Perhaps this was the time he should.

Something ain't right.

Yet, the deer was lined up in his rifle scope and all he had to do was take the shot. He'd done it a hundred times. Maybe even a thousand. Not only on animals but on humans too. This stag was different though. It wasn't standing still like it should have been. It was shaking its head around wildly like a swarm of bees was attacking it.

Andre saw no bees. He saw nothing irregular other than the deer going batshit crazy.

"What's wrong with eem?" Carl asked, his strong southern drawl seeping into his whisper.

Andre ignored him and focused on his breathing. When the moment was right, he held his breath as he squeezed the trigger.

"Got eem," his cousin, Carl, announced. "Got eem good, Cuz."

Andre wasn't sure about the hit. Like everything else, it didn't feel right. Usually, when he struck something, a red mist erupted from it. This time, the deer just collapsed as soon as he'd pulled the trigger. All its wild head thrashing stopped, and it dropped to the ground. That didn't seem right at all.

"Looks like dinner tonight," Carl continued.

"Keep it down," Andre said.

"But you got eem."

"Did I?"

"Sure looked it."

It looked more like I hit a slab of frozen beef.

Carl high-stepped, dancing his "we nailed it" jig, all the way to the carcass. "This gon' be dinner, yessir."

His cousin was still a full-bred country boy, straight from their West Virginia holler. He even bore the scar to prove it. It cut across his left cheek and served as a reminder that teenagers should never ride lawn mowers drunk. He should have never been drunk in the first place, but his daddy made moonshine for a living and made so much of it he often lost track of a bottle or two.

Carl fully embraced small-town living. Andre, however, had outgrown the lifestyle. He'd joined the U.S. Marine Corps, learned to shoot properly, and was only home because he'd injured his leg and didn't want to serve in Uncle Sam's elite forces if he wasn't up to par. He had too much pride to ride a desk or teach. He knew the saying. Those who can't, teach. Even if he couldn't, he wouldn't.

Carl was right though. He'd sniped that buck.

Where is the blood?

"Carl, step away from it," he ordered, this time digging deep and finding the loud, commanding voice he'd used in the battlefield.

Like an obeying soldier, Andre's cousin backed up a step or two and waited for Andre to meet him a few feet from the dead animal.

"It looks weird," Carl said.

He was right. From up close, Andre could see no blood seeped from the bullet wound, but a hundred or so minuscule red dots covered its fur. It looked like it had been bombarded with tiny pinpricks or syringe injections. Its eyes were white, cloudy, like both were plagued with cataracts. "I don't like it. Leave it."

"Leave it? Are you nuts? You're fixin' to waste all that meat?"

"Carl, leave it. Some things ain't worth the hassle. I got a bad feeling about it. Might have caught something. Rabies or whatnot. Look at the eyes."

If he could take back the order, he would, but it was too late, and he'd already started to turn away from the deer when he heard Carl say, "Damn, look at them puppies. Its eyes are freaky, ain't they?"

Andre turned back to his cousin, who was holding a stick and was about to jab one of the eyeballs.

"Don't touch it," Andre warned, but he was too late.

Before the stick came in contact with the animal, a strange skittering sound emanated from it, like a bunch of pissed off crickets had been shoved inside the animal's gut and were ready to be freed.

"Carl!" Andre yelled.

His cousin glanced back at him with his face scrunched up in confusion, and as he did, his stick touched the deer's gelatinous eyeball. Like he'd pushed a trick button in some cursed tomb, it released something.

FSSSSST!

The skittering sound grew louder and angrier. A black cloud burst forth from the animal's fur and shot toward Carl.

Carl screamed, dropped his rifle to the ground, and spun in circles.

"Get it off me!" Carl yelled.

Andre rushed to his cousin's side, but he didn't get any closer when he saw the cloud dissipate. It sank right into Carl's head. The man stopped spinning and stared back at Andre with a look of confusion. His brow furrowed. His mouth twisted and his eyes blinked rapidly.

Carl breathed deeply.

Sighed.

Groaned.

His eyes rolled back, and his hands shot to his head where he clawed at his hair.

He groaned again, but he didn't scream. His fingernails dug into his scalp and thin trails of blood ran down his forehead and from the sides of his head over his ears. His face was a scarlet chandelier.

Andre moved around his cousin and saw blood trickle down the collar of his shirt. It was like an invisible crown of thorns had been slammed onto his head so hard it planted itself there and sent a crimson cascade flowing down.

The man's mouth opened so wide it seemed his lips might stretch over his nose and chin. He wanted to cry out, but all that came was a guttural sound like someone had pressed against his stomach and let loose an agonizing gasp.

"Carl," Andre said. It was all he could think to say. He couldn't ask if the man was all right because he clearly wasn't all right.

His hands remained at his head and his fingers dug through his hair so hard and so fast it seemed the flesh beneath it was starting to tear away. He scraped at his scalp with the frantic intensity of a dog digging up a bone. Finally, his gasp transformed into a scream. His shriek was so loud it would have driven away any living creature in the forest if they hadn't already fled the scene.

Andre stepped back and stumbled over a tree branch lying across the forest floor. Even as he tripped and struggled to regain his balance, his eyes never left his cousin. Blood rained down from Carl and Andre knew if he hadn't already, his fingernails would soon reach his skull.

Carl dropped to his knees, looked up to the sky, and kept clawing at his head. Andre winced from the man's screams and for a second, he considered putting a bullet into him to ease his pain. It was only a fleeting thought, as he could never shoot his kin, but the agony his cousin was in was undeniable.

Then, as sudden as it had come on, it seemed as if the pain had been plucked away.

Carl's arms went slack, falling to his sides like two dropped bags of groceries. His mouth remained open for a moment before he clamped his jaws shut. His eyes were watery, and his face seemed frozen in a post-stroke grimace. Drool slipped from his lips and Andre thought he looked like a patient in an insane asylum who'd been given a lobotomy.

When Andre backed up a few steps, Carl shimmied forward on his knees, creeping closer.

"Carl stop," Andre said as he took a few more steps back.

His cousin obeyed, then reached up to scratch his head again.

"You ain't right, cousin," Andre said. "I don't know what's wrong with you, but we need to get you some help. And you gotta quit scratchin' your head like that. You're gonna hurt yourself really bad."

Carl moved closer on his knees a couple of steps.

"Hey now! I said stop!"

Carl didn't listen. He lifted his right knee and set it down in the mud a few inches further.

"Carl!" Andre yelled, now lifting his gun in his cousin's direction. "Please."

Carl stopped.

"I don't know what's happened to you, man, but this ain't right. You do what I say, and I won't shoot you, but if you come any closer, you're gonna force me to put a bullet in you. A bullet I can't take back. So, please, cuz, do what I tell ya. Walk toward the truck."

Carl nodded. Then he slowly lifted one leg and put his foot down on the ground. He did the same with the other. He rose sluggishly and smiled. Andre had known his cousin all his life, and he'd never seen a grin like this one.

"Go on," Andre said, eyeballing the rifle Carl dropped when the black cloud descended on him. He wasn't sure if he should pick it up. He didn't want to touch anything that had come in contact with the man.

It was that fucking deer. Why did he have to touch that fucking deer?

"Carl, walk to the truck."

Carl hadn't said a word since he'd touched the deer with that stick. He was either in a serious stupor, the way he was whenever he got involved with the other meth heads in town, or he'd screamed so loud he'd damaged his vocal cords and couldn't speak. Andre could see that being the case. He'd never heard a scream like that before.

From behind, Andre marched his cousin out of the woods. He was acutely aware, once again, of the silence, and he wondered if everything else in this forest was as afraid as he was right now. Were the birds hiding out in the tree limbs? Were the frogs burrowing into the mud? Were the bears taking their cubs far away from this place? That deer should have followed them.

Carl stepped carefully ahead of him, like a drunk man trying to fake his way through a field sobriety test. If Andre were a cop, he'd definitely haul his drunk ass in. It was his erratic behavior. The way his fingers opened and closed, and his head shook back and forth like he was vehemently disagreeing with someone unseen. He kept scratching his head, and his skin seemed to have a slight sheen to it like he was sweating even though they hadn't done any uphill hiking or anything else strenuous.

At this point, Andre wasn't thinking of *it* as his cousin anymore.

It was a *thing*.

Something he might hunt given the opportunity.

You ain't never hunted anything like this before.

"Keep going," Andre said, only because he felt the need to break the silence.

That awful quiet.

Some folks prayed for an end to the noise, for a chance to experience a total hush, but not Andre. He hated it. Ever since he was pushed into a swimming pool as a kid and suffered the complete and utter quiet of being underwater and realizing he should have learned to swim the previous summer. A bigger boy saved his life. Come to think of it, that boy was Carl. This sudden realization brought with it a surge of hope. He wasn't going to call an ambulance once they reached the road and better phone reception. He was going to drive his cousin to the hospital himself.

Perhaps he'd been concentrating too hard on the past because Andre didn't even realize Carl had turned around and was staring at him. The sun was a dull pastel orange at this point. The tree branches up and behind Carl were black at this angle. They were charcoal limbs of skeletal beasts ready to pounce on him. Carl was their leader, and he grinned back at Andre with the excitement of a madman.

"Turn around!" Andre ordered.

Carl laughed.

"I'm warning you, cousin. Turn around, or I'll be forced to—"

Carl leaped at him, and Andre reacted as quickly as his injured leg would allow. He limped backward, raised his rifle, and shot his cousin in his right thigh. As the man pitched forward, Andre saw something small and black fall from the top of his head, like dark dandruff. It hit the ground, and Andre imagined it crawling toward him, whatever it was. It had to be a part of that black cloud he'd seen earlier.

"Stay back!" Andre yelled.

Carl groaned, but he didn't cry out the way any other man would when taking a bullet to the leg.

"I fuckin' told you to turn around, Carl. Why'd you do that, dammit?"

Carl rose to his hands and knees. On all fours, he glanced up at Andre with saliva dripping from his lips. His eyes were bloodshot red. He had to be in pain, yet his face didn't register it.

Andre remembered taking several bullets to his leg and the pain he felt. Searing hot coals like the Lord himself reached into his leg and planted them there. It hurt like hell.

Carl smiled up at him again.

"Get to your feet and keep walking," Andre tried again.

He knew, without a doubt, that his cousin would be able to stand and walk again, even with a bullet in his leg. Whatever was wrong with him had given him a newfound strength. Like Andre thought, Carl rose to his feet. For a second, it looked like he might try to lunge at him again, but then he turned and continued walking.

They reached Andre's Chevy pickup as the sun waved its final goodnights and plunged them into darkness. Carl continued onto the paved road like he didn't even recognize the truck. For a moment, Andre watched his cousin stumble onto the street, showing none of the wisdom ingrained in him since he was a kid. All the times Aunt Becky told them not to go wandering in the street. To stick to the sidewalks or the sides of the roads. "Drunks and pedophiles are drivin' around everywhere!" she'd warned them. They never walked down the center of the street, but there Carl was, right smack dab in the middle of it, walking to nowhere in particular.

"Carl!" Andre yelled.

The man that used to be his cousin stopped walking.

"Carl!" he tried again.

Carl turned around but didn't look directly at him. It was almost like he couldn't see him. It seemed to get dark faster than usual. Andre didn't want to be out here with Carl at all, and he dreaded the darkness. He feared it, and Andre had never feared anything before.

As he stood there and watched the Carl thing look around in every direction except the right one, Andre wondered if he should simply leave the man out here by himself. If he did, he could go home, shower, and forget this day ever happened.

This is your cousin, man. He's family. You can't leave him out here like this.

If it were anybody else, he knew he would have fled the scene, but this was his big cousin. As dimwitted as Carl was, and as many times as Andre had to pull him out of a drugged-up or drunken stupor, he would never be frustrated enough or *afraid* enough to leave him stranded or in harm's way.

"Carl," Andre said once more. "I'm over here, buddy."

His cousin seemed to home in on his voice and began to walk toward him. The shadows covered his face, and Andre was thankful they did. He knew what he'd see if they didn't. That crazed, drool-dripping grin.

"Carl, listen to me," Andre said. "I want you to climb into the back of my truck. Go ahead. Get in there in the bed."

Andre expected to see bloody footprints leading to his truck, but there were none. There wasn't nearly enough blood. His cousin should have been bleeding out at this point. If it were any other man in any other situation, Andre would have put a tourniquet on him, but he wouldn't dare get close enough to his cousin to try that.

As Carl slid into the back of the truck, only a light smear stretched from the tailgate to the back where Carl had propped himself up.

Andre moved to the door of the truck. "The other side," he said. "Move to the other side. I ain't lettin' you get near me."

Carl didn't budge.

"Get to the other side of the fuckin' truck, Carl!" Andre ordered.

He was losing his shit. He'd wanted to beat the darkness and he'd already lost that battle. Now, he was stuck out here with this crazed lunatic cousin of his.

Luckily, Carl obeyed and slid to the passenger side of the bed. Andre glanced at the truck frame and made sure nothing had moved from his cousin to the metal. It was some kind of bug. He'd seen the black cloud leap from the deer to his cousin's head.

That shit ain't happenin' to me. Fuck these bugs or whatever they are.

When he finally got in the truck, he locked both doors and made sure both windows were rolled up tight. He nearly forgot the small window that led to the truck bed. He locked it too. Through it, he could see his cousin sitting there staring up at the sky. That stupid smile was still on his mouth.

Andre tossed his rifle onto the seat next to him. Carl's was still out there in the woods. That was another reason he knew his cousin wasn't his cousin anymore. The *real* Carl would have never left his rifle behind like that. He would have thrown a fit if Andre didn't let him bring it with them. This *thing* sitting behind him wasn't normal.

The hospital was a good forty-five miles away, so Andre stepped on the gas and planned to speed the entire way. He only needed to make it back to Clydesville. The hospital there wasn't huge like major cities, but it would do. All he wanted to do was drop Carl off so he could say he'd done the right thing.

And you want to get him help.

Of course, he wanted his cousin to get help, but deep down he didn't believe it was possible. Something was seriously wrong with him. A hundred movies he'd seen flashed through his mind.

In The Blob, a meteor crashed and when a homeless man poked at it with a stick, it leaped onto him.

In Night of the Creeps, slugs jumped into people's mouths and turned them into zombies.

In The Thing... Oh, God, so many bad things happened in The Thing.

None of the people in any of those movies was saved in a hospital, but that was where Andre was headed. He looked in the rearview mirror and saw Carl still seated in the back. Still staring at the sky. The way he sat reminded Andre of an animal. Hunched over but seeming to enjoy the wind the way a dog does when it sticks its head out a car window.

Andre felt like he wasn't in the real world. He'd felt that way all afternoon. Since he'd noticed how silent the woods were. Now, he wished another car would fly past him on the road. At least that would remind him he wasn't alone in the world.

All was silent, and that kind of deep quiet wasn't Andre's friend. Too many thoughts came with the absence of sound. He glanced in the rearview mirror. Carl was still looking at the sky.

The stereo can fix the silence.

He mashed his palm against the stereo dial and it instantly came to life right in the middle of the song he and Carl had been listening to when they parked the truck. 'Big River' by Johnny Cash played and its upbeat, guitar picking sound instantly livened up Andre's mood.

Andre was thrumming his fingers against the steering wheel when he glanced in the rearview mirror again. Carl's face filled the space, grinning back at him from the other side of the glass. Andre jumped, jerked the wheel, and nearly took them off the road.

The pickup kicked up gravel as it slid over the side of the road and then arched back onto the street.

"Jesus!" Andre yelled.

Carl's palm slapped the window softly like he wanted to get Andre's attention.

"What is it, Carl?" Andre asked. "I damn near killed us both."

Carl's hand curled into a fist and knocked slowly and steadily.

Knock… knock… knock…

"Cut it out and sit still!"

Knock… knock… knock…

Through the rearview mirror, Andre could see his cousin staring back at him, grinning. His knuckles tapped at the glass. Soft at first. Then a little harder and harder still.

"Carl, stop!"

Knock… knock… knock…

"I'm taking you to the hospital so you can get help with your leg," he reminded the man in the bed of the truck.

He wasn't sure if the words got through the glass, especially with the commotion of Carl's persistent knocking and Johnny Cash belting out his tune. He considered shutting off the music, but that would leave him alone with Carl's noise. This *thing* behind him was pounding on the glass, and Andre knew they wouldn't make it to the hospital.

"I said stop it, dammit!" he yelled, losing his cool.

The pounding ceased. The truck engine grumbled as Andre pushed the gas pedal down harder. He didn't care if he got pulled over by cops. He'd prefer it actually. Anything to stop him from being alone with the *thing* in the back of his truck.

He had to be pushing eighty miles per hour when the real thumping started. Carl pounded against the window with a heavy fist.

It spiderwebbed, starting at the center with small cracks spreading out.

Andre had to make a decision fast. He could slam on the brakes, hop out, and if he was quick enough he might be able to put a few more bullets in his cousin, or he could keep driving and hope Carl wouldn't be able to do much damage to him from the bed of the truck.

The Carl thing decided for him when he slammed his head against the glass, and it shattered. Andre, in an attempt to grab his gun and stay away from the *thing,* let go of the wheel for only a second. The truck was moving too quickly down the highway. It cut left and flipped.

Tires screeched.

The truck went over with a loud thwomp.

Andre was weightless and then he wasn't.

Weightless and then he wasn't.

Weightless and then he wasn't.

The truck kept tumbling as it tore through the guardrail and plummeted down the side of the mountain. It was a small decline. Metal struck rock and the truck jerked to a halt in a small ravine. If he'd been wearing a seatbelt, Andre would have been upside down with the rest of the truck, but he'd turned halfway and now lay on his back.

Andre's ears rang and Johnny Cash sang 'God's Gonna Cut You

Down.' It was an odd thing, thinking about the change in song, but he realized he'd never heard the track switch. One second Carl was drumming on the back window, way offbeat, to 'Big River.' Now God was going to cut him down. And it felt that way. Every bone in his body ached.

He didn't see where the Carl thing went. He would have been flung far away with the truck's first flip. This couldn't be the end of it though. That thing was strong. It would continue after him, Andre had no doubt, and his current position wasn't the best to be in when that happened.

If he remained in this spot, he would die. He was sure of it. For a moment, and it was only the briefest of moments, he considered accepting his death and riding it out. Every inch of his body hurt. Death would be the easiest way. Yet, he'd seen what Carl had become, and death no longer seemed certain to him.

"Fuck," Andre muttered through his torn, tattered lip.

His teeth had bit through it and his cheek was sliced open. The copper tang of blood filled his mouth. But he could move his arms and legs. That was a good thing. He was alive. Maybe the Carl thing wasn't. Dragging himself free of the truck cab wreaked havoc on his body. Everything in the truck was crushed. The frame was bent so badly he could barely fit his body through the driver's side window. The front windshield and the passenger side were mangled.

He was nearly out of the truck when he saw his rifle outside on the ground. It was a miracle. That thing could have flown out anywhere, but it landed here beside the truck. It gave him a new sense of hope like he might actually stand a chance out here.

2

This is bad. You don't get up and walk away from something like this.

Halogen Williams wasn't liking his first night on shift. As a new park ranger, it was his duty to make sure nothing bad happened in these woods, and a wrecked pickup with a missing driver would be considered *bad* to most people. Things of this nature didn't really fall under his responsibilities, so he was glad when the state troopers showed up.

"You said I had a boring area," Hal said as he spit a black wad of tobacco onto the muddy ground.

Last night, Hal had ridden around with his boss, Gus, during an unofficial – which really meant unpaid – practice run. Gus was an asshole by nature and wasn't too shy to admit he was ready to pawn this "shitty shift" off on Hal.

"What's so shitty about it?" Hal had asked.

"What's not? It's boring here. You ain't gonna see no college girls skinny dippin' in these parts of the woods. Nope. It's all quiet nights with the animals and insects."

"Well, I'll do my best to keep this part of the park safe and clean."

Stonewall National Park was a labyrinth of dirt roads zipping between Virginia pines, slippery elms, green ash, and a handful of other trees. It came complete with a couple of rivers, two lakes, and the old Stonewall Forge battleground now turned into a field trip destination during the more pleasant months of the year. The rest of the time, it was nothing more than a set of abandoned buildings.

This week was one of the biggest conferences Stonewall Forge hosted. Some kind of teenage leadership thingamajig. Hal didn't know much about it, and he didn't care to. As long as they stayed on the campus, they would be safe from wildlife, and he wouldn't have to get involved much.

Now, standing in front of the crushed pickup, Hal was reminded of his days on the police force. He'd only worked a few years in Nashville before deciding law enforcement wasn't for him. Lawmaking wasn't what it looked like on TV, and he wasn't going to be able to outrun his dead wife and daughter's memory by pulling over speeders, arresting drunks, and fighting with gangbangers. When he was a young cop in Summersville, West Virginia, he'd been good at it, but those days were gone. It just wasn't in him anymore.

He'd moved back to his wife's hometown of Clydesville to face his demons. This was where *it* happened. Sheila had always loved it here, they both had, and he had no other place to go. So he returned. Life moved at a much slower pace here than it did in Nashville. Even slower than it did in Summersville. It was almost painfully slow, but he'd decided he liked it this way.

"You done shined that light of yours on a real mess here, Halogen," Gus said. Hal had only known the man a couple of days and he was already sick of his light bulb jokes. "You really illuminated this shit-show," he continued.

"Funny," Hal replied.

"Your parents done slapped a real doozy of a name on you, didn't they?"

"My dad was drunk, and my mom was high when they decided on it."

"And they couldn't have changed it when they were sober?"

"Apparently they both liked the name and thought it was a good idea."

"Well, it wasn't."

Hal glanced right at the older, self-righteous asshole. Gus clamped his mouth shut, which was good for him. Hal wasn't one to mess with. Clydesville was a small town and he already had that reputation. For some reason, Gus seemed to think his position of authority over him gave him the right to throw verbal jabs in his direction.

"Keep it up," Hal warned him.

"Oh, don't get your panties in a bunch. Come on. Let these troopers take over this mess. Ain't got nothin' to do with us anyhow."

It just so happened the highway was where Halogen's area ended, but the truck had flipped right into his zone of responsibility, or ZOR as Gus liked to call it. There wasn't much a park ranger could do in this situation, so Hal was lucky enough to walk away from it. Yet, it bothered him.

Where is the driver of the truck? And what would make him flip like that?

Had to be alcohol. Nothing would make a man run away from his own wrecked vehicle like drunkenness. If Hal were a betting man, he'd say the cops would get a call later that this truck was stolen. It wasn't, but the owner would claim it was so he could walk away free from blame. If the cops had any sense about them, they'd see the driver's bruised and battered face and know he'd been driving the truck when it flipped.

That had to be the case. The driver had gone home to sleep off his drunken stupor. Tomorrow was Saturday. By Sunday those bruises would surely set in and Hal wondered if he'd see somebody around town who looked like runover dogshit. That would be the driver. The funny thing about small towns is you can never keep a secret for long.

Hal liked Clydesville though. He liked West Virginia as a whole. Sure, he'd left to try that short stint in Nashville, but he was home now, and he liked this small town. Everyone was polite. Well, everyone except Gus. People here nodded hello to each other in Walmart. They helped one another in times of need.

They tried to help you when Sheila and Susanna were taken from you.

Hal walked with Gus back to their trucks parked on the main gravel-covered road that circled the entire park.

"Hey," Gus said. "Remember, the kids are arriving at Stonewall tomorrow. Don't be accidentally shooting anybody thinking they're deer or a bear or whatnot."

"I won't," Hal said.

The truth was, he had no intention of drawing his gun, ever, unless it was absolutely necessary. It was *his* gun that killed Susanna, and it was a gun that killed Sheila as well. It might as well have been the same one. Susanna was only twelve when she pulled the gun on her cousin, Gabe.

Nobody knew why. That was the story, and everyone stuck to it.

But Hal knew the truth. Gabe was fifteen and had a history of perverted ways. He'd tried something with Hal's little girl, and she'd been brave enough to defend herself. That was the truth about what happened. Sheila didn't last very long after that. She blamed Hal. It was his gun after all. She shot herself three months to the day after Susanna died.

Hal wanted to follow suit. He'd almost gone through with it, but he'd been too much of a chicken shit. Sheila had always been the strong one in their relationship. He might have been able to hunt and fish like nobody's business, but she was the one with the true grit. She wore the pants. Now, she was gone.

If it weren't a job requirement, Hal wouldn't even carry a gun. The way he saw it, if a bear wanted to wrestle with him, maybe he'd get lucky and the bear would knock his head clean off his shoulders. That would sure be a way to go. He might not be able to put a bullet in his own skull, but he wasn't afraid of death itself. It might lead him back to his wife and little girl.

Gus assured him he'd probably never need to fire a gun on this job anyway. Some nights he might catch black bears digging in garbage cans, but they were harmless for the most part and could be easily chased off with his truck's horn or siren.

This was an easy job. That was what mattered. It kept him working through the night when he usually woke up drenched in sweat, reliving a moment he wasn't even there to see in person. In his nightmares, Susanna screamed for her life while nasty, now-dead Gabe pulled his teenage pecker out of his pants and stroked it in front of her, telling her she needed to touch it. When she tried to leave the room, he grabbed her and threw her onto the bed. Susanna reached for the gun in the nightstand drawer and pulled it out, but Gabe was quick and almost pinned her down again when the gun went off between them. He took the first bullet in the gut, but his adrenaline was going strong and he forced her to put a bullet in her own stomach next. They both bled out with Susanna crying and calling out to her father.

"Daddy. Daddy. Daddy." He could hear her even now, crying for him as she lay in a puddle of her own blood.

"—You know what I'm saying?" Gus finished saying something.

Hal missed the first part of his question but figured the older man hadn't said anything of any importance, so he nodded his head and added, "Ain't that the truth."

"It sure is," Gus replied.

Whew. Works every time. Ain't that the truth covers just about anything.

"*These kids are running me ragged. They might be the death of me.*"

"*Ain't that the truth.*"

"*Dinner's gonna get cold if we don't hurry up and get home to eat.*"

"*Ain't that the truth.*"

"*That sure is one gorgeous woman.*"

"*Ain't that the truth.*"

"*He is one stubborn son of a bitch.*"

"*Ain't that the truth.*"

Hal stood for a moment and watched as Gus hopped into his truck, fired up the engine, and drove away. His taillights were fading in the distance and the state troopers were picking through the remains of the wreck. For a moment, Hal felt like he was outside of it all. Life felt like that a lot right now. Like he was an observer instead of an active partic-ipant. His reasons for living were long gone and now he was only taking it day by day until the good Lord saw fit to reach down and free him from all *this*.

His eyes scanned the damage once more, and he shook his head, feeling sorry for the poor soul who'd once been inside that truck.

Whoever climbed out of it must be in a world of pain.

Gus was right about one thing. Hal's shift was boring. He patrolled the perimeter road every hour, as expected, and drove the interior maze of dirt and gravel during the time in between. At a little after two o'clock in the morning, he parked near one of the lakes and ate his dinner. It was during that time, when he had his windows rolled down and was enjoying the cool breeze coming off the water, he heard splashing.

Giggles.

More splashing.

There wasn't supposed to be anyone in this part of the park. Not right now anyway. It was too close to the Stonewall Forge campus. Kids would be arriving, if they hadn't already, way too close to here. This was the kind of nonsense that could get him in trouble on his first night.

Hal blew out a breath and stepped out of the truck. It occurred to him that he could drive away right now and pretend he hadn't heard anything. If he'd never taken his lunch break here, or if he'd driven away even five minutes earlier, he would have had no idea anyone was back here. Pretending was easy.

If you turn your head once, you'll turn it a hundred more times.

It wasn't adults he was worried about. If those kids had arrived at Stonewall Forge, some of them could be sneaking away for some nighttime skinny dipping. That was something he would have done when he was in high school. Water moccasins, copperheads, and rattlesnakes were around these parts. God forbid a kid get bit on his watch. That would be bad. First, a truck takes a tumble off the highway and then a snakebite incident?

No, thank you.

With his flashlight out in front of him, Hal stepped carefully through the brush. The moon was bright overhead but came and went as patches of grey clouds drifted in front of it and then moved on. It was like a strobe light effect. The moon blinked at him in Morse code.

Another giggle and Hal shook his head. He hoped he didn't push through this last patch of tree branches to find a naked teenage girl hopping around on the beach. Gus would probably pray he did. He was a perverted son of a bitch.

Ain't that the truth.

The blonde he stumbled upon as he came out of the trees was young, but she wasn't a teenager. If Hal had to guess, she was at least twenty-two. She was probably a college girl, and Hal didn't mean to catch a peek at her big, obviously fake, breasts. It took the girl a moment to realize she needed to cover them up. She'd been about to step into the water when she heard Hal's approach and turned to face him.

"Oh, Lord," he said. "Ma'am… I'm sorry."

"Oh, shit!" she exclaimed as she crossed her arms in front of her chest.

Her pink panties were soaked through and Hal only caught a quick glimpse of them before realizing he needed to look beyond her and over at her friends. Next to the woman, was a stark naked man who was about the same age as the blonde. He covered up his pecker with a cupped hand.

These kids sure didn't have any shame. He wouldn't be caught dead stomping around naked in front of his friends, and these two were cavorting around as nude as they came out of the womb.

The other two people seated on the beach were fully dressed. Hal thought he recognized the young man as one of the guys who worked at the local bait and tackle shop. Next to this couple were two small tents. One was orange and the other blue. These couples were planning to spend the night if not the whole weekend.

"Damn," the guy said. His name was Kip. Hal was pretty sure of it.

"Kip, that you?" Hal asked.

"Yes, sir," he replied.

Kip was a handsome young man with a bit of a mullet. Believe it or not, they were coming back in style. His long, black hair flowed loosely in the back. Sitting beside him was a pretty brunette.

By now, the blonde and her boyfriend were both frantically getting dressed. Hal kept his eyes on Kip and the brunette so they could have some sense of privacy.

"Y'all know you're not supposed to be out here?" Hal asked aloud to nobody in particular.

"I know," Kip said, "but Gus never bothered us before."

"You mean you've done this before?" the girl seated next to him asked. "Becky," she called out to the blonde, "I knew we shouldn't have trusted these assholes."

"Hey, come on now," Kip said. "I ain't ever done this before. Lenny has but not me."

Lenny, who now had his shorts on, defended himself as the blonde Becky slapped his arm.

"You made it seem like it was your first time camping out here, Lenny," Becky said.

Lenny pinned her arms down and wrapped her up in a hug. "I'm a jerk. I know."

The girl squealed. Hal realized he'd seen Lenny before too. He worked the drive-thru at one of the fast-food restaurants in town. Becky worked there too. Hal hadn't recognized her at first because she always wore a hat at work, but she was a flirtatious one. She always winked at him when she handed him his food. Only the brunette was a stranger to him.

"So, Gus knows about this?" Hal asked.

It didn't surprise him. The old man had probably snuck through the trees and jerked off watching these cute young women bobbing around on the beach.

"He should know," Lenny replied. "I paid him fifty bucks to leave us alone."

"Fifty bucks?" Hal asked. "That's steep."

He almost asked why they didn't get a hotel room for that amount, but then he remembered hotel rooms weren't all that cheap anymore.

Plus, nothing beat the great outdoors when it came to spending time with a woman.

You can't skinny dip in a hotel room.

"We ain't bothering nobody, man," Kip said. "I know we're not supposed to be out here, but we ain't gonna cause any trouble. We'll just be out here tonight and tomorrow night and then we'll be on our way."

Hal was working tomorrow night too. He wasn't sure who was on the day shift though.

"This is my post now," he informed them. "It could cost me my job. I don't know who's working the day—"

"Arnold works the day shift and he has my other fifty bucks," Lenny said with a chuckle. "Come on, man. Really. This cost me a lot. I don't make all that much."

"I know you don't, buddy," Hal said.

Fast-food workers weren't paid top dollar. He felt bad for the kid. He'd been in his position before, trying to impress Sheila when they were young twenty-somethings. It was a night not too unlike this one that resulted in baby Susanna being born.

"All right," Hal said.

Both young men squeezed their fists and whispered something along the lines of, "Hell yeah."

"I've got twenty bucks on me," Kip said. "For your kindness."

"You keep it, buddy," Hal said. "But be careful out here, all right? You know there's snakes and bears and all kinds of critters. Y'all armed?"

Kip reached into the orange tent and pulled out a shotgun. He held it up for Hal to see clearly.

"Good," Hal said. "Just don't be firing that thing for fun. Alcohol and guns don't mix."

"Yes, sir," Kip said. "And thank you again."

"Kip," Hal said with a nod. He turned to each of the others and said their names with a tilt of his park ranger cap. "Lenny. Becky. Ma'am." He still didn't know the brunette's name.

"Rachel," she said.

"My name's Hal. Y'all be careful, have fun. Behave."

They all laughed. Hal wasn't expecting them to listen, but the parental side of him felt the need to say it.

As he walked back to his truck, he cracked a smile.

Oh, to be in my twenties again.

"We goin' back in the water?" he heard Becky ask.

"Damn right we are," Lenny replied.

Hal laughed.

Man, ain't that the life.

3

Annie Freemont hated her husband, Jeb. She hated Jeb Junior too. In fact, she hated every male Freemont. Only her daughter, eleven-year-old Jessica was worth a damn, and all *she* did was lie around and play with her phone. "Mommy, watch this. Mommy, watch this. Mommy, watch this."

So help me God if I have to watch one more video of some idiotic kid doing something dumb to amuse the masses...

Something slimy slid between her fingers and she squished it between her fingernails, feeling the crunch as it split in two. Green pepper. Annie always put green peppers in her meatloaf. She knew it was what made it kind of runny, but she didn't care. That was the recipe she found online nearly five years ago, and it was the one she was sticking with. Her mother never did pass down any of the family recipes, so she was creating some of her own.

"This one's gonna be good," she said aloud knowing nobody was listening.

Jessica giggled at the table behind her.

Another one of those stupid videos.

"Jess," Annie called out.

Her daughter ignored her or didn't hear her. Both were unacceptable.

"Jessica!" she shouted.

"Yes, Mama?"

"Hand me that seasoning salt."

"Mmmkay."

Annie reached one slimy hand out to accept the bottle from her daughter when she glanced out the kitchen window and into the front yard. The patio light didn't work like it was supposed to. Jeb never got around to fixing anything. He loved to claim how he was a maintenance man extraordinaire, a real Mr. Fix-It. Yet, he didn't fix a damn thing around here.

And here he was, staggering drunk through the yard. The moon showed his silhouette as he did, what, make his way to the shed to fiddle with his riding lawnmower again? It seemed he was always out there playing around with that thing. She was pretty sure that wasn't what he was doing at all. More than likely, he was watching pornography and jerking off.

Lord knows he never uses that thing of his on me.

It had been nearly a year since the last time they'd made love. Making love wasn't the right term to explain it at all. Poking around in the dark was a better description.

"Your daddy's goin' out to the shed again," Annie said aloud as she accepted the seasoning salt, flipped it upside down, and doused her gooey meat concoction.

And he didn't even turn off the damn TV... again.

She could hear one of his stupid sports shows playing in the living room. He could watch ESPN all day and all night. He tried reliving his youth by watching through blurred vision as muscular studs ran down a football field, smashed a baseball into the stands, and dribbled a ball down a court. At first, she'd felt sorry for him. He'd been great at sports when they were younger, but then he hurt his back in a logging accident.

He resented her and the kids for having to stick around town and take care of them. Annie knew that, but she also knew he'd be lost without them.

Annie found herself in the midst of a mental argument that never happened in real life. She did this often. She imagined herself walking out the door and yelling at him from the front porch.

Jeb! Don't you go out there and start fiddling with that lawnmower again.

It ain't the lawnmower I'm fiddling with, woman!

I know it ain't. Why don't you come in here and fiddle with me?

Maybe I don't want to.

Well, why not?

Because I don't find you attractive no more! That's why.

I fucking hate you, Jeb!

The feeling is mutual.

The argument never occurred in real life, but that didn't matter. Annie smashed both fists into the bowl, mashing the meat into mush with her knuckles, pretending it was her husband's face in there. She sneered as she looked out the window and saw he was no longer in the yard.

"That's it," she said aloud, turning on the sink and washing the goo off her hands.

"What's *it*, Mama?" little Jessica asked.

"You just watch your videos and be quiet," she hissed at her daughter before drying her hands on a towel, throwing it onto the countertop, and storming out the side door that led to the backyard.

She moved slowly down the porch steps until she stood on the patch of dirt at the bottom. The yard was quiet. Inside the house, she could hear the sound of an announcer breaking down the latest basketball game, but out here where Annie stood, all was silent. She focused her attention on the shed, but it appeared the light was off in there. No trace of illumination seeped out the bottom of the door like it normally did when her husband was in there. This made her even angrier. She imagined him in there watching porn by the dim phone screen.

"Jeb!" she yelled. "Jeb, get in here and spend time with the kids while I get this meatloaf into the oven!"

Her husband didn't answer. No light flicked on inside the shed. No door creaked open.

"Jeb!" she yelled.

Nothing.

"Jeb!" she tried once more.

"What is it, woman?" came the voice of her husband, so sudden and so loud it caused her to jump with fear. She turned to see Jeb standing in the doorway, looking out at her.

"You…" she started, "you… I thought you was out there in the shed."

"You can't hear the TV in the living room?" he asked. "I'm in there watching my damn show while you're out here hollering my name."

"But I saw you—"

Jeb was behind her, standing in the doorframe, when the silhouette of a man moved through the darkness from behind her husband's pickup truck. This man walked funny, hunched over slightly, stalking toward her.

"Jeb," she said, her voice barely coming out.

Her husband wouldn't be able to see the man from where he stood.

"I'm going back to watch my show," Jeb said. "I thought you needed me or something."

"Jeb," she squeaked out as she backed toward the porch steps.

The man coming toward her growled. He wore dark, camouflaged hunting clothes. As he moved into the porchlight, she saw he had a long scar on one side of his face, and his forehead was all scratched up. His face was covered in dried blood that looked to have dripped down from the top of his head.

"Jeb!" she screamed.

She heard her husband burst through the screen door and come pounding down the steps.

"What the fuck?" he yelled. "Buddy, you best—"

Annie stared in fear as the stranger's hair shifted, moved, like it was shivering. A strange, almost cracking sound emitted from it like when a windshield spiderwebs and begins to shatter. He reached for her with his arms outstretched and his mouth dripping drool. Bloodshot eyes grew wide with hunger, and her shock turned into horror.

Her scream caught in her throat and then erupted all at once in a sound so loud it made her ears ring. Annie panicked, stepped backward, and tripped on a water hose left screwed into the faucet.

Why isn't Jeb saving me?

It was the last thought she had as the grotesque man in the yard rushed at her and leaped on her. His mouth drove into her shoulder, and she thought he was going to rip a chunk of her throat off, but he didn't. She would have preferred it to the reality.

His head drew close to hers, so close she could hear his groans, and he bit down on her shoulder. It wasn't the bite that sent blinding hot pain through her body. Something else happened. She didn't understand it at first. She never fully did. The skittering sound coming from the man's hair grew louder.

Then a hundred tiny razorblades dove onto her head, sifted through her hair follicles, and nicked at her scalp. Each blade sawed back and forth, cutting through her skin. She reached to her head, trying to stop them, desperately needing to grab hold of whatever was chewing through her scalp, but there were so many.

One of her fingernails pierced her skin, and she dug at that spot, feeling like if she could only remove her scalp, she could rid herself of the pain. Blood pooled at her fingertips, and she kept digging, even as her nails broke and her skin peeled back.

Annie's head could have been doused in gasoline and set ablaze and she wouldn't have been in such agony.

She screamed through it all.

Jeb jumped into the fray, trying to come to her rescue, and then she heard him scream and knew whatever was happening to her had reached him too.

My kids!

All her thoughts went to her children and how vulnerable they were.

"Mama? Papa?" little Jessica asked from up on the porch, and Annie knew she'd be dead soon too.

4

"Bangladesh!" It was the first country that started with a "B" to enter her mind.

"Canada," Robbie Boyd said in his usual laid back, calm voice. The game didn't stress him out in the slightest. It seemed nothing did. Life was easy for this kid. Into his phone, he recorded a message to one of his many girlfriends. His tone was pleasant, sweet, and he seemed sincere even though Nitsy was sure he was full of it. "Baby, it's only for a few days and then I promise I'll pick you up and take you out."

He made her stomach turn. Robbie was everything she thought was wrong with the world. A world she'd vowed to appreciate much more now that she'd beat the beast as her mom called it.

Natasha "Nitsy" Porter tried to be positive. She really did, but Robbie irked her. The way he always took the easiest route. So many countries began with the letter "C" and he, true to his lazy ways, would choose Canada. Why Canada? Because it was the first thing to come to his mind and that was how Robbie was built. Go with the path of least resistance. Don't stress.

How about Cambodia, Cameroon, or even Chad? Why is he even on this trip?

Nitsy screamed her frustrations out on the inside while smiling and trying hard to focus on the other students' answers on the bus. She heard Dominican Republic, Egypt, and French Guiana.

There we go. French Guiana. That's a boy who deserves to be here.

The kid who'd impressed her was tanned, had a high-top fade, and wore glasses. His T-shirt read: I paused my game for this. That made her laugh. Unlike Robbie, this kid clearly deserved to be here. After all, he'd paused his game for this.

This was the opportunity of a lifetime. Only one male student and one female were chosen from random counties throughout the nation. Her school, in Ft. Lauderdale, Florida, was the only one in all of Broward County to be a part of it.

How Robbie had been chosen as the male student to represent their school was a complete mystery to her. Sure, he was a jock, one of the best players on the baseball team, and he was a popular guy, but surely his essay hadn't been anything worthy of winning this trip. Dennis Dean deserved to be here if anyone did. He was sure to be the valedictorian next year. Even Anthony Puzzo, who was the leader of their branch of Future Business Leaders of America, could have been by her side on this trip. It was a *leadership* conference. Yet, Robbie had been chosen.

You're being judgmental. You don't like it when people do that to you.

Nitsy worked hard to get good grades. She'd practiced putting together the typical five-paragraph essay until she thought she'd go mad. She'd even devised a game to help her classmates learn the procedure. Musical plates. Like musical chairs, but paper plates were placed on the floor with an essay prompt written on one side. Students danced around in a circle until the music stopped. The student without a plate would have to give three supporting topics from the prompt on the last plate removed from the circle. It was fun. Her classmates had a blast, and they even seemed to understand essays more after playing it.

Even Robbie seemed to like it. He'd drawn the prompt: Batman faced only three villains who stood a chance at beating him.

"Oh shit!" he'd blurted out in class.

Mr. Myers didn't appreciate it but didn't scold him either. That had become the case with most of the teachers in their school. Some even took the "if you can't beat 'em, join 'em" approach to profanity and would tell the students to, "Sit the hell down!" The word *fuck* was still a bit taboo.

"Easy," Robbie had continued. "The Joker, hands down. Bane. And... uh... Deathstroke!"

"Great," Mr. Myers replied, "Now, if this were an actual essay topic, you'd need to provide reasons these three stood a chance at defeating Batman. You're arguing a point, so get that point across and nail it down so well nobody else can possibly challenge it."

The game definitely earned Nitsy points in her English class. She needed as many as she could get since she'd missed so much school lately. Most of her junior year had been spent going in and out of clinics. She was on the mend now and felt great. Her mom didn't like the idea of this trip, but she was a growing woman – as she explained to her mother – and she deserved the chance to get out and experience something most teenagers never would.

The Stonewall Forge Leadership Conference.

It was her chance to meet some of the future leaders from around the country. There would be kids here from as far west as Hawaii and as far north as Alaska.

Back at school, people treated her like the poor, unfortunate weakling who had to be handled like a fragile glass sculpture. There was a time she'd considered trying out for the volleyball team. She'd been tough and had even practiced ballet and tai chi. Then she got sick.

Nitsy hadn't realized she'd sunk into a daydream until the girl seated one seat closer to the front of the bus than she was nudged her with an elbow and said, "Hey, your turn again. I said Turkey. You've got "U."

"U," Nitsy repeated. "Um..."

"Uruguay," Robbie whispered from the next seat.

Please, you're only choosing that country because Veronica is from Uruguay and you've been trying to get in her pants all year.

"No, Uzbekistan," Nitsy said proudly.

"Whatever," Robbie said. "Vietnam."

Or Vanuatu.

She realized she was being mean now. Vietnam was a pretty good answer and she should have been proud of her teammate. Was that what they were? Were they on the same team? Or would they be split up and placed on teams with other attendees? Nitsy realized she had no idea how this was going to work, and she wasn't sure how she felt about that. As much as she hated the idea of being teammates with Robbie, she feared the unknown.

What if you don't like your teammate? But you don't like Robbie, so who cares?

Robbie was... safe. She hadn't considered that before, but yes, she felt comfortable knowing she'd be on a team with someone she was at least familiar with.

Typical Natasha.

Everyone at school called her Nitsy, but he never understood why. To Robbie, Natasha was a much more beautiful name. It fit her perfectly. With her long, auburn hair and cold, grey eyes, he thought she could easily be a model. Not the traditional kind for clothing companies in Paris. She'd never grace the billboards for mixed drinks on exotic islands. But she was something else.

She was pretty. That was the best word to describe her. It was a lame thought, he knew that, but that's what he thought of Natasha. She could easily be the pretty mom in a mac & cheese commercial. She was that soccer mom type.

And, as usual, she had an attitude problem. Robbie knew his reputation often caused girls to think down on him, but it seemed like Natasha, or he supposed he ought to think of her as Nitsy like everyone else, despised him more than most. He watched her as her cool grey eyes moved around the bus. He imagined she was some sort of android and her eyes would show her that digital display of stats for each kid on the bus.

With her eyes fixed on a boy seated about halfway down the bus aisle, Robbie imagined it would say something along the lines of: Timothy, age 16, allergic to pollen, loves pizza and video games.

"Next," she would think. No way would she be into a kid who played video games.

What IS she into? I bet she sits and writes out song lyrics on notebook paper that she keeps in a giant binder. But not just any song lyrics. They'd be deep, sad songs usually performed in coffee houses. She probably has a shelf full of those old Precious Moments dolls that she's enhanced to make them edgier... with a paint set her parents bought her for her thirteenth birthday.

He remembered she'd spent a considerable amount of time in the hospital. At one point, it seemed like she wasn't at school at all. Not that he was keeping tabs. She had blonde hair back then. Now, she had long red hair, kind of wavy, and he liked this look better.

That's it. She likes to sit and fill out Sudoku books or force her way through one of those giant brain games kind of puzzle books. That's the kind of stuff you do in the hospital.

None of these thoughts came with any disrespect. It was the opposite really. Yes, Robbie liked to play sports. He enjoyed the action and the competition. And, sure, he dated a lot of girls. Most of the ones attracted to him weren't very deep though. Conversations always turned to the sexual side of things or to talk of clothes or other kids at school.

Truth was, Robbie was a bit of a nerd at heart. He enjoyed watching horror movies, playing video games, and reading mystery books. Sex was great. No kid his age would deny that. Yet, it wasn't the *only* thing he wanted in a relationship. He wondered if any of the girls here would be something special. Nitsy would never give him the time of day, so he decided to turn his attention away from her.

The bus hissed to a halt and in the seat ahead of him, Nitsy looked out the window. Robbie's eyes followed until they settled on a wooden sign with red letters carved into it. It read: Stonewall Forge: A Legendary Battlefield where Leaders are Forged.

"It's like going to summer camp, isn't it?" he asked.

Nitsy flinched, and he realized he'd scared her. He chuckled and touched her shoulder softly. Her head turned and her eyes fell upon his hand. For a second, Robbie thought she might bite him.

He remembered the words of his buddy, Max, back home: "Nobody lays a hand on Nitsy Porter."

They'd both laughed at the time, but now he wondered if there was truth to that statement.

She didn't growl at him. She didn't smack his hand away like he feared she might. She only smiled and said, "Summer camp for the elite."

"And only for three days. Man, I hope there are some hot chicks here."

Something in her face changed, and he wished he could take the words back. It was a douchebag remark and he'd promised himself he'd try like hell to be less douchebaggy.

"I'm sure you'll find someone you like," she replied.

"You too," he said.

Is Robbie Boyd talking to you? Like not staring at his phone while he does it but actually talking to you?

He was sure she'd find someone she likes here? Was this for real? Robbie had never spoken more than a few words to her, and she'd always assumed he thought he was too good for her. Perhaps she'd misunderstood and he was actually a nice guy.

"Oh, shit," Robbie said. "Look at that ass."

And just like that, he totally deconstructs the image you were forming of him. That's what you get for letting yourself be blinded by his charm.

She glanced left to look out the tinted window and saw what had stolen Robbie's attention. A young woman, probably one of the college girls from WVU or Marshall – both schools were sponsors of the Stonewall Forge program – here camping for the weekend, was walking alongside the road with her companions. Her bikini bottom had soaked through the light-yellow fabric of her jean shorts. Her boyfriend held her hand but walked ahead of her as if having to drag her along. Another couple was ahead of them.

"I love West Virginia," another boy on the bus said. "God bless this state."

"They sure know how to grow 'em in these parts," Robbie agreed.

"Yeah," replied the other boy, "we don't have anything like that in North Dakota."

Both boys laughed. Instant friends.

"You guys are ridiculous," Nitsy muttered under her breath.

"What?" Robbie asked, his attention still on the girl outside who was now waving at the bus. To her, they were probably cute kids on the way to a field trip. She had no idea they were horn-dog boys checking out her ass. The girl's boyfriend understood exactly what was going on and scowled at them before wheeling around to kiss her passionately.

On the bus, the boys cheered him on.

Boys are incorrigible.

"I don't think it matters if a guy has a high IQ or a low one," the girl seated in front of Nitsy said, "because their little head seems to do all the thinking most of the time."

Nitsy laughed out loud, covered her mouth, and nodded. "So true."

"I'm Phyllis," the girl said. She was cute, with her black hair up in two tight rolls atop her head. Her name matched her perfectly as Nitsy thought she looked like a grandmother in training. It was something about her flowered dress and kind smile.

"Nitsy. This fool behind me is Robbie. We go to the same school."

"He's cute," Phyllis said.

Of course, he is.

"Don't tell him that," Nitsy replied and both girls laughed again.

Kids her age seemed to be all about relationships. Either they were proud to be single and made sure every post on social media reflected that. Or they were in a relationship and wanted the world to see how special that was. Then there were people like Nitsy. Those who weren't dating anyone and weren't excited about being on their own. She tended to post about food or her cat or pretty sunsets.

"He is cute though," Phyllis said.

She couldn't fault the girl. The truth was, Nitsy would have liked to find a Stonewall Forge romance herself. Nobody wanted to date a sick girl, and she'd been sick so long she nearly forgot what it was like to feel healthy. At least here, nobody knew her past, so it was like she was starting with a clean slate.

Nitsy's memories weren't like normal girls. Hers were doctor visits, injections, and IV drips. She'd missed all the school study sessions, weekend parties, and Saturday night dates. She'd never experienced those secret phone chats in her bed or sneaking flirtatious text messages to the cute boy in class.

While most girls her age fished for "likes" on social media, Nitsy scrolled by the posts of the others and wondered if their lives were as glamorous as they made them out to be. Was anyone else feeling as lost as she was?

"You should smile more, Nitsy," Robbie said as he stood up from his seat to line up with the others.

Nitsy hadn't even realized the bus had stopped. She'd slipped into another daydream. This one consisted of all the selfies she imagined herself taking. On the beach, at night on some bridge, or in a restaurant surrounded by her friends. In all of the scenarios, there was a boy with no face. But she wasn't alone. Someone was with her, whoever he was.

"You have nice lips," Robbie added. "Happy looks good on you."

She couldn't help but flash him a smile. Of course, he was known for flirting. Nothing that came out of his mouth could be taken seriously, but still, he could have chosen to withhold those words and didn't. If nothing else, she was glad he'd chosen to be nice to her.

"Thank you, Robbie," she replied.

"Don't mention it."

He smiled back at her and she decided she wouldn't mention it again. He'd meant nothing by it, and she couldn't afford to let her guard down with a guy like him. Phyllis, who'd noticed the exchange, shot her a wink and a smile. Nitsy shook her head and laughed.

Outside the bus, Nitsy noticed there were three types of kids attending. The ones like her who were proud to be picked as representatives of their school. They understood the importance of this monumental moment. Even thinking it seemed cliché, but it *was* important.

Then there were the teenagers like Robbie who were nonchalant about it. Sure, it was cool, but it was no big deal. This group might have even included some of the kids who were so smart they weren't easily impressed. This was just another day for them.

The third type was the kids who didn't belong here at all. They were the ones who were too witty for their own good. They cracked jokes, easily found others like themselves, and bunched together so they could heckle the teachers or make snarky remarks at the other two types of kids.

Nitsy heard whispers from all the groups.

Group 1: "Oh, my God. This is great." "I can't believe I'm here." "This is going to be awesome!"

Group 2: "I'm sure this will be all right." "I wonder what the food is like." "My squad's competing online tonight, and I can't play because I'll be here doing *this*."

Group 3: "Look how Big Titties over there is waving her hands to get us all to line up." "This is going to be fucking boring." "Somebody's mom dressed him."

Nitsy was ushered into a line without having any choice of her own. A big, bald man with glasses tapped her shoulder and said, "Over here, please." So, she followed his lead and lined up behind one of the boys who'd been on her bus. She wasn't sure why, but she found herself scanning the crowd for Robbie. As expected, she found him behind a beautiful blonde girl. They seemed to be enjoying each other's company.

You've been given the gift of life, Nitsy. Don't squander it thinking of all life's negatives. Always see the good in people, things, and situations.

Pastor Jean's voice echoed through her mind, and she found herself smiling. She was no longer going to be "Negative Nitsy" as her cousin used to call her. She would find the positive, even if her default mode seemed to be sorrow, frustration, and anger. She could battle it and overcome it.

Once more she glanced over at Robbie and saw his beaming smile focused on the pretty girl. She was smiling back at him and twirling a finger through her hair. They were hitting it off.

Good for you, Robbie. Good for you.

And she meant it. She was happy for the boy. She couldn't quite call him a friend, but he *was* an acquaintance.

"Looks like we're on the same team," Phyllis said as she filed into line behind Nitsy. "Where are you from?"

"The Fort Lauderdale area. Florida. Wilton Manors to be exact."

"Cool. I've never been to Florida. I'm from Gary... Indiana."

The two girls talked some more while the other kids took forever lining up. Each group had a leader who was not in high school. These guides ranged from young college kids, maybe nineteen to twenty-two years old, to ages well over that. The bald guy in charge of Nitsy's group had to be at least twenty-five. Each guide wore a bright red jacket to make him or her stand out from the pack.

"Ladies, gentlemen, my name's Eggo," the bald guy started once it looked like he'd snatched up the right number of teenagers. Nitsy counted and there were ten in her line. "Yes, like the waffle. That's what they call me anyway. I'll be your group leader. That means any issue you have, you come to me. We'll get you squared away. As soon as we wrap things up here, we'll get you into your rooms in time for an early dinner. We'll be showing a movie in the conference hall tonight. Something scary from what I've been told."

Eggo went on to explain a few more details about their stay at Stonewall Forge, but Nitsy felt her attention drift away and settle on a young man who was bagging fallen leaves not far away. He was a muscular boy, soaked in sweat, with black hair stuck to his brow. His black t-shirt seemed to struggle as it stretched around his biceps. Grass stains adorned the knees of his jeans. The way the kid stared at her made her a bit uneasy.

An old man in blue jean overalls and a filthy white long sleeve shirt walked over to the boy and slapped him on the back of his head. The kid winced and rubbed the spot while the old man said something to him. She felt bad for the boy, but her attention was pulled back to her group by cheering.

"What… what is it?" Nitsy asked Phyllis.

"You're my roommate," she replied. "Well, I'm claiming you since I've met you already. The other two girls can share a room too and the boys in our group will be split up three and three."

"Great," Nitsy said.

"We're gonna have a blast," Phyllis said.

Nitsy did her best to mimic her new friend's enthusiasm while glancing back at the boy who'd slung the bag full of leaves over one shoulder and was following the old man off the lawn. He glanced back once at Nitsy and smiled. She returned the gesture and followed her team as they walked through the gate and into the Stonewall Forge Leadership Conference.

5

"What did I tell you about peeping on them young girls here for the conference thang?"

This was the first time Thomas cared to check out the girls. Last year, he'd gone on about his job and hadn't even glanced once at any of them. He hadn't been interested. With *her*, he felt a stirring *down there*. She was a stranger. Maybe that was what made her so exciting.

He was eighteen now, practically a grown man, and where he lived, it was hard to find a girl who wasn't family. Not because they didn't exist, but it was a small area, and he didn't have a lot of friends since he'd dropped out of school to help his old man take care of Stonewall Forge. The town gave them quite a bit of money to take care of the place.

So, Thomas mowed lawns, raked leaves, trimmed trees, picked up garbage, and did whatever else was required of him.

Yep, she was different all right.

Not that his family was into dating its own, but he did have two uncles who were married to second or third cousins. The Hallahan name was common around here. It seemed everyone was related somehow. In his holler, Thomas was practically a prince. He was the best looking around, and he'd noticed some of the neighbor girls looking whenever he took his shirt off to work in the yard, but he'd already been warned by his mother.

"Ain't none of these girls 'round here good for you," she'd said. "Every single one of 'em is attached to your name somehow. If it ain't a cousin, it's a cousin of a cousin. If you's even thinkin' of datin' one of 'em, you come tell me who she is, and I'll find out if she's family."

This girl, the one he couldn't keep his eyes off of earlier today, she would have a name he'd never heard of. She was probably a Miller or a Beauchamp or a Gibson. Something like that. She'd have a rich girl's last name. She probably went to a private school and everything.

"Huh?" Pa continued on. "What did I tell you?"

"You told me I'm gonna get us both in trouble by looking at 'em," Thomas replied.

He'd remained quiet enough and Pa wasn't one to ignore.

"And?" Pa asked.

"If we get in trouble, they'll find somebody else to be caretakers of the property," Thomas replied.

Outside, Moses, Thomas's Labrador, barked. He was always barking at something, but when he got going like this, Pa tensed up and usually yelled at Thomas to go shut the mutt up. For the meantime, the argument at hand seemed more important, so Moses kept yapping while Thomas's mom decided to jump into the fray.

"And somebody else to run the kitchen when they have these conferences," Ma added. "You think I want to be out of a job? I only get to work when they have these shindigs going on. You want to take that extra money out of our pockets?"

"No," Thomas replied.

"No, what?" she prodded.

"No, ma'am."

Thomas had a strict upbringing. When he was younger, he'd often have to go outside and pick his own switch off a tree for Ma or Pa to give him a proper lashing. Now, he was too big. They seemed slightly intimidated by his size, but it didn't stop them from giving him hell all the time. For a second, everyone stood silently. Thomas kept his hands behind his back and stared down at the floor. Moses continued to bark.

"Go on and wash up for supper," Ma said.

"Yes, ma'am." Thomas was on his way to the bathroom when Pa finally couldn't take the barking any longer.

"Damn possums," Pa said. "Got Moses all riled up. Dumb boy too busy washing his hands to help with his own damn dog. Looks like I'll have to go outside and kick that lazy hound 'til he shuts up."

He wouldn't kick the dog. Pa was a mean, grumpy old bastard, but he wouldn't put a serious hurting on the dog. They needed Moses. He kept the rats and other pesky vermin away. Without him, possums would be in the fridge and coons would be in the cupboard. Those animals were assholes with no respect for humans. Thomas laughed at the thought of furry rodents flipping his parents the bird.

"Pa, be careful out there," Colleen called out to him.

The boy called her Ma, but to Pa she was Colleen. Pa, on the other hand, went by Pa. Plain and simple. Everyone called him that. Cleon down at the gas station called him Pa, Sara over at the ice cream shop called him Pa, and even that dumb boy Kip at the bait shop called him Pa.

"All right, keep it down. Keep it down." He was grumpy, and it wasn't a show. He really did despise most people and detest most things. At some point in his life, Pa stopped giving a shit what everyone else thought. He ate what he wanted, drank what he wanted, and he smoked cigarettes like he wanted, regardless of what Dr. Vince said.

Vince. What a stupid name for a doctor. Sounds like some Italian out of New York City.

Pa pulled his pack out of his pocket, stuck a cigarette in his mouth, and lit the end. This was his favorite part of the day. After work, when he had no more responsibilities, he could inhale that warm heat and blow away his worries. That's how he felt about it and why he liked smoking so much. It purified him. Each inhale grabbed a few more of his problems and tossed them out on the breeze. He held up his cigarette and looked at the cherry on the end.

They taste like shit. But I love 'em.

He'd kick the boy's ass if he ever caught him with one, but it was his guilty pleasure, and he didn't feel guilty at all about it.

Moses stopped barking when he saw Pa, and when Pa sat down on his favorite wooden crate to relax, the black Labrador meandered over to him and sat back on his haunches. It stared at Pa with its tongue lolling out. He was begging for food, and Pa didn't have any. Not yet. Supper would be on the table in a few minutes, but even then, he wouldn't give this dumb dog any.

"What you barking at, boy?" Pa asked.

The dog didn't answer. Of course, he wouldn't, but sometimes he'd at least turn and run toward whatever was bothering him. Once, he'd cornered a copperhead and the snake, for some reason, refused to pounce. Moses got lucky that time. If it had been a rattlesnake, there'd be no barking tonight. There'd be no barking for any other night either. That would be one dead dog.

Tonight, Moses sat still and watched the old man. Pa took another drag on his cigarette and blew the smoke at the dog's face. He loved doing that. Usually, Moses would back up and bark at him once. Only once. Like it was the dog's way of saying, "Fuck you, too." This time, he didn't budge.

Moses was quiet. Too quiet. In fact, the whole forest was silent. Pa spent so much time in this holler he never even noticed all the little sounds around him, but he knew they were there, like one big outdoor orchestra. Right now, the conductor had allowed the musicians to set down their instruments.

All was silent. Pa became suddenly aware of all those noises he usually ignored because none of them were making a peep. This wasn't natural. Even in the winter, there were sounds in these woods.

Pa didn't even realize he'd been holding in the smoke from the last drag on his cigarette. He'd been sitting there with his lips pressed together tightly, straining his ears for any sound out there. He might have even been satisfied with noise from inside the house, but Colleen must have been calmly plating dinner.

Finally, Pa blew out the smoke and blasted it in the dog's direction. The mutt only sat up straighter, appalled by the gesture, and Pa thought he might have seen the dog's hair move ever so slightly. Like a stiff wind raking over its hide or a hand petting its fur.

A death rattle sounded off. That's what it sounded like to Pa. Like a giant letting out its final breath.

No, it was skittering, like a bucket of beetles had been set down beside him and they were all crawling over each other to get out. The clicking sound made his jaw clench tight, and he nearly severed the cigarette butt from the rest of the stick.

The sound was unnatural.

"What is that, boy?" he asked the dog.

Moses didn't answer. He only sat still and watched him from his seated position a couple of feet away.

"Well you're good for nothin', ain't ya?"

The dog didn't budge.

Pa took one more drag off his cigarette.

He leaned forward and blew another cloud of smoke, but this time, as soon as it hit the dog's snout, its eyes shot open wider than Pa had ever seen a dog's eyes open. Something, a whole lot of something, leaped from the animal's fur and landed on the top of Pa's head.

His initial reaction was to claw at it, to rake at whatever had landed on him. He didn't even scream. Real men didn't do that. He was a real man, and he would never allow himself to—

Pa screamed as what felt like tiny dentist drills cut through his scalp.

A race of miniature piranhas burrowing into his skull, chomping at his flesh.

No, they had to be worms.

Parasites.

Pa screeched and clawed at his roots, digging in where the hair follicles met skin. He picked, pawed, and tried to peel back his scalp. Blood trickled down around his head as whatever was up there fought to eat its way through the bone and into his brain.

Hot coals burned at him.

His skin sizzled, but only he could hear the crackling of invisible flames.

Pa hit his knees and begged silently for the pain to end.

So many holes being drilled into his skull.

Then, at a spot close to the crown of his head, one of the tiny razor-toothed lice succeeded. Like the one sperm to win the race to the woman's egg, it ate its way through the skull and dropped onto the brain, burning into his mind like radio-controlled battery acid.

Pa's eyes shot open and a moan emitted from his gut. He couldn't control it. The pain was so immense he pissed himself.

His fingers curled up into claws and locked that way.

A white milky substance ran over his eyes and blurred his vision. Tears mixed with them and landed on his cheeks.

He was only a passenger now.

Scorching hot blades raked at the insides of his arms and legs as tentacles reached into his extremities, taking control of them, and forcing his legs to move and his arms to lift and wobble around.

It was inside him, and it hated him. Its rage was so thick. Its hunger to kill so strong.

Pa was no longer in control.

They were. *It* was.

Only the rest of them were still lodged in his scalp, waiting for him to get close enough to another lifeform so they could pounce. Only one could win each race. Only one could control the body. The others would wait. The process would repeat until *they* were satisfied.

It would find another lifeforce.

But where?

Those that remained on the dog's fur would wait too. The dog ran off into the woods. It was on the hunt.

Which way should *it* move? Where should *it* go?

"Pa, I can smell that smoke!" a voice called out. "Hurry up and get in here for supper."

There. The source of that sound. That was where *it* needed to go.

6

The folks inside the Cloud 9 Trailer Park always knew how to have a good time. Most of the people living there were in their early to late forties. They were the stable ones anyway. Those younger than that were typically meth heads or hooked on pain pills. They partied too. Those older had been around so long they typically liked to watch TV during the day and then join the others outside at night to sip wine and smoke weed. Marijuana was illegal in the state, but that didn't stop people from getting their hands on it.

Peter and Kev were a gay couple living in Cloud 9 and loving the free-spirited ways of their neighbors. They'd driven down from Trenton, New Jersey because Peter's mom wasn't doing so well on her own. She was an alcoholic who spent more time in the hospital than she did at home. This left her little terrier, Kit Kat, to fend for himself quite often.

Now that the guys had purchased their own trailer and were only a few lots away from Peter's mom, they could take care of the dog whenever she went away.

Tonight, the guys were with the rest of their new friends at Cloud 9. The 'Circle of Hope' they liked to call it. It was a circle of lawn chairs and coolers, but who were they to burst the trailer-bubble.

The truth was, people here were nice to Peter and Kev. Not everyone in Clydesville seemed to appreciate their relationship. In fact, it seemed downright frowned upon. Not that they walked around holding hands and trying to rub it in anyone's face, but they were legally married, and they hated having to hide it from the locals. At Cloud 9, they didn't have to.

Right now, they sat side by side at that lawn-chair ring, staring at the small fire going at the circle's center. Peter was excited about life. This was all he needed. His mom, Pam, was seated across from them, smoking a blunt with her friend, Saucy. An ex-stripper with big, hair-sprayed hair that looked like a do straight out of the 80s, Saucy liked to joke that any young man who was willing could get the "sauce." Peter *did not* want that sauce, but it didn't stop her from grinding her ass against him every chance she got. For now, she was busy getting high with his mom.

Kenny Chesney played on a tiny boombox and the song made him feel like they should be sitting on a beach right now. He should have his toes in the cool water. He should be drinking a margarita or a piña colada instead of a canned wine cooler.

Glancing to his right, he couldn't help admiring the way Kev stared at the fire. Light played at his lips and Peter, as he often did, thought how lucky he was to be with a man as handsome as his husband. His hair was always perfect, high up on his head with perfectly manscaped sideburns. His brown eyes sparkled, and he laughed with such ease.

Back home, in Jersey, he'd been different. He'd always seemed stressed about life. Bills were piling up, their families wanted little to do with them, and there was nothing to do for fun other than going to a nightclub or a casino.

This. This outdoor, fresh air, West Virginia life was the best.

"Anybody else getting hungry?" Del, an old man with multicolored rubber bands keeping his beard in braids, asked as he stood up and raised his beer as if in toast.

The others in the group raised their beers. Kev lifted his glass of whiskey. Peter followed suit and hoisted his canned wine up to join them.

"To hunger?" Kev asked, jokingly.

"To fuckin' burgers, my friend!" Del announced.

"To burgers!" some of them called out, including Peter and Kev.

"To fuckin' burgers," Saucy yelled a little too late.

Del staggered as he walked toward his trailer and his wife, a blonde woman his age with pink feathers roach clipped to her hair, yelled, "You're gonna bust your ass again, Del. Be careful."

"Be careful with our food!" Peter's mom added.

It was a fine night. Most of their nights were. Every once in a while Dan and Casey would smoke too much or drink too much or pop too many pills and they'd end up throwing punches at each other. The two twenty-somethings now ate on only Styrofoam. Real dishes can only take so much high flying.

At the moment, the two young wildlings seemed madly in love. Dan lifted the brim of his Mountaineers ball cap and leaned down to kiss Casey.

Even the psychos are calm tonight. Speaking of psychos—

Lizzy Pete wasn't crazy, but she didn't interact with the rest of them much. Her husband had gone hunting with his cousin, Carl. Now, Carl was a crazy son of a bitch. He didn't seem to like Peter or Kev too much. He always gave them nasty looks and made gay comments and told gay jokes from time to time, always glancing over at them as if to gauge their level of shame. There was none here. Both guys were proud of their love for one another.

Andre wasn't bad at all. He'd sit and hang out with the rest of them. He didn't drink because he was a recovering alcoholic, but he'd still sit by the fire and gossip with the rest of them. He was a nice guy. Too bad he hadn't come back from that hunting trip.

"Hey, Peter," Lizzy said softly as she sat down on top of the cooler to his left.

Peter was surprised she decided to come so close. Oftentimes she'd stay inside the trailer while her husband joined them outside. He said she didn't feel well most of the time. She suffered from terrible migraines.

"How's your head?" Peter asked.

"You know... same ol' same ol,' but I'm dealing."

"I can imagine it's rough. Still no word about Andre?"

She shook her head and wiped at her eyes. "It's not like him, you know?"

"What do you think happened?" Peter wasn't trying to be an asshole by asking the question. He simply didn't know what else to say to the woman. Her husband's disappearance would be the only thing on her mind, so why dodge the subject?

"I'm afraid to say," she replied. "The police said maybe a bear got him, but not my Andre. He was a crack shot and they said his gun was missing too. It could've gotten thrown from the truck, but they would have found it by now."

"Bear," Peter repeated, shaking his head.

He couldn't imagine what that would be like. Crashing your truck, tumbling into a ravine, and then having your mangled body dragged out by a bear, only to be chewed up like a steak dinner. That had to be one of the worst ways to go. Maybe right after the pain of being burned at the stake. *That* would be the worst. Feeling the flames start at your feet, licking at your arches and heels, slowly climbing its way up the rest of your body while you can do nothing but stand there and scream.

Peter got the chills and shook gently.

"What is it?" Lizzy asked.

"Nothing," he replied. "Just a thought."

"What do you think happened to him?" she asked.

He hadn't been expecting that question. Of course, he'd thought about it, but he didn't know which version would be the least horrible. One came to him and he figured it wasn't as bad as the rest, so he went with it. "Maybe he was flung from his truck and hit his head so hard he got amnesia. Then he woke up and started walking."

"Just started walking?" she asked.

"Yeah."

"Where would he go?"

"I don't know. There has to be a cabin or something nearby. Maybe an old ranger station. He'd go somewhere and maybe he wouldn't understand what happened. So he'd just sit. They'll find him. Don't worry."

"All I do is worry."

"Hey, we've got company!" Del yelled as he stepped out from around the side of his trailer carrying a plate of beef patties. "I may need to make some more."

"Who is that?" Saucy called out.

Everyone looked toward the asphalt path that circled the inside of the trailer park, making it easy for the mailman to drop off their mail. The entire place was one big circle with one entry and exit. Cloud 9 was a mountain community, up on its own hill, and its residents were always keen on company.

"Is that ol' Jeb?" one of the other men seated around the fire asked. "I'd recognize that dirty-ass flannel jacket of his anywhere.

"I think that is Jeb," Del said, shielding his eyes as if the porch light beside him would help him see the silhouetted figures moving their way a little better.

Peter counted four of them. There was definitely a hefty man, then what appeared to be a woman, a teenage boy, and a little girl.

"Jeb, what you walkin' up here for?" Del called out. "Car trouble?"

Jeb didn't answer. Peter wasn't very familiar with this Jeb guy they all seemed to know, but he thought it was quite rude for him to ignore everyone. Everybody in town was polite, so this was a little strange.

"Well, hell, maybe that ain't them," Peter's mom mumbled as she took another toke.

"That ain't like Annie at all," Saucy agreed. "You know her. If she smelled this shit here, she'd be running over here asking for a hit of it."

Both women laughed as Peter's mom handed the joint over to Saucy.

"Yo, Jeb Junior!" Dan hollered as he lifted Casey off his lap and got up to go see his young friend. "You 'bout ready for baseball season?"

Jeb Junior didn't answer either. Peter knew Dan was an assistant coach at the high school and all players knew to respond when their coach spoke to them. He couldn't put his finger on it, but Peter knew something wasn't right. Everyone else seemed unfazed by the family approaching in the darkness.

"You want some, baby?" Kev asked as he handed his joint to Peter.

Peter didn't want any of it and swatted it away with his hand. Apparently, he'd knocked it from Kev's hand because he heard him say, "Aw, come on, clumsy. That wasn't cool."

"Kev, get up," Peter demanded as he rose to his feet and reached for his husband's hand.

"Okay," Kev replied, smiling, oblivious to the fact that something unearthly loomed only twenty feet away.

Light from the fire at the circle combined with that of the lamps outside the trailer homes to finally reveal the faces and hunched over bodies of the family members marching into Cloud 9. This clearly wasn't the Jeb the rest of them knew. Del grimaced and dropped his plate of hamburger meat. His wife nearly fell out of her lawn chair. "Annie?" she asked.

Annie didn't seem to know her own name anymore, and she wasn't interested in sitting around the fire with old friends. She crept forward, hands out in front of her, knuckles bent forcing her fingers into claws. Beside her, little Jessica growled like a hungry dog.

Big Jeb picked up his pace and rushed straight at Del. Usually, the old man would have a gun or a knife at his hip. Nearly every man in small town West Virginia did, but Del was at home. They all were. This was the place to rest, to relax, to feel at ease and out of harm's way. Jeb was only a foot away from Del when the old man threw his hands up to his head and screamed. His arms flailed frantically, like he was swatting away a swarm of bees.

Peter froze with his hand locked around Kev's. Behind him, his mom yelled, "Hey, get off him." Saucy, who seemed to understand the attack was much more serious, screamed. Annie barreled right at her, like the sound was a beacon calling her home. Saucy was drunk, but she wasn't stupid. She reached for a small cooler at her feet and leaped at Annie, smashing the oncoming woman in the face. Her forward momentum continued and soon Saucy was on top of Annie, and she too was screaming and swatting at the sky.

Everyone around ran to their friends' aid.

Dan, as expected, did have a gun at his hip. He was young and full of bravado. He wouldn't go anywhere, not even right outside his front door, without a firearm. But he seemed to go numb when he saw the frantic rush at his friends and heard the screaming. He turned to watch and took his eyes off Jeb Junior for only a second. That was all the time the young man needed to get close enough.

"Dan!" Peter yelled. "Get back!"

It was too late. Whatever was attacking the others was now on the young man, and as his girlfriend ran to his aid, Jeb Junior's sister, Jessica, ran at Casey and leaped on her.

Casey screamed and shook the child off her.

She turned toward Peter and reached for him. She started to run, her mouth open in a scream, when he saw her eyes light up. Like someone had stuck a hot branding iron to her back, her face twisted into a look of pain. For a second, no sound came out of her mouth, but then she let loose a shriek Peter would never forget.

His mom, who was to his left trying to help Saucy, let out a similar wail. It was the agonizing scream of someone who'd had a pot of boiling water thrown in their face.

"Peter, come on!" Kev yelled.

This time it was him being saved as his husband pulled on his arm and yanked him toward their trailer.

As they ran around to the side, where the door was located, the sound of something hitting the far wall and then scrambling up to the hood, or roof, of their home could be heard. It sounded like a monkey was bounding up above them.

Peter's hand was on the door when he heard what sounded to him like a rattlesnake's rattle. Kev was at his side, and he screamed. By the time Peter glanced up it was too late to flee from the little girl grinning down at them. Something pounced from Jessica's head and landed on them both. She remained on the roof, looking down at them for a few seconds, watching them as the pain set in. As Peter's eyes blurred over, she ran away, pounding her way down the trailer.

The party raged on, moving from trailer to trailer. The interesting thing about Cloud 9 was the amount of nighttime gatherings that took place and the sheer number of times things got out of hand. With so many relapsed junkies and people unwilling to address their addictions at all, fistfights often broke out. Wild yelling and even full-on screaming were a nightly occurrence.

So, nobody batted an eye when the sounds at the Circle of Hope turned sour.

No one called the cops. Most of the residents at the trailer park who weren't there at the party slept with earplugs or with music softly playing beside their bed. Or they too were passed out after a private party inside the comfort of their home.

When Jeb, Jeb Jr., Annie, Jessica, Del, Lizzie, Dan, Cassie, Saucy, Kev, Peter, Peter's mom, and all the others went door to door, there wasn't a single complaint until it was too late.

It was a massacre at Cloud 9, and *they* would continue to spread.

7

Hal yearned for a drink. He wouldn't take one, of course. Mostly because if he did, he would have to stand up in next week's meeting and tell everyone about it. Some of his friends, if he could even call them that, had gone through that embarrassment.

"Fuuuuck... me," he complained, lifting up onto his elbows to look out at the filthy trailer he called home.

Packets of peppered beef jerky and empty cans of Mountain Dew littered the kitchen counter. His only towel lay draped over the knob of the bathroom door.

Once upon a time, he and his wife owned a four-bedroom house on eight acres of land. Sheila kept the place spotless, and he mowed the lawn. Life was in order. He didn't have to look outside to know the grass looked like shit now. It was a pitiful patch of earth, but it was where he called home. For now.

Glancing over at the nightstand next to his twin-size bed, Hal stared at the invitation to the church gathering tomorrow night. It was some kind of end-of-summer festival. He had no plans to attend, but he might stop by before work if he felt the temptation for a chili dog and one of those funnel cakes—*no, don't go there, brother. Don't think too much right now.*

His head crashed back onto his pillow. He reached for the invitation and flung it through the air, watching it Frisbee twirl until it landed on the ragged carpet beside the door.

The fact was, he hadn't attended any kind of fair, festival, or even party since *they* were taken from him. He tried not to blame God for their deaths, but he couldn't help it sometimes. They'd gone to church as a family and they'd prayed together before meals. Wasn't that what was required?

The Lord works in mysterious ways.

Hal heard different variations of that each time he tried church again. It was one of the reasons he refused to go anymore. He couldn't sit peacefully and soak up the good word now. Every time he tried, somebody approached him either before or after mass to express their sympathies and to try and comfort him.

You can shove that comfort up your ass.

He wished like hell he'd left an emergency bottle of one of the brothers around here somewhere. Those brothers would be Jack Daniels, Jim Beam, or even their foreign cousin Jose Cuervo. The thought of that family reunion was really nice. He would drink away his sorrows and not show up for work tonight.

His job seemed pointless really. He needed the money, and it was easy work, but driving around the forest all night made no sense to him.

He eyed his pistol on the table, right where he'd left it at eight this morning before settling down to a turkey with gravy TV dinner and season three of *24*. Hal had the entire show on DVD. It was the last gift Sheila gave him for Christmas. He'd always been a fan of that show. He wondered what its star character, Jack Bauer, would do in his situation. Would he bite a bullet?

It was a tempting thought. All he had to do was put the muzzle in his mouth and pull the trigger. Then all this would go away. He might not make it to where his angel was, but he'd be able to meet up with Sheila again. It was that fear of the unknown that stopped him from doing it. *What if?*

What if you pull the trigger and somehow don't die?

What if you pull the trigger, you do die, but you never see your daughter again?

What if you pull the trigger, don't see your daughter, and can't find your wife?

The truth was, he was a coward. That's why he didn't do it.

Deciding not to waste his time with thoughts of things he'd never accomplish, he shuffled his worn-out, lazy carcass over to the freezer and pulled out a couple of blueberry waffles. He stuck them in the toaster and then crossed the trailer to his reclining chair. It was the only piece of living room furniture he owned other than a coffee table and the stand holding the TV.

Having slept all day, Hal was left with only the news to watch on his rabbit-eared TV. He refused to pay for cable when there was never anything on. Instead, he retrieved his waffles and ate them without syrup while watching the horrendous events going on around the world. It seemed there was always some kind of terrorist attack, race riot, war... the list went on and on. Gone were the days of seeing stories such as "neighborhood kid sees a classmate in trouble and runs to the rescue" or "a family in need is given assistance by unknown strangers."

Hal glanced back at his gun once more and considered leaving the world behind.

This place is becoming a dumpster. Someday, maybe someday soon, something is going to come along that will force us to unify. Race won't matter, sex won't matter, religion won't matter... only the human race will matter.

He chuckled as he imagined the spaceships from the movie *Independence Day* hovering over West Virginia.

"Ain't nothing here worth blowing up."

With his finger on the power button, Hal was about to turn off the day's negativity when a picture of the pickup from last night flashed on the screen. The camera was positioned right around the same spot he'd been standing.

"Yes, Mark, authorities are saying the truck must have flipped over the guardrail and plummeted down here into the ravine. With signs of no other vehicle present, exactly what caused this accident is unknown. The vehicle has been identified as belonging to Andre Pete from right here in Clydesville, but there has been no sign of Andre, so exactly what happened is very much a mystery. If anyone knows Andre's whereabouts, please get in contact with the police department so they can verify his wellbeing."

The scene flashed to a cop Hal recognized. He'd gotten pulled over once by him when he was still hitting the sauce pretty hard.

"It's kind of crazy," the cop said. "There's quite a bit of blood on the scene, but it's almost like he just got up and walked off. Anyone who knows Andre knows he's one tough son of a gun, but he really needs to get checked out in the hospital."

Andre Pete. What happened to you, man?

"Again," the reporter continued, "if anyone knows the whereabouts of Andre Pete, please get in touch with authorities. Back to you, Tom."

The next few stories passed in a blur. Hal was worried about Andre. They weren't friends, not really, but they'd attended AA meetings together. Andre had started drinking while still in the military. His injured leg made him feel inadequate, and as it usually did so well, the rum made him feel invincible even if only for a little while. Hal had gone for coffee a couple of times with Andre and some others from the group.

Andre was the type of man who didn't understand people who were capable but weren't willing. Once, they'd even argued about it, over coffee, when Andre asked Hal why he wasn't a cop anymore. Hal told him the truth, and Andre said, "I don't understand you at all, man. If I were able to go back into the field, I'd do it in a heartbeat. I think it's pretty pitiful that you're able to do the policing but just don't feel like doing it anymore."

They didn't go for coffee anymore after that, but that didn't mean Hal wished him dead. He might be a little too opinionated, but he was a good man.

Overwhelmed by the feeling something bad had happened to Andre, Hal prepared for work early. He knew where Andre lived and wanted to stop by his house before clocking in. Once, after one of those post-meeting coffee meet-ups, Hal dropped Andre off at his trailer only a few blocks away. Andre's car was in the shop at the time. They talked a little, mostly about hunting and the right to bear arms, until Andre started talking about his next get-rich-quick scheme. This time it had something to do with selling ladybugs to organic farmers. The whole concept was ridiculous, but Hal sat and silently listened. Hal had become the quiet type. He spoke when spoken to or when in need of information. Other than that, he felt better keeping his thoughts to himself.

His beliefs didn't always mesh well with the opinions of others.

If you won't eat the fish, throw it back.

Be kind. There ain't no reason, nor is there time, to waste with meanness.

Watch when someone's laughing. Remember that face they make. You'll miss it when they're gone.

If you can eat more, ask for seconds. It's a great compliment.

Apologize when you're sorry.

Only shoot what you'll eat.

Hold the damn door open for the person behind you.

Wash your hands after you piss.

Tell your loved ones how much you love them. All the time.

Fight hard... until you win. Then your fighting should be done.

Those were the rules he followed. If others did the same, the world would be a much better place.

Driving up the hill to the Cloud 9 trailer park, Hal wondered how some of these people made it up such a steep incline in the winter. He could imagine someone gunning it from the bottom, speeding up the hill, and then sliding on ice all the way into the living room of some poor soul's trailer. That would never happen though. Folks around these parts were so well-versed on snow driving. The changing of the seasons meant very little to them other than the fact they couldn't go mudding on backroads or kayaking on the lake.

At the top of the hill, Hal drove around the giant circle at the inside, noting the Circle of Hope at its center. He'd partied there a few times himself. Twice when he was still drinking. It wasn't the best place for a recovering alcoholic, so he kept his distance now. The last time he was up here, some chick named Saucy kept trying to get in his pants.

"You can have the sauce anytime you want it," she'd offered.

He'd turned her down politely, but he had to admit, if he'd had two more drinks he would have gone back to her trailer to show her his business. That was the reason he'd left when he did. He neither needed two more drinks nor a late night rendezvous with the Cloud 9 hussy.

"Where the hell is everyone?" he asked himself quietly as he drove to the front of Andre's trailer and parked.

The place was never hopping during the day the way it always was at night, but this was unusual. Old Man Paulson, as everyone in the area called him, was always outside picking up trash or mowing the few patches of grass that remained in the place. Yet, the outside was riddled with beer cans, paper plates, and other clutter left over from last night's festivities. The old man must have been out of town or sick. He'd never let the place look like this so late in the afternoon.

Moseying up the three wooden steps leading to Andre's front door, Hal couldn't help feeling like he was being watched. He turned quickly, expecting to catch someone in the act, but he saw nobody around. Andre was an acquaintance, but he wasn't a good friend, and if the cops hadn't located him yet, Hal stood little chance of digging up his whereabouts. These were his thoughts as he tapped his knuckles against Andre's door.

All was silent on the other side of the door. He recalled Andre's wife's name starting with the letter "L," but, for the life of him, he couldn't remember her name.

Leslie? Leeanne? Layla?

He knocked again, but nobody called out from the other side of the door. The ex-cop part of him wanted to try the doorknob and see if it was unlocked.

And if it is?

That was the problem. If he tried and found it open, he would feel the need to peek inside.

And what if she's sitting on the toilet? What if his wife is in the shower? She's not expecting company.

With his hand on the knob, he fought the urge to turn it and pop it open. More than likely, even if she wasn't home, it would be unlocked. Hardly anyone locked their doors around here. There was a mutual respect in Clydesville. Nobody took things that weren't theirs, not even in a place with so many drug-addicted residents. It simply wasn't done. People were raised right. They were God-fearing folks and stealing was a sin.

Nashville had been entirely different. There, you needed to keep *everything* locked. That place was too wild for him. He supposed things would be worse in some other cities like Los Angeles or maybe New York, but Nashville was rough. The world knew it as the home of country music, but what they didn't see was all the bloodshed in the shadier parts of town.

Pop the door open and call out for her. If you hear the shower running or she tells you she's in the bathroom, you apologize and leave. What's the harm in that?

Behind him, a dog's collar jingled. Hal turned around to see a German shepherd prancing through the center of the Circle of Hope. It stopped, sniffed something on the ground, and then turned its attention to one of the trailers.

Hal wasn't worried. More than likely the dog belonged to one of the people who lived at Cloud 9. It was probably friendly. Hal decided he'd knock once more. This time, as he did, the big dog barked in unison, suddenly aware of his presence, and from the way his snout rose up over his gritted teeth, he didn't like Hal.

The dog stepped forward, and Hal knew he must be seeing things, but it seemed like its fur shifted. Like a strong wind blew through it and made it move.

But it's a German-fucking-shepherd, man.

Its fur was short and smooth. The wind wouldn't make it shift like that.

Hal's desire to check in on Andre's wife faded as he glanced at his truck. It was only three steps down and the passenger side door was only three feet from there. Approximately six feet would see him safely inside.

The dog growled and launched itself forward, sprinting toward him.

Hal wasn't in good enough shape to leap off the stairs, but he took the three steps as quickly as he possibly could, hearing the sounds of the dog's paws galloping toward him on the other side of the truck. It was close. Too close.

His boot hit mud at the bottom of the stairs and his right leg slid back, forcing him onto a knee. The dog would round the corner any second. If it did, he was a goner. The beast would leap on him and go right for his throat the way dogs always did.

He reached out, grabbed the wooden staircase banister, and hoisted himself back to his feet. The second he reached the passenger side door handle, the dog sped around the back of his truck and dove for him.

Hal slid inside and slammed the door.

It didn't close, but bounced off the dog's ugly, enraged face as it struggled to get inside the truck.

Its eyes were bloodshot.

Its mouth dripped saliva.

Its growl ripped through its throat and told him it would kill him if he let up even an inch.

But none of that bothered Hal like what he saw at the top of its head. Its fur shifted again, moved the way he imagined an overhead view of a cornfield would look if someone were running through it. Something wasn't right here. This wasn't only an angry dog. It was sick or... or possessed.

Hal hated to hurt an animal. It wasn't in him to do so, but this was life or death, and as much as he'd considered suicide in the past, he wasn't ready to die here today.

Pulling his aching knee back as far as he could, he thrust it forward and slammed his heel against the dog's snout. It whined, growled some more, but slipped out of the doorway, allowing Hal to slam the door shut and lock it. He scrambled to the driver's side and mashed the lock down on that side as well.

It's a dog. It's not going to open the doors.

That didn't matter right now. He needed those doors locked. It felt safer that way. He was safe now.

A sudden *boom* rang through the air and Hal felt his entire truck shake. A second strike and he realized the dog was ramming its head against the passenger door.

You're not safe. You're not safe at all.

He turned the key, threw the truck into drive, and drove around the circle.

The dog wasn't finished with him though.

It raced toward the opposite side, planning to cut him off.

This dog is fucking crazy.

Hal floored it, pressing his foot against the gas pedal while at the same time keeping his eyes on the dog racing across the Circle of Hope, leaping over a plastic cooler, and charging toward him. Whatever was driving that ferocious little fucker forward wasn't going to stop until it had its jaws clamped around Hal's throat.

Not today, son. You ain't eating me today.

The pickup was only ten feet from the dip that would take him downhill and away from Cloud 9 when the four-legged monster caught up with him and leaped forward. Acting on instinct alone, Hal waited until the mutt was only a foot or two away and threw open his door. With the dog's momentum carrying it forward, the door clipped its jaw and swatted the angry bastard away. Its head spun, its ass hit the side of the truck, and the rest of its body bounced off the pickup's frame.

If it wasn't dead when it hit the ground, it sure as hell wouldn't be getting up and chasing anybody else for a while.

Hal checked his rearview mirror as he descended the hill and saw he was no longer being chased.

His hands shook from the encounter with the dog, but he chalked it up to a mean hell hound protecting its territory. In the back of his mind, he wondered if the dog belonged to Andre. Maybe it didn't like that he was about to walk into the trailer.

He decided he'd call animal control later. Maybe even the cops.

Somebody needed to go up there and make sure that dog didn't attack anyone else.

If it's even alive. You nailed that damn thing right in the jaw.

Hurting animals wasn't his thing, and he felt horrible for having hit the dog, but he was convinced that thing wasn't right in the head. In his mind, there were only two reasons to ever hurt an animal. For meat, if you're a hunter and for safety, if yours or anyone else's life is in danger.

Damn mutt.

Hal was angry with the dog, but he was also angry with himself. Maybe if he'd left a few minutes earlier, he never would have had that encounter with the beast.

Nah. It was coming for you. It needed to be put down.

Hal shook his head in disappointment as he shifted into a higher gear and headed toward work. There was only one place Andre could be hiding that might have made a lick of sense. It was close to his crash site. Yet, right now it was crawling with teenagers.

He needed to visit Stonewall Forge before his work shift began.

8

"What do you think the group was missing in last night's movie?"

When the head of the conference, Mrs. Leyla Price, asked the question, Nitsy smiled because everyone else had gone to bed after the sci-fi horror flick. To most of them, it was simply a fun night with new friends. Nitsy knew there was more to it than that. In a place like this, there was always a lesson to be taught. The movie wasn't scary. Not really. It was some alien film and the reason they'd been made to watch it was clear. Leadership. That was what this conference was all about, and in the movie, the crew of a spaceship suffered from having faulty leadership. Too much squabbling between the captain and co-captain.

Nitsy raised her hand.

"Yes?" Mrs. Price asked, pointing one of her long, blood-red polished fingers at Nitsy. The woman was kind looking with big, frizzy black hair and a smile that was almost too big, kind of clownish. Her charcoal suit was ironed and was shiny from all the starch she'd used. Mrs. Price was a professional through and through, and she was waiting for Nitsy's answer.

"The crew of the Falcon was lacking in leadership," Nitsy replied proudly.

"Excellent," the conference leader exclaimed. "Exactly. The Falcon crew had its own drama from within, which definitely wasn't helping when the alien parasite snuck aboard their ship. So... that will be today's theme. In your groups, you will find a place to work. You will be given a list of crew positions and responsibilities to distribute. You will need to come up with a name for yourselves... like 'The Falcon.' Draw, paint, or digitally create your group's spacecraft. I want to know all about it. How you get your food and water, what kind of protection system your ship has... all the information is in the packet you'll be receiving. Use your time wisely and most importantly, have fun with this."

Group members instantly began whispering ideas. Nitsy waited to hear the end of Mrs. Price's speech. Every word was important. She couldn't wait to get started. That captain position was going to be hers.

"Ladies and gentlemen," Mrs. Price continued, "when we reconvene tomorrow morning, I want to be wowed. Your team leader, or captain, must be prepared to answer questions and your team should be ready to handle any alien lifeform I throw your way. The captain of the winning crew will have a shot at running for this year's Stonewall Forge President." Mrs. Price walked away and could be heard saying, "This is going to be so exciting."

Nitsy was elated. She'd never been involved in an activity like this one. The teachers at her school seemed to believe the only good lesson came from a book, or if a student failed a test, they'd add that failure was the best teacher. Of course, not all her educators were lazy. Mr. Henshaw, the science teacher, was pretty good at coming up with dynamic ways to help students learn, but he'd never challenged them with anything this exciting.

After a short team meeting where it was decided Nitsy would be the team leader, the students were ushered off to lunch. Kids shuffled slow step by slow step through the buffet-style line. Robbie was a few feet ahead of her when she heard him grumble to the lady serving food, "Ma'am, I'm sorry, but I'm type 2 diabetic and I was wondering if you guys have anything that's not pasta."

The attendant, who was about to dump a heaping ice cream scooper full of chili-mac onto his plate, pulled her hand back and pointed to the next counter. "There's sandwiches over there."

"Anything without bread?" he asked.

The woman rolled her eyes, so Nitsy stepped in front of the few people ahead of her in line, grabbed Robbie by his arm, and said, "There's a salad bar over here. I guess I should be eating better too."

He smiled at her. "Thanks."

"I didn't know you were diabetic," Nitsy said.

Robbie turned around and his face was red. "It's kind of new. I was having dizzy spells and well, you know, parents rush you off to the doctor and bam, just like that, you have a new health issue."

A new health issue? What other health issues does he have?

As he piled fresh lettuce and other vegetables onto his plate, he said, "Please, don't tell anyone about this."

"About what?" she asked.

"You know… me being diabetic."

She hadn't realized it was something he was embarrassed about, but she would never tell a secret that wasn't hers to tell.

"I promise I won't," she said.

Robbie smiled, and from that point on, Nitsy knew they would be friends. She was shocked to find he wasn't as immune to the problems of the common man as she'd believed him to be. He had issues too. Only, he kept his secret, and she was pretty sure she knew why. He wouldn't want everyone on his baseball team knowing he was diabetic. It was silly really. It wasn't like having issues with sugar made him weak, but in a young boy's mind, he couldn't be Superman anymore if the world knew his kryptonite.

"So, you going to be the leader of your group project?" Nitsy asked as she followed him to an empty table and sat down across from him. He was the leader type and if anybody could handle the job, it was Robbie, so it surprised her when he shook his head.

"Really?" she asked.

He stabbed a cherry tomato with his fork. "Why do you seem so surprised?"

"No reason. You'd be good at it, that's all."

"Nah, not me. I don't feel like being hit with a bunch of questions later. Plus, I'm not into public speaking. I get all marble-mouthed when I have to speak in front of a crowd."

She almost spit out her food. By the second, Robbie was tearing down this tough guy image she'd always had of him.

"*You* have a fear of public speaking?" she nearly yelled.

"I take it you don't."

Now that she thought about it, she didn't like it much either. Her palms always got sweaty and her throat would get dry. If she took on this leadership role today, she'd have to speak later. She decided she needed to face this demon if she had any shot at slaying it. She'd confronted death this year, and she figured she could go face-to-face with public speaking too.

"I wouldn't call it a fear," she finally answered. "I'm not exactly excited about it, but I can handle it."

He chuckled as he stabbed a cucumber slice and shoved it into his mouth. "Man, you really are a tough chick, aren't you, Nitsy?"

He thinks you're tough.

"I can hold my own," she said.

"Mind if I sit with y'all?" came a voice with a sweet southern accent.

Nitsy looked up to see the blonde Robbie had been talking to as they'd lined up at the entrance yesterday. She was even prettier up close. Finally, Nitsy said, "Sure."

Robbie was clearly happy to see her. He wore the big dumb grin all guys wore when they were close to a pretty girl.

He doesn't grin like that when he's near you.

Of course, he didn't. He didn't like her. He was consumed by the hot blonde now seated next to him.

"I'm Bianca," the girl said.

Of course, you are.

Nitsy, who was nice to everyone she met, waved a polite hello to the girl. Inside, she was kicking and screaming. Why? She wasn't sure. It wasn't like she was crushing on Robbie or anything. Maybe she simply felt Bianca was too perfect, and it reminded Nitsy of all her own imperfections. That had to be it.

She'd barely touched her salad when she found herself standing up from the table and saying, "I have to go. I need to take care of a few things."

Typical to Robbie's carefree nature, he didn't question it but nodded and said, "Okay, it was great talking to you, Nitsy. Hope your team does well in the competition."

"Yours too," she replied.

Nitsy took her tray to the garbage collection area and angrily separated her leftover food, her utensils, her plate, and her cup into the correct bins. She didn't realize until she was finished that Phyllis was standing next to her, bug-eyed, clearly concerned about the dramatic manner in which she was disposing of her lunch.

"What?" she asked the girl, unable to control her negative attitude. She was suddenly in a pissy mood and she wasn't sure why.

"What has you all riled up?" Phyllis asked.

"Riled up? I'm not."

"Really, 'cause you were softball pitching your garbage into the bin."

Nitsy laughed.

"We could go egg people's houses," Phyllis continued, "or rob a store if you still need to let off some steam."

"Stop it," Nitsy said. "I'm fine."

"If you say so."

Robbie didn't know what to think. It seemed like Nitsy was flirting with him a little bit. Not so much in the words she spoke, but definitely in the sidelong glances she gave him and the way her lips kept creeping up into smiles at the oddest of times. He'd been with enough girls to know when one liked him, and he was getting the feeling Nitsy might actually be into him.

What a breath of fresh air.

It was cliché, he knew, but he felt like he could breathe easier when Nitsy was around. Unlike so many other girls, she talked to him like a human being, like an equal, and he kind of dug that. So many girls his age treated him like a superstar when he hadn't really done anything to deserve it.

And she knows your secret now.

It wasn't that he was embarrassed about being diabetic, but he didn't want to be treated differently. His parents had given him a note to pass to the coach, but Robbie tossed it into the garbage can.

This was his junior year. This was when college recruits would be out looking for the best of the best. If it was known he had health conditions, they might try to stop him. That happened to his buddy Matt. Matt had asthma, and he tried to play anyway, but the coaches treated him like he was different. He ended up sitting the bench more often than he played, even though he was one of the best on the team.

Robbie couldn't handle being a Matt. He was a starter. He was great at every sport he played. Some kids could tell you everything about the universe, some were mathematical geniuses, some could dance across a stage or sing every note needed in chorus, and some, like Robbie, were natural athletes.

Nitsy seemed to understand, and it was yet another reason to like her.

But can you seriously see yourself dating her?

Yes, he could. Would he catch some shit for it? Obviously. People would ask why he'd chosen to date a nerd. That would have bothered him when he was a freshman or a sophomore. Something changed in him right before his junior year. It was around the time he found out he needed to control his sugars. He didn't care all that much what others thought. He only wanted to play sports and be a kid for a little longer. He wanted to run until his chest hurt, play video games until his fingers throbbed, and maybe even fall in love. Real love. Not the sexual lust he'd had with his last two girlfriends.

Nitsy could be a real girlfriend. She even thought Robbie had leadership potential. He could never do it. Speaking in front of people made him nervous. He could stand in a locker room and get his team excited before a game, but he could never stand on stage and do it with a crowd of spectators gaping at him.

He sincerely wanted to ask Nitsy out. Not to date here at the conference, but to maybe go grab a burger and see a movie when they got home. It was that smile of hers. He loved it. Her dimples were adorable.

"Mind if I sit with y'all?"

Bianca's voice caught him off guard. He'd met the beautiful blonde by the buses when they were first ordered to line up before entering Stonewall Forge. They'd bumped right into each other in that crowd of teenagers. She was gorgeous. Smooth skin, silky blonde hair, and luscious red lips.

She's the type you always go for.

Then he saw the way Nitsy was staring at him. Without saying a single word, he'd pissed her off. When she got up and left with her tray, he felt like he should say something that would make her stay, but he also didn't want to make his slight infatuation with her too obvious.

He wasn't leading Bianca on. In fact, he'd only met the girl yesterday. They were only friends.

A friend you would hook up with in a second if given the chance.

No, a friend too much like the girls he'd hooked up with in the past, so making the same mistake again would be stupid. This was true, but it didn't stop him from moving his hand when he felt Bianca's brush his on top of the table. If she had interlaced her fingers through his, he still wouldn't have pulled his hand away.

Why?

Because Bianca was hot, and Nitsy was out of reach. Why not pursue something much more likely to happen? All he needed was to spend his time trying to win the affections of one of the most unapproachable girls at school, only to have her go back and tell everyone on campus how he'd tried to date her on this trip.

You know that's not like her.

It was like most girls.

She's not most girls.

His internal voice was bugging the shit out of him. He didn't realize he'd been ignoring Bianca until he noticed she was waiting for an answer to a question she'd asked him. So, Robbie did what he always did at a moment like this. He tilted his head slightly to the side, grinned, and said, "I don't know," followed by a slight chuckle.

"What do you mean you don't know?" Bianca said, slapping his hand. She rolled her eyes and added, "You know exactly what I'm talking about. Don't play shy."

To this, he added one more head tilt, one more grin, and one more chuckle. Then he stood and helped her with her tray.

———————

Nitsy led Phyllis back toward the conference center. The campus was huge, easily large enough to have once been a college. The history of the campus was never explained to them, but Nitsy could imagine this once being a university at some point. The name of it, Stonewall Forge, meant there must have been Civil War history around here. Stonewall Jackson was an important general and Confederate leader. There were probably places all over West Virginia named after him.

"I wonder if anyone died here," she said as they walked the long corridor that led back to the conference room.

To walk the circumference of the entire campus would probably take at least thirty minutes. That would be at a brisk walk. The center's red brick walls formed a large square with stairs at each corner and halfway between each wall, leading up to the second floor. Both floors contained classrooms and other locked doors that Nitsy assumed were probably apartments or dormitory rooms like the ones they were staying in on the second floor.

At the atrium of the building was a giant chrome statue of Thomas Jonathan "Stonewall" Jackson standing proudly and watching over the main campus gate. Inside the walls, a dirt path circled the statue where people could drive in through the gate, circle the statue, and drive out. During the conference, while so many teenagers were meandering about, no vehicles entered the gate.

"Died *here*?" Phyllis asked, her face going blank and her eyes shooting open wide. It was clear the thought had never occurred to her, but it would now, probably every day and every night until they left.

"Yes, here," Nitsy replied. "You know this place has to have Civil War history. *Stonewall* Forge?"

She pointed at the statue's back.

"Oh, wow," Phyllis said. "Like double wow. I bet you're right. I bet there are ghosts all over this place. In fact, I heard things last night outside our room. Sounded like footsteps and chains dragging."

Nitsy rolled her eyes and laughed. "Yeah, the Ghost of Christmas Past was outside our door."

"Huh?"

She didn't get the reference, so Nitsy added to it, "*A Christmas Carol...*"

Phyllis still wasn't getting it.

"Not even the Disney one? The cartoon? With Goofy dragging the chains and Scrooge McDuck playing Ebenezer Scrooge? Oh, girl. You're helpless."

"Whatever, I heard chains."

"A friend of mine is missing," a booming voice called out from the other side of the statue.

Nitsy put an arm out to stop Phyllis, keeping them behind a brick column where they hid. Nitsy peered around it to see who was talking. One of their instructors, a man named Mr. Hayes, a very proper gentleman wearing a sweater with a dress shirt and bowtie beneath it, was talking to a park ranger. The ranger was a huge man, nearly twice Nitsy's height, with brown, slicked-back hair.

"He's a big guy, kind of rough around the edges. A hunter. Ex-military," the ranger said. "His truck crashed over by the highway and the cops haven't found him."

Mr. Hayes shook his head. "Haven't seen anyone like that."

"Maybe the caretaker has. Is he around?"

"No, and we're pretty upset about that. He's usually very good at his job. His wife too, but she didn't show up today to unlock the doors and he hasn't gotten rid of the beehive in the back. It's not like them.

We had to use the spare keys in the office to open the conference room this morning. Mrs. Price wasn't too happy about that."

The park ranger nodded his head every now and then but Nitsy was pretty sure the guy didn't care much about the boring happenings at their conference. He'd just said a friend of his was missing and Mr. Hayes was going on about pest control.

"Any idea where the caretaker lives?" the ranger asked.

"Somewhere down that street is all I know," Mr. Hayes replied. "They always drive off in that direction. Other than that, I'm afraid I can't help you."

"Thank you for your time."

That was Nitsy's cue to keep walking. She grabbed Phyllis by her wrist and yanked her down the hall. Eavesdropping on one of the instructors wasn't something she wanted on her record. She was hoping her group would do so great in their challenge she'd be a fron-trunner when it came time to vote in a conference president.

Nitsy and Phyllis were the first ones back to the conference room. Eggo was in a meeting with the other group leaders and Mrs. Price. He waved at the girls when they entered. Mrs. Price glanced over and noticed them.

Another point. She saw you were the first one back from lunch.

"Girls, you're back early," Mrs. Price said.

"I was always told if you're not early, you're late," Nitsy replied.

Mrs. Price turned back to the group leaders and said, "Oh, I like this one. We'll finish up later during dinner. You've got your group responsibilities, you've got your packets, now let the students shine. Make sure everyone's having a great time." She clapped her hands together and the leaders dispersed.

"Welcome back, Captain," Eggo said to Nitsy as he approached the girls. "We're going to be moving into the classrooms, so the team captains are hanging around here so they can send the rest of the team to the correct room. We'll be in 12-A. Upstairs."

With that, Eggo left Nitsy alone. Soon after, students started piling in at the exact time they were due to return from lunch or a few minutes after. As her teammates entered the room, Nitsy pointed them in the direction of room 12-A. Once everyone was accounted for, she joined them.

"So," Eggo began as soon as she entered and took her seat, "you've chosen your captain." He pointed at Nitsy, who couldn't help but blush. "We'll need to fill all the other positions too. But first, I've got some fun news. Each team is responsible for a duty around here. These duties help keep the place tidy and in order."

A few moans and groans went up in the group.

Eggo laughed. "Don't worry. I can promise you've scored the easiest, the best duty on the entire list." Eggo clapped his hands and rubbed them together. "Well, I should take that back. It's only the best if you're a morning person. If you hate getting up early, you won't like this one at all."

Nitsy had to think about this. Was she a morning person? She didn't particularly like getting up super early, but she was never any crankier when she had to.

Sure. You're a morning person.

As of today, she would be one, whether her body liked it or not.

"We're the wake-up crew," Eggo informed them. "We get to go up and down the halls at five o'clock in the morning and bang pots and pans together to wake everyone up."

"Seriously?" Phyllis asked, laughing and clapping her hands together the same way Eggo had. "Oh, can we please wake up Andrew? He's from my school and I know he's gonna be up late playing his video games every night."

"Is he the one who paused his game for this?" Nitsy laughed as she asked. Phyllis didn't seem to get it so Nitsy added, "You know, the t-shirt he wore on the bus?"

"Oh, yes!" She opened her eyes wide and grinned devilishly. "We have to wake him up. He'll hate me even more."

Nitsy liked the girl and could already see they'd be great friends.

"Tomorrow morning, you will become the most hated team on campus," Eggo promised them. "And you're going to love it. While some crews have to stay behind to make sure the cafeteria is tidy after every meal and some have to walk the grounds to pick up garbage or straighten up the seats in the conference room, you get to make every-body angry each and every morning."

"But we also have to wake up earlier than everybody else," a boy named Todd squeaked out from his seat at the back of the classroom. He was a tiny, mousy boy with feathery blonde hair. He looked more like an eighth-grader than a junior in high school.

"Very true," Eggo said, "but you have to get up early anyway around here, so why not be the one who gets to have some fun with it?"

Eggo's energy was infectious and soon they were all laughing.

After that, it was all business. They needed to assign positions to everyone else in the group. Their briefing inside the packet given to them by Mrs. Price was a list of key positions. Ten positions. One for each person in the group. Eggo could not play along. Nitsy, being the captain, got to choose her co-captain, and she went with Avery, the one person who'd challenged Nitsy for the lead position. She was the pret-tiest in the group, with long black hair that hung down in tangles, and wasn't afraid to speak her mind.

Communications and Information Officer was easy. Phyllis never stopped talking. She was perfect for the position. Structural Engineer went to Bradley, whose attire screamed anime and manga. He was the artist in the bunch, so it would fall on him to draw the spacecraft. Ashley, who seemed to blink constantly, would be the crew Medical Officer. She wanted to study medicine in real life, so... why not? The list went on and on. Soon, they also chose their Pilot and Co-Pilot, their Security Officer, their Data Collection Specialist, and their Lead Scientist.

From that point on, everyone worked on his or her portion of the packet with feedback from other group members. Afternoon faded into evening with a short dinner break and then right into night. It didn't occur to Nitsy how late it was until she started rubbing at her eyes. A yawn escaped Phyllis. Eggo played on his phone through most of the work session since he really couldn't add any information. He was only there as a moderator, to keep them on track. Now, even he was looking at them with heavy eyelids.

"Y'all ready to wrap this up?" he asked.

"We're not done," Nitsy said. "Oh, how I wish we were finished, but we still need to go over the security info for the ship and make sure we all understand how we'll answer questions. They could be slow and relaxed, or they could be rapid fire."

Eggo nodded and chuckled. "I'd expect at least some rapid fire. Mrs. Price is tough enough but wait until she opens up questions to the rest of the groups. This is a competition. That part can get pretty ugly. You all should be thinking of questions you'd like to ask opposing teams, too."

"Bradley's ship is awesome at least," Phyllis said.

It was. The boy had created something Nitsy couldn't imagine any of the other teams coming up with. It was beautiful, but it was also strong and sturdy.

"Yeah," Nitsy agreed. "We've got the ship design aspect in the bag."

Bradley blushed. Earlier in the evening, when he'd come close to her to get her opinion on a few design elements, Nitsy thought he might have been flirting with her. He was definitely friendly.

A few minutes later, Eggo clapped his hands together and said, "I think you all should call it a night. You're Wake-Up Crew, so we need to meet up downstairs, outside the entrance, at 4:45 in the morning. If you're late, we're waking everyone up without you and our team will lose points for not fulfilling our duty."

"Eggo, we're not done though—" Nitsy started to argue.

"You'll be fine," Eggo interrupted. "This happens every year. No team is ready this early. Do your wake-up duty in the morning, then get ready and shower, eat breakfast, and come back to this classroom. The morning session won't be until ten, so you'll have a few hours to finish."

Nitsy wasn't happy about this. She wanted to be prepared. Her teammates were used to staying up late. All teenagers were. If they were at home, they'd be playing a video game half the night, or they'd be watching movies. They definitely wouldn't be going to sleep. She considered talking to them on the side and asking if they wanted to meet somewhere to finish their work. They'd all scooted out of the room ahead of her, and she was about to rush out after them when Eggo pointed at her and said, "Don't even think about it. I see it in your eyes. It's against the rules to meet unsupervised. Teams have tried and every team has failed. Don't do it."

She laughed and rolled her eyes. "Busted. That's exactly what I was thinking."

"I know," Eggo replied. "Want to know how I know? Because the brightest kids are the hardest workers, and somebody tries it every year. I don't want your team to be this year's example. You have to follow the rules if you want a shot at winning."

"Sometimes the best leaders are rulebreakers," Nitsy argued.

He shrugged. "Not here they're not. Finish up tomorrow."

Nitsy left the room feeling defeated. They had a lot of work to complete in the morning. She knew her mind wouldn't shut down the way she needed it to. More than likely, she would be up most of the night thinking about the project and what she might say tomorrow in front of Mrs. Price and everyone else attending the conference.

She was so stuck in her thoughts that she didn't even realize she was the only person in the hallway. Above her, one lamp shone brightly down on her, but up ahead, where the motion sensor lights picked up no movement, the hallway was pitch black. The others were gone. Even Phyllis had left her.

At her feet, the lime green tile flooring was shiny beneath the lamp. The cement wall to her left bounced the sheen of the overhead light back at her. On that wall, a bulletin board was only half visible. The rest of it was obscured by the darkness ahead and off to her right where the wind rattled the trees out in the open courtyard.

Talent show, Saturday night, 8 p.m., let us see you shine.

Nitsy read the postcard-sized advertisement on the bulletin board aloud, and her voice carried down the hall, echoing so loudly she thought the other lights might pop on. As much as she wanted to show off her leadership skills, she had no desire to get on stage and sing, dance, or recite poetry. She hoped the talent show had nothing to do with the president position.

Student Board Meeting to discuss new curfew and other matters of importance.

This flyer seemed old. Its corners were raveled and some of the wording had faded. Most of it was too dark to see, but it made Nitsy wonder once again about the past at Stonewall Forge. Was this once a college campus?

Her mind kicked into overdrive, a problem she often had when lying in an MRI machine. That loud, constant noise. It was like a jackhammer to the brain, but it changed pitch and tone often. Sometimes she'd imagine bad things happening throughout the hospital. Each scene moved to the beat.

In one, there was an after-hour party and all the doctors were dancing to the beat. Everyone was drinking. No one noticed the lunatic who'd escaped his restraints and was now enjoying the party with them. He boogied his way over to one of the nurses, a brunette that looked kind of like Nitsy's new Co-Captain, Avery. The nurse lifted her glass to cheer when the lunatic brought a scalpel around and slid it across her neck. Then he moved on to one of the doctors and jabbed at him to the beat.

When the MRI tone changed, she saw a girl dancing on a stage. Ballet style. She was beautiful, around the same age as Nitsy, in a pink leotard. Her graceful legs pranced around the open space while a row of judges watched her. One of the judges reached for a dial on the table in front of him. It looked like the kind on the oven in Nitsy's kitchen. The judge cranked the heat up all the way and suddenly the stage glowed red and the ballet dancer screamed. She leaped to the MRI machine's beat, screaming with each step as her feet sizzled on stage.

Then there was the one Nitsy hated, but it always appeared when she was in that white tunnel of solitude.

WOMP... WOMP... WOMP... EEK... EEK... EEK... WOMP... WOMP... WOMP.

Over and over again the noise beat at her brain until she imagined creepy crawlies inside her body fighting to escape the sound. Cockroaches that had been snacking on her brain cheese scattered down and out her nose. Worms swimming in her intestines couldn't take it any longer and burst through her belly. Spider babies that had hatched in her ear canals skittered out her ears and ran along her shoulders. Gnats popped out the jelly of her eyes and fled from her screams as much as that insistent hammering from the machine.

This was the havoc Nitsy's mind played on her when she was alone... in the dark... like she was now. Down the hall, she knew something must be waiting. In a place as old as this, with the bloody past of the land surrounding it, and with the possibility of drunken parties gone wrong when it was once a university campus. Young women would scream while frat boys held them down. Ghosts would want to play in this place. Maybe even poltergeists. Demons would dance in these dark halls, unable to force the motion sensors to come to life, leaving them forever prancing in the blackness of night.

Even the living would roam these grounds. Terror lived on forever, and all the sorority girls who'd screamed for help would manifest into something horrible. Nitsy imagined pale white women roaming the halls, barefoot, in ripped nightgowns, and if you got to close to them, they'd open their mouths and scream the way they did that night when the boys played too rough and their virgin innocence was ripped from them.

Silence. Total silence. It was almost as loud as the MRI machine's hammering.

A door popped open behind her and Nitsy nearly screamed.

Eggo stepped out of the classroom and locked the door behind him. She'd forgotten he was still in there. Everyone else had left, but Eggo stayed behind, playing on his phone, waiting for them to flee back to their rooms.

Nitsy paused with her hand at her chest, choking back the scream that almost belted forth from her gut. Eggo seemed almost as frightened by her presence. The keys rattled in his hand.

"Jesus," he said. "What are you doing here?"

"I... I was reading the flyers on the board," she said.

"You scared me, man," he admitted.

"Got me too."

They both laughed.

"Now, go to bed," Eggo ordered. "At 4:45 you better be ready to wake up the world. Nobody else even knows what's coming. You guys will be the most hated crew here."

"Great," she replied, "and right on time to be hit with questions."

He shrugged. "Gotta laugh in the face of your enemies, Nitsy. Get some rest," he lowered his voice and added, "so you can scare the shit out of everyone in the morning."

"It's on," she assured him, with a confident nod of her head.

"It's on," he replied.

Eggo turned and walked in the opposite direction of Nitsy's room, leaving her once again to face the darkness alone.

Nothing's here with you. Walk to your room. That's all you have to do. Walk.

With the workshop room on the second floor, the same floor where her room was located, she only needed to continue down the hall to get where she was going. So she did. She took one step at a time and made her way past the next classroom. The lights were off, the room was dark, and so was the hallway—

POP. The light above her flashed on and even though she was expecting it to, the way it cut through the black space so quickly and so harshly caused her to flinch and tighten her fists.

Somewhere in the distance, she heard giggling and feet slapping the tile floor, but it wasn't scary. It wasn't the playfulness of ghostly children in the halls. It was one of the other teams wrapping up their project session and headed back to their rooms.

The next light popped on as she moved under it. There was still so much hallway ahead of her.

She quietly made her way down the dark corridor and tried her best to force hideous images from her imagination. It was of no use. Ahead of her, in the next classroom window, she thought she saw a pale face, and she knew it would be grinning at her as she passed, daring her to turn the knob and join it in there.

Don't look. Keep walking.

Her eyes were on her shoes as she stepped past the window. The light turned on and she still refused to glance up. It would be there. She knew it. Smiling a jagged-toothed grin. It might even call out to her in a gravely, throaty voice. "Come in and play."

Keep walking, keep walking, keep walking.

Nitsy picked up her pace and finally lifted her gaze to see how much further she needed to walk. Around the next bend would be the hall full of dorm rooms. Hers was the fifth down on the left. She was almost there.

Why didn't Phyllis wait for you? You're going to give her so much hell when you get to your room.

Nitsy froze.

Behind her came the chittering of what sounded like crickets. Inside the building. Too terrified to look back, but too nervous not to, Nitsy stood in the space between one light and the next and thought about it. The light behind her turned off. The one in front of her hadn't yet illuminated.

Total darkness.

Crickets.

No, not crickets. Like hissing cockroaches.

And it wasn't coming from behind her now. It was somewhere ahead of her.

She couldn't wait any longer, she marched forward, her legs moving on their own now, too afraid to allow her mental images to slow them down. The sound was far enough ahead of her that she could detect it before getting too close.

Before she knew it, she was rounding the corner and on the last leg of the walk to her room. She had only five doors to go. The lights came on as she walked, and she was moving so quickly more than one light was on at a time. She felt better, more secure until she saw the figure at the end of the hallway.

Nitsy halted again and peered into the darkness at the end of the hall. The hissing of the roaches was there in the darkness, and she thought she saw a man standing with his legs slightly apart, his right arm stretched out, his fingertips touching the wall while his other arm hung loosely at his side. The man looked like he was struggling to hold himself up, like a drunkard walking home from a bar.

There is a man.

She couldn't make out his features. He was too far away. Nitsy crept forward quietly. She was at the third door now and only needed to go a little further. She was almost there.

Is he watching you?

The closer she grew, the less sure she was that it was a man at all. He stood so still that he could have been a mannequin propped up at the end of the hall. She didn't remember seeing one there during the daytime and she couldn't imagine why there would be one there at all.

The clicking and hissing grew louder as if some*thing* sensed her proximity. Whatever was making that noise wanted to pounce on her. She could feel it.

It's your imagination again. You're not in a damn MRI machine, Nitsy. You're at Stonewall Forge Leadership Conference and you're safe.

But was she? The park ranger had said his friend was missing. And the caretaker and his wife hadn't shown up for work.

It's only a coincidence.

Nitsy was only a few feet away from her door when the figure at the end of the hallway moved. The hand touching the wall scraped against it, digging its fingernails in. The free hand reached out to her. And the clicking and hissing practically screamed at her.

She turned the knob, yanked open her door, and closed it behind her. She didn't slam it out of fear it would only make the figure come to her door. She hoped that by being quiet maybe it wouldn't follow her.

"Hey!" Phyllis called out from behind her. "I was wondering where you were."

Nitsy looked at her new friend in her flowered pink pajamas and fought back the urge to scream at her. Finally, she got control of her breathing. "You left me."

"Left you where?"

Their other roommate, Megan, who'd been assigned the role of Data Collection Specialist because she was always on her phone "researching," stared down at them both from her bed on the top bunk and said, "We only came back to the room."

"Something's out there," Nitsy whispered. "Keep your voices down."

"You're just trying to scare us," Phyllis insisted. "Like earlier when you were talking about ghosts and stuff. Now's not the time. We need to sleep so we can do well on our project in the morning."

Nitsy shook her head. "I'm telling you, there's something out there."

Phyllis put her hands on her hips. "Are you trying to get me to look out there?"

Nitsy shook her head again.

"Good," Phyllis said, "Because I don't want to. I want to go to bed. And you want to know why I left you?" When Nitsy didn't reply, Phyllis continued, "I left you because Bradley walked me back to the room. I think I kinda like him."

Of course, Nitsy was happy for her. Any other night, she would probably ask for all the juicy details, but she knew something was on the other side of her door. She had no idea what it was or what it wanted, but she sensed it wasn't good, and she knew it was standing out there right now... listening.

Megan plopped earbuds into her ears and threw her head back onto her pillow. "I'm getting some sleep. You two can chit chat all night if you want."

Nitsy had taken the bottom bunk, leaving Phyllis the free twin-size bed across from them. Nitsy didn't even change her clothes. She would do that in the morning. For now, she only wanted to wrap herself up in her comforter and feel safe and warm. She would not be leaving this room until morning, even though the shared female bathroom was a couple of doors down. She would pee herself if she had to, but she wasn't going out into that hallway.

As Megan whispered the lyrics to whatever song she was listening to and Phyllis began to snore softly, Nitsy swore she heard footsteps retreating down the hall.

9

While Nitsy closed her eyes and prayed the thing in the hallway was only a figment of her imagination, downstairs and three doors over, a group of teenagers seemed to have forgotten about the project at hand. Robbie was one of them.

When he'd returned to his dorm room following his group's meeting, he found his roommates freshly dressed. The room reeked of cologne.

"What are you guys doing?" he'd asked as he plopped down on his bed. Robbie had gotten stuck with the bottom bunk.

"Dude," Trevor, his wisecracking, wannabe tough guy roommate started, "do you know who's in the room like right above us?"

Robbie didn't.

"I heard from a reliable source," Trevor continued, "that Misty, that cute chick with the purple hair, Desiree, and your girl, Bianca, are upstairs. I got their room number. They're in 214."

It turned out Trevor had a bit of a crush on Misty, a raven-haired goth girl who'd been somewhat flirtatious with the boy at lunch. Robbie had spent the entire day with all three of the girls, and as much as he liked Bianca, he was ready to shower and get some sleep. Trevor, who hadn't been lucky enough to get "all the hot chicks" on his team, wouldn't take *no* for an answer. The boy was dying to spend time with Robbie's "team full of hunnies."

"Dude, if we get caught, we're gonna mess things up pretty badly," Robbie said.

"Tell me," Trevor said as he stood on the one single bed in their room. His soapbox. "What do you really think this is going to do for your future, man? Aren't you a sports star?"

Robbie, looked up at him from his seated position on the bottom bunk across from him and said, "Star? Bro, I said I play baseball."

"Too bad it's not football," the kid on the top bunk said. His name was Steven, and Robbie thought he was a bit of an asshole. "It's the football players who get all the chicks."

"Do you play football?" Robbie asked, looking up at the boy around the edge of the bed.

Steven was tall and muscular. He claimed to be a martial artist. That was enough to stop Robbie from crossing the line, but it wasn't enough to keep him from stepping right up to it.

"Nah, man," Steven replied. "I wouldn't play a sport that requires me to wear a bunch of pads. I like to meet my opponents head-on."

Robbie wanted nothing more than to stand up, grab hold of Steven's neck, and yank him over the bed and onto the floor.

And where would this plan go from there?

That was a problem. He'd never had to fight much in his life. He was well-liked by most of the guys where he lived. Plus, he hung out with a lot of bigger guys. He'd made it through high school so far unchallenged and unscathed. Besides, it seemed the days of fistfights were over. People seemed to be resorting to violence less and less. Heated discussions were more likely to occur at his school. Robbie, who was exhausted, wasn't in the mood for an argument.

"Hey, eyes up here," Trevor announced.

Robbie tore his eyes from the asshole above him and shifted them back to the kid with the slicked-back hair and denim jacket covering his torso. It was the kid's mustache that drew the most attention. It looked ridiculous in all its barely-there glory. Trevor often stroked it as he spoke, running his fingers over the shadow like he might will it to grow more fully by touching it with magic fingertips. With his attire and nearly non-existent facial hair, it was clear Trevor wanted the girls at Stonewall Forge to know he was one of the bad boys.

But is he?

He was here, after all, and that made Robbie think he was nothing but a poser. His punk rock T-shirt wasn't fooling him. You could only be so bad and receive an invite to a conference like this. Yet, the kid was willing to risk the entire thing on meeting some girls.

"Are we really going to waste this weekend sitting around and studying?" Trevor continued. "Pretending we're on a spaceship for fuck's sake? I think not. I'm headed upstairs to Misty's room. You, Robbie, should be thinking about Bianca right now. And, Steven, I think you could totally nail Desiree."

Nail? The thought made Robbie laugh. These chumps weren't going to have sex with either of those girls. It wasn't like they were at some sleazy nightclub or a drunken frat party. They were juniors in high school on a school field trip.

"You do realize we're at a fucking *leadership* conference, right?" Robbie asked. "These are leaders."

"Yeah," Trevor replied, "well, I'll lead these *leaders* to the water… and make 'em drink."

That didn't even make sense. Robbie stared at him with one eyebrow raised. It was his "what the fuck are you talking about" look.

"Oh, I wouldn't miss this for the world," Steven said as he leaped down from the top bunk, inches away from Robbie's head.

Even Steven seemed to realize how ridiculous this was, but he was willing to tag along. Robbie felt like he didn't have much choice in the matter. Sure, he could stay in his room and let the other two boys go alone, but he felt an odd sense of camaraderie with these boys. He couldn't ditch them. He was the third musketeer. He was the drummer while Trevor was the wild frontman and Steven was on lead guitar. Robbie imagined them as a three-person band on stage and laughed.

"What's so funny?" Trevor asked. "You don't wanna get laid?"

"We're not getting laid," Robbie said as he stood from his mattress and shook his head, "but I'll go with you."

"My man!" Trevor announced as he whipped his hand out to slap Robbie's.

A high five? We're really doing this?

He couldn't leave Trevor hanging, so he met the boy halfway and slapped hands with him, which turned into one of those automatic *bro* handshakes. Robbie knew this was a bad idea, but he had to admit it would be fun sneaking out and paying Bianca a visit. He wondered how she'd react. She might freak out and tell him to get the hell out of her room, or she might invite him in.

You know who else is on that floor. Nitsy's probably only a few doors down.

Nitsy would punch him in the nose if he showed up at her room this late at night.

"Fine," Robbie said, "but only for a few minutes. Unlike you, I actually do care about this conference."

"Right," Trevor said, "only a few minutes. I don't know about you two, but I usually take a little longer than that."

The hallway was pitch black, and it seemed the plan would be easy. Hide in the shadows until they made it to the stairwell and then quietly head upstairs.

"Piece of cake," Trevor said. "These people are idiots."

As soon as he took two steps, an overhead light popped on and caused the boy to jump and sprint for the stairs. Robbie froze in place for a second, realizing it was his last chance to turn back and return to his room. They were still on the male floor. Here, he stood no chance of getting in trouble, but once he stepped foot on that staircase, if he got caught, it would be obvious where he was going.

"Come on, man!" Steven whispered loudly. "You're gonna get us caught."

Robbie snapped out of it and followed the other boys to the staircase, where they fought to contain their laughter.

"That light scared the shit out of me," Trevor admitted. "I thought we got busted already."

"Motion sensor lights," Steven said. "Fucking figures."

When they reached the second floor and found the girls' room, 214,

Trevor knocked softly. Desiree answered the door in a pair of silk paja-mas. Her pink shorts were really short and outlined with black lace. Her top had spaghetti straps and was the same material. It was clear she wasn't wearing a bra underneath. Robbie shook his head when Trevor froze up with his eyes glued to the girl's nipples.

"What are you doing here?" she asked.

The girls, after a short debate, allowed the boys to enter the room. Robbie sat at a desk chair in the corner. Bianca was on the top bunk looking down at him, smiling. She wore green shorts and a T-shirt designed to look like a Green Bay Packers jersey. As he checked her out, he realized he was still wearing the clothes he'd been in during their project meeting.

What a loser. You couldn't at least change clothes like the other guys?

In his defense, he hadn't been given much time.

Trevor and Misty sat side by side on the single bed. Steven sat on the floor with his legs crossed. Desiree didn't seem interested in him at all.

"So, what now?" Bianca asked.

"What do you mean?" Trevor replied.

"Y'all came all the way up here. For what?"

"To get to know you better, man," Trevor replied as if it made all the sense in the world.

Bianca scoffed. "You do realize if we get caught with you in our room, we're screwed, right?"

Bianca was their voice of reason the same way he had tried to be for his group.

"That's what I said," Robbie replied.

Bianca smiled at him and Trevor rolled his eyes.

"We could play cards," Steven suggested, holding up a pack he'd pulled from his pocket.

"I don't know any card games," Bianca admitted.

Neither did Robbie. He hadn't played cards since he was a kid. War and Go-Fish were the only two games he remembered. Again, he found himself thinking this was a horrible idea. He wanted to go back to his room and rest. He'd only tagged along because he thought maybe he'd get somewhere with the pretty blonde on the top bunk, but unless he decided to climb up there with her, he didn't see that happening.

"Maybe we should go," Robbie suggested.

Bianca whined, surprising him, and said, "No, don't go. Not yet. You just got here."

Trevor grinned. "Thought you wanted us to leave."

"Well, you're here now," Bianca replied.

Trevor winked at Robbie and said, "Truth or dare?"

"I know that one," Bianca replied.

"Sounds like fun, I guess," Misty said.

Desiree shrugged her shoulders.

Typical teenagers and their kissing dares. It bothered Robbie for some reason. He'd played this game a ton of times. He'd either be dared to kiss Bianca or to remove some piece of clothing. If he chose truth, he'd be asked if he liked anyone in the room.

He wondered if Nitsy would play a game like this. He figured she probably wouldn't. She was too good to allow herself to be kissed on a dare. A guy needed to earn it with her.

Why are you thinking about Nitsy when you're right here in a room with Bianca?

The truth was, Robbie wanted to leave the room. This wasn't his plan for tonight. He wanted to rest and do well in the competition tomorrow.

If this were a movie, every male member of the audience would throw popcorn at the screen.

He knew this was the lamest way to leave the room, but he couldn't be in a place, doing things he didn't want to do, with a girl he wasn't sure he wanted to do it with. These were the typical teenagers, and he wanted to believe he was something more. Bianca was beautiful. Any guy would be lucky to have her, and perhaps he'd still pursue something with her, but if he did, he didn't want to do it like this.

Risking it for both of them wasn't a good idea.

"Hey, I'm really sorry, guys," Robbie announced, "but I'm

exhausted, man. Tomorrow's competition is kind of important, and I want to do well."

Bianca frowned at him, looking quite sad. Trevor booed him. Steven laughed.

"Will you stay?" Misty asked Trevor. "A little longer?"

"Damn right I will," Trevor announced.

"Me too," Steven said.

They could stay and entertain the girls, but Robbie felt good about his decision to leave. Bianca climbed down from the top bunk and met him at the door.

"Sure you don't want to stay?" she asked.

Her blonde hair was pulled back into a ponytail and Robbie thought she was gorgeous. He was doubting himself.

Stay. She wants you, man. Stay and get some.

If he played Truth or Dare, he'd end up making out with her. She seemed fine with that. Any other teenage boy would probably stay and take advantage of the situation, but Robbie felt strange about it, like he needed to go. Nitsy came to mind again. Their conversation at lunch and the way she seemed to be nervous around him. He liked that. He liked her. It was then that he realized why he wanted to leave the room so badly. Because he couldn't be with Bianca without thinking he was somehow stabbing Nitsy in the back.

But you're not even dating that girl!

His internal frat boy wanted to punch him in the face for making this decision, but he nodded and said, "Yeah, I want to go back to my room. I'm tired. We have a big day tomorrow. You should get some rest too."

She frowned and looked over at Misty who was practically sitting on Trevor's lap. Steven was now sitting next to Desiree on her bottom-bunk bed.

"I don't see myself getting to sleep anytime soon," Bianca said. "I could use some company."

It was so hard telling the girl no, but he did with a shake of his head.

"Robbie," Bianca said, "you sure are a confusing boy." She leaned forward and kissed his forehead. "If you can't sleep, you know where I am."

He smiled and left the room.

When he closed the door behind him and stepped out into the dark hall, all was silent except the muffled sound of laughter coming from within the room at his back. Robbie never considered himself someone who scared easily, and there really wasn't much reason to be afraid, but he did feel a sudden sense of dread in the hallway.

With his back to the door, he stood in the darkness and glanced to his right, away from the staircase. He wondered where Nitsy was. She could be in the room right next to him and he would have no idea. She was probably already asleep or reading a book while listening to Mozart. She was that kind of girl. He bet she listened to classical music all the time and read all the books the English teacher tried to force on them like *Pride and Prejudice, A Tale of Two Cities,* and *Wuthering Heights.*

If teachers would include more books with sports or with... zombies—

His thoughts were interrupted by a strange sound. It was an insect's chirp. But more like a clickety-clack. He didn't like it. It didn't sound natural. It was coming from his right. He peered in that direction once more and thought he saw something at the end of the hall.

Robbie froze. A man stood there watching him. If it was a teacher, he was busted. He'd stepped out of the girls' room only moments before. The teacher would have seen that. If he made a run for it now and quietly slipped back into his room, he'd never get caught. He could get into his bed and shower tomorrow morning.

The man at the end of the hall moved forward, slowly, and Robbie waited for the overhead light to pop on. If it did, he'd be able to see which teacher was watching him. Then again, if the light came on, the teacher might get a better look at him as well.

On the count of three. One... two...

Heavy footsteps sounded off as the man moved toward him, stumbling forward.

Robbie didn't wait for the lights. He dashed down the hall, hit the stairs and took them three at a time, and was back in his room with the door shut and locked in a matter of seconds. With his heart pounding in his chest, he slid to the floor and sat with his back against the door. He waited for the teacher to come knocking, but he never did.

Bianca stood at the door pouting. Robbie was exactly what she wanted, and she didn't want for much. She was the kind of girl who usually got what she desired. That didn't make her a bitch. Some of the girls at her school thought so, but it wasn't true. In fact, she cared more about what others thought than most of her friends. She hated being hated. She loved being loved. So, boys like Robbie were confusing. He was somewhere in the middle. Of course, he didn't hate her, but it was clear he wouldn't be falling in love with her anytime soon.

"I can't believe he left like that," Misty said.

Bianca had a feeling Misty didn't like her. Desiree seemed okay with her, but Misty had made a few comments throughout the day that got on Bianca's nerves. Like when Bianca came to class a few seconds late, Misty said, "The girl with all the dough can't afford a watch?"

Sure, her family had money, but that didn't mean she flaunted it. She was a nice girl. She spent a lot of time making sure everyone knew that. She volunteered at the children's hospital every Saturday and spent Tuesday evenings at her church's youth choir.

"I know," Bianca said. "I guess that's what makes him kind of special."

"That he'd ditch you?" Desiree asked. "Sounds like an asshole to me."

"He's just tired," Bianca defended him. "I have to admit, I am too."

Bianca was about to climb the ladder to her bed when there was a thump at the door behind her. She smiled.

"Ohhh sounds like lover boy might be back," Trevor said. "I had a feeling he'd regret leaving."

"Don't open it," Misty told her.

"What?" Bianca asked. "Why not?"

"Let him wait a bit," Misty replied. "Being in our room is a privilege. He's lost that privilege."

Desiree and Steven both laughed. They would make a good match. Desiree was a tennis player who always kept her dirty blonde hair up in one of those headbands tennis players wore. Steven was obviously a jock. If she had to guess, she'd say he played one of those sports she'd never actually seen anyone play like polo or lacrosse.

Something smacked against the door.

"He's desperate," Misty said. "Hear that? He's slapping the door now."

"Oh, let's let him in," Bianca said.

"No, a little longer," Desiree suggested.

"I say don't let him in at all," Steven added. "He's kind of an asshole. If he wanted to go back to our room so badly, I say let him."

Sounds like you're the asshole.

Bianca hadn't had any reason not to like the boy before, but now he seemed like a total jerk. What had Robbie ever done to him?

"No," Bianca announced, "I'm going to let him in."

She turned, threw the latch on the door, and pulled it open despite her friends' calls to keep the door shut. As the door opened inward, she saw a shadowy figure standing in front of her.

"Robbie?" she asked.

She knew it wasn't him. Her first thought was they were busted. A teacher had heard all the noise from the other side and was here to check on the disturbance. They would all be in trouble. She wondered if they would call her parents or handle this internally.

"Who is it?" Misty asked.

Bianca gasped when she heard the sound emanating from the man. She couldn't describe it, and she couldn't move to close the door even though she knew she should.

It was loud.

Angry.

Hungry.

Determined.

And it pounced on her. Like a hundred hot droplets of acid on her scalp, instant sizzling-like pain bit into her head and seemed to be quickly driving deeper and deeper into her skull. Bianca fell backward and right into the arms of Trevor who'd stood to check on her.

"What the fuck?" he asked. "Are you okay—"

His voice caught in his throat, and Bianca knew he was feeling the pain too. The way his body locked up caused them both to crash to the floor. There, on her back, Bianca rolled away from Trevor and stared up at the old man she recognized from the day before. The caretaker. He'd been working on the lawn. Now, he stood in her room, drool dripping from his mouth.

Bianca's body spasmed and her back arched so hard she felt a muscle rip. The stinging and burning were like a thousand nails shot from a nail gun and riddling her scalp. Her hands flew to her head and her fingernails clenched at her hair, pulling so hard clumps of it came off in her hands.

And she dug. Her nails bit down into her flesh and she skewered herself, digging into her skin and pulling back, desperately trying to peel the pain away from her body.

Behind her, Trevor screamed in agony, and she realized she was screaming louder.

"Who are you?" she heard Steven yell.

Through blurred vision, she saw the big boy rush at the old man. The two went down on Misty's twin-size bed. Then there was more thrashing around and more screaming.

Bianca fought to free herself of the miniature, squirming insects chewing their way through her skull, racing toward her brain.

The door slammed shut, locking them all inside with the deadly visitor.

Then all went black.

10

"Yeah, at Cloud 9," Hal said into his phone as he cruised around the woods, doing his normal checks of his area. The cop on the other end of the line was one of the smuggest, cockiest assholes Hal had ever had the pleasure to meet. It was the same cop that caught him driving under the influence. "I don't know where everyone was, but it was quiet."

"Quiet?" the cop asked.

"Yeah, it was weird, man. Can y'all just go check on the place?"

"You want us to check on a 'quiet' trailer park?"

"This isn't a joke."

"I'm not saying it is, but you have to understand how that sounds. Hal, we've got only two officers on duty at night. You know how things are around here. They're *quiet.*" He put emphasis on the word as if to further make fun of him. "This means we don't really have the manpower to go checking on things unless there's an actual problem. Now, I'm not saying there isn't, but none has been reported to me."

"I'm reporting it to you now," Hal said. "I was attacked by a damn dog. A mean motherfucker, too. He wasn't normal. I'd say that thing had rabies. What if he attacked the people at the trailer park?"

The phone became muffled on the other end like the cop had

placed his hand over the speaker. Hal was sure he heard laughing on the other end.

"Well," the cop came back with, "I can assure you we'll take care of this."

"You'll send somebody over there then?"

"We'll take care of it."

That was as good as it was going to get. Hal was pretty sure they'd do absolutely nothing. Some of the daytime cops were good guys. They took the job seriously, but the nighttime guys, unfortunately, were lazy assholes. They dealt with very few *real* situations. Every once in a while they probably got called to a domestic dispute, but this was a town with little to no violent crimes occurring. People here were good people who policed their own.

Hal hung up his cell phone and threw it on the seat next to him. He wasn't going to go back to Cloud 9 himself. Of course, he was worried about the people who lived there, but the cop had a point. Nothing seriously out of the ordinary had occurred other than a dog trying to attack him for walking into what could have been its owner's house.

He laughed out loud and said, "Damn good guard dog, that's for sure."

A memory came back to him that made him laugh even harder. It was from a long time ago.

They were lying in bed together after making love. Sheila's head rested on his chest. She wanted a pet. She thought it would do Susanna good to have an animal to take care of. It would teach the girl some responsibility. Hal knew the truth of it. Kids never did well with that kind of responsibility. It would end up being he and Sheila cleaning up after it.

"How about a turtle," he'd suggested.

"Boring," Sheila said. "Plus, they grow too fast."

"A bird?"

"Birds are meant to fly free. It's mean to put one in a cage."

"A gerbil then."

"Eww. Might as well get her a rat."

"A rat then."

She slapped his stomach and he flinched, laughing.

"I think we should get a cat," Sheila suggested. "Amy's cat had kittens. She'll give one to us, I'm sure."

"Cats are fuckin' mean," he said. "They're evil."

"No, they are not!" She looked at him with her mouth wide open, having a hard time digesting his words.

"Let's get a dog," he said. "At least that way we can let it run around in the yard—"

"And cover our yard in dog shit," she argued.

"It's better than filling our house with the fresh aroma of kitty shit in a sandbox."

"It's a litter box."

"Dogs are better for security anyway," he said.

"Cats are good for security too."

"How?" This time he had to sit up. He couldn't believe she was suggesting a cat was a good security measure.

"They meow when there are intruders."

"Ha! Do you know what a fuckin' dog does when there's an intruder? A dog barks and goes nuts. Even the smallest dog goes apeshit when there's an intruder!" Hal snarled and attacked Sheila's neck, pretending to bite it. She squealed and laughed. "You know what a cat does when there's an intruder?" he added. "It runs for its fucking life. It says, 'fuck this family' and runs."

Sheila laughed.

And they picked up one of the kittens the very next day.

"What do I know?" Hal said aloud as he continued on his route.

Going down his checklist of nightly areas he needed to make sure were safe and secure, he started with the bathroom area near the lake. The lights were on, the stalls were empty, and it seemed everything else was in order. Nothing to report.

He continued on his route. He looked around the Green Briar campsite, the Overlook campsite, the Carlsbad campsite… all seemed fine. A black bear was spotted making its way through the Flagstaff campsite, but it wasn't bothering anyone. None of the campsites were even open to the public, so Hal left the animal alone. It was looking for food, and it wouldn't find any. He considered throwing it a piece of the cheeseburger he had for lunch, but he decided against it. He was supposed to be deterring the bears, not feeding them and teaching them to come looking to people for food.

When it came time to eat lunch, he decided he'd go check on the college kids and see if they were still looming around, illegally camping next to the lake. Tonight was supposed to be their last night according to what they'd told him yesterday. He wasn't going to bother them, he only wanted to make sure they were okay.

"Everybody dressed this time?" he asked as he stepped out of the bushes.

Hal was met with silence. The kids were nowhere in sight.

Their campfire had started to burn down. Soft music flowed from inside one of the tents.

"Hello?" Hal called out.

A sickening feeling hit his gut. Where were they?

He didn't hear the sexual sounds of anyone getting busy inside the tent, only the music.

What if something happened to them? And you let them be here? This is your area. This is your Zone of Responsibility. Fuck the zones. Where are these kids?

A squeal came from the water and Hal whipped his head left to see Lenny pop up out of the lake. His blonde girlfriend, Becky, swam away from the boy and splashed water at him as she retreated. They were laughing and having a good time.

"For fuck's sake," Hal muttered. "Thank God."

"Sir?" a voice came from his right.

Hal glanced that way and saw Kip's head sticking out of the tent.

"I'm sorry," Hal said, "I didn't mean to interrupt."

Kip laughed as he opened the flap. His girl for the weekend, Rachel, was next to him, covering her chest with what appeared to be his T-shirt.

"Good to see you again, sir," Kip said as he raised a beer. "We're staying out of trouble."

"I know you are," Hal replied. "I just wanted to stop by and make sure y'all are okay."

"Everything's fine here," Lenny, the slightly goofier one yelled from the water. Becky swam over to him and held onto him.

Now that is one lucky guy.

Hal wasn't a pervert, but from the way she was facing him that close, holding onto him, it was pretty clear she wanted the boy. Lenny would be getting lucky tonight. Hal, feeling like some kind of peeping Tom, turned his attention back to the tent.

"Tonight's your last night here, right?" he asked Kip.

"Yes, sir," Kip replied. "We were just talkin' about how sad we are to go."

You were in there talking. Right.

"Work sucks," Kip added.

"So bad," Rachel said.

"I have to agree with you," Hal said. "I'm doin' it right now."

"I suppose I couldn't interest you in a beer, right?" Kip asked.

"Kip," Rachel said through clenched teeth. It was clear she wanted to get back to what they were doing when Hal so rudely interrupted.

"I appreciate it," Hal replied, "but I have to decline."

"Work," Kip said, nodding his head.

"Exactly." Hal wasn't going to tell them it was much more than his job stopping him from putting one of those cans to his lips. "Seen any snakes out here?"

"There was a water snake down by the lake," Kip informed him, "but it wasn't poisonous."

"Keep your eyes open for copperheads," Hal reminded the boy. "They're startin' to poke their heads out now. Shouldn't bother you, but you know how it is. Check your sleepin' bags before you get in 'em."

"You check my sleeping bag before I get in it," Rachel said to Kip.

"I will, baby, I will," the boy replied.

They seemed like good kids. Once again, Hal thought back to when he was their age. Smoking weed and drinking by the lake. That was a great time. He was lucky he didn't end up a father at sixteen. He hoped Kip and Lenny both were smart enough to wrap it up.

"Saw a black bear out by one of the campsites," Hal told them, "so keep your food put away. Y'all know the drill, right?"

"Absolutely," Kip replied. "We been campin' since we were kids. We're all right."

"Y'all got the number to call in case of an emergency?"

"I've got Gus's number," Kip said.

Hal figured that would be okay. They could always call Gus who would get a message to him pretty quickly. Worse case, 911 worked too. He doubted they'd need it, but shit happened. He couldn't shake the thought of his visit to Cloud 9. If a damn dog could try and take his head off, there were a variety of animals out here that could do the same to one of these kids.

"Be careful," Hal added as he backed away from them.

"We will be, sir," Kip said.

Hal decided he liked that kid. He was respectful. His parents had done right.

Back at his truck, Hal climbed inside, fired up the engine, and was driving away when he noticed a black Labrador heading toward the college kids' camp. Once again, thoughts of Cloud 9 came back to him. This dog seemed relaxed though. Its tongue lolled out as it meandered toward the lake. He didn't recall seeing the dog the last time he visited these kids, but maybe they'd let the dog roam around. Having one at the site was probably a good thing. It could scare off some of the other smaller animals that might try to scavenge their site later on.

He remembered wanting a Labrador when he was a kid. That was his dream dog. His buddy, Patrick, had one. Hal had always wanted either a lab or a golden retriever. Maybe it was time he got one for himself. As he told Sheila so long ago, they were good for security purposes, and this world was quickly turning to shit.

11

—————

"Get back in here, please," Rachel demanded.

God, she was gorgeous. Kip liked this one a lot. She was polite, smart, and had been raised right. Better yet, she was a bit of a freak after having a few drinks. She'd been reaching into his zipper since her second beer of the night. He was buzzing pretty good himself right now and couldn't wait to put her on her back again.

She was in nothing but her bright yellow bathing suit, which contrasted with her tanned skin and drove him wild. Instead of taking her suit bottom off, he'd simply pulled it to the side and was tonguing her clit when he'd heard the park ranger arrive.

The ranger was a nice guy, but seriously? He had to arrive now? Right when shit was clearly about to go down? The entire time the ranger was outside, Kip had fought back the urge to scream at him. He'd offered the guy a beer knowing he would never accept it while on the job. Hearing that Rachel was impatiently waiting for him turned him on even more.

Now that the ranger was gone, Rachel was all his. He zipped the tent most of the way down, leaving only a small space at the bottom for some of the breeze to get through. Then he sat back and looked at the beautiful young woman he had in front of him.

He felt no shame as he dropped his hand to his swim trunks and stroked himself over the fabric. His hard-on was clearly visible, and Rachel smiled as she watched him.

"'Do you want a beer, sir?'" she said, mimicking him. She rolled her eyes and added, "I could have killed you."

"I knew he'd say no."

"But what if he didn't?"

"Then you'd have to wait a little longer."

"I'd fucking kill you," she joked. "You can't warm a girl up like that and then leave her to cool down. That's cruel and unusual punishment."

"I'll show you cruel and unusual punishment," he replied.

Rachel slid back in the tent and reached for the string that kept her bathing suit top on. She pulled on it and tugged the top off slowly as she said, "I... dare... you."

Her tits were small, but he kind of liked them like that. He was more of an ass man, and she definitely had a nice ass. The way she leaned back on her elbows, knowing how enticing she was, drove him mad with lust. Her dark nipples, swollen from the cool breeze, made him throb even harder.

"Can we get back to what we were doing before we were interrupted?" she asked.

"Yes, please."

With that, she slid off her bathing suit bottom and said, "So you don't have to pull it to the side this time."

Kip was in awe. He'd been with a couple of girls, but he'd never had one lie back and open her legs for him the way Rachel was now. She didn't seem nervous or even slightly hesitant to give in to him. She wanted him.

"Mmm," was all he could think to say, but she looked absolutely delicious.

Never one to rush into it, Kip started at her knee. He kissed her there and let his tongue dash out to lick her flesh. She leaned her head back and smiled.

"Keep going," she said.

So, he slid up a little further and did the same. He noticed the higher he went, the more her back arched, and the louder her sighs became.

"You're driving me crazy," she whined.

He liked the sound of that. She'd been doing that to him since the first time he laid eyes on her. She was a tease too. She'd kissed him and felt him up on a couple of occasions, making sure to give his cock a squeeze at the end of their last date, but she'd never given in to him completely. This was their first time actually going for it.

When Kip reached the crease between her thigh and her pussy, he spent a little bit of time there licking her silky skin. The way she bucked her hips and edged closer to him made it clear she wasn't fond of the way he was stretching it out. She wanted him to come at it head-on. He had to fight back a chuckle when she humped the air, doing her best to drive herself into his face.

With his hands, Kip held her legs still. He pried them open and finally moved left, dragging his tongue over her trimmed mound and up to her clit. He flattened his tongue out and scraped it against the tender nub, feeling her legs tremble as he went to work.

"Oh, God," she whimpered.

Her moans made him so damn hard he couldn't think straight. It was good Lenny and Becky were out in the water. He was sure those two would be fucking before the night was over, but right now he didn't want to have to keep things quiet. Reaching for the small stereo he had inside the tent with him, he cranked up the volume so none of their noises would be heard.

The music did the trick. It seemed she felt better with the tunes masking the sounds of her pleasure. She gave into him completely and whined, moaned, and groaned as she thrashed and grabbed hold of his head to force his face into her fully.

Kip couldn't breathe so well. She was strong, almost violent in the way she tried to fuck his face.

"Yessss, baby," she whined. "Right there."

He was about to rip off his swim trunks and slide between her legs. He couldn't take it anymore. Rachel was an animal in the tent. He held onto her legs, wrapped his arms around them, and dug his fingernails into her inner thighs as he drove his tongue into her.

That was when he felt something strange against his foot. He jerked away from it and pulled his mouth off her in time to see a black Labrador at the tent flap, lifting its head against the zipper to force it open. It was on its belly, sliding into the tent.

"What the fuck?" Kip asked. "Hey, get the fuck out of here."

"What is it?" Rachel asked. "Why did you stop?"

"It's a damn dog," he said.

"Don't stop," she ordered. "Just push the dog out with your foot."

He tried that, but it kept coming in.

Rachel leaned her head back and lifted her hips to give Kip easier access. She was clearly not about to let a dog ruin her good time. Kip once again tried to ease the dog out of the tent flap, but the thing was persistent. In the shadowy entrance to the tent, it was hard to see the dog's face, but Kip thought its eyes seemed strange. Kind of lifeless. And its tongue lolled out.

"Get out," he tried once more, but the dog was already halfway in the tent when its fur made a strange clicking sound. "Out of the tent, boy... or... girl," he tried again. A skittering sound competed with the music blasting from the radio speakers, and Kip leaned closer to the dog. He swore he saw its fur move, almost like it was dancing to the music. Some of it leaned one way and then leaned the other.

"Forget the dog," Rachel whined. "Pay attention to me."

"Rachel, this thing is—"

His face was too close to the dog. So close he saw the small cloud burst from its fur and come right at him. He closed his eyes and swatted at the air, but it was too late. It rained down on his head.

"Ah, what the fuck?" he cried out.

"Push it out with your foot," Rachel complained again, lifting her hips and bringing her pussy closer to Kip's face.

The young man couldn't concentrate on her. He leaned away from her and threw his hands to his head where he ruffled his hair, scratching at his scalp and trying to shake off whatever had landed on him. It itched at first but that quickly changed to pain as it felt like shattered glass was being jammed into his scalp. Kip cried out and his head fell forward. His hands scraped at his head, which had fallen close to his girlfriend's trimmed mound.

Kip thrashed and screamed, his face splatting against her wet pussy, and his hands frantically scratching at his bleeding scalp.

Rachel kept herself trimmed, but the hair in her pubic area wasn't short enough. Some of the lice leaped from Kip's head and did what they did best. Clenching onto the tiny pieces of hair, they climbed down and into her skin, biting, and tearing their way through the thick flesh at her mound and into every place where a follicle led into her body.

There was no brain there, but the lice didn't care.

Rachel was in pure ecstasy when Kip was going down on her. She'd only been with a couple of guys in the past, but none of them were as skilled as this one. The way he used his tongue. How he caressed her with it. It was like he'd studied the art of cunnilingus.

Then that damn dog came in. First the park ranger, now this dog. Why did it feel like the universe was against her having an orgasm tonight?

But Kip was a champ. He kept going. He didn't let the mutt stop him from eating her out. He pushed the dog with his leg. He did all he could while he continued to come back to her.

When Kip started screaming, Rachel didn't know how to react. She didn't understand what was going on. Had the dog bitten him? And even if it did, it wasn't a big dog. What would cause so much pain?

She tried to slide away from him. He was clawing at his head and face, digging into his head. Her screams caught in her throat as she watched him dig into his scalp. Blood ran down his face and he was in so much pain. She fought to get out of the back of the tent, but she couldn't break through the fabric.

His face fell between her legs where only moments before she'd experienced so much warmth and pleasure. Now, it felt like a handful of thumbtacks were pushed into her skin. Tiny pinpricks that hurt so bad. She screamed so hard she tore her vocal cords.

And she screamed even louder.

Something was wriggling between her legs, fighting to get inside her. A bunch of them. Tiny, vicious things that ate their way into her through the pubic hair above her pussy. She kicked Kip's face, forcing him away from her, and she swore she heard his neck crack.

The pain.

The pain.

The pain was so fucking immense.

Like microscopic piranhas chomping their way into her body.

Kip moved. He writhed on top of her, still crying out in pain, but his screaming had stopped. Hers grew louder. The agony continued, and now *he* was sliding over her body, making his way up closer to her.

Both of her hands were between her legs, clawing at whatever was trying to get inside her. Demonic fire ants had mistaken her pussy for their home, and they were ripping into her. She pulled her blood-soaked hands up to try and push Kip away. The way he moved on top of her was like he'd forgotten how to use his body. He slithered over her, and he was too heavy to push off. Every time she tried, her slick hands slipped off his stomach and chest, causing him to land on top of her, each time harder than the time before.

She swung at him with closed fists and clawed at him with curled fingers. She tore at one eye, feeling her fingernails dig into the jelly-like substance. She heard the pop and felt the ooze, but he kept coming. Nothing would stop him.

And his hair. It was moving, shaking.

Lenny and Becky were in the water, splashing around and having a good time. Drunk off watermelon moonshine, the two could barely tread water at this point. Now in the shallower water, he was able to stand, and Becky had her legs wrapped around him. He wanted her so bad. Once the ranger left, they'd both thrown their swimsuits onto the beach.

Now they were naked, and every time she wrapped her legs around him, he felt his cock pressing against her. He'd always thought sex in water would be easy. That it would make everything wet and lubed up, but it was the opposite. It was hard to push himself inside her when they were in the lake.

Plus, he wasn't sure he wanted to. He remembered hearing something a long time ago about the rivers in Vietnam and how soldiers who pissed in it sometimes had parasites swim up their dick hole and then... he wasn't sure what happened after that, but it was enough to stop him from pissing in lakes and rivers. Pools were still fair game, but any natural body of water?

Nah, fuck that.

"I have to pee," Becky complained.

"Go in the lake," he said.

The thought made him laugh. He wasn't going to do it, but he didn't care if she did.

You're such an asshole.

He was. He knew that. He'd been told that his entire life. He was an asshole at birth when he tore his mother open. He was an asshole as a toddler when he pushed Ben Brockner off the monkey bars and broke his collar bone. He was an asshole as a teenager when he knocked up Diana Dunne and talked her into getting an abortion. And he was an asshole now when he wanted Becky to pee and take the chance of getting parasites in her pussy hole.

He was an asshole and he owned it. Chicks who fucked him knew they weren't getting a boyfriend out of it. He was one of the best-looking guys in Clydesville, he knew that, and any girl who rode his cock knew they were simply getting off. That was all. They'd get one mighty good orgasm and then go tell their friends about him. With a dick the size of his, he could get away with anything. It didn't matter. He was a straight-up asshole and women were lining up to get a piece.

"I don't know about pissing in the water," Becky complained.

"Then don't," he replied. "I don't care. Go piss in the bushes. Go piss on the fuckin' road. Just don't piss on me."

Her jaw dropped. "You're an asshole."

"It's my nature, baby. Sorry, not sorry."

"Fuck you," she spat as she pulled away from him and swam toward the shore.

She'd be back. She'd howled so loud last night he'd been afraid she'd attract wolves. He'd had to clamp a hand over her mouth as he fucked her. She didn't know how to shut up. She'd do the same tonight, no matter how mean he was to her.

She had daddy issues and he had mommy issues. His mom left when he was a young boy. She'd told him he was a worthless piece of shit like his father and then stormed out of the house. He'd never seen her since.

His therapist told him every woman he hooked up with was his mother. That's why he didn't care about any of them. He'd laughed about it at the time, but now, he thought she was probably right. It could be why he only dated blondes too. His mother was blonde. Maybe treating all these women like shit was his own way of getting back at her. Whatever it was, he liked doing it, and he'd continue to do so.

Tonight, he'd fuck the shit out of tight little Becky, and then tomorrow he'd drop her off and never see her again. He'd see her, as in bump into her at work and the high school football games, but he wouldn't give her the time of day. At some point, she'd beg him to fuck her again. They always did, but he never went back for seconds unless he was super high or ridiculously drunk.

"It's cold out here," Becky complained as she reached the beach.

This dumb bitch was going to get fully dressed to take a piss, wasn't she? This aggravated Lenny because he knew if she got dressed, she probably wasn't going to come back into the water, and he wasn't ready to get out yet. He liked it in here.

You know what? Fuck it. I'll stay in with or without her. She'll either come back in to be with me or she'll have to wait out there until I feel like getting out.

Lenny was underwater when Becky crouched down to take a piss in the bushes. Her shorts were around her ankles, because like he'd expected, she'd gotten dressed before going to take a piss. This was the position she was in when the dog approached.

With his head underwater, Lenny couldn't hear her scream. He didn't hear *anything*, and when he finally popped his head up after holding his breath for a full minute – maybe less since he kind of sped up his counting as he struggled to hold his breath – he didn't see anyone on the beach.

"Becky!" he yelled.

He wouldn't have been able to hear her reply even if she did respond. That damn music coming from Kip's tent was so loud. Who had sex to Metallica? Lenny had always liked either slow country music or R&B. Hard rock didn't do it for him in the bedroom. He reserved that shit for when he was working out or punching the heavy bag.

Surely Becky hadn't finally gotten so pissed off at him that she'd left. Besides, they'd parked pretty far away, and he'd driven her out here. Kip was the only other person with his car nearby.

Nah, she's probably taking a shit.

Thinking of the pretty blonde squatting and pinching one off turned his stomach. Of course, everyone had to crap, but he didn't want to think of his girl doing it. For a second, he imagined her behind a bush, her shorts around her ankles, wincing as she forced it out.

Ah, that's fucking nasty.

"Becky!" he tried again.

Now, his thoughts turned to her trying to finish while standing up tall enough to yell out, "I'll be there in a minute."

Her answer never came, and he refused to get out of the water. She was either going to come back in or he'd stay out here all by his damn self. Lenny floated on his back, looking down at his own body and thinking his dick looked like a submarine periscope. He pretended his body was a massive underwater ship and tiny people were preparing to man their battle stations. The water was a bit cool, so he was suffering shrinkage, keeping the little guys' viewing port right at the lake's surface. He needed Becky to hurry back so he could expand his periscope.

"Where the fuck are you, man?" he asked aloud, smacking the water with both hands as he finally gave up waiting for her and waded toward the beach. "You really are out here taking a shit or something, ain'tcha?"

The damn music blasted, filling the air with James Hetfield's vocals followed by a guitar riff. His first order of business would be to tell his friends in the tent to turn the damn radio down.

"Kip!" he shouted. "Turn down the fuckin' music, man. You tryin' to wake up all the animals?"

He imagined pissed off raccoons, bears, and even snakes making their way to their camp to smash that radio. His mind was an immature, completely random place.

He'd just stepped out of the water when Becky moved out of the woods and stood between him and Kip's tent. The campfire had died down, leaving her mostly in the shadows.

"I knew you didn't leave," Lenny said.

She didn't reply, and Lenny didn't like the way she was standing. She was slumped over slightly, her arms dangling at her sides.

"Wore yourself out with that shit, did ya?" he joked.

Apparently, Becky didn't find it funny. She wasn't in the mood for his bullshit tonight. Even he had to admit he was being a bit of an asshole. Maybe he should tone it down if he hoped to get some tonight. So far, she'd been a pushover, but he'd overheard the girls talking earlier this evening, and he was pretty sure Rachel was telling Becky to have more respect for herself.

"I was only kidding," Lenny finally said.

He'd stopped walking and stood across the way from her, the dying fire between them.

"You wanna get back in the water with me, baby? It's cold out here." He looked down at his shriveled dick and added, "As you can clearly see."

She refused to answer him. He'd really pissed her off. He thought back to what he'd said throughout the night and couldn't come up with anything that would have made her this angry with him. He'd said worse, he was sure of it.

It was Becky who moved forward next, and as she did, Lenny got a closer look at her. He still couldn't see her very clearly in the dark, but her head was tilted at an odd angle and it seemed like she had rivers of black ooze coming down from the top of her head. He backed up a couple of steps and felt his heels touch water. The lake was at his back.

Becky raised her arms and held them out to him, perfectly straight, like a deranged Barbie doll asking for a hug.

Behind her, Kip and Rachel stepped out of the tent.

"Guys, I think something's wrong with Becky!" he yelled.

They didn't answer, and he realized they too were standing weird. Their arms hung at their sides. It occurred to him that this was probably some kind of dumb joke. Kip was always watching horror movies. He could have told the rest of them to play along while they pranked him.

"Are you fucking with me?" he asked.

This would have been the perfect moment for Kip to start laughing hysterically while yelling out, "Gotcha!" But he didn't, and Becky continued to step forward.

Lenny was busy looking past her, at his other two friends, when her fingers reached his chest. The shock of feeling her sudden touch caused him to step backward too quickly, hit the water, and fall in. Lenny's ass splashed down, and he landed on a rock. His mouth shot open and a howl erupted from him, letting lake water pour through his lips and down his throat.

"Becky!" he yelled, through a mouth filled with water. "Get the fuck away from me!"

He kicked his legs and swam away from her. She fell forward onto her hands and knees and crawled into the lake that way, like a rabid animal desperate to catch its prey. Lenny was only a few feet away, swinging his arms, trying to gain distance on her, but she was closing in on him quickly. In all his panic, he'd nearly forgotten how to swim.

Finally, he latched onto reality and remembered he needed to turn and flee from her into the water. Lenny spun around, kicked out his feet, and swam. Becky was right behind him. He could hear her splashing through the water and growling at him. He glanced over his shoulder and saw her rise up onto two feet and then pitch forward, still coming after him. Her head ducked underwater this time, and as it did, he saw a puddle-like substance, frothy and bubbling, leave her head and move toward him.

"What the fuck!" he yelled, scrambling against the water to get as far away from her as possible.

Now, he was afraid to not look back at her. Knowing she was back there, and something had left her body in pursuit of him drove him forward at a frantic pace. It was dark and difficult to see, but the teardrop-shaped frothy cloud was making its way toward him, skimming across the surface of the water. His eyes shot open and he turned once again, swimming as hard as he could.

Behind him and gaining on him quickly, came the sound of fizzing, like whatever had come off Becky's head was chomping at the water, wiggling through it, biting at the air the way acid popped when it did its damage.

Lenny couldn't swim quickly enough. He was trying, but he couldn't move any faster, and whatever was in the water with him was fast. Clouds moved in front of the moon, blotting out the only light the boy had to illuminate the water's surface.

Whatever was in the water behind him disappeared in the dark, but they didn't slow down.

Lenny's head went under as he struggled to swim.

Moonlight broke free from the clouds, and Lenny was nose deep in the water when he saw the frothy puddle only a foot away from his face. Frantically, he slapped his hands down against it, breaking the strange shape into pieces. Now, the thing came at him from different angles. He swatted at the parts converging on him from the right, but in doing that, he took his eyes off the rest.

The lice found his long hair underwater and climbed swiftly to his head.

Razorblades bit into Lenny's scalp. Razorblades with an agenda. He felt them saw at his skin. As afraid as he was to reach up and try to tear them away, the searing hot pain caused his hands to react on their own, and soon he was ripping into his own flesh.

The lake was doused in blood.

Lenny went under.

Lenny rose back up to the top, and then he waded toward the beach, his arms dangling at his sides.

12

"Did you go check Cloud 9?"

Officer Milton Owens was half asleep when he heard the voice of his commanding officer, Sheriff Mike Morris. Of course, he hadn't gone to check on the trailer park. Why would he? Because park ranger Hal demanded it? He didn't follow orders from drunks on the mend, especially when this had nothing to do with the park he was responsible for rangering.

Rangering. Is that even a word?

If it wasn't, he was making it one tonight.

Yet, he didn't want to admit his lack of doing his duty to his boss because he knew Morris took every call seriously. He took *everything* seriously. Milton liked it much better before Morris came into power. Back in the day, when Aaron Weeks was the sheriff, work was so much more relaxed. Weeks never did shit. This was a town with little to no drama. Most of the crimes consisted of drunk driving and even those traffic stops usually resulted in zilch since all of the cops in Clydesville were friends, or at least acquaintances, with the other town residents. Only folks with out of state license plates felt their wrath.

"Yes, sir," Milton lied. "I drove over there, and everything was fine. You know how that place is. Everyone was hungover from last night's hoorah, but other than that, there was nothing but a barking dog getting on my nerves."

"And the dog didn't attack you?"

"If the dog attacked me, I woulda shot it."

"Right. Shut up."

Both men laughed. Of course, he wouldn't have shot the dog, but it was part of his personality to act like a badass at all times.

"It's been quiet tonight," the sheriff said.

"It's always quiet, boss," Milton replied.

"Yeah… seems quieter than most other nights though, right? I don't think we've had a single call. Not even from Drunk Jimmy."

Drunk Jimmy was an ex-cop who'd been kicked off the force for slipping whiskey into his coffee every night. Everyone knew he had a drinking problem, but nobody wanted to push the issue because he was a big, ex-Navy SEAL with an attitude. His problem could no longer be overlooked the night he wrapped his patrol car around a tree.

"The night is still young, sir," Milton reminded him.

"True enough. I'm going back to my office to take care of some old paperwork. Keep an ear out for the phones and the radio?"

"Sure."

Fucking dammit!

Milton hated phones and he hated monitoring the law enforcement desk. He was an officer of the law, not a secretary. During the day, they had Junie around to take care of this crap. It was the dayshift that dealt mostly with traffic accidents, the occasional shoplifter, and any other minor mishap that went on in Clydesville. Usually, Bill was here at night to take care of the desk. He was a cop too, but he was a shitty one and was better off doing clerk duties.

And now you get to do them, Milton. Why? Because you didn't want to go out on the road like you should have done.

They were short-staffed tonight. Bill hadn't shown up at all and wasn't answering his phone. It was unlike him, but it wasn't like it hadn't happened in the past. They used to have a guy named Weathers working on the force. He missed work all the time.

The force. What kind of force is this? We've got three of us on shift tonight.

Not that it took more than three of them to handle the town's issues. With Sheriff Morris, Riley who was out on patrol right now, and himself, they had more than enough personnel for the job.

Milton was considering hiding out in the bathroom, pretending to take a crap while playing with his phone, when Riley walked through the door holding a cardboard carrier with three cups of coffee and a paper bag in his hand. The youngest guy in the department was on a health kick, so there wouldn't be donuts in that bag. More than likely it was celery or some shit.

"Brought y'all some coffee," Riley announced.

Sheriff Morris walked out of his office with his thumbs in his belt, his large gut hanging over his buckle, and a big ol' grin on his face. The man had a coffee addiction. He'd brought his own, as he always did, in a giant metal thermos, but he'd never pass on fresh hot joe.

"What's in the bag?" Milton asked, accepting his cup without thanking the young man.

As far as Milton was concerned, it was the youngest in the department's duty to do things like this. He was supposed to kiss his superiors' asses. Technically, Milton and Riley were the same ranks, but Milton had been here longer, so he'd earned the coffee by right of seniority.

"Wraps," Riley answered. "Got to The Diner before Sally closed up shop. Hope y'all like tuna."

"A tuna wrap, great," Milton said. He didn't care if the boy caught the sarcasm in his voice. He should know not to order nasty shit like tuna. He would have rather had plain ol' toast with butter on it than a seafood wrap.

"It's good," Riley said. "Have you ever had one?"

"Tuna?" Milton asked, trying to figure out if he'd heard the young officer correctly. "Are you asking if I've ever tried tuna?"

Riley didn't answer. Sheriff Morris laughed and said, "I'll take one, Riley. Thank you." Suddenly the boss man clutched his belly and winced. "Oh, boy. I'll be back in a little while, guys." He reached for the nearest magazine off one of the waiting room tables – not that anyone ever had a need to wait in that room – and headed straight for the bathroom, calling out over his shoulder, "Nature calls."

"You gave him the shits," Milton informed the younger officer.

"He didn't even drink his coffee yet," Riley said in defense.

"It was all that talk of tuna. You should be ashamed. Next time get the typical cop treat. Donuts."

"That shit will kill you," Riley informed him.

"At least I'll die a happy man."

"Are you ever a happy man?"

This made Milton laugh. Finally, a bit of sarcasm from the rookie. There was hope for Riley yet.

Riley had his back to the front door and floor to ceiling window. The blinds were open, and Milton saw something in the parking lot that he found quite strange. A group of people was walking toward them, coming out of the surrounding forest. He peered out into the brightly lit parking lot and watched as they emerged from the tree line and headed straight toward their door.

"What in the hell is that?" Milton asked aloud.

"What?" Riley replied, finally setting the last remaining coffee cup and the bag of wraps onto the counter.

Milton couldn't answer him because he wasn't quite sure what to say. He leaned over the counter and stared through the glass. Riley turned around to see what Milton was staring at. His hand went to his gun, but he didn't pull the pistol. He only rested his palm against it and nervously said, "Wha... what is that?"

If this were a major city accustomed to large groups of protestors, this might not have seemed so odd, but it was rare anyone visited the police station, yet alone flocked to it in a group this size.

"Lock the door," Milton said.

He would have done it himself, but he was on the other side of the counter and it would take too long to get to the door. He wasn't even sure why he said it. Was this a threat of some kind? He wasn't sure, but his instincts told him this wasn't good.

"Lock the door?" Riley asked, turning toward Milton, surprised by the request.

The people outside were getting closer and closer, and Milton didn't like the way they all walked with their arms hanging down, their backs slightly hunched, and their heads tilted forward. They looked dirty and ugly and... Milton stopped his judgment of them long enough to realize he recognized a few of them.

That was Jeb. He knew that ugly face anywhere. He'd been called to Lumberjacks Lounge a few times because Jeb had gotten ornery after too many beers. That was Annie, his wife, too. Milton also recognized nasty ol' Saucy and Del who both lived up at Cloud 9.

The park ranger warned you something was going on out there. You didn't listen.

"Lock the fuckin' door!" Milton yelled.

Riley finally snapped into action and ran toward the door, but it was too late. The crowd had picked up its pace. Men, women, and—

Are those kids? Is that Jeb Jr. and his sister?

Riley reached the door as Jeb Jr. ran at it full speed, like a fullback on a football field, and bashed the door inward. The officer was caught off guard and slammed against the wall behind him. Riley slid down that way, a smear of blood following him from the brute force that had knocked him against the concrete wall. As he slid, he reached for his gun, but it was too late. The first two people through the door dove at him and the rookie screamed.

Milton couldn't react quickly enough. The mob was already inside. He pulled his gun, and he fired at the first one he saw. The bullet struck Del in the forehead and the guy went down with only a red polka dot as proof he'd been hit. Blood didn't fly the way it should have.

Each of the monstrous figures entering the police station wore a crown of blood. It was dry and caked to their foreheads and faces, but it was definitely blood.

Milton turned and fired at the next one, shooting Annie in the face. The woman went down.

The crowd seemed to come at him all at once. Two of them reached for him and flipped over the desk and onto the floor. He pulled the trigger and caught one of them in the back of the head, but the other stood up quickly, and as he turned to shoot that one, the people on the other side of the counter reached for him, grabbed hold of his shoulders and arms, and pulled him backward.

He still had room. He reached back and shot someone, but then he felt it. The miniature buzz saws digging into his scalp. His eyes went wide, his hand shook, and he dropped his gun. The last thing he saw as his eyes blurred was Sheriff Morris stepping out of the bathroom with his mouth open in mid-yell, because *they* were climbing over the counter, and they'd be on him in seconds.

Two miles down the road and an hour later, nurse Mallory Mills was outside on her break, smoking a cigarette. She had to do it quickly because any second now, Dr. Baelish would be calling for her and if he smelled the smoke on her – or God forbid actually walked out here and caught her red handed – she would receive the tongue lashing of the century. The truth was, she hated the taste of these things, but they calmed her down, and with her two kids both on a trip with their dead-beat father, her ex-husband, out to Myrtle Beach, she was stressed the hell out. It did give her some time alone with Dr. Baelish though.

She preferred calling him that in bed too. Of course, outside the hospital, she didn't have to, but she had enough responsibilities in her life already. When it came to sex, she didn't want to be in control. She wanted the good doctor to give her orders. Her favorite was when he treated her like a surgery patient. How he made her lie down on the mattress, naked, while he slid his scalpel carefully over her flesh and told her how he would need to open up each piece of her to *fix* her.

He would never harm her. She knew that, but she liked the thought that he had all the power.

Bad habits weren't acceptable, and she knew he would throw a fit if he found out she'd gone back to smoking. She hadn't actually *gone back* to it. It was more like a temporary coping mechanism. Rodney had offered her one last night on break. He was the EMT on night duty.

When he wasn't riding around aimlessly in the ambulance, wasting gas, he was usually at the hospital… wasting time. He wasn't bad looking either, and Mallory thought if she weren't with the doctor, she might like to try him out. At least with him, she wouldn't have to kick this habit.

She looked at the lit end of the cigarette, and blew on it, watching the embers fire up for a second before she crushed it out and threw it into the ashtray next to the door.

Sniffing her hands, she winced and whispered, "Fuck."

Out of her pocket, she pulled a small bottle of cinnamon sugar scented hand sanitizer. She hoped it would mask the smell. She'd used it last night and *he* didn't seem to notice the smoky aroma left behind by the cancer sticks. Her breath was another matter. She pulled a small bottle of mouthwash from her other pocket, poured a little into her mouth, swished it around, spit it out, and then popped in some strawberry gum.

Mallory was about to walk back into the hospital when she heard what sounded like dragging coming from the parking lot. She wheeled around to see someone walking with a limp, kind of dragging his foot forward, scraping it against the pavement. The side entrance of the hospital was an odd place for a patient to be entering. This was where most of the staff took their breaks. It wasn't a main entrance.

"Excuse me," she said, wondering if she should walk away. She wasn't security and she had no responsibility to keep people from entering this way. When the man didn't answer, she said, "I think you want to go in the other way. This entrance is for staff only."

An overhead parking lot lamp shone down on him, and Mallory saw it was a cop. She noticed the uniform and was pretty sure it was the new guy. He was a cutie. Riley was his name. She was pretty sure of it.

Now you think he's cute too?

She'd been a straight-up horn ball since divorcing her husband. It was like she'd been given a new sexual lease on life. It had become her responsibility to have as many orgasms as she could with whatever man she wanted.

"Officer Riley, is that you, hun?" she called out. "What happened to your leg?"

She heard him mumble something, but she wasn't sure what it was, so she stepped forward.

"I couldn't hear you, hun," she said.

The officer growled and grumbled. She couldn't make out any of his words, but she could see he was injured.

"Looks pretty bad. Let's get you in here and have you looked at."

If it were anyone else, she would have made them go around to the main entrance or over to the ER, but this was a cop, and she needed to make sure he was taken care of. He would do the same for her if she were hurt. He needed a hand, so she rushed toward him. She was only a couple of feet away and was about to reach out, throw his arm around her shoulder, and help him navigate the rest of the parking lot when she noticed he didn't look so great in the face either.

His eyes were lazy, and his head was tilted a bit. He looked sickly.

"What happened to you?" she asked.

Behind him, from around the corner of the building, came at least ten others. She recognized Milton and Sheriff Morris... and they were coming right at her. She wasn't expecting it when Riley jumped on her. A slight growl escaped him as he dove at her with his good leg.

He grabbed her by the shoulders, pulled her in close, and bit into her shoulder.

Light flashed behind her eyes as her entire body went into panic mode. It was an attack, but why? Why would he do this to her?

His teeth tore into her flesh, and she heard something near her. Something abnormal. It sounded like a pool of angry insects stepping over each other to get to her. All clicking and hissing. Mallory screamed, pulled away from him, and then sprang forward and bit his nose. She pulled back and ripped it clean off. Blood flung wide, but his grip didn't loosen. It was like he didn't even feel the attack. He had her tightly in his clench, and when she spit out his nose and looked back at him, her eyes were drawn to his hairline.

There, in his short, cropped hair, she saw something move. Tiny bugs, like minuscule maggots, writhed through his hair, causing it to ruffle.

Mallory screamed again, but it only made it halfway out her mouth before catching and turning into a gurgle. The maggots leaped from his head and landed on hers. There, she felt *everything*. The bugs clawed at her hair, laid eggs at the roots, planting them in the soil-like flesh of her scalp. Then they began to dig, pressing past their egg-engulfed, infant children and biting into her like miniature torpedoes burrowing into her skull.

Her eyes rolled back in her head, and she passed out.

A minute or two later, Mallory dragged herself alongside the others as they entered the staff entrance of the hospital and went after every living being inside.

13

"Wake up, sleepyhead," Phyllis called out from the center of the room.

Nitsy rolled over and looked at her new friend. She was not about this morning crew life. Yes, the rest of the campus would be waking up soon to the sound of their banging on pots and pans, but that wouldn't be for at least another thirty minutes. They still had to brush their teeth, get dressed, stumble outside to meet the group, pick up their pots and pans provided by Eggo, and then go from floor to floor being royal pains in the asses to everyone who wasn't a part of their crew.

She would rather take these thirty minutes to rest peacefully, but then again, she would not enjoy waking up to the racket her crew was about to make.

"You're way too cheerful," Nitsy said through a mouthful of pillow.

"This is exciting, isn't it?"

"It's not."

"It's so not," their other roommate, Megan, agreed. She too was face down in her pillow, refusing to get up and get ready.

"I'll get to see Bradley's sleepy face," Phyllis said.

Nitsy rolled her eyes. The girl's infatuation with the artsy kid from their group wasn't reason enough for her to get out of bed. Nitsy didn't need to be a part of their romantic, leadership-conference fling.

It must have been obvious Nitsy wasn't going to change her mood, because Phyllis switched to, "And Robbie's?"

"You don't even know what room he's in," Nitsy said, trying to hide the excitement in her voice. If anything could get her out of bed, it was the thought of seeing Robbie when he first woke up. Not only because she thought he was handsome, but she could snap a picture of him looking his worst and threaten to use it against him. She'd never do that, but he didn't know that. It would be fun holding that over him.

Plus, she still hadn't decided whether she trusted him or not. She'd started the trip so frustrated that he'd been chosen to attend the conference with her. She was sure he was an asshole. That he was a high school jock who thought he was God's gift to women. She'd judged him. Perhaps a bit unfairly considering she'd never had a full conversation with him before. Could he really be a nice guy or was this all a ruse? She hoped it was the former.

"Let's go see Robbie," Phyllis sang.

Thirty minutes later, Nitsy was outside the dormitory hallways, standing next to the statue of Stonewall Jackson. Eggo had a big box of old pots and pans, tea kettles, a trash can lid, serving spoons, ladles, a jar of nuts and bolts, and other random items that could rattle, clink, and clank.

With two metal skillet lids in hand, held out like symbols, Nitsy followed Phyllis. They strolled into the halls like bandmates about to put on the Super Bowl halftime show. Most of the boys in their group headed straight up to the girls' floor. Of course, they would. As Nitsy contemplated the predictability of the boys, Phyllis and she remained on the first floor, and she realized they weren't much different.

Everything, whether they liked it or not, had to do with attraction. They were excited to rouse the male students.

Maybe if you're the first thing Robbie sees when he wakes up, he'll think of you all day.

Why was she worried about Robbie? At what point did this become a schoolgirl crush? She'd made it through the airport and had flown all the way to West Virginia without a single romantic thought about the boy. She'd even sat near him on the bus to Stonewall Forge. That was when it happened. She remembered the exact moment she'd realized how attractive he was.

She'd been staring out her window and happened to glance left. She saw his reflection in the window and then he looked at her. It was only a second, in that shimmering sunny reflection, but their eyes caught. She wasn't even sure he noticed it. He could have been staring at the trees that lined the road or the mountains in the distance, but his eyes were directed at her, and she saw something in them.

Innocence.

That's what it was. Yet, at the time, she'd fooled herself into believing it was arrogance. Her opinion of him had formed a long time ago. Now, after having discussed his diabetes with him and hearing the soft tone of his voice when he talked to her, she realized he had a childlike innocence.

He *was* here for the right reasons. Like she was. She may have been the more intelligent of the two, but he definitely had a charisma she lacked. Nitsy smiled as she reevaluated the reasons he might have been chosen for this conference. She hadn't understood it before, but now she did. He was charming, he was witty, and he was smart.

Is he though?

Yes, she decided, he is. He may not have been book smart like she was, but he had a different kind of intelligence. She wasn't sure if it was street smarts, as she doubted he'd ever really fought his way through the mean streets, or just an overall wisdom about him.

Nitsy and Phyllis weren't the only ones on the male's floor. Some of the other girls on their team, and one of the guys, had made their way through the corridor. She wasn't sure which room was Robbie's exactly, but she was pretty sure it was close to the entrance. She couldn't remember seeing him enter a room, but she thought he'd disappeared rather quickly one time after a break.

"They'll get the doors at the far end," Phyllis suggested, "so maybe we should start down here."

"Sounds good to me," Nitsy agreed.

They started with the third door from the entrance. Glancing over at her teammates, Nitsy held up her hand and counted, "One... two..." They didn't even make it to three before the kids on the second floor started making their commotion. Nitsy shrugged and crashed her lids together, making them clang as loud as she could.

Phyllis rattled a metal spoon inside of a pot.

All down the hallway crashes and clatters sounded off. The noise was nearly deafening.

The boys living in the room nearest where Nitsy and Phyllis were standing stepped out. One was shirtless and ripped with muscle.

"Oh wow," Phyllis said aloud, then quickly covered her mouth in shame.

"What the hell, man?" the boy asked.

"It's time to get up!" Nitsy sang.

"Is this a joke?" one of his roommates asked from inside, still in bed.

"Nope," Phyllis said. "We're your wakeup crew. It's our duty. Every day at this time."

"Jesus," the muscular boy said.

Out of the next door over, a familiar face emerged. Robbie rubbed at his eyes. His hair was a mess. He wore a yellow Average Joe's T-shirt with navy blue pajama pants. Nitsy took one look at the red font on his shirt and laughed.

"*Dodgeball*?" she asked him.

"Huh?" He was clearly still half asleep.

"Your shirt," she said with a finger pointed at his chest. "I love that movie."

Average Joe's was the name of the gym owned by Vince Vaughn's character in the movie. She'd know that shirt anywhere. She'd only seen the flick a hundred times. It was one of the few DVDs she had available to her when she was in the hospital. The WiFi went out too often to be able to depend on streaming shows and movies, so her small collection of discs kept her sane.

"I'm sorry," he said with what Nitsy thought was the most adorably groggy voice she'd ever heard, "but what are you guys doing out here?"

"Waking you up," Nitsy said with a smile.

"Waking us up," he repeated.

"Every morning," Phyllis added. "We're the wakeup crew."

"Got it," he said. "So, I can't go back in there and go to sleep."

Nitsy shook her head and smiled. Robbie glanced into his room and then back at her.

"Did my roommates come out here before me?" he asked.

"Nobody came out here but these guys right here," Phyllis said, pointing at the now closed door of the muscular boy and his roommates.

"Hmm," he replied. "Weird. Okay. I'll be out in a bit. You goin' to breakfast?"

Nitsy glanced down at her pajamas, pink pants with white clouds on them and a grey T-shirt, and said, "Yeah, after I shower and get dressed."

"Meet you there?" he asked.

Nitsy couldn't hide the smile growing on her lips. Butterflies were doing all sorts of summersaults and stuff in her stomach. She wished they'd calm down so she could concentrate. Was he asking to sit with her at breakfast or only acknowledging that they both required substance for their stomachs and they'd both get that substance in the same cafeteria building?

"Save me a seat?" she asked, deciding she would make it official if he wasn't.

He rubbed his eyes once more and said, "Deal."

When Robbie closed his door behind him, Nitsy went to clap her hands in glee and forgot she still held the two lids in her hands. They clanged together once more.

"Sorry," she said aloud to no one in particular.

"That was awkward," Phyllis said.

"What was?"

"The amount of drool you dripped on the floor. That and the fact I didn't really exist during that entire time you two were talking."

Nitsy wanted to apologize to her friend, but she couldn't. She was happy. For the first time in a long time, she had a serious crush on a boy, and it seemed he wasn't oblivious to the fact. In fact, he seemed to be welcoming it.

You cannot date Robbie Boyd. Are you looking for trouble? Are you looking for disappointment?

Here, in a land where they were alone and everything seemed possible, dating a hunk like Robbie wasn't too farfetched. Back home, where everyone talked trash and every day was a popularity contest combined with a fashion show, Nitsy didn't stand a chance. Even if he happened to like her back – which couldn't be the case – he would crumble once he was surrounded by all his jock friends and bitchy girl-friends.

How many of them is he talking to on his phone at night? And what about the blonde bombshell, Bianca?

Nitsy glanced toward the ceiling and wondered how they were doing waking up the girls on the second floor.

Bradley thought he should have stayed downstairs with Phyllis. He had a slight crush on her. Instead of hanging out with her, he'd opted to follow the other guys in the group up to the second floor where all the girls slept. Like they might be awarded a sneak peek at a girl – one who happened to sleep naked in a room full of other girls – they'd run upstairs with all the elatedness of children on Christmas morning.

"Maybe we'll see some tits," Elias, their space mission security officer whispered as they headed up the stairs.

"Yeah, maybe," Bradley had replied, only because of peer pressure. He'd never really been "one of the guys" and felt the only good answer was to agree with the boy.

Once upstairs, they did their thing, banging on stuff and knocking on doors. Eggo had never really told them to touch people's doors, but it only made sense to do so. If they were the wakeup crew, they needed to make sure people were awake. Elias smacked every door in the hallway on his way to the far end. On his way back, he made sure to slap every window.

Only four of them were upstairs, so they fanned out and each made as much noise as they could. Bradley rattled his cowbell with a big spoon outside the first door he came to. Elias and the others were further down the hall.

The first girl to open the door looked mad as hell, and he couldn't blame her. He wouldn't have enjoyed being woken up by a nerdy kid with a cowbell. His sister used to call him Urkel, like the kid on the old 90s sitcom *Family Matters*. He'd never really seen the resemblance. Now, cowering in front of this pretty girl, who'd apparently gone to bed in the shortest shorts he'd ever seen on a girl his age, he felt every bit the dork his sister said he was.

"What the fuck, man?" she asked.

"Who the hell is that?!" one of her roommates asked.

Bradley couldn't see her.

"That's not a funny joke, asshole!" a third roommate yelled.

For being the top students in their schools, these kids sure have mouths on them, don't they?

Bradley rarely used foul language. It wasn't that it offended him, and it wasn't for some religious reason. He simply enjoyed knowing he could find better vocabulary to express his disinterest, aggravation, or astonishment.

"I'm sorry," he said. "This isn't a joke. My group has the duty of being the wakeup crew, so we'll be doing this every day."

"Every day?" the girl who'd answered the door asked.

"You gotta be kidding me!" one of her roommates yelled.

"Every single one," Bradley informed them. "So, unless you want to be woken up like this, I'd suggest you set your alarm for about five minutes before now... for tomorrow morning."

"Yo, did you get this one already?" Elias asked, pointing at the next door over, room 214.

He hadn't. Bradley had spent his entire time here. He shook his head and then smiled at the girl in front of him. She poked her head out the door and looked at Elias.

"Good luck waking those assholes up," the girl called out to Elias. "They were up *all night* partying. I'm talking yelling, screaming, whooping, and hollering. They're our future's finest, that's for sure."

"Oh, I'll wake them up," Elias assured her.

"Sorry about the—" Bradley started to say when the girl stepped back into the room and slammed the door in his face. The room number, 215, was an inch away from being branded across his forehead.

Elias laughed at him and pounded on his door. Bradley passed him on his way to the stairs. Everyone else had already descended. It seemed they'd successfully awoken all the female students, and Bradley had only gotten to see *one*.

"Whoa," Elias said, "there's some strange noises coming from inside this room." He looked over at Bradley and his eyes lit up. "No way. You don't think... three girls, one room?"

"Come on, man. You tried to wake them up. Let's go."

"No way. You gotta hear this. Sounds like moans and groans."

"Do you know the girls in that room?" Bradley asked.

"Nah, not really. I think that hot kinda goth girl, Misty, is in this room."

"If something is going on in there, you're gonna piss them off."

"Hey, it's my job to wake them up."

"Whatever, man. I'll meet you at breakfast."

Elias crashed his pot and pan together a couple of times and then went back to knocking on the door while yelling out, "Wakeup crew! Wake up! Wakety wakety!"

Bradley laughed and was about to turn the corner to the stairs when he heard Elias yell, "Whoa, hey!" He turned around and Elias was gone.

It was strange. Only a second ago, the boy had been standing in the hallway, right outside that door. Bradley walked slowly toward it. Were the girls playing a prank on them? They'd probably yanked Elias into their room and were now waiting for Bradley to go check on his buddy so they could douse him with – he wasn't exactly sure what girls would pour all over him to be mean – flour or honey or fruity-scented lotion.

"Elias!" he called out.

Far off in the background, he heard a girl slam her door, probably still angry about being woken up as she headed for the shower. Downstairs, a few pots and pans banged together haphazardly. Probably a few of his crew members lingering in the halls, not willing to give up on their first day of being pains in everyone's asses.

"Elias?" Bradley said again as he approached room 214.

The window blinds were pulled tight, and he couldn't see any shadowy movement on the other side. The sun coming up behind him, blasting its way across the hallway, was making that impossible. No breeze blew through the corridor, but that didn't stop Bradley from feeling a sudden chill. He didn't like this.

"Elias," he said once more, this time barely above a whisper.

He approached the door and put his ear within a couple of inches of it. This would be the perfect time to yank the door open and throw something on him. The door didn't budge, and with his ear close to it, Bradley listened intently. He even held his breath as he did, thinking that might help him make out even the slightest movement or words spoken on the other side.

A scraping sound came from within the room. It sounded like someone sliding across a floor.

Bradley's heart hammered inside him, but he couldn't leave the boy unless he was sure he was okay. He did his best to hold his nerves steady as he placed his ear against the door, feeling his cartilage crackle as he pressed it too hard. Now, any sound would be muffled, so he eased up a bit.

THUD! Something crashed against the door, something solid, and Bradley jumped. He was about to shove his way into the room when he heard a moan.

He backed up and cocked his head to the side.

Well, shit.

Stepping closer once more, he held his breath and listened to the groans, the grunting, and other noises that to his overworked teenage brain, sounded extremely sexual. Bradley chuckled and backed up a few more steps.

Elias, you stud. Looks like you got what you wanted. The hot goth girl must have had a pretty erotic dream last night to pounce on you like that.

And she had two roommates. For a second, he wondered what would happen if he went in there. Would her roommates try something with him? He knew it was doubtful, but he was a virgin whose sole sexual experiences came from watching porn on incognito mode.

Strange things happen in porn. Maybe they'll happen in real life too.

Then it came down to whether or not he wanted it to happen. Did he want his first experience to be an orgy with three girls he'd never seen before and a guy he hardly knew? Probably not.

"You are the man," Bradley said loud enough that Elias might be able to hear him from the other side of the door.

Then he walked away, laughing to himself at his friend's good fortune. Maybe, someday, he'd be lucky enough to enjoy an experience like that himself. For now, he needed to go back to his room, get changed into something more presentable than these silly pajamas, and try to get to the cafeteria before they ran out of chocolate chip muffins.

Elias, you are a lucky guy, man.

14

Wind blew the one traffic light along Main Street, causing it to dip and swing, bouncing its blinking yellow light off the damp road and then back at his windshield. It was always quiet this early, but Grant Pope couldn't help thinking today was different. Each morning, he went to The Diner to read his newspaper, have exactly two cups of coffee, and eat a blueberry bagel slathered with peanut butter. He always parked his truck at the curb. Sheriff Morris didn't mind it. None of the cops did. They knew him well enough. If anyone else decided not to park around back in the tight confines of The Diner's tiny parking lot, they'd be served a ticket mighty quick. But Grant Pope was a good man, had lived in Clydesville all his life, and never bothered anyone who didn't deserve a little bothering.

"Damn, it's quiet," he grumbled as he threw his truck into park. It seemed darker than usual too. He knew that wasn't the case, but it felt darker somehow. Glancing up at the sky through his windshield, he didn't see any storm clouds. The sky looked pretty clear.

But damn if it ain't dark.

He glanced right as the neon pink *open* sign popped on. Inside, the lights were dim. Grant could see Sally at the counter refilling the salt and pepper shakers. It was her morning ritual. Next, she'd move on to the ketchup bottles and the napkin dispensers. She was a woman on a mission, and nothing got in the way of her routine. Grant liked that about her. She was in her late thirties, and even though he was at least twenty years her senior, he'd often considered trying to get to know her better.

What more do you need to know? She's pretty, she's smart, and she's kind.

He wasn't confident she liked him though. She was familiar with him, sure, but could she see a romantic spark with him? He doubted it. He wasn't much of a looker. Sure, he had plenty of money with his disability compensation – due to a slip and fall that shattered his right knee – and the money he made creating custom furniture and wooden signs.

Grant was a handyman. He would have his breakfast, talk to Sally a bit, and then he'd go home and get back to working on the fish tank stand he'd been commissioned to craft for the Fish & Things down the street. He furnished a lot of the local shops, and he always did mighty fine work, but this thing was going to be a real piece of art. He thought he might focus on fish tank stands for a while. He might even be able to sell some of his work to the bigger shops in the city. They'd pay more. His priority would always be to the local stores though. That was the American way, and Grant Pope was a true American.

Damn, it's really quiet out here.

Poe's Pets still had the lights off inside. Poe wouldn't open up shop until at least ten. His dad used to be up before dawn taking care of the animals in there. The newer generation didn't respect hard work. They slept in until the last possible moment and closed shop as soon as they could.

The Smoke Shop, which was now called The Smoke and Vape, wouldn't open until noon.

It's a wonder these places make any damn money around here.

A car turned into the small parking lot behind Lyle's Barber Shop. Old man Lyle would be stopping by The Diner too. He was one of the few people in town Grant got along with.

Grant finally got out of his truck and made his way into The Diner.

The bell rang above his head as he entered. Sally glanced up, smiled, and waved hello.

"Sally," he said.

"Grant."

"See I'm your first customer."

"You're always our first customer."

He took a seat at the counter. Sometimes he picked a booth, but today he wanted to be closer to her. She continued doing her chores but stopped long enough to pour him a cup of coffee. It was an easy and quick interruption since he drank his coffee black with no sugar. Grant wouldn't dare blow on his cup or take a cautionary sip the way other people always did. He liked it hot, and when it was blazing enough to burn his tongue, he enjoyed it even more.

Grant sipped and then winced, savoring the sting that scorched his throat.

"Mmm, nice and hot," he said.

"You always say that."

"'Cause your coffee always is."

"I know how you like it," she flirted.

"You damn sure do."

If anyone else were around to hear the conversation, they might have thought the two were engaged in dirty talk. This was their usual way. He'd say something normal, she'd spice it up a bit and toss the ball back to him, he'd add something on top of that, and it would go on like this until one of them ran out of stuff to say.

"Ready for something to eat?" she asked. "I'm sure Roy's got the grill heated by now."

Roy was a big ol' country boy who'd been working at The Diner nearly as long as Sally. He wasn't much of a talker though. He enjoyed cooking and hardly ever left the kitchen.

"In a bit," Grant said. "Right now, I'm just here to enjoy the view."

Sally blushed and looked down at the counter. If there was a moment he fell in love with her, it was right then. Her dimples were more pronounced than usual and that sparkle in her eye woke him up better than any cup of coffee ever could. He wasn't ready for breakfast because he was filled with a fondness for her.

Fondness. Really? Fondness? That's the best you can do?

Their flirting was always interrupted at some point, and this morning, it was interrupted by an elderly couple stopping in for breakfast.

Grant glanced over his shoulder, saw them, and returned to his steaming hot mug. "Kind of early for regular customers, ain't it?"

Sally shrugged. "You ain't the only person in my life, Grant Pope. I got others."

"I knew it."

"Keep that in mind if you ever decide to do me wrong."

"Noted."

They both laughed as she walked over to the couple now seated in a booth.

"We just need some breakfast," the old man said. "We need to get on the road. Visiting our granddaughter at Marshall today."

"Oh, that's great," Sally replied. "You mean Anna?"

"No, she's at WVU," the old lady replied. "Leeanne is at Marshall."

Grant didn't mean to eavesdrop, but they weren't exactly speaking in hushed tones. This was another reason he was infatuated with Sally. She knew and cared about every person who walked through that door. She didn't even own The Diner. Guy Miller owned the place but was too old to make frequent trips through his restaurant doors. Grant always wondered if Guy would leave something to Sally when he passed. With no kids of his own, she was the closest thing he had to a daughter.

Maybe Sally will end up owning this place someday. It should be called Sally's Diner anyway.

As Sally took the couple's order, a younger couple entered and sat in a booth not far from the first. It seemed breakfast time was starting a little earlier than usual today. This younger couple told Sally something about visiting a family member at Marshall too. It must have been one of those open house days. It made sense folks would want to get an early start then.

Fifteen minutes and a fresh cup of coffee later, a few other patrons were seated. Ronald Mosley read his newspaper at the corner booth the way he always did. Harrison and Constance sat together sharing a giant plate of biscuits and gravy. They came in for breakfast a few days a week. Harrison made Constance breakfast at home the other days. Her dementia had taken its toll and Harrison now took care of her the way a dad might have to look after his daughter. They were a sweet couple though.

"Ready for another cup?" Sally asked as she swung back around his way.

She was a great waitress. She never missed a beat.

"Two is fine for me. You know, three and I get jittery. Need my hands to be calm so I can work."

"What are you building now?"

"Finishing up a fish tank stand."

"Don't forget you promised me a coffee table."

He had, and he hadn't forgotten. He wanted to make that table for her so badly, but he got nervous thinking about it, and Grant never got nervous. Something about her excited him, and he was terrified he'd make a mistake and ruin it.

"You promised me if I made it, you'd invite me over to watch a movie and set my feet on top of it," he reminded her.

"I did promise that. Seems that wasn't enough to get you working on it." She slapped his shoulder with a folded over newspaper as she walked away.

Grant wasn't much of a reader, but he did enjoy some of the classics. He'd read *The Great Gatsby* once, and he remembered his tenth-grade teacher giving him an assignment involving that damned green light in the book. He'd hated the assignment, but now, as he thought about the coffee table, he realized it was *his* green light. Having that possibility of building it and spending time at Sally's house with her almost seemed too fragile. Like if he touched that dream, it might shatter and cease to exist. So, he didn't build the table. If he did, it would be like grabbing hold of that green light. Once he did that, it was all over.

Or maybe it all begins, you dummy. Maybe that's when the dream truly begins.

He wanted to believe that would be true, but he had a feeling even if Sally gave him a chance, she'd grow tired of him soon enough. He was boring, he didn't have energy like he used to, and he was pretty set in his ways. Women didn't like men like that. She deserved better.

Grant's thoughts were disturbed by the bell jingling over the door. Another customer had entered. Only this one didn't look so great. She was slumped forward, her fingers curled, and it looked like drool was dripping from her mouth. Her hair hung down from the sides of her head, practically covering her face, and it looked wet. Like she'd swam through a river to get here for breakfast.

"Hey, good morning," Sally said to the woman. It was clear she sensed something *off* about the customer too, because her voice cracked as she added, "Ma'am, are you okay?"

"Sally," Grant said, standing from his stool.

The Diner went silent. Everyone stopped chatting to see what was going on. It was the usual town gossip manner in which the people here conducted themselves. They were sweet, charming people, but they loved to tell stories, and they needed to hear the facts if they were going to pass this one on to their families and friends.

Sally took another step closer to the woman, but Grant was right there behind her, grabbing hold of her shoulder and gently pulling her back.

"She ain't right," Grant whispered. "Back up a bit."

"Ma'am?" Sally repeated.

The woman didn't answer. She only inched forward, sliding her feet one at a time. Grant glanced down and noticed she was only wearing one shoe. The other foot was bare and filthy.

Through the window behind the woman, Grant saw a man stumble into the middle of the street. The man dropped to his knees and scratched at the top of his head, screaming in agony.

The old couple about to visit their granddaughter at her college looked out the window and saw him too. The old man pointed at the window, but no words came out of his mouth.

"My lord," his wife said as she stood from the table.

She was closer to the new customer than Sally was. The customer turned, and the light caught the side of her face. A large, deep gash ran from her forehead across her cheek and all the way to her chin. It was opened so wide her teeth could be seen beneath the flesh. It was like someone had taken an ax to her face.

"Oh my God," Sally said.

"That man outside is screaming," the old lady said, clearly forgetting about the new customer standing right next to her.

They couldn't have been any closer than four feet when Grant saw movement at the strange woman's head.

"Do you see her hair?" Grant whispered.

Sally nodded. "Mrs. Floyd? Why don't you back up a bit?"

The old lady looked over at Sally, and as she did, it looked like something passed from the strange woman's hair to the old lady's. Mrs. Floyd's short grey hair moved a bit like a light wind was blowing against it, and then the old lady's eyes opened wide.

She stared down at her husband, who looked confused, and said, "James?"

James took her hand and pulled her onto the seat next to him.

"James, it hurts," Mrs. Floyd said.

Then her face twisted in pain and she screamed.

Grant's reaction was to grab Sally by the hand and pull her deeper into the diner, as far away from the front door as possible. The other patrons could fend for themselves. He had only enough time to make sure she was safe.

Glass exploded as the front door crashed inward. People ran through it, and all Grant heard was screaming. Over his shoulder, he saw Ronald Mosely throw his newspaper onto his table and run at the door. He was a big, proud man and wouldn't go down without a fight.

A hunched-over man with blood dripping from his head dove at Ronald and the two collided. Ronald swung a heavy fist at the man, but this wasn't a fight. It was a slaughter. Ronald was on top of the man and when he brought his fist down for a second time, the man beneath him opened his mouth and chomped down on Ronald's fist. Teeth shattered, and blood ran. Suddenly Ronald's back arched, and his entire body went rigid. He fell off the man and rolled onto the floor, screaming and clawing at his head.

Harold and Constance were still seated at their booth. A woman with long, scraggly hair was on top of their table, on all fours. Constance's arm was in her mouth, and the woman was yanking back and forth, thrashing as blood flew from the old lady's forearm. Harold was fighting her off. There was so much screaming.

"The kitchen!" Grant yelled as he pulled Sally behind the counter and through the double swinging doors. The last thing he saw was the old couple's plate of biscuits and gravy hit the floor and shatter into a broken, muddy mess.

Sally just made it through the door when a hand shot through and reached for her hair, catching the collar of her shirt instead. She screamed and jerked back on Grant's arm. He turned and threw his body against the doors, stopping them from opening all the way, but putting himself dangerously close to whoever was on the other side, clawing at Sally through the three-inch gap it had created.

It thrashed wildly at her, and Grant was too busy trying to hold the doors closed to help much. Through the circular, bubble-like window set in the door, Grant saw his friend, Lyle the barber, with his face twisted in rage. Bloodshot eyes looked like they might burst from their sockets at any second. Blood trickled down his forehead and face.

"It's Lyle," Grant said through shaky breath.

Roy, the cook, left the grill and ran to them, prying the hand away from Sally. He was a bull of a man, with his head completely shaved except for a mohawk on top. Crucifixes were tattooed on each side of his head.

"Let him in," Roy said. "I got something for him."

"Roy!" Grant yelled. "This ain't the time for tough-guy antics!"

Roy picked up a hot frying pan filled with oil. "Let him in."

"I hope you're right about this," Grant yelled as he let go of the door and ran.

Sally joined him as they made their way toward the rear exit. Grant glanced back in time to see Lyle barrel through the swinging doors.

Roy stood his ground and dumped the pan full of hot oil on the old man's head. Lyle screamed and fell to his knees, clawing at his face, which instantly blistered under the searing liquid.

Grant heard the old man's wails and felt bad for him for a second. He might have been trying to attack them, but that wasn't the old man he knew. Something had changed him into an animal.

Through the old man's cries, Grant was sure he heard something else.

A high-pitched screaming that wasn't coming from the barber's mouth.

It came from his head.

As he watched the old man crumple up on the ground and go silent, he still heard the scream of what sounded like a hundred crying kittens burning alive in sizzling oil.

His attention was on the old man for only a moment when a second and third growling customer ran through the door, stepping over the body of the dying old man, and launching themselves at Roy, who was only quick enough to grab a kitchen knife and plunge it into the first man's throat.

It was Ronald Mosley who made it past the knife and wrapped his body around Roy. Then Roy's screaming began.

"This way," Sally whispered as she pulled Grant out the back door.

Inside the diner, everyone was either screaming, growling, or both. Grant would never forget the sounds, and he knew Sally wouldn't either.

They ran alongside each other, racing toward nowhere in particular. Grant's truck was in a dangerous place. The streets were no longer safe. As they ran along the backs of the shops on Main Street, they peered through the alleyways and saw the same thing at the end of each one.

The silence Grant noticed earlier that morning existed no more.

Downtown was dying, not in sleepy silence, but in agonizing wails.

15

Nitsy's eyes burned. She needed Starbucks for a day like this. Whatever coffee the staff at Stonewall Forge was serving wasn't doing the trick. Today was the big day. She was going to stand in front of her peers and discuss their project. She and the rest of her team had worked together, scrambling all morning to create a security protocol since the person she'd put in charge of security, Elias, was a no-show.

She swore she saw him this morning during their wake-up crew meeting. She was sure of it. He'd gone upstairs with the rest of the guys. Bradley should have seen him, but the kid denied it. The goofy grin on his face told a different story though, and Nitsy was going to get to the bottom of it. Was he simply skipping out for the day? If so, where would he go?

It's not like we can hop in a taxi and go to the local mall.

Nitsy was pretty sure there was no mall nearby. There probably wasn't one for a hundred miles at least. It was probably a girl. The opposite sex was always the reason teenagers did stupid things. Speaking of opposite sexes, Robbie had been flirting with her all morning.

During breakfast, they'd sat together and sipped coffee while eating the least sugary items on the cafeteria menu. Hardboiled eggs with bacon. She really liked him. They talked about a lot of stuff, especially the kids back home. The entire time she sat with him, she expected Bianca to stroll over to their table and interrupt. She didn't. The pretty blonde was nowhere in sight, and Nitsy thanked God for over sleepers and underachievers.

Now, she caught herself stealing glances at Robbie out of the corner of her eye. He was the one making her anxious. She could speak in front of the others. She'd be nervous, but she could get it done. But, for some reason, knowing she was going to have to do it in front of Robbie made her want to throw up.

He seemed too good to be true. How could he suddenly like her just because they were on a field trip together? Was there a trick up his sleeve? Was this the moment when his and Bianca's dubious plan would be revealed? Was she going to become Stephen King's *Carrie* and find herself doused with pig's blood the moment she opened her mouth to speak?

Robbie's too nice for that. You're being a jerk thinking he's going to do something wrong.

She looked at him again, and this time he had his head leaned back. Nitsy realized she wasn't the only one who must have had a long night. But why was he so tired? Had he snuck out to go see Bianca?

Nitsy felt her heart pick up its pace. She opened and closed her fists over and over until she realized it was jealousy she was feeling. Why was she jealous? Robbie and she had made no promises to each other. He owed her nothing. If he wanted to talk to Bianca—

Over my dead body will he talk to that girl.

Nitsy's eyes shot open and she grinned. It was a devilish smile, not because she had devious intentions but because she realized she was experiencing real, raw, teenage emotion. She was no longer worried about which pills to take at what time. She didn't have to think about the appointment her mom scheduled that conflicted with the time she expected to hang out with a friend. She wasn't nervously awaiting test results.

This was petty teenage drama, and she was finally feeling it. She couldn't even count the times she heard her friends complain about boy drama or saw social media posts that made her eyes roll so hard she thought they might leave the house and travel the country. She'd always hated the ridiculous angst-ridden problems of her youth. Why? Because she wasn't feeling them too.

But you are now.

It gave her an instant feeling of excitement and energy. She was ready to do this speech, and if Bianca thought she could dig her filthy talons into *her* man, she'd find out soon enough that Nitsy fought back, and she would not give up easily.

While Nitsy mentally conjured manipulative ways to strike down Bianca, Robbie sat back in his seat and closed his eyes. His head was pounding. This always happened when he didn't get enough sleep, and it didn't help that all those jerks came pounding on pots and pans down the hallway this morning. He'd opened the door ready to knock someone's head off his body, but then he saw Nitsy, and his morning changed.

Even at first light, her hair burned fiery red. Her skin was so smooth, and her lips were so soft. Her eyes... those eyes... even thinking about her almost made his morning wood from earlier return.

Thank God she didn't notice it.

He was pretty sure Nitsy's friend did because her eyes kept dropping to his crotch.

It was a teenage problem that had plagued him since he was fourteen. It seemed to spring up around that time and had continued launching at early hours ever since. First, it was boners in class. They tended to always show up a few minutes before the bell rang to signal the end of the period. He'd had to cover himself with his backpack so many times.

Most of those hard-ons had stopped occurring. Now, it was mostly early morning. That and any time a girl touched his leg. His inner thigh was super sensitive.

Last night, he'd actually had a dream about Nitsy. They were alone together in class, back home, and they were discussing math. He remembered jotting down numbers that probably wouldn't have made sense in real life, but Nitsy seemed to understand exactly what he was talking about. While they worked on whatever mathematical equation would save the world, Robbie felt Nitsy's hand touch his thigh beneath the desk. Next thing he knew, her hand was in his zipper and she was rubbing him hard while whispering in his ear, "I want you to take me right here on this desk."

He would have taken her right there on that desk too if it weren't for the sound of pots and pans outside his room. It had taken him a second to understand what was going on. First, he'd woken to an empty room. Neither of his roommates was there with him.

Then, of course, there was that God-awful banging.

Once Nitsy was gone, with the promise to meet her for breakfast, Robbie had felt his erection die down as he thought about his roommates. Had they stayed the night in Bianca's room? Had they gotten lucky? He couldn't help imagining Steven fucking Bianca. It made him angry, mad enough to decide right then and there he didn't need to talk to her again. She wasn't the one he wanted anyway. He had his sights set on Nitsy.

His roommates were assholes. They'd stayed the night with the girls. He was sure of it, and the more he thought about it, the less he cared. Robbie was better than that. Even if they came back and told him about the wild orgy they experienced last night, he would know he'd made the right decision. They might have gotten away with it this time, but maybe not.

Maybe that's why they're missing. Maybe they got caught and were immediately escorted off campus.

He liked the idea but knew it wasn't the case. If they'd been forced to leave, all of their belongings would be gone. Yet, all their stuff was still in his room.

"Cell phone, please," a man holding a big, white bucket asked. He wore the jacket most of the team leaders had on, so Robbie didn't argue with him.

The kid seated next to him did. "Why? I don't trust anyone with my phone."

"Orders of Mrs. Price," the team leader replied. "Phones in the bucket. You can lock it or whatever, but we had a lot of issues with kids using their phones during the meeting yesterday, so we've been asked to collect them all. You can get it back at the end of the day."

"At the end of the day?" the boy asked, shocked.

"I'm sure your phone will be fine," Robbie said.

"Fine," the kid replied, locking his phone and then gently placing it in the bucket. "If something happens to my phone—"

"Excuse me," a young man said into the microphone, interrupting the kid's idle threat. He, too, was part of the staff. "Excuse me, can I have everyone's attention?"

It took a little while – as it always did with teenagers – for everyone to settle down, take their seats, and be quiet.

"Good morning," the young man continued. "We should be getting underway here shortly. It looks like we're missing quite a few students. Can someone please go check the cafeteria to see if we have any students lingering about? Mrs. Price would like to get started soon."

Robbie's body reacted before his mind could wrap around the question. He stood up and raised a hand.

"Excellent," the young man said. "Please do a quick search of the cafeteria, and if nobody is in there, go through the dormitory hallways quickly to see if you hear anyone in any of the rooms. Maybe shout out that we're getting started. There's always a straggler or two and we wouldn't want them to miss the meeting."

"Sure," Robbie said.

He glanced over at Nitsy and saw her staring back at him. She stood and said, "I'll go with him. It'll be faster with two people."

Robbie smiled. He was pretty sure she liked him too. If he played his cards right, maybe he'd leave here with a girlfriend. Of course, Daphne and Angelica, who were the two girls he talked to most on social media, wouldn't be too happy about it. But they were only friends. Flirtatious friends, but still only friends. With Nitsy, he could see something different.

When they met at the door, Robbie said, "Are you sure you want to go with me? You said earlier you were pretty excited about this."

"Nervous," she admitted, and once again, her smile melted him.

"You can hang out somewhere and practice your speech if you want," he suggested. "I promise I won't tell anyone."

"No, I've practiced as much as I can. If I practice more, I'll stress myself out to the point of not delivering my speech at all. What made you volunteer to do this?"

"My roommates are still missing," Robbie informed her. He paused for a second, trying to decide how honest he wanted to be. This was one of those moments in life where a white lie might serve him well, but he hated lying at all. Some of the kids at school might think he was a smug asshole, but they couldn't say he was untruthful.

"Do you know where they went?" Nitsy asked, making it even worse.

To answer with anything but the truth would now make him a liar. He couldn't just withhold information.

"Yeah," he said, looking down at his feet.

He didn't mean to do it, but it was kind of his natural reaction when feeling ashamed. Nitsy was one of those perfect girls. She would have never snuck out of her room. So, the fact that he did was bad enough. But to see Bianca?

"We snuck out last night," he finally managed.

"Are you crazy?" she whispered, then laughed. "You are crazy, but I guess that's kinda cool too—" She stopped talking and her whole demeanor changed. "Wait, why did you sneak out? To see *her*?"

The way she said it reminded Robbie of one of those stupid soap operas his mom always watched. Like he'd been caught cheating in the past, and they'd swept it under the rug only for him to get busted a second time. *Her*. The emphasis had been on that word. Even though Robbie and Nitsy had never really discussed having a relationship together, nor had they spoken about having one with someone else, he knew exactly who Nitsy was talking about, and he hated that she was absolutely right.

"Bianca," he admitted.

Nitsy backed up a step. "You risked this whole conference on *that* girl?"

"That's kind of hypocritical, don't you think? A second ago, you thought it was kind of cool."

"Yeah, before I knew it was for her."

When she pouted, her bottom lip stuck out a little past the top, and Robbie thought it was the cutest damn thing in the world. Nitsy walked away from him, headed toward the cafeteria, and he hurried to catch up with her. As she put her hand on the cafeteria door handle, he wrapped his arms around her and whispered into her ear. "I left though. I went with them to her room. My roommates wanted to hook up with hers."

"Right," Nitsy said. "You left. Look, you don't owe me an explanation. You really don't."

She refused to look at him, so he had to lower his face and speak into her neck to reach her ear. She placed her forehead against the door, and even though he couldn't see her face, he knew she was opening up to him.

"I did see Bianca last night," he said. "I thought I wanted to talk to her."

"You're not helping matters. Just leave me alone."

"I left though."

"Sure."

"I left because I realized it was you on my mind."

Nitsy didn't move. She kept her forehead against the door and only breathed, sighing as she exhaled.

"You don't have to do this—" she said but was interrupted when he turned her around to face him.

He put his forehead against hers and said, "I know I'm not your usual type..."

The sentence lingered there, giving her time to reassure him, and Robbie was disappointed when she didn't. What should he say now? That was the prime opportunity for her to make it known that she liked him too. This was embarrassing. He should just forget it and—

Nitsy pressed her lips against his, and Robbie nearly fell into her.

"I know I'm not your usual type…"

Robbie left it at that, and Nitsy had to think about it. He was right. Surely, he was, but what was her type? Did she even have one? She'd never even had a boyfriend before. Words escaped her, and his face was so close to hers. Not only had she never been on a real date, but she'd never been kissed. So, she went for it.

Her lips mashed against Robbie's, a little too hard at first, but then it was perfect. She'd seen enough movies to know how this was supposed to happen, and he didn't disappoint. First, their lips met. It was soft but kind of awkward. Then she felt his tongue at her lip barricade, and she forced herself to relax, open up to him, and meet him tongue dash for tongue dash.

She crashed against the door and reached up to his face, holding his cheeks as he reached for her shoulders. It was wonderful. His body pressed against hers, and for a moment, she lost herself. She forgot where she was. If this had happened at the end of a long date, back home, she would have never wanted it to end. But this was outside the cafeteria door at Stonewall Forge. This could get them in serious trouble.

Nitsy pulled away from Robbie and nearly fell over. She'd never actually swooned before, but her knees were definitely wobbly now.

"Whoa," she whispered.

"I know," he replied.

"That was nice."

"It was."

"Too bad it won't last past this trip."

"What do you mean?"

"Robbie, you know what I mean. When we get home, and you're around all your popular buddies, and you have all your hot, beach-bodied, selfie-taking model type girls crowding around you… where will that leave me?"

He paused and it took him too long to respond.

"Exactly," she added.

She turned and opened the cafeteria door. The lights were off. All was silent. She stepped in and made her way to the main seating area. Light shone through the windows, so the space wasn't completely dark. She could see the room was empty.

"Nobody's here," she said.

She'd figured as much. Nobody would hang around after everyone else left. In this kind of place, people followed the crowd. Nobody would want to be that kid who walked in late. Maybe a few seconds or so, but at this point, the meeting was supposed to start nearly fifteen minutes ago.

"We should go up and down the hallways," Nitsy said, turning once again toward Robbie.

He grabbed both of her arms and kissed her again. This time it was a short but passionate kiss. When it ended, he said, "I don't know what home will be like, but you want to know a secret? I've kind of had a thing for you for a while."

"A thing for me?" she asked.

Nobody had ever had a *thing* for her. He nodded.

"You're so full of shit," she said.

"Ouch," he replied. "That wasn't exactly the response I was hoping for."

"What *were* you hoping for?"

"I don't know. That maybe we'd see how things go. Ride it out, you know? I like you and I think you like me, so why not?"

Because I don't know if I can handle having my heart broken. That's why not.

Her thoughts said one thing, but her voice said, "Okay, sure." They started toward the cafeteria doors when she added, "I guess we should go check your *other* girlfriend's room first."

Robbie laughed and she did too.

With everyone inside the big conference auditorium, the campus was eerily quiet. The sun beat down over them as they crossed the courtyard, passed the big Stonewall statue, and headed toward the dormitory wing. Nitsy thought the weather was beautiful, but she'd seen how quickly it changed in West Virginia. It could be sunburn weather one second and raincoat the next.

The bugs were what fascinated Nitsy most. Like most girls her age, she didn't want to be close to *any* flying insects, but she did find the new variety to be spectacular. She'd never seen such heavy bees in her life. Back home, they were the common garden variety most people steered clear from, but here, they had giant bottoms and were black, almost purple looking. It was like she'd been transported to some other planet. One flew past them as they walked and she squealed, moving quickly behind Robbie. He threw his arm around her and pulled her in close.

"They won't sting you," he told her.

"How do you know?"

"I think they're carpenter bees. My uncle lives in Pennsylvania and they have them there too. They're just pests."

Nitsy swatted at a fly. "West Virginia sure has a lot of pests." She pushed Robbie away teasingly and added, "present company excluded."

"Oh, I'm a pest, am I?" he flirted back, pulling her close to him once again. "If you think the bugs are bad, you should watch out for the snakes."

Nitsy stopped in her tracks and got dead serious for a second. "Snakes?"

"Copperheads for sure... rattlesnakes too I think."

"You're serious?"

"Very. You'll be fine as long as you stay here on campus. Then again, people do sometimes find them in their houses so... you never know I guess."

"How much longer is this trip?" she joked.

They'd reached the dormitory wing and stopped. They stood quiet for a second.

"I don't hear any kids goofing around," Nitsy said.

"I'd imagine they'd be pretty quiet if they were skipping the meeting."

"They should do a rollcall and find out who's missing. It would be pretty easy. Then search the rooms of the absent kids."

"You sound like a pretty good leader. You should suggest it when we get back. Might score you some leadership points."

She liked the sound of that.

"I guess we should go ahead and take a look at Bianca's room," Nitsy said, pouting as she did.

"I really don't want to."

"Sure, you don't."

"I don't. I told you. I like *you*."

Nitsy beamed at the sound of that. His flirtation game was strong, and she didn't mind it at all as long as it was directed at her. This morning, at breakfast, she'd stopped him from eating a glazed donut. She'd hated being the motherly figure to him, but she'd found herself genuinely concerned about his wellbeing. She didn't need to watch her figure, especially after all the hospital stays where red and green Jell-O was her main meal, but she cut the sugar out of her breakfast too, so he wouldn't have to eat that way alone.

"Well," she replied, "I did give up the bowl of Frosted Flakes I wanted so badly this morning."

"I gave up my donut, so I understand."

"That was for your health, creep! I gave up my sugar for *you*!"

"We need to find you one of those saintly robes—"

"You're an asshole," she said as she slapped him playfully on the shoulder.

They ascended the stairs to the girls' floor and Robbie said, "I think we're the only ones making noise out here."

He was right. The corridors were dead silent. This was going to be a waste of time. She only hoped they hadn't started the conference without her. She wanted to be a part of the questioning process, so she could hear the questions asked of the other leaders before it was her turn.

A loud bang came from somewhere on their left.

Nitsy jumped and Robbie laughed.

"Sounds like someone's up here," he said.

"Please tell me that was a slamming door and not a knocking head-board," Nitsy replied.

"If that was a headboard, Lord help the poor girl in that bed."

"Why does it have to be the poor girl?"

Nitsy's face went red with the look he gave her. It was the first time she'd made a sexual joke, at least the first time she made one with a boy.

My God. What will he think of you now?

She doubted Robbie was a virgin. There was no way. What if he didn't think she was one? What if he thought she was some girl who'd climb right into bed with him?

The door slammed again. They were in the hallway this time when it happened. A steady breeze rattled the trees to the left of them and blew against the corridor from the open courtyard. Nitsy glanced over the railing and could see the door to the auditorium in the distance. They needed to hurry back before she was too late to participate in the morning's activities.

One of the dormitory room doors swung open in the wind and then slammed shut. They approached cautiously. Nitsy wasn't aware of Robbie's thoughts, but she knew something was wrong. It looked like the door was splintered, as if the lock had been kicked open.

She squeezed Robbie's hand and said, "Maybe we should stop and tell one of the teachers."

Nitsy had read once in one of those teen magazines that nothing built excitement in a new relationship like a creepy situation, but she didn't like this. She couldn't quite explain why the broken door scared her, but it was enough to make her want to flee and go get an adult involved.

"That's the door to Bianca's room," Robbie whispered.

There shouldn't have been a broken door on campus, and even if there were a good explanation for it, it bothered her that it was Bian-ca's room. The room Robbie visited last night with his roommates. The roommates who were missing.

"Let's just look a little closer," Robbie said, "that way we have something to tell them when we go back."

"We can tell them the door is broken," Nitsy whispered. "That's weird enough, isn't it?"

"How about you stay right here," he suggested, "and I take a closer look."

"Robbie…"

"It'll be fine. I won't go in the room. I'll only peek."

"We should go back."

"Just a sec…"

Nitsy let go of his arm and took a few steps back while he took a few forward. She wished he didn't feel the need to try and be brave in front of her. *This* wasn't going to earn him any points. She would much rather have him here, holding her hand, than over there pretending to be Sherlock Holmes.

Robbie's shoe crunched on the ground, and he stopped. He looked down at his feet and then over at the window. He backstepped carefully, much quieter than he'd approached, and looked over his shoulder to say, "There's glass all over the ground. The window's shattered."

He didn't look so brave anymore.

"Did you see anything?" she asked.

His face was pale. "Blood… all over the wall. And on the bed." He leaned forward and looked a little closer. "The railing is broken too. Like someone fell down to the first floor."

Nitsy looked over the railing and saw nobody below, but the bushes that ran along the bottom floor looked disturbed. The flowers at that part of the shrubbery were scattered. Someone *had* fallen from the balcony.

"Robbie, come on," she said.

Heavy footsteps thudded against the floor behind her, causing her to whip her head around and nearly leap out of her skin.

"Nitsy," Robbie said.

Behind her, maybe twenty yards away and blocking the stairwell, was a young man she was familiar with. It was the kid who was supposed to be in charge of her security team. He'd startled her at first, but now she was ready to lay into him and give him a piece of her mind. She'd spent all morning coming up with a plan he should have already put together.

"Elias," Nitsy said, "I have a bone to pick with—"

She stopped. Elias had shuffled forward a few more steps and now she could clearly see his face. He looked grotesque. His neck was tilted at an odd angle, and his eyes were bloodshot. Drool dripped from the corners of his mouth. He raised his arms out to her in his strange, stuttered Frankenstein walk, and she saw the fingernails on two of his fingers were peeled completely back, sticking straight up toward the sky.

"Nitsy, back up," Robbie said.

"What's wrong with him?" Nitsy asked.

Elias glared at her and growled. He was a big boy, and when he suddenly ran straight for her, Nitsy froze in fear. Robbie ran to her, grabbed her arm, and yanked her away from Elias. Robbie was a baseball player. He was fast, and he was in great shape, but Nitsy wasn't, so she struggled to keep up with him.

The stomping of Elias's feet behind her kept her going. They'd reached room 214 and Nitsy's shoes slapped against the broken glass. She couldn't help but look to her right and see the blood-covered walls of the dormitory room beside her. That was all the time it took for Elias to catch up with her.

He reached out and slammed one of his heavy hands against her shoulder. She squealed, alerting Robbie, who spun around and drove a fist into the face of the bigger boy. It caused him to stumble back only a step or two, and when Nitsy turned to follow Robbie, she felt another heavy hand swat her to the side.

The broken railing gave way, and like a swinging door, it allowed her to pass through.

"Nitsy!" Robbie yelled.

She tumbled forward, arms out, ready to break her fall on the bushes when she felt a heavy body slam into her on her way down.

Her first thought was Elias had followed her down. She screamed and swung her arms wildly as she crashed into the shrubbery. Robbie groaned beside her. He'd followed her over the railing. She rolled away from the bushes and tumbled onto the grassy lawn.

"Robbie," she muttered.

"That hurt," he replied as he too found his way out of the bushes.

They'd just stepped away when they heard a loud roar and glanced up to see Elias pitch forward in his attempt to chase after them.

Nitsy caught a glimpse of his face as he fell. He seemed completely oblivious to the fact that he was falling. He simply went over, headfirst.

"What's wrong with him?" she asked for the second time.

Elias plummeted toward the ground, and he didn't seem to have the wits about him to break his fall. He came down hard and landed on his chin. The crack of his neck shook Nitsy to her core. She screamed. Robbie yelled and covered his mouth with a hand. Elias lay crumpled on the ground, his head twisted the wrong way, his eyes closed.

Robbie stepped closer to him and was only a few feet away when Nitsy noticed Elias's hair move. It shook like there was something inside it.

"Robbie, don't," she yelled as she grabbed his arm and pulled him away.

"Yeah," he agreed. "Holy shit."

The crunching of glass above alerted them to another presence. They looked up to see Bianca walking along the second-floor corridor. Her head was tilted to the side. She wore the same dead expression as Elias.

"She's the same way," Nitsy whispered.

"Come on," Robbie replied as he pulled her toward the auditorium.

16

Robbie tore through the auditorium door with Nitsy by his side. Momentarily blinded, it took him a second to understand what was going on. The brightness of outside clashed with the dark room where his peers were watching a film on a giant screen. Through squinted eyes, Robbie saw John F. Kennedy standing at a podium delivering a speech. It was a leadership film, probably meant to keep the kids busy while he and Nitsy searched the school for their missing classmates. Only they weren't missing.

They're zombies.

With the sunlight at his back and the door closing behind him, cutting a slice of daylight through the darkness, Robbie saw quite a few teenagers looking his way. The sudden normalcy of the scene in front of him made him doubt what he'd just experienced. Like Elias's fall and broken neck might have been all in his imagination.

"Stop the movie!" Nitsy yelled.

She stood at his side. He hadn't even noticed her there, but her voice thundered through the auditorium with the command of a great leader. She demanded everyone's attention. He needed to do the same.

"Stop the movie!" he yelled, mirroring her authority.

An adult might have handled the situation differently, but he wasn't one, and he had no idea how to deal with a zombie apocalypse. With Robbie's outburst, the rest of the kids watching the movie gasped and turned to look at him.

"Lock the doors," Nitsy said, going back to the entrance and searching for a way to secure them.

Eggo, who Robbie knew was the leader of Nitsy's group, joined her at the door.

"Nitsy, what's going on?" he asked.

Voices went up all around him, and Robbie felt faint. None of this made sense. This was scary movie shit. This wasn't the kind of thing that happened to teenagers in real life.

"He... uh... he..." Robbie tried to explain when Mrs. Price made her way over to him and grabbed hold of his shoulders.

"Calm down," she said, "and tell me what happened."

"He broke his neck," he finally found his voice. "He broke his own neck."

Mrs. Price put a hand to her mouth and stared at him. She looked over at Nitsy. "What is he talking about?" She was nervous. "Did someone get hurt?"

"Mrs. Price," Nitsy took over, and Robbie was so thankful she did because he didn't think he could explain it in a way that made sense. "Something has happened to the missing kids. They're... they're like—"

"Zombies!" Robbie announced. "Elias and Bianca and who knows how many others. They're zombies."

One of the wisecracking boys Robbie had never had the pleasure of speaking to was seated nearby. As soon as he heard the word *zombie* he burst out in laughter and stomped his feet on the carpet in extreme exaggeration. Like he might laugh himself to death.

"Did you hear this kid?" the boy asked. "He said they're zombies. Zombies, man!"

A few others laughed. Some of the kids in the crowd were afraid. They weren't saying much. Robbie felt his blood boiling as the boy continued heckling him.

In the background, John F. Kennedy prattled on, speaking proudly to the American people while inside this auditorium, young people were freaking out.

"Will someone please stop the movie?" Nitsy asked.

Somewhere, someone did. The film paused on Kennedy's face as he raised one finger to explain an important point that wouldn't make a lick of difference in what was happening today.

"Yo, were these zombies like dragging their feet and stuff?" the wisecracking boy asked.

Robbie snapped. He leaped over an empty chair, grabbed the boy by the front of his T-shirt, and pulled him in close. "Do I look like I'm fucking joking?" he hissed through clenched teeth.

The boy's eyes went wide and he shook his head. "Nah, man. Nah. You don't."

"It's not a joke," Robbie declared as he let go of the boy. He looked at the rest of the students. "Something very wrong is going on out there."

"That's enough," Mrs. Price announced. "You, sir, need to sit down."

She was talking to Robbie.

"Mrs. Price, he's telling the truth," Nitsy said. "We need to lock the doors."

"Wait a second," she replied. "I'm sure something *is* going on out there, but I'd be willing to bet it's a sick joke. It might be a prank by your peers. Don't you think that's possible?"

Robbie turned toward her and thought about it. No, it wasn't possible. She hadn't seen the way Elias had come after them and how he'd fallen on his neck. She hadn't seen the room splattered with blood.

"Room 214 is a bloodbath," Robbie said.

Everyone fell silent. Robbie had never used the term bloodbath before, but it certainly held some sort of power over the staff and students alike.

"A bloodbath?" Mrs. Price asked.

"Let me go check that room," Eggo said. "Robbie, I'm sure something's going on. Let me go confirm the things you're saying."

"No!" Nitsy interrupted. "Are you kidding? Aren't you even listening to us?"

"I'll go," one of the other male staff members announced as he pushed past Nitsy and exited out the main doors.

"Don't let him—" Nitsy started but quieted down as she realized he was already gone.

"Nitsy, please find a seat," Mrs. Price said. "Mr. Dale will be back in a few minutes once he's assessed the situation. In the meantime, I think we should continue playing the film if for no other reason than to calm everyone's nerves."

Robbie couldn't believe it.

There are zombies outside, and she wants to watch a fucking movie?

"Nitsy?" he said, returning to her side and taking her by the hand. "Can you believe this?"

"I want to get out of here," she whispered.

"I said please take a seat," Mrs. Price ordered.

Robbie pulled Nitsy toward two empty seats high up in the auditorium. As they sat down, he scanned the crowd. Most of the kids were fidgeting in their seats. He wouldn't have expected any less. How could anyone calmly watch an ex-President speak at a time like this? While everyone else kept his or her eyes on the screen, Robbie was busy looking for potential exits. To the right, about halfway between where they were sitting and the front of the auditorium, was an emergency exit.

He wasn't sure where it would lead, but he thought he'd seen a second floor at the cafeteria. This door might lead that way, which would be fine by him, at least he knew that part of the campus was clear. That was where he and Nitsy had experienced their first kiss.

"What are you thinking?" Nitsy asked.

"I'm thinking this is fucked," he said. "That guy, Mr. Dale, he's in trouble."

The auditorium was silent except for the sound of President Kennedy delivering his speech and spectators cheering at the end of nearly every one of his sentences.

"Do you see the way he commands respect?" Mrs. Price spoke out over the sounds of the film. "Look at the way he—"

The main entrance door, the one Robbie and Nitsy had come through earlier, crashed open with a loud bang.

In stepped the large silhouette of Mr. Dale. His shadowy frame just stood there.

"Mr. Dale?" Mrs. Price asked.

Two more figures pushed through the doors and stood at his side. Robbie couldn't help thinking they looked like the figures people cut out of paper and hung on their Christmas tree. Three featureless people, side by side, stood inside the entrance as the doors closed slowly behind them, bringing the room back into total darkness aside from the light of the movie screen.

"I see you found a couple of the students," Mrs. Price said.

"Do you see how they're standing?" Nitsy whispered to Robbie.

They were hunched over, their shoulders down, and their heads to the side. The same way Elias looked earlier.

"I think we should go," he replied.

"Well, Robbie and Nitsy, do you feel better now?" Mrs. Price asked as she turned toward them.

Mrs. Price had her back to Mr. Dale and the two others when they stepped toward her.

"Mrs. Price!" Nitsy yelled. "Get away from them!"

Robbie stood and grabbed Nitsy's hand. It was too late. The *things* were inside the auditorium. He'd called them zombies earlier, but that sounded too corny. Too cheesy. Too unrealistic. These things were something else.

Nitsy struggled in Robbie's grasp, trying to pull away, trying to warn the rest of them, but it was too late.

Mr. Dale grabbed Mrs. Price's arm and the woman gasped. It was like he'd made a sexual comment or said something she found disgusting. That was all. Nothing more than a gasp.

The kids seated near her didn't move at all. Not at first.

Then Mrs. Price moaned. She fell to her knees and cried out. Her cry turned to a scream as her fingers reached for her scalp and dug in.

It took a second for a reaction from the students. They sat still, caught between watching a movie and trying to understand the scene unfolding in real life.

Over the voice of President Kennedy, Robbie thought he heard something. A sound like insects. Crickets maybe. Or possibly cockroaches climbing over each other. It started over by the door, but then Mr. Dale and the two people with him, two kids still shrouded in darkness, moved closer to the seated students.

And the sound amplified. It went crazy, like a million bugs riding a tidal wave that washed over the entire student body. It started close to the door but quickly made its way over the sea of seated teenagers. With it came the groans, grunts, and screams.

Robbie yanked Nitsy toward the exit door.

"Run!" he yelled.

Some of the kids near them stood and followed as they ran for the door. The sounds coming from behind them as they made their escape were those of hell. Like people being tortured for eternity. Robbie knew he'd never get those cries out of his head.

The creaking, skittering sound of insects.

The deep, guttural howls.

The metallic clatter of chairs being thrown.

The thudding of bodies tripping over each other and hitting the floor.

The screams.

As they reached the door and pushed through it, Robbie glanced back to see kids tumbling over one another and flipping onto the carpet.

One boy's eyes ran bloody tears.

A girl clawed at her own face, raking at her cheeks with long fingernails. Deep grooves were already cut into her flesh, and she kept digging, searching for something she might be able to pull free of her own body.

Mrs. Price leaped onto the sarcastic kid Robbie had yelled at earlier. The boy reached out to them as if he expected Robbie to shoot across the auditorium, scoop him up, and carry him to safety.

His outstretched arm weakened with his screams, and then it went limp.

Like the hands of hundreds of screaming spectators at a college football game, the wave started near the doors and fell toward them.

"We have to go!" Nitsy yelled, pulling him out the doors as it crashed down only a few feet away.

The last thing Robbie saw as he raced out the door was a teenage girl reaching out to him as a male student hugged her legs and climbed up her body. The boy's hair moved. He kept climbing. The girl began to scream, and her hopeful expression changed to desperation and then, as she clawed at her own head, it changed to hunger. She reached out to him because she wanted him. *It* wanted him.

17

Hal hadn't felt right all day. He woke up later than usual, feeling hungover again, despite the fact he hadn't had anything to drink. It had to be a lack of water. Every time he had a doctor's appointment, he was reminded of the same few things. He was supposed to watch his sodium intake, be careful with the amount of sugar he consumed, and drink lots of water. Hal followed none of that advice. He barely wanted to live at all, so why would he choose to live such a horrible life. He loved salt and sugar, and he hated drinking water. Coffee kept him going. It was one of the few substances loyal to him, and in return, he was loyal right back.

He'd tried to call Gus earlier that afternoon but hadn't been able to reach him. He'd tried the day guard too. The one who worked his post when the sun was up, but he'd had no luck getting him to answer his phone. He couldn't get the nagging feeling something wasn't right to leave his mind. It was those damn kids camping by the lake. If he'd only turned them away the first night, everything would be fine, but no, he'd had to be the *cool* guy, the *nice* park ranger.

You should have been an asshole and told them to go have sex someplace else.

"What the hell is taking so long?" he said aloud, drumming his fingers against the steering wheel.

The sun would be setting soon. He needed to hurry and get to work. The streets were really quiet today. He'd hardly passed any other cars on the way to the Burger Bin. This local fast food joint was a nice, hip diner on the inside. It was the local place to take dates for a burger and a shake. They'd recently added a drive-thru window, and this was where Hal now sat, idling, waiting behind three other cars so he could pick up something quick to take with him to work.

He hadn't moved an inch since joining the other cars in line.

"I swear they must have had to fly to North Carolina for the beef," he said barely above a whisper.

If his stomach didn't rumble to remind him of his hunger, he might have pulled out of the line and left. There wasn't anything else to get for dinner, especially not this late. Sure, he could go into the grocery store and see if they had any of those rotisserie chickens they sometimes had ready for take-out, but most of the time they ran out by this time of evening. Then what? He'd be stuck eating Pop-Tarts or Doritos for dinner.

No, he'd stick around a little longer. All it took was one asshole to order a ton of irregular stuff for a family of eight to make this line take forever.

As he waited, Hal's eyes traced the scenery around him. Further back in the parking lot was the grocery store and along the plaza was a bakery, a tattoo parlor, a shoe store, a discount clothing store, a cell phone provider, and all the other usual shops you'd expect to find in an outdoor strip mall. Other than this burger joint, there was a bank located on the other side of the parking lot. The DMV was around the corner, along with a car dealership, and the most upscale townhomes in the area.

He always thought it was weird seeing these two-story, cream-colored buildings pop up right next to all the metal and discount painted on prices at the dealership. Right now, a man was walking five dogs all at once. Hal couldn't help wondering if he owned all those dogs himself or if this was some kind of business of his. He'd heard of dog walkers before but thought that was only a thing in New York City or maybe in Los Angeles.

"Come on," Hal heard the man say as he tugged the leashes of the dogs, leading them to a patch of grass between the townhomes and the plaza.

Hal looked at the shopping center again and over at the windows of an electronics store. At this hour, the place should have been open, but the lights were off. Next door to it, the cell phone provider had its lights on but there was nobody inside. That wasn't all that odd, given that it was a small town, but he didn't even see employees inside. As he looked through his rearview mirror at the rest of the parking lot, he thought it looked quite sparse.

There was that thing going on at the university, so he knew quite a few people were headed out of town for that, but he'd never seen Clydesville this void of life. The grocery store always had a decent crowd. There wasn't much else for people to do. Curiosity got the best of him. Nobody was behind him in line, so he pulled his car out of the drive-thru and drove toward the bingo hall at the end of the plaza. *Everything* else in town could be empty, but that would *never* be the case at the bingo hall. Half the town's elderly spent their retirement checks in there.

Sure enough, as he rolled his window down at the curb, he noticed there were people inside the bingo hall. Only they didn't seem to be playing bingo at all. The frosted windows didn't allow him to see much of what was going on, but he could tell people were roaming about. Usually, everyone was seated and trying to win money.

"Is it a break between games?" he asked aloud.

He wasn't into bingo himself, but he'd visited the hall once out of boredom. He couldn't remember there being a time where the old folks moved aimlessly about.

As he sat in his truck watching the place, one of the people inside approached the window and slapped the glass. The shadowy palm slid downward, and it gave Hal the chills.

He pulled out his phone and dialed the police station. Of course, there wasn't much to report. Nothing at all really, but he was curious if they ever checked out the Cloud 9 trailer park. He figured he could ask about that and gauge if the cops mentioned anything weird.

The phone rang and rang until Hal finally hung up.

Weird. Someone always picks up.

This place wasn't exactly the crime capital of the world. There should never be a reason for the phone to go unanswered.

Hal's stomach rumbled and he looked once more at the drive-thru he'd left only a couple minutes before. The line still hadn't moved, so he drove back to the line. This time he didn't pull to the back but instead drove alongside it.

He came upon the red sports car that had been idling in front of him first. Because of its tinted back window, Hal hadn't been able to see the occupants of the car. As he pulled up alongside it, he realized it wouldn't have mattered either way because there weren't any occupants. The car was empty. It idled there, parked, with nobody behind the wheel.

"What the fuck?"

The next car was the same. So was the truck in front of it.

"What in the actual fuck is going on?"

The drive-thru window was empty too. He glanced beyond the truck idling at the window and stared into the brightly lit interior of the Burger Bin. Usually, there would be a teenager with a visor on manning the window. This evening, the inside of the burger joint was empty.

The barking of dogs pulled his attention to the right where he watched the man walking his dogs try to hold them back from an approaching beagle.

"Come on, now," the young man said, pulling back on the leashes clutched tightly in his fists. "Back."

The beagle continued toward him and the other dogs, seemingly unafraid of their threats. Something about the dog seemed wrong. It reminded him for a second of the dog he'd seen headed toward the young people camping at the lake. It looked rough like it hadn't been washed in a long time. Its fur, for being as short as it was, looked like it was blowing in the wind.

Hal rolled down his window. There wasn't any wind.

His mind went back to the trailer park and the ravenous mutt that attacked him with so much fury Hal still couldn't open his driver's side door without giving it a serious boot each time he pulled the handle. That dog really fucked up his truck.

"Stay back now," the man with the dogs said to the approaching beagle. "I don't want you to get hurt, little guy."

The man's expression changed. He was seeing something extraordinary. He squatted down and stared at the dog in awe. Then he flinched. It was a slight jerk of his head like he'd been splashed with water from a kid's toy gun, but it was enough to set Hal's internal alarm to high.

Hal slapped his palm against his horn, hoping to make the beagle flee, but it didn't.

The young man with the dogs fell back onto his ass and clutched his head. Then the other dogs really lost it. They began to bark and thrash wildly on their leashes. The beagle was unfazed by their wild manner.

Hal honked his horn again and the beagle turned its head toward him. It stared at him and Hal knew he'd seen that look before. It was the same cold stare the dog at the trailer park had given him.

The man with the leashes fell onto his back and let go of them all. Five dogs took off running in different directions. Not like they were afraid, but more like they were on a mission. Only the beagle remained, and it was glaring back at Hal. He honked his horn once more and it, too, fled the scene.

Hal sat there, shocked, watching as the man who'd been walking the dogs sat up and stared at the ground for a moment. He seemed confused, and Hal wondered if he needed help.

Then he picked himself up off the ground. He stood slowly to the upright position, but with his shoulders slumped slightly. The man's head turned to the left where he seemed to be scanning the parking lot, searching for something. His gaze steadily moved to the right. When he reached the Burger Bin, he stopped with his eyes set on Hal. This man would have no reason to approach Hal. They didn't know each other. But the man seemed interested in him, and the way he stared back at the truck gave Hal the chills.

What the fuck is wrong with this guy?

Hal pulled his gun out of his glove box and set it on the seat next to him. He couldn't imagine having to use the gun, but he would if he needed to.

He shifted his truck into drive and was about to speed away when he heard and felt a heavy thud against his truck's tailgate. Hal looked through the rearview mirror and saw a woman behind him, her entire body bathed in the red glow of his break lights. She snarled at him and moved around to the side of the truck.

Hal reached for his gun and for only a second wondered if he had grounds to pull the trigger. Nobody had physically assaulted him in any way. Not yet. But he wasn't about to let it get that far.

The man who'd been walking the dogs reached his passenger side window and slammed a fist through the glass. Hal's instinct was to step on the gas, and as he did, the man's forearm hit a large shard of glass at the bottom frame of the window and was skewered there. It dug deep into the man's arm as the truck dragged him through the parking lot.

Any normal person would have screamed and cried. They would have begged for their life. This guy only grinned with gritted teeth, growled back at Hal, and thrashed around wildly. Blood trickled from the wound on the man's arm instead of gushing the way it should have. The man seemed unfazed by the pain and kept trying to climb his way into the truck.

Hal jerked the steering wheel and swerved. As he did, he heard another thud on the left. The woman was now holding on to that side of the truck. Both of these maniacs were being dragged through the parking lot. They banged on the truck, howled, and shrieked.

"Get the fuck off my truck!" Hal yelled.

The man to his right, the one at his window, pulled his one arm free, tearing the broken piece of glass away from the frame. It was deep in his arm and blood splattered the seat next to Hal.

On the left side of the truck, the woman kicked wildly, thrashing around. She was too far back to really attack him, but a glance through the side mirror showed she was hellbent on reaching him. She was shimmying hand by hand, getting closer and closer to him.

Hal reached for his gun just as he noticed the man trying to climb in his window had something wrong with his head. His hair moved oddly and there was a strange sound emanating from it.

"Ahh!" the woman to his left yelled.

She'd reached the back door and was about to open it when Hal swung his truck wide to the left and stepped on the gas, bringing the truck toward a large green metal trash dumpster.

"I said get the fuck off my truck!" he yelled as he drove so close he thought he might ram right into the dumpster. He didn't, but she did. The woman on the side of the truck hit the large, metal container so hard she nearly lost her arms.

Hal lost his side mirror in the process, but a quick glance over his shoulder and he saw her tumbling across the ground.

A loud roar came from Hal's right and he saw the man was nearly in the window. The guy roared again. Adrenaline flowed through Hal. He'd had enough of this bullshit. He reached for his gun, pulled back the hammer, and shot the man right between his eyes.

The man flew out of the truck, but something fell from his head in the process.

Hal looked down at his seat and saw at least five tiny bugs. They were white, almost like maggots, but black in the back. He heard the noise again and realized it was coming from the bugs.

He turned back to the windshield a second too late.

Hal drove right through the front window of the shoe store. Glass exploded all around him. The world went black.

18

They'd found an old music classroom with only one window high up in the ceiling and a metal door that bolted from the inside. It was the perfect hiding place or the best they could find when running for their lives. Seven of them were now seated on the floor. The room had chairs in it, but Nitsy thought it felt less like hiding when leaned back in a desk. Curled up on the carpet felt safer, like when she was a kid and would throw her blanket over her head to hide herself from monsters. Back then, her parents told her they didn't exist, but that was a lie. Monsters did exist. They were at Stonewall Forge, and she was one of the lucky students from across the United States who got to see them up close.

These are the real monsters.

No blanket over her head would hide her now. There would be no calling for her dad to check her closet. She was alone with only six others. Robbie was here, of course, and he would do his best to protect her. Like now, he had his arm around her and was pulling her close to him.

The room was nearly completely dark with only that one small window to cast moonlight in on them, but her eyes had grown accustomed to the dark, and she could see the other kids now. Their features weren't sharp, but she could see them.

Lance, who she'd never met until this moment, was a big kid who carried a harmonica with him everywhere he went. Nitsy was terrified he'd forget their circumstances and nervously belt out a tune. He'd taken on kind of a leadership role, demanding they find shelter in one of the empty classrooms. He'd admitted to sneaking into this music room with one of the girl students.

Bradley had followed them out the auditorium and was now seated across from her, his legs tucked under him as he rocked back and forth. His glasses were crooked and Nitsy wanted so badly to reach over and fix them for him. He had a childlike quality and she remembered Phyllis had a bit of a crush on him.

Phyllis was here too. Nitsy had started the morning seated next to her friend in the auditorium, waiting for the day's big challenge to begin. They'd sat as a group. Everyone was in attendance except Elias. If she hadn't left to go search with Robbie, she might not have made it out of that auditorium at all. She would have been as confused as everyone else.

Nitsy blinked and remembered the faces of students scrambling for their lives.

One boy had turned toward her in his effort to flee, but something or someone had grabbed hold of his leg. He seemed to lose hope instantly like it was too late already, and then it was. His mouth fell open in a painful cry as his body pitched forward and scattered the seats around him. An infected girl crawled onto his back.

A female student was nearly at the door, had almost escaped with the rest of them when an infected boy jumped onto her back. His hand reached over her forehead and Nitsy watched in horror as the boy's fingernails dug into her eyeballs. The girl screamed and reached out to her, but it was too late. The boy continued to claw at the girl's face as Robbie yanked Nitsy out of the auditorium.

Even if she made it through this and returned to her home, she knew she would never close her eyes again without seeing those faces. So many more haunted her. The way the infected, zombie-like kids spread through the group so quickly was unlike anything she could ever fathom. It seemed like whatever was happening was jumping, not moving through bites like in all the horror movies. It was so much faster.

She and Robbie had been their only warning. If only they'd listened to her. They could have had a head start. There might have been more than seven of them cowering in this classroom now.

The other two kids with them she didn't know. The girl looked too young to attend the conference. The boy looked too old. They definitely knew each other. The two held hands and the boy whispered to the girl often.

"Are you two from the same school?" Nitsy whispered to them.

They froze as if her sudden interruption of the silence might bring the creatures down on them.

The girl nodded.

"What are your names?" Nitsy asked.

"Shh," Lance warned her.

"Don't shush her," Robbie warned him.

"Fuck you, man," Lance shot back. "We need to be quiet."

"Well you're being louder than I ever was," Nitsy replied.

Lance scoffed and scooted away from the rest of them. He stood and made his way to the door. Nitsy knew he wouldn't be dumb enough to open it, but she didn't trust that he wouldn't accidentally make a loud noise and alert the monsters. He was bossy by nature, and Nitsy didn't need to ask to know he was the leader of his group. He would have been her competition if they'd ever gotten to the point of explaining their projects to Mrs. Price.

Mrs. Price. She's dead too. They're all dead.

"Her name is Yasmin," the older boy answered, pulling Nitsy from her thoughts. "I'm Beau."

"Where are you from?" Nitsy asked.

"Portland, Oregon," Beau replied.

"I wanna go home," Yasmin whined.

Beau squeezed her tighter. Nitsy hoped the young girl would make it home. She wondered if any of them would. She wanted to be back at her home in Florida, sitting at the dinner table right now, about to help her mom clean the table before sitting down to watch a TV show. She wished she'd never shown interest in this program. She'd been told she was one of the lucky ones. She didn't feel so lucky now.

"They're out there still," Lance whispered as he returned to the rest of them and plopped down at a desk. "I didn't hear any footsteps, but they're near. It sounded like someone screamed."

"Someone screamed?" Phyllis asked.

Lance nodded. Nobody needed to mention what that might mean. If any of the others had escaped the auditorium, the monsters might have caught up with them. Nitsy closed her eyes and tried to focus on her breathing.

What if this place isn't good enough?

What if they break down the door?

We'll be trapped.

"I don't like staying in here like this," Nitsy said.

"We did what we had to do," Robbie reminded her. "We didn't have a lot of time to plan it."

She shrugged. "I guess. We could have run away from the campus."

Lance laughed and tapped his fingers on his desk, way too loud for comfort. Robbie glared at him and it was clear he wanted to give him a piece of his mind but held back, probably out of fear of a commotion starting. That was all they needed. Some stupid fight that would get them all killed. If the monsters never found them, they might make it for a while, but if they all came crashing against that door at the same time, they were done for.

"We'd never make it out there in the woods with those things chasing us," Bradley said, surprising everyone. He hadn't said a word since they'd fled the auditorium. He tucked his face back into his knees.

"Maybe," Robbie agreed.

Bradley lifted his face again. "You said you saw Elias break his neck?"

Robbie nodded.

"I was with him this morning," Bradley said, "for wake-up crew."

Everyone sat still, silently waiting on the rest of his story.

"The girls wouldn't come out of their room," Bradley added. "We knocked and tried to wake them up, but they wouldn't come out. Elias was convinced there was something... I don't know... sexual going on in there. I turned my back for a second and then he was gone. He'd entered the room." Bradley was silent and then he wiped at his eyes, getting rid of his tears. "I thought he was the luckiest guy in the world. I thought he was in there... you know... doing stuff with those girls."

"Room 214?" Robbie asked.

Bradley lifted his gaze and nodded, wiping at his eyes once more.

"Bianca's room," Nitsy said.

"I should have told somebody," Bradley said, "but I didn't want to get him in trouble. I thought he was just skipping out on the conference for a little while so he could hook up with the girls."

"It wasn't your fault," Nitsy said, doing her best to comfort him but knowing it wouldn't help.

Bradley buried his face in his knees again and mumbled, "I should have said something."

"Well, you didn't, bro," Lance whispered. "So, suck it up, and let's get through this."

Lance was *that* kind of leader. The kind who belonged in the military, not in politics. He would be the kind of coach to tell him to, "Put some ice on it." Nitsy hated those kinds of people. It was the reason so many teenagers were afraid to share their true feelings. They had fathers who'd raised them to toughen up and shut up.

"You're a lot of help," Nitsy said to Lance.

"And holding his hand is supposed to get us through this mess?" Lance shot back.

"Back off," Robbie warned him.

Lance stood. "Or what?"

Robbie met him eye to eye. "Really? You want to do this now?"

"Boys," Phyllis said. "Now's so not the time. Nobody cares who's tougher. Not unless the tough one is willing to go out there and lead those things far away from the rest of us so we can have a chance to escape."

Lance and Robbie both stared down at the girl.

"I think I know how it spreads," Beau, the older boy said.

Everyone turned their attention to him.

"I was sitting next to our team leader, a girl named Andrea, when it happened. Yasmin was to my right. My mind is quite… analytical, let's just say, and while everyone else was freaking out, I paused to try to get a closer look. If it weren't for Yasmin, I'd be one of them out there." He pointed at the door.

"So, what did you see?" Lance asked.

"Just before Yasmin pulled me to safety, I saw a girl scream and fall backward out of her seat. She got trapped there in the aisle as everyone else ran for safety. One of the girls who'd already been turned crawled across the floor toward her, and I swear it, I know this is going to sound crazy, but it was like her hair was leading her. Wisps of it were out in front of her like her hair was reaching out to the girl."

Lance scoffed again.

"Go on," Nitsy said.

"I swear I saw something jump from the girl's hair onto the hair of the other girl," Beau finished.

Nobody spoke for a while.

Finally, Nitsy broke the silence. "That makes sense."

"It does?" Phyllis asked.

"I thought I saw Elias's hair move when he was coming toward me," Nitsy informed them.

"And that sound," Robbie added. "It sounds like bugs trampling each other."

"It's in their hair," Lance said. "So, we shave off our hair."

"Sounds like a good plan," Robbie said, "if anyone has hair trimmers in their back pocket."

"All we need is a knife," Lance said.

"Do you have one on you?" Robbie replied.

Lance shook his head.

"And this room is empty except desks," Robbie added. "We'd need to get to the kitchen."

"Risking it out there *with* those things to get the thing that would maybe, only possibly, keep us safe *from* those things seems kind of counterproductive," Phyllis said. "Don't you think?"

"Getting our phones would be the smartest thing to do," Nitsy suggested.

"Our phones?" Yasmin asked, shaking her head wildly.

"Our phones are in the auditorium," Bradley reminded them. "There's no way I'm going back in there."

"That would be crazy," Robbie agreed.

"Fuck that," Lance said.

"If we can get our phones, even one of them, we can call for help," Nitsy reminded them. "How long do you think we'll survive in here without food or water?"

Beau rubbed his head. "Not long."

"Not long," Nitsy repeated. "I'll go for a phone."

"Nitsy," Robbie said, grabbing her arm, "you know I'm with you, no matter what, but come on. That's crazy."

"There's literally a bucket," Nitsy reminded them. "A single bucket... full of our phones."

"And you're going to run all the way from the auditorium back to here with a big bucket in your hands?" Phyllis asked.

Nitsy lowered her head. The more she thought about it, the crazier it seemed. She didn't even know where the bucket was. What if it had been locked up somewhere? That would be the smart thing to do with expensive possessions like kids' phones. Yet, she couldn't imagine anyone would go through the trouble to lock up a bucket of phones. It was probably there in the auditorium, on the floor, near where Mrs. Price always sat.

"Does anybody have a better idea?" Nitsy asked.

Nobody answered.

"So, we either go to the kitchen to find a knife and painfully shave everyone's head... hoping that'll keep us safe from the zombie horde outside, we go to the auditorium and get the bucket of phones, or we sit here and do nothing."

"We could make a run for it," Beau said, "try to get to the woods."

"And then what?" she asked. "It took the bus a long time to get to campus, and we don't even know how far the main road is from civilization. You want to hike all that way with these things on our asses?"

Beau shook his head. "No."

"I say we go for the phones," Nitsy said.

"There's a lot of *we* talk going on," Lance replied. "Who is this *we*?"

"Her... and me," Robbie informed them.

Nitsy smiled. She couldn't believe he'd risk his life to go with her.

"It might be better if I go alone," she said.

"Not gonna happen," he said.

"Robbie..."

"You're not gonna talk me out of it. In fact, I think *you* should stay."

She held up a hand to stop him. "Fine, we both go."

She stood up from her spot on the floor.

"Oh," Robbie said, "we're going now?"

He suddenly seemed nervous.

"I want to get out of here," she said.

19

This was a hell of a first date. Grant and Sally had escaped Main Street on foot. Grant could have gone back for his truck, but it was too risky. Those *things* were everywhere. They'd spent the daylight hours hiding out in an antique furniture store where Grant often sold his wares. The old lady who owned it never used an alarm. Most people in Clydesville didn't. Nobody was going to break in to steal her old tables and chairs.

The phone inside the store worked, so Grant tried calling the cops. Nobody answered, and that didn't surprise him. They would be out there dealing with the situation. The police force was rather small, and they definitely weren't equipped to handle something of this scale. This was the kind of thing seen in 80s horror movies where military trucks would roll in any moment with scientists clad in white hazmat suits and face shields.

If that happens, they might shoot everyone still alive.

That, too, always happened in those movies.

Sally cried quite a bit at first. She was worried about her family. Her parents were both in their seventies and her younger sister was twenty-two. Their home phone rang and rang. Their cell phones went to voicemail.

If this thing had already infiltrated the Clydesville neighborhoods, things were seriously fucked. Grant had believed it was unique to the Main Street, or downtown, area. Now, he wasn't so sure.

"We need guns," Grant said aloud, for at least the third time since they'd entered the store. "Dammit, we need some guns."

"Then what?" Sally asked, peering out onto the dark street.

"Then we shoot the bastards in the head," he replied. "Like in the movies. I mean, they're zombies or somethin', right? That's what you do with them. You ain't ever seen *Night of the Living Dead*?"

Grant knew he was dating himself. Of course, there had been countless movies and TV shows about the rising dead, but he wasn't much of a movie buff. He spent most of his time in his house, so if it wasn't something that came on basic cable, he probably hadn't seen it. He appreciated shows like *Antique Roadshow* and *Storage Wars*. Television programs with furniture on them often gave him ideas for projects.

Jesus, you really are a boring son of a bitch. What would a woman like Sally see in you anyway?

Here they were, crouched down behind a big oak bookshelf, hiding from whatever sickness was spreading on the other side of the shop window, and he was thinking about romance. In his mind, he might somehow become the hero of this situation and win the girl's affections in the end.

"It's dark enough now, I think," he said as he stood from their hiding place and made his way over to the door.

Sally didn't budge. "Wait, what? We *are not* going out there."

"We can't stay in here forever."

"Forever? It's only been hours."

"It's been all day. I know where we need to go. It's not that far away and in the darkness, we should be able to hide."

"Hide? We're hiding now." She looked at him with her eyes watering. "I don't even know if my family is okay."

He crossed the room and held his hand out to her. She refused to take it at first but then accepted it and rose to her feet.

"We ain't gonna be able to check on your family from in here," he said.

"We don't even know if those things see, hear, smell... I mean they're human, right? They should be able to do whatever humans do."

"Sure as hell seemed like it back at the diner."

Grant walked to the floor-to-ceiling glass window and peered out at the dark street. He was surprised he didn't see burning cars or anything else destroyed the way things always were in scenes of the aftermath of riots or other periods of mass hysteria. From where he stood, Main Street looked no different than it would any other night. In the dark, it looked quite peaceful.

The streetlamps were on a timer and they popped on as he stared out, causing him to jump away from the window.

"For the love of God!" he yelled.

Sally giggled behind him, and when he turned toward her, he saw she had her hand over her mouth, laughing into it. It was the sweetest thing he'd ever seen, and soon after, he was laughing with her.

"You should have seen how high you jumped," she squealed.

"Scared the bejesus out of me," he admitted.

She stepped toward the window, still laughing, and stood next to him. With the street illuminated, all didn't look as safe as it had seconds ago. The sidewalk across the street was stained with blood, a spray of it, like someone had gotten cut badly. The body it belonged to was nowhere in sight.

"Do you think they eat the bodies?" she asked.

"Back at the diner, it looked like they take over the body, like some kind of blood-sucking parasite."

"Vampires?"

It was his turn to chuckle. This time she didn't join him. He hadn't meant to be insensitive, but the word *vampire* sounded childish. Like something out of a scary book. He didn't think Clydesville was being overrun by the fanged undead.

As if staring into an underwater view through one of those thick glass viewpoints at Sea World, Grant felt safe inside. The sharks were on the other side, with the fish, not in here where it was warm and dry. Did he really want to venture out there onto the street? Did he really want to put Sally's life at risk? He didn't. He preferred the company he had. For a moment, he considered staying put. They could ride out the initial phase of this storm and then maybe those *things* would starve to death or kill each other or maybe simply fall down and die. Maybe the damn army would show up and wipe them out.

And what if they don't? You can't stay in here forever.

He'd zoned out only for a moment, lost in his thoughts when a bloody hand slapped the window in front of them. The thwack was so loud and so unexpected that Grant and Sally both jumped this time.

Dragging himself down the sidewalk was one of the creatures. It looked like a man. Of course, it did. They all appeared to be human. This one wore a ripped and bloody park ranger uniform.

"Don't move," Grant said softly from the corner of his lip.

If they didn't budge. If they remained stoic, maybe the *thing* would think they were mannequins. Maybe it sensed movement and by not giving it anything to chase, it would continue down the sidewalk in search of someone else to attack.

Grant's heart pounded in his chest. He'd seen how strong and how fast they were. If it turned toward them now, it might be able to throw itself through the window. Then what? They could run. They could try to make it to the back door. Sally was faster than he was, so he might be able to save her if she ran and didn't look back, but then he would become one of them, wouldn't he?

"Grant?" Sally whispered, her voice quivering with fear.

"Don't move," he repeated.

It slapped its bloody hand against the window once more, leaving a red handprint a few feet away from the first. It could barely hold itself up and needed the window for support.

The thing had long, greasy hair and a beard. Grant thought he recognized him. Or who he used to be before he was changed. He didn't know the man personally, but he'd seen him around. He was one of those folks who left Clydesville at some point and then decided to move back. A lot of people did that.

They would be okay. The *thing* was almost past them. He wasn't going to see them.

It slapped the window again, leaving another red palm print on the glass, and this time it was so close to Sally's face, she accidentally flinched.

The thing whipped its head to the right and glared right into Sally's eyes.

She screamed.

It slapped the window harder.

"Let me in!" *it* demanded.

"Back up," Grant ordered.

Sally stepped back, and he grabbed her by the hand. They would run for the door.

"Please," the man outside said, "let me in."

His eyes weren't angry. They'd been determined. Now, they were hopeful. The man pulled a gun from his belt and pointed it at the glass.

"Grant!" Sally cried.

"I'm not one of them!" the man outside said. "I promise. Please. Let me in. It's dangerous out here."

"What do you think?" Grant asked Sally.

"Hal?" she asked.

"You know him?" Grant asked.

Sally didn't reply. She went to the door, unlocked it, and pulled the door open for him.

"Oh, thank God," Hal said as he fell through the door and landed on the floor.

He was hurt. His hair was matted with a mixture of sweat and blood. Sally dropped to her knees beside him.

"Hal, what are you doing out here?" she asked.

"I wrecked my truck," he said. His lips were dry and cracked. His tongue stuck to them as he tried to speak.

"He needs water," Sally said.

Grant only stared down at the man. He didn't know Hal, but he knew the man was beat the hell up. He'd been out there on the street, in the war zone, and had seen things that had him practically paralyzed with fear.

"Water," Sally repeated.

Grant snapped into action. At the rear of the store, next to a small card table with two plastic chairs, was a small refrigerator. Sally and he had found bottles of water in there earlier along with a bag of apples, a jar of pickles, and some banana popsicles in the freezer. The old lady who ran the store was wise enough to keep snacks. Scooping up a couple of the water bottles, Grant made his way back to Hal, who was now lying on his side, exhausted.

"We have to get ahold of the police," Hal said.

"We been tryin'," Grant informed him. "Done called at least fifteen times. Ain't nobody answerin' that phone. If I had to guess, I'd say they're already out on the street takin' care of business."

"They ain't takin' care of *shit* out there. I came all the way from Burger Bin," Hal informed them.

Grant handed Hal a bottle of water. Hal twisted off the top and swigged the cool liquid, then winced as it ran down his throat. "Cold," he said. "God, that tastes good."

Sally stared out the window. "We were at the diner. I was working. Grant came in as he usually does. Then everything went crazy. I can hardly remember how it went down, yet I can't get most of it out of my head. I know it doesn't make sense. It's like... my timeline is all messed up. I can see the people changing and hear the screams, but I have a hard time putting events in order."

"I get it," Hal said.

"Not me," Grant replied. "I remember it all, in order, every single damn word spoken before it went down and everything that came after."

Hal sat up. His strength seemed to be coming back to him. "I was trying to get a bite to eat and some guy walking a dog attacked me. And the dogs... they all went nuts. Wrecked my truck, crawled away, and stumbled all through town trying to get to the police station."

"That's a long walk," Grant said.

It was. It had to be at least three miles between the Burger Bin and where they were now. On foot, with those creatures out there, that was a hell of a long way to travel. Grant decided he liked Hal already. He'd continue to like him as long as he didn't try and squeeze his way in on Sally.

Stop thinking about the girl and focus on the real problem.

"You're hurt," Sally said.

"It ain't that bad," Hal replied. "Got a nasty gash on my side and hit my head pretty hard when I crashed, but I'll be fine."

"We need guns," Grant announced again.

"You keep saying that," Sally replied.

Hal set his gun on the floor. "He's right. Or at least some ammo."

Grant picked up the gun and found it empty. "Great."

"I used it all out there," Hal informed him.

"You shot people?" Sally asked, moving away from him as if repulsed. "What if they can be changed back? What if this is temporary?"

"I don't mean to hurt your feelings, Sally, but I wasn't going to let any of those assholes get close enough to me to find out. Out there, it's either run faster than they can and farther than they can or hit 'em right here." Hal touched the center of his forehead.

"Think we can make it to Clementine's?" Grant asked.

Hal stared at the floor and then slowly shrugged. "I honestly don't know. The thought of going back out there scares the shit out of me."

"It's only about four blocks that way," Grant said.

"Yeah, I know where it is, but those things are everywhere. That's why I was pressed up against this building, trying to blend in with the shadows. I still can't figure out if they got senses like humans or if they're able to smell us, hear us, or see us better."

Sally picked up the gun and hefted it in the palm of her hand, letting it fall slowly. She could have been playing with a feather. "I think it's safest to assume all their senses are better. I say we stay in here 'til the army arrives."

"We haven't called the army," Grant reminded her. Then he turned his attention to Hal and said, "Any idea how we call the army?"

Hal chuckled. "No. But damn if they don't make that look easy in all the movies, right?"

"911 doesn't seem to do it," Grant said with a snicker of his own.

"I'm glad you guys find this funny," Sally said and then laughed a little herself.

Grant was still laughing when he noticed movement outside. He turned toward the big window and hesitated for a second, trying to make sense of what he was seeing. From across the street, he thought he saw somebody approaching. It was a big bull of a man rushing toward them.

Hal and Sally both followed his line of sight and tensed up as he said, "The hell is that?"

The time it took him to get those words out was all the time he had. The man coming at them launched himself at the glass.

The window exploded inward.

He roared, his face a bloody mess, as he fell through the shattered glass, arms flailing, reaching for anything he could get his hands on.

Sally screamed.

Hal yelled.

Grant let out an "oomph" as he stood too quickly and toppled backward over the desk behind him. He regained his composure and climbed to his feet in time to see Hal swing a metal lamp at the thing's head.

Sally ran for the back door while Grant and Hal worked together, grabbed the nearest bookshelf, and shoved it down onto the man.

His growl never stopped, even as the heavy piece of furniture pinned him to the floor.

"Stay away from him!" Sally screamed from the back of the room.

"Look at his hair!" Grant said, pointing down at the tufts sticking out from under the bookshelf.

The man's long, scraggly locks moved on their own, reminding Grant of the old tales of medusa. It seemed to slither, searching, trying to find something to attack.

"What's wrong with his hair?" Hal asked, staring down at it with his mouth agape.

It wasn't only moving, but it was whining in some strange insect language. Clacking and clicking to itself.

"Come on, man," Grant said as he grabbed Hal by the arm. "Don't get any closer."

Hal looked back at Sally and shook his head in disbelief. "Did you see it?"

"I don't wanna see it," she replied.

Grant passed him and followed Sally to the back of the store. "Let's get out of here."

20

"Remind me why we're the ones doing this," Robbie whispered as they stood at the music room door, trying to get up the nerve to leave.

"Because we're brave," Nitsy said.

He passed her a smile and shook his head. "Yeah, that must be it. Brave Robbie and his girlfriend Nerves-of-Steel Nitsy.

Your girlfriend? Oh, she's definitely going to notice that. No take-backs now, man. She's your girlfriend.

"Girlfriend?" she asked, not missing a beat. "Shouldn't you ask a girl, first?"

It was dark, but he knew if he could see her face she'd be blushing. She had an adorable grin, and he wished he could see it now. It might actually relax his nerves a little. Her face remained hidden in the darkness, refusing to step out and calm him.

"You're trying to take my mind off this stupid plan to go get the phones, aren't you?" she asked.

He chuckled and shook his head. "Not a chance. If we get out of here alive, I need you to be my girl."

She leaned forward and stood up on her tiptoes. He met her halfway, putting his forehead against hers.

"I'll be your girlfriend right now," she said, "how about that?"

"I don't know," he replied. "You gonna ask me first?"

She pulled away from him, but he grabbed her around the waist and held her tight. He pressed his lips against hers.

"You're mine, all right?" he asked between their lips.

She kissed him hard and backed up a step. "Absolutely. Now, stop trying to waste time, and let's go get these phones."

"If I die out there, I'll be so disappointed."

"You won't be the only one."

"You definitely won't be the only one," Lance added from behind them. "We'll all be pretty disappointed.

Robbie had almost forgotten about the rest of the kids waiting on them to leave. He didn't care though. They were going to be here, safe, secure in this room while he and his girlfriend would be out there risking their lives to search for this bucket of cell phones. Its whereabouts? Nobody knew for sure. They'd be traipsing around in the dark, blindly seeking something that could save their lives.

This whole ordeal started early this morning, as far as Robbie could tell. It was the longest day ever. How could it have been this morning that he'd been woken up by Nitsy and her morning crew? Was it really only today that he'd shared breakfast with her before the big meeting? It seemed like so long ago.

When death comes in waves the way it did in the auditorium, death itself seems to take on a whole new meaning, or its own persona. It becomes death as a whole. So much death. The individuals get lost in it, and for the first time since it started, Robbie thought about some of the faces he'd seen in the crowd. He remembered conversations he had with kids, nameless companions, excited to be a part of this big leadership conference. The laughing, the joking, the elation. All positive energy.

They were all dead now. Or worse, they were those *things*. Their parents were at home looking forward to seeing their children again soon. Waiting to hear all the stories. Excited to watch the digital recordings promised by the program. Only thirty dollars each if the kids wanted to bring home a video of their experience here at

Stonewall Forge. Robbie's parents had paid the fee. He was sure Nitsy's had too.

He'd never seen a cameraman on site, which meant there were cameras around. The thought had never crossed his mind before, but he bet the auditorium had a few. Would anyone ever see what happened in there? Would the local news get ahold of it? Would the government reach it first? This seemed like one of those situations that would result in a cover-up.

They could die right now on their way to get these phones and there was a good possibility nobody would know the truth.

What would the story be? He imagined it would be something like contaminated water that poisoned them all. No, it would be a gas leak. Then *they* could set the place ablaze and the story would be that an accidental spark ignited the gas and the entire student body went up in flames.

"Are you ready?" Nitsy asked him.

He nodded, but he wasn't ready. He could never be prepared for something like this. The only thing he knew for sure was they needed to get the hell away from the campus before something like that "accidental" explosion wiped them off the face of the earth. He'd never had a reason to not trust his government before, but whatever was happening here, this information would need to be locked up and never shared with the public.

Robbie had seen his fair share of conspiracy theory videos on YouTube. He was still sifting through mental debris when Nitsy popped the door opened softly and listened with her ear at the crack in the door. Everyone behind them remained perfectly still. Only silence filled that dark void beyond. No howling, no crying, and no screaming. Wind blew past the corridor and ruffled the flyers posted on the corkboard next to the door.

Nitsy peered up at him, waiting for his encouragement. Robbie nodded and watched her close her eyes, take a deep breath, and then gently pull the door open further, but only wide enough for the two of them to slip through.

Here they stood, hand in hand, unmoving as they tried to get a sense of where they were and what was around them. Nitsy surveyed the area. Robbie did too. He needed to make sure they could get back to the room in a rush. The first time, they'd run blindly through the campus halls until they came upon the unlocked music room. If they were chased this time and ran in the wrong direction, they may never make it back.

When the door behind them was closed, probably by Lance, the click echoed through the hallway and might as well have been a bullet shot from a .44 Magnum. It cracked so loud, Robbie was sure it would awaken and alert anything sleeping or quietly stalking the halls.

"Fuck," he muttered under his breath.

They remained still for a moment. If anything growled, Robbie would turn and bang on the door behind them. They could return to their safe slumber. It wasn't too late.

He listened intently.

No growl.

No scream or shriek.

No voices.

Nothing.

Finally, when he was sure the door's click was unheard, he pulled Nitsy by the hand in the direction he was sure led to the auditorium. She followed, which meant he was right. If not, she would have yanked him down some other path. It was already clear to him that she was someone who liked to be in the lead.

It's why we're the ones out here looking for the phones.

As they crept down the hall, something caught Robbie's eye out in the courtyard to their left. It was parked near the statue of Stonewall Jackson. It was a wheelbarrow and sticking out of it was some yard equipment. He saw the handle of a shovel and a rake.

Leaning in close to Nitsy, he whispered, "Just a second."

She shook her head when she saw where he was going, but he didn't care. Those were potential weapons, and he wasn't too fond of being out here unarmed. He carefully pulled out the shovel. He was about to go for the rake when he saw a rust-stained machete inside the wheelbarrow.

You've got to be kidding me.

He pulled the machete out, and it scraped the bottom of the metal wheelbarrow so hard he was sure *everything* and everyone in West Virginia heard him.

"Fuck," he swore again under his breath.

Nitsy raced toward him and grabbed him by the arm, whispering into his ear, "Are you crazy?"

"Weapons," he said as he handed her the shovel.

The rake might have been a better weapon, but it was long and awkward. The shovel was heavy enough to cave in a skull. She accepted it, and he held the machete up proudly. She shook her head again.

Something roared nearby.

It could have been a lion for how ferocious it sounded. It was far away, but it sounded like it was on the hunt.

A growl sounded off a little closer than the roar.

"We should go back," he said, knowing he was the wimp here, but also knowing this wasn't the time to feign bravery. This was about staying alive.

"You've got a machete now," Nitsy reminded him. "And I've got…" she looked down at the makeshift weapon in her hands and continued, "… a shovel. I've got a shovel. This will have to be good enough. If you're too afraid, you can go back, but we need those phones and I'm capable of getting them. I *have* to do this."

A look flashed across her face, and it took Robbie a moment to understand it. Her jaw muscles flexed, and her eyes squinted. It was determination, and he wasn't sure why she felt she needed to take it upon herself to save them. Why was it her responsibility? He couldn't answer that now, and he figured if they made it through all this, he would ask her about it. For now, he would have to trust her, and there was no way he was letting her do this on her own.

With a quick kiss on her lips, he said, "Lead the way."

Each step they took had to be slow, cautious, and planned. Robbie found himself holding his breath from time to time, so he could hear better. The beating of his heart and his own panting made it hard to decipher sound.

A gunshot sounded off from far away and Robbie wondered if it was the distant sound of hunters, young drunks shooting beer cans in a backyard somewhere, or had this thing stretched beyond the campus and now people were out there fighting for their lives? He'd been thinking *this* was confined to the Stonewall Forge campus, but if this spread to the nearest town, it could keep going. Whatever *this* was.

They weren't far from the Stonewall statue when lights popped on all around them. It was the courtyard lights, and Robbie figured they must have been on an automatic timer. That meant the motion sensor lights for the hallways would be on too. This could be bad. More than ever, he considered turning back and hiding inside the music room. They could do this in the morning.

Nitsy froze in place with him as the lights popped on, but then she continued walking toward the auditorium, her fingers interlaced with his.

The hall around the corner from the music room was dark when they entered. At the far end was the auditorium entrance. To their right was the dormitory area and to the left, all along the corridor, were classrooms.

No people were in sight, which meant none of the creatures were either.

Nitsy took another step into the hallway and the lamp above their heads popped on. In reality, it was only a slight flicker, but it seemed so loud. Bathed in light without warning, Robbie was forced to put a hand over his eyes and squint. When his vision cleared, he saw the wall between two classes, to their left, was slathered in blood.

It started with a handprint like someone had slapped the wall, but then the hand kept going, smearing the mark several feet before stopping and slapping the wall again a foot or so later.

A few feet ahead, on the concrete walkway, they came across a puddle of blood.

More blood on the wall a few feet further.

As the corridor opened up to the same grass-covered area Robbie and Nitsy had run from earlier, bodies came into view. None were on their feet. Elias still lay in the bushes below the broken balcony. Other bodies littered the lawn.

The closest to them looked as if its fingers had tried to claw the hair right off the top of its head. Like the kid had dug at his own scalp so hard he'd nearly peeled it off. Skin hung to the side of his head like a haircut gone horribly wrong. The barber put the clippers too close to the skin and sliced it right off in a jagged groove. His face was crushed at the nose and jaw like someone had taken a baseball bat to him.

Maybe we weren't the only ones to survive.

It looked like this kid, this *thing* had tried to attack someone, and the attacker blasted him in the face with a pipe.

A few other bodies were in the same condition. Their skulls were broken open like someone hit them hard to finish them off.

The heads. Just like fucking zombies, man. You have to go for the head.

He'd always known he was right. They were zombies. Brain-seeking zombies. And here they were trying to find a bucket of phones. All it would take was one bite and they'd be goners. They couldn't let these things get that close.

Robbie gripped the handle of his machete and followed closely behind Nitsy. His eyes were still on the dead body-riddled lawn when she stopped in place, causing him to bump into her. He unwittingly made an "umph" sound as their bodies collided. When he looked ahead of her, he saw why she'd stopped.

A figure stood at the end of the hall, past the auditorium door, silhouetted in the lamplight at its back, staring right at them.

"Do you see it?" Nitsy whispered.

He couldn't miss it. It stood hunched over, long hair hanging down at both sides of its face, and its hands were out at its sides, fingers curled, like it was a feral beast waiting to attack. Its shoulders rose up and fell down with each strained breath.

"It's looking at us," she added.

"We knew we were going to have to take them on," he said. "Now's as good a time as ever."

His words sounded tough and brave like he was a badass zombie killer, but inside he felt bile rise to the top of his throat. He was seconds away from vomiting all over the place. He knew they would face these things, but he hadn't counted on seeing one this early, this clearly, and this calmly waiting for them to advance. He'd imagined them like they were in the auditorium, rushing the mob, growling, and screeching as they devoured their prey.

That's what we are. We're prey.

Robbie had been afraid several times in his life. Bad things had happened to him. He'd once gotten stuck at the top of a Ferris wheel. He'd been with a date, too, which only made matters worse. He'd never been afraid of heights, but he wasn't very fond of them either, so when he looked down and saw the people in the amusement park looking up at them, he was scared. But, he'd known someone would eventually get them down.

Another time, when he'd hopped over a fence to swim in a neighbor's pool with his friends, they'd thought the neighbor was gone for the weekend. It turned out the whole family left except the dad. He pulled a shotgun on the trespassing hoodlums. Robbie thought he'd shit his pants in that pool, but he didn't. He was confident the guy would do nothing more than call the cops. Of course, he wouldn't actually shoot them.

This time, standing there staring at the infected woman at the end of the hall, he felt none of that faith things would work out. He'd seen so many kids attacked in the auditorium, many of whom probably called out to their parents or God, and they hadn't made it out unscathed. Robbie and Nitsy did because they ran.

If they ran this time, it would mean they'd failed.

"Walk slowly toward the door," Robbie suggested, realizing they needed to go ahead and get this over with. The longer they stood in one place, the more likely they were to encounter more of the creatures.

As they stepped softly toward the auditorium door, the infected woman at the end of the hall didn't come closer. It was like she wasn't aware of their presence. The woman's body moved in mechanical-looking jerks like whatever had possessed her body wasn't capable of manipulating it in smooth motions.

Her head tilted and she stared up at the ceiling while raising her left shoulder. Then her shoulder fell and her right lifted. Each stuttered move seemed thought out, one right after the other, like someone was controlling her with a joystick.

Bizarre. And how isn't she seeing us right now?

Nitsy continued down the hall, and Robbie followed with his machete raised. If the woman suddenly saw them and came running, he'd be ready.

She never came. Nitsy reached the auditorium door and leaned against it. Robbie nodded to tell her to go ahead. She closed her eyes and pushed the door inward. It opened smoothly, without any noise, and plunged them into darkness once again. Robbie closed the door carefully, and it let out an audible click as it secured itself.

Robbie squeezed Nitsy's hand with the sound and stared into the darkness. If any of the creatures were in here, this would be the moment they would attack. But the room remained silent.

The only light inside came from the film that was still on pause. On screen, President Kennedy had his finger raised in mid declaration. Bluish light shined across the rows of scattered chairs where Robbie was sure he saw bodies strewn about.

Bodies of kids who'd actually died instead of being turned.

Some would have been trampled, a few might have broken their necks in the fall, or perhaps they even had fright-induced heart attacks. Robbie wasn't sure if that were possible, but he'd seen the fear on the kids' faces as the infected lashed out at everyone in the auditorium, and he imagined it could've stopped their hearts.

Now, the place seemed void of the creatures.

"Where did they all go?" Nitsy whispered to him.

He shrugged.

The place was empty of the infected.

Or was it?

The entire perimeter of the circular room was hidden in darkness. Robbie imagined the zombie-like students standing with their backs against the wall, waiting for the right opportunity to pounce on them. Were they that smart? Were these things intelligent?

"The phones," Nitsy whispered.

He nodded and followed her to the spot on their left where Mrs. Price and her crew had set up shop. This was where they watched the students and waited for their turn at the podium. It was where the computer sat on a table that was now controlling the Kennedy flick. The bucket of phones had to be over there too. It was the only place that made sense.

Nitsy moved with purpose, stepping over the body of a fallen student and walking stealthily over to the laptop on the table. Robbie stood behind her and acted as a guard while she squatted down and searched the area around the floor for the bucket.

While she was busy under the table, Robbie thought he saw something at the rear of the auditorium, way back near where he'd sat earlier with Nitsy. Where they'd made their escape. It was so dark back there, but Robbie thought he saw a girl standing with her arms at her sides. Perfectly straight, as if she were a statue frozen in time.

Robbie tapped his foot softly against the floor to try and get Nitsy's attention. He wouldn't dare take his eyes off the shadowy figure at the back of the auditorium. Yet, he wasn't sure if what he thought he was seeing was real at all. His mind could be playing tricks on him. If one of the creatures were back there, wouldn't it have attacked them by now?

The one outside didn't.

"Found it," Nitsy whispered from under the table.

She reached up to the table and grabbed hold of it to pull herself up, and when she did, her fingers accidentally mashed the spacebar on the laptop. President Kennedy's voice came to life, finishing his heartfelt moment, and throwing Robbie and Nitsy into the frying pan.

"Shit," Nitsy said as she realized what she'd done and hit the space bar again to pause the video.

The sudden disappearance of sound seemed louder than the video popping on at full blast. Nitsy stood up, beside Robbie, with her arms hugging a big white bucket. Her shovel was on the floor. Robbie wanted to tell her to just grab a few of the phones, but what if those few were locked and were useless. It was better to bring the whole bucket. Robbie's eyes were on Nitsy when he heard it.

"Huh," came a noise at the back of the auditorium.

It was the shadowy figure Robbie thought he'd seen. Its head jerked up and to the left, like the woman outside.

Nitsy held the bucket in her arms and stood next to Robbie, staring out at the sea of scattered chairs where one by one figures emerged from the floor. Shadowy strangers popped up to their feet as if they'd been sleeping or lying on the floor in confusion. Now, everywhere, at least fifty of them were staring back at Robbie and Nitsy. But none of them moved.

Robbie jerked when loud banging suddenly came from the door behind them. Growling followed and Robbie knew it was the woman outside in the hall. She'd heard the sound of the movie, and now she was furiously pounding on the door.

The noise from the door threw the others into action. It seemed to excite them, and suddenly they all shrieked at the ceiling and started forward. Running at full sprints, the creatures fell over chairs and kicked them out of the way as they charged toward Robbie and Nitsy.

"Run," Robbie told her.

Nitsy turned to flee. The only way out was through the door they'd entered. They would have to barrel right over the woman outside. If any others were out there, they would be fucked, but it didn't matter. That was their escape route, and Robbie raced beside Nitsy as they headed for the door.

From seemingly out of thin air, one of the creatures pounced on them from the left. Robbie reacted quickly and swung his machete down at the crown of its head. He kicked the creature's chest and yanked his machete free, but in trying to save them from the attacking monster, he took his eyes off Nitsy.

21

Nitsy was almost out the door when she felt claws dig into her left shoulder blade. One of the things was on her, digging its fingers into her flesh. She tried to reach for Robbie. He was close but slightly ahead of her, holding onto the door when one of them came at him and he struck with his machete. Blood rained down over her, hitting her lip, and covering her hands.

The world seemed to move in slow motion. Behind her, the *things* were coming fast. She heard their footsteps, shrieks, and growls. Metal and plastic crashed as they threw things out of their way to get to her, and she was stuck running with this plastic bucket in her hands.

When she reached for Robbie again, her fingers couldn't keep hold of the bucket, and then the weight of the other creatures was on her, pulling her down. The bucket slid from her hands and crashed to the floor. She tried to reach for Robbie, but she couldn't get her hands on him. Then she was on the floor with creatures piled on top of her.

The sound of the insects crawling around so close to her made her scream.

She couldn't become one of them. She wouldn't.

"Nitsy!" Robbie called out to her.

For only a moment, through the crowd swarming all over her, she caught a glimpse of him swinging the machete again.

He looked at her with his brow furrowed and his mouth open wide with horror.

"No!" she screamed.

The buzz and the clicking from the insects rang in her ears. It was over. They had her. She would become one of them.

Infected bodies smothered her, and as they moved, she caught quick flashes of Robbie swinging his machete. He wasn't giving up. He wouldn't leave her.

She tried to scream, to assure him she was still in here, but her breath caught in her throat.

A heaviness fell on top of her head.

The insects were on her. She could hear their gnashing, feel their squirming, and smell the foul rot of their tiny bodies.

Nitsy's body went slack. Her chest hit the floor, and then she noticed something. There was wiggle room beneath all the creatures. They'd piled on top of each other in their efforts to attack her, and in doing so, they'd left a hollowed-out spot beneath them. She grabbed hold of whatever limbs were in her way and pulled, dragging herself across the floor.

Now that the bugs were on her, it seemed they'd lost interest in her. They began to crawl away from her, and she headed toward the door.

Tears streamed down her cheeks. Her nose ran. Slobber fell from her desperate, crying mouth. She only wanted to get away from them.

But they were on her. They were there, digging their way into her scalp. She could feel them.

Realization hit her as she crawled on all fours and fought her way back to her feet. Her fingers dug into the mouth of the creature Robbie had hit with the machete and her left palm pressed against the back of another fallen monster. They were everywhere around her, and she knew she needed to get away.

Finally, Nitsy found her feet and yanked open the auditorium door.

"Robbie!" she yelled as she watched him swing the machete into the face of the infected woman who'd been outside.

Up on the balcony, a creature fell into the bushes. This one didn't break his neck like Elias. It rose to its feet quickly and charged after her.

Nitsy's shovel was gone. She'd dropped it when she went for the bucket of phones, which was also gone.

"Nitsy!" Robbie yelled. "Your hair!"

She felt the squirming on top and realized the little maggot-like lice were struggling to get to her scalp. Reaching for her hair, she roared with anger as she pulled her wig from her head and threw it onto the ground.

They will not fucking infect me today!

Under her wig was the cap she wore to keep what little of her real hair she had tamed beneath the wig. Ever since going through chemotherapy, she'd been trying to grow her hair, but she'd become known for her fiery red mane and had opted to wear the wig until her hair grew longer.

Now exposed, but uncaring of what she looked like at the moment, she ran toward Robbie with the wind whipping over her sweaty hair. Her real hair. The hair free of infection.

Robbie stared at her with disbelief on his face.

"Wha... what? I don't..." he couldn't get the words out.

It wasn't that difficult to understand. At least she hadn't thought it would be.

"Cancer, dummy," she reminded him. "It's why I was out of school so much. I told you I'd been sick."

"Behind you!" he shouted as the creature that had fallen from the balcony made its way toward her.

She moved out of the way just in time for him to swing the blade and set it in the skull of the oncoming beast.

Robbie was steadily backing away from the auditorium when Nitsy said, "The phones."

"Fuck the phones!" Robbie yelled.

"We have to go get them. It's the whole reason we came out here."

He grabbed Nitsy and pulled her close to him. "You almost fucking died in there, Nitsy. Fuck those phones."

"I'll get them," she argued, but as she got the words out, the auditorium doors opened and out spilled every single one of the infected students trapped inside that room. Nitsy shook her head when she saw them and said, "Fuck the phones."

Robbie pulled her back in the direction of the music room.

They ran. Moving faster than she ever had in her life, Nitsy sprinted beside Robbie, turning left and right, doing their best to lose the crowd of attacking infected. They couldn't lead the horde back to the others. The roaring, growling, and shrieking was far behind them when they finally found the music room and banged on the door.

"Who is it?" Lance asked from the other side.

"Are you fucking kidding?" Nitsy yelled. "Open the door!"

"Are those things following you?" he replied from the other side of the door.

"Dude, open the damn door!" Robbie yelled. "If they were behind us, it's more dangerous to leave us out here banging on the door!"

The hissing and grunting of the creatures were close. Right around the corner. If they didn't get into the classroom soon, they'd be done for.

"Do you have the phones?" Lance asked.

"No, I dropped them when they came after us," Nitsy replied.

She hated admitting it but felt she needed to be honest. She knew the second the words left her mouth that she should have lied.

"Just open the door," someone else yelled. It sounded like Phyllis.

"I'm sorry," Lance replied, "I'm sorry that you dropped the phones. I... uh... I can't open the door. It's too dangerous for us."

"You fucker!" Robbie yelled.

They had no more time to waste. If Lance wouldn't open the door, they'd need to hide somewhere else.

Nitsy banged on the door with both fists. "If you don't open this door, I'll lead them all to you and you can see how long this flimsy little door holds them back!"

Robbie pulled her arms away from the door. "They're coming. Come on. They won't let us in."

"They can't do this!" she screamed. "They can't do this to us!"

"Open the door, man!" someone called from the other side. It sounded like Bradley. Then a struggle broke out. The sound of wrestling, an overturned table, shouting back and forth.

"You open that fuckin' door and I'll kill you, man!" Lance shouted.

"Let them in," the other boy replied, breathing heavily.

"You open it," Lance said, "and I'll kill you. Try me if you think I'm lying."

"Don't do it," Robbie yelled to the boys on the other side. "Don't open it. We'll survive on our own."

"Nitsy!" Phyllis yelled from inside.

"Phyllis," Nitsy whispered. "Robbie, where do we go?"

She knew he had no idea. How could she expect him to answer a question like that? She was supposed to be the leader here. It was why she'd gone for the cell phones in the first place. She'd been given a second chance at life, and she knew she hadn't fought all those years in so many clinics and hospitals just to die here at a stupid leadership conference.

Robbie was looking around the campus, trying to come up with a place to hide. The creatures were too close for comfort. They'd be on them in seconds. Now, it seemed they were coming from more than one direction. They were coming from everywhere.

The cafeteria.

It was the only place she knew would be clear of the infected. Or, it should be anyway. It was the last place she and Robbie had been together before they'd stumbled upon the creatures in the dormitory hallway. They'd been inside the cafeteria and it had been empty.

"Follow me," she told Robbie as she ran across the courtyard, stopping to grab the rake from the wheelbarrow. At least now she'd have some sort of weapon.

"Where are we going?" Robbie whispered at her back.

"The place where we shared our first kiss."

Nitsy prayed the cafeteria would be empty when they yanked open the door and stepped inside. It was dark, the way it should be at this hour of the evening. Robbie looked through the small rectangular windows in the door to see if any of the creatures had followed them.

"Looks like we're okay," he said.

He threw the bolt on the door. It wouldn't hold against a bunch of those creatures, but it might keep one or two out.

"Be careful," Nitsy whispered. "We don't know if any of them got in here before us."

She considered turning on the light to make it easier for them to search but realized it might shine out the windows and draw the creatures to them. She was pretty sure they were more interested in sounds, but it wasn't a risk she was willing to take.

"Hello? Anyone in here?" If they were attracted to sound, it would draw them out. She knew that, but she was more worried about accidentally running into one of them in the cafeteria. If one came thrashing its way out of the kitchen, they could flee from it.

She and Robbie remained silent, listening for any stray sounds. None came.

"Hello?" she said a little louder. "Is there anyone in here?"

"Shh, keep it down," someone replied.

"Someone's in here," she said as she turned to Robbie.

From out of the kitchen, squatting down and duck-walking their way as if standing up straight might give him away, came a shadowy figure headed their way. He held a metal pole in his hands. It looked like it might have come from the side of one of the classroom desks. As he grew nearer, Nitsy realized she knew him.

"Eggo?" she asked.

The man stopped duck-walking and looked up at her. "Nitsy?"

"Eggo," she repeated as she squatted down next to him and hugged him. "I thought you died in there with the others."

"No, thanks to you guys," he replied, looking up at Robbie and nodding in his direction.

Nitsy shook her head. "Nobody believed us."

"Would you have?" he replied.

She wouldn't have. Or at least she didn't think she would have. She'd barely believed it herself when she'd run in there and made the announcement.

"No," Robbie admitted.

"I believed you," Eggo said. "Maybe not fully, but I knew something was wrong. I've been to enough of these conferences to recognize a prank when I see one. Nobody would go through such extreme measures to pull one over on their colleagues." Eggo paused for a moment and then said, "I'm sorry I have to ask, but what happened to your hair?"

"It was a wig," she admitted. "Those things jumped on it, so I had to throw my hair off."

Eggo chuckled. "Damn. You don't fuck with a girl's hair."

Nitsy laughed.

"Well, I don't have any hair," Eggo added, running a hand over his bald head.

"Why didn't you have the door locked?" Nitsy asked.

"It was locked," he replied.

"No, we walked right in," she said.

Eggo stood and made his way over to the door. He jiggled the handle and the door opened easily.

"Shit," he said. "It must be broken."

He looked at her rake and said, "I'm sorry to ask you this. We can probably find something else in here to block this, but..."

Nitsy knew the rake would do the trick, so she handed it over. He slid the wooden stick through the two handles, locking it in place. Again, it might hold against one of the creatures, but not against the whole group of them. She only hoped they weren't smart enough to track them down.

"Have you seen anyone else alive?" Nitsy asked.

He shook his head. "I went to try and check the auditorium for living people, but I got attacked outside."

"Those bodies on the grass were from you?" Robbie asked.

Eggo nodded his head, but he wasn't proud. It was clear he felt badly about what he'd done. "Yeah, they just kept coming." He paused and asked, "Have y'all seen anyone else?"

"A few of the students are hiding in the music room," Nitsy replied. "Bradley and Phyllis from our group—"

"Oh, I'm glad they made it," Eggo said.

"And some asshole named Lance and a couple... uh... Beau and... uh..."

"Yasmin," Nitsy finished for him.

"I don't know most of the kids," Eggo admitted. "I mean you were in my group, so I know you, but..."

"We went to get the cell phones you guys collected from us," Robbie said, "at the auditorium, but we got attacked."

"Any idea what we can do?" Nitsy asked Eggo.

He shrugged. "Stay right here and wait for help?"

They'd gone from one locked room to another. At least in this one, they'd have food and drinks. Maybe hiding out and waiting for rescue was the right answer. Robbie joined them in sitting on the floor, and she held his hand while putting her head against his chest. At least they had each other, from back home, to help each other through this.

22

"Right there," Grant said as he, Sally, and Hal crouched behind a parked Buick.

Hal could see the sign even though the lights were off. It read: Clementine's Cannons. It was the local gun store. The only place in town to get a gun legally.

"The street looks empty," Hal said. "I think we can make a run for it. Try our best to stay out of the streetlights until we reach the door."

Grant nodded. "If she ain't in there, then what?"

"Can't break the window," Sally warned them. "You'd bring every one of those things down on us."

"Is there a back door?" Hal asked.

"I don't know, man. I don't hang out there."

Hal was starting to dislike this guy. It was clear he was a jealous man and didn't like him talking to Sally. Hal had known Sally for years. He got a lot of his pre-work meals from The Diner. Sure, she was a good-looking woman, but he wasn't searching for a lover or a spouse. He liked being by his lonesome. So, Grant could kiss his ass.

"You don't have to be an asshole about it," Hal said, never the one to let someone talk trash and get away with it.

"You think I'm being an asshole? I'm just sayin' I don't know the ins and outs of Clementine's Cannons."

"How about we try the front door before y'all get to arguing," Sally recommended.

She didn't wait for the boys to agree or disagree. It was clear she didn't need their approval. She stayed low as she rushed to the gun store's door. She jiggled the handle as the two men raced to catch up with her. The door was locked.

Sally knocked on the door. Hal wished she'd do it more softly. If even one of those *things* heard her, they'd all come running.

When simply knocking on the door didn't work, Sally pounded, and as Hal was about to tell her to stop, a face appeared on the other side of the glass. Clementine was a plus-size woman with hair that had been box dyed at home so many times it now was the color of sweet tea and was as dry and brittle as could be. She used to attend the meetings with Hal and had even flirted with him a bit.

Since her husband's death, she'd been running the gun store all on her own and lived in a small room at the back of the building. Hal knew this because she'd once offered for him to come over after a meeting and share TV dinners with her. Of course, he turned down the invitation.

"Sally?" Clementine asked from the other side of the door. "Grant? Hal?"

"Open up," Hal said, "before we get attacked out here."

"What if you're not really you?" she asked.

"Look at my hair," Sally said, leaning her head forward until it touched the glass.

"What the hell does your hair have to do with anything?" the shop owner shot back. "I don't give a damn about your hairstyle. You might wanna eat me."

"I don't want to eat you," Sally said, "I promise. Now, open up."

"They get in your hair," Hal informed her. "They're little bugs that get in your hair—"

"And change you into a zombie," Grant added.

"Really? In your goddamn hair?" Clementine asked.

"We really need to get in there, babe," Sally said. "I don't want to die out here on the street."

"Or get your hair taken I suppose," Clementine said as she stood up and unlocked the door.

"They don't *take* your hair," Grant mumbled.

Hal had a sudden image of these things ripping the hair off of people and wearing it as their own, like some kind of fashionable parasite.

Once inside, Grant was the first to speak up about the guns. "I know we just got here and all, but we really need some guns and ammo."

Clementine rolled her eyes. "I figured as much. Ain't like y'all come around to visit when you don't want something."

"You ever swing by the diner when you ain't hungry?" Sally asked.

Clementine had to think about that for a second. "No, I suppose I don't."

"Well, there we go," Sally replied.

Clementine chuckled under her breath and said, "You sure done grown up to be a real spitfire. I told your mama you would." She paused and watched as the two men loaded up with weapons. "So... they get in your hair? That's really messed up."

"It's awful," Sally said. "And it happens so fast. They took over the entire diner in no time at all."

"What kind of monster goes after your hair?" the older woman asked. "Well, head lice are a bitch, so it don't surprise me something that goes after your hair is as well."

"They are like head lice," Sally agreed.

"I wonder if, you know that stuff they sell at Walmart... that uh... permethrin!" Clementine shouted and then remembered the situation they were in and lowered her voice. "That's it. It kills lice, right? I wonder if we sprayed that stuff on all them things if that would make 'em go away."

"That's the dumbest thing I've ever heard," Hal said under his breath. He was not going to get close enough to these things to spray head lice ointment on them. Then what? Was he supposed to sit beside each one with that tiny comb and try to scrape them out of their hair? It was a dumb idea.

"Now, wait a minute," Grant said. "It's not really the worst idea. I mean it could work, right?"

"I don't think so, Grant," Sally said.

"I think it's a great idea," Clementine said.

"Only because you thought of it," Hal replied. "Come on. It's not a good idea."

"I say we try it," Grant said.

"I say *you* try it," Hal shot back.

He'd already gotten so sick of Grant and his smart ass comments. As far as he knew, this guy created furniture for a living. He wished he'd build himself a chair, sit in it, and stay in it. Sally did not need to be getting within spray bottle distance of these things. The whole idea was reckless.

Thirty minutes later, after loading supplies, weapons, and ammo into the back of Clementine's pickup parked at the back of her shop, they pulled up in front of Walmart and parked at the curb. Hal hated the idea. Sally seemed to be on his side, but the other two were convinced this would work. Without a real plan of his own, other than to drive around shooting people in their heads, he didn't have much of a say in the matter.

Clementine and Sally sat in the front of the truck with Hal and Grant in the bed. As soon as the truck came to a halt, Grant hopped out and headed toward the store's doors. The lights were on inside, which was a good sign, Hal supposed, but that also meant the *things* could have been attracted to the light. He wondered how many of them were in there.

Sally stopped on the sidewalk and waited for Hal. Grant and Clementine were hopped up on adrenaline, ready to run through the door.

"What's the plan?" Hal asked.

Grant held his shotgun up and said, "What do you mean? We go in to get the head lice shit and we blast anybody who gets in the way."

"Any*body*?" Hal asked.

"You know," Clementine stepped in, "any of those zombies."

"Are you going in, Hal?" Sally asked.

He glanced at the parking lot and saw none of the bastards running toward them. From where he stood, he could see the other side of the street where he'd wrecked his truck earlier this evening. He knew some of those things had to be out here roaming about, looking for their next victim.

"I suppose we're better off staying together than splitting up," Hal said.

Grant nodded. Clementine threw an arm around Sally's shoulder and pulled her toward the door. Hal followed with a pistol tucked in his belt and a rifle in his hand.

Inside, there was no greeter, which was to be expected. The self-checkout lanes were empty. The tiny sandwich shop tucked in its own corner to the right had nobody working the counter and no customers dining. It was too late for that anyway. In fact, the diner should have been closed already, as in the floor mopped and the chairs stacked on top of tables. The store was twenty-four hours, but the sandwich shop wasn't.

"That isn't a good sign," Hal said. Nobody else seemed to pick up on what he meant so he added, "Stay alert. They've taken over the staff."

Grant raised his rifle and carried it out in front of him like the point man in a military fireteam. It looked like he was about to lead them in clearing a house instead of searching for head lice ointment.

This is so stupid. It's dangerous. And for what?

Clementine held two shotguns, one locked into each armpit, and Hal couldn't help thinking the world had surely gone to shit. They'd become a rogue team of post-apocalyptic bandits. This was *Mad Max* and they were in the thunder dome.

For the first time, seeing the untouched shelves in front of him, Hal wondered if they should take as many supplies and as much food as they could pile into the back of the truck. If this thing reached beyond town limits, they could be plunged into darkness. It could become *every man for himself.* What was their plan once they left the store? To ride around and blast these creatures with head lice spray? If that didn't work, then what? Shoot them? Or go hide away somewhere? If they were going to hide, they would need to stock up.

Grant looked back and waved for Sally to follow him. He wanted her by his side, and that was the first thing he really respected about the guy. He was doing his best to take care of his girl. If she was his girl. Hal wasn't even sure. Now wasn't the time to ask simple kinds of questions. If it didn't involve saving the human race, it probably wasn't a good discussion.

"It should be back near home and garden," Clementine whispered. "With the pesticides and stuff."

Hal was glad she knew where she was going because he had no idea where they'd find the shit. He couldn't even remember the name of it. He'd heard of Nix, but that was about it. He figured that would probably be somewhere over by the pharmacy.

"I need to get me a carton of smokes while we're in here," Clementine added.

He wasn't a smoker, but he had been in the past, and he could imagine himself saying something so dumb at a time like this. They were in here now, so whatever she needed to grab to make herself feel better, she might as well get it.

Grant was out front with Clementine close behind. Sally stayed behind them and Hal brought up the rear. The home and garden area was to the left, past the women's clothing, the jewelry, the kitchen and bathroom supplies, the pharmacy, the toys, and the beauty care products. Hal could see the barbecue grills from where they stood near the cash registers.

If this were a regular shopping run, he wouldn't have thought twice about the distance they needed to cover, but this was anything but normal. Between them and their destination lay countless shelves these creatures could hide behind. His heart hammered in his chest as they passed the women's clothing.

Deeper into the store was the men's clothing, the shoes, and the socks and underwear.

Hal knew this store well. He did all his shopping here. Sometimes, when lonesome and sorrow hit him hard, he'd walk up and down every aisle. He'd look at the yarn and remember how his wife used to knit sometimes as they watched TV. It calmed her nerves. He'd run his fingers along the young adult books in the paperback section. His daughter used to shut the world away whenever she was grounded from her phone. She'd curl up under a blanket and stay in her room all day and all night reading books. She'd told him once it was her way of drowning them out. She didn't have to look at her mother or father if she was concentrating on the words in front of her.

Sadness hit him now as he thought about how much time was lost. He wished he could go back and unground her. He'd spend every one of those seconds with her talking, laughing, listening...

A groan came from somewhere in the back of the store. Probably at the electronics. He imagined one of those creatures knocking over the books his daughter might have picked out. Soiling the paperback covers with its disgusting hands. Its hair wiggling, searching for another human to infect. Human or animal. He'd seen the dogs too. The dogs were worse because they were smaller, faster, and more aggressive than the infected humans.

Hal could outrun some humans. He couldn't outrun a dog.

Grant waved at the back of the store, completing his military image. He made hand gestures Hal didn't understand but knew it had something to do with the sound he'd heard at the back. It looked like Grant was waving in that direction. If he thought Hal was going to go looking for the source of that growl, he was out of his damn mind.

As they all kept their attention on the rear of the store, Clementine stepped on a bag of Cheetos that had been knocked off a rack and lay on the floor. It popped as her weight came down on it and then the foil package crackled and the chips inside it crumbled. The sound was way too loud and way too sudden.

Oh shit.

Clementine looked back at Hal and mouthed the word, "Sorry."

Sorry wouldn't cut it. The growl they'd heard before now turned into a high-pitched wail. Then, to the right, near the bread aisle in the grocery section, a shriek sounded off. That led to a monstrous roar back in the auto supply area.

"Go!" Hal ordered.

Grant didn't argue. He raced toward the home and garden section. Hal followed, but he really wanted to hightail it back to the front door and get the hell out of the store. It was too late though. He'd already committed to getting the permethrin. The others stormed ahead, paying little attention to the aisles on their left and right. Hal was all too aware. He wasn't moving as quickly as the others out of fear something might pounce on them.

The others had already passed the greeting card aisle when Hal approached and heard the ruffling of cards and envelopes being knocked off their racks. He glanced right and saw it. A huge man, easily 6'4" and over 250 lbs., stumbled toward him. He walked with his hands outstretched, using his fingers to guide him, and the cards fell at his feet like congratulatory confetti. Hal was the lucky winner, and this creature was hissing at him, its hair clicking, as it came to give him his prize.

His first thought should have been to pull the trigger and blow him away, but he froze for some reason. The scene in front of him was surreal. Almost beautiful in its insanity. A card flew in front of Hal's face and he was able to read it: Happy Father's Day, Daddy. Your princess loves you.

As it fluttered to the ground, the big man's face came into view behind it, and Hal considered doing absolutely nothing. Maybe the card was a sign from his daughter telling him it was time to come see her. It was time to let go of this cruel, nasty world and come be with the one person who loved him unconditionally. He raised his gun and pointed it at the creature, and then turned it on himself.

He would let the creature get to him, and as those tiny writhing bastards thought they had a new host, he would blow his own fucking brains out. Grant, Clementine, and Sally could finish their plans without him. He wasn't much a part of it anyway. He lived a loner, he'd die one.

Come on, you bastard.

The creature was five feet from him when he heard a voice say, "Hal, what the fuck?"

A blast so loud he thought it might have blown out his eardrum screamed next to him, and the big man's head exploded like a ripe melon. Blood and bone fragments sprayed across the cards.

Hal stood stunned, not only shocked at the creature's explosion, but at the realization that he had been willing to die right now.

"What's wrong with you, buddy?" Grant asked as he tugged on Hal's shirt at the shoulder.

"I don't know," he replied, and as his eyes drifted down to the fallen cards, he read another one.

It was covered in blood and read: Live life to the fullest.

A shriek came from only a few aisles away and pulled Hal out of his trance-like state. He shook his head, cleared his senses, and ran ahead of Grant toward the others.

Clementine found the permethrin and held it up. It was in a yellow bottle with a black nozzle. Grant handed her an empty duffle bag and she shoved about ten bottles of the stuff in there. Grant grabbed two big jugs full of the stuff and Hal grabbed one himself. Clementine slung the duffle bag over her shoulder and kept her shotguns pointed out in front of her.

The sound of items being knocked off shelves was heard near the rear of the store making its way toward them. Clangs, clattering, bangs… something was making its way toward them quickly.

"We should go out the exit by the patio furniture," Sally said, pointing into the adjoining room where Hal knew the store kept its lawn chairs, barbecue grills, and outdoor decorations.

She was right. They should get out of the store as quickly as possible.

"One of 'em's coming," Clementine announced, speaking the obvious.

"I think we should try this stuff out," Grant said.

"You go right on ahead," Hal said. "I'm headed toward that exit. Ain't no need to be getting ourselves killed so soon. I'd like to live to fight some more."

"You sure about that, buddy?" Grant asked. "Didn't seem like you were up to fighting a second ago."

Hal glared at him. The man was right, but there was more to it than he knew. It was only a moment of self-reflection. Now, he knew what needed to be done. He needed to kill these things.

"I know I want to fight," Grant said as he pulled one of the spray bottles out of Clementine's bag, turned the nozzle to "on" and held it out in front of him. "So, might as well start now."

Sally scratched at one arm nervously. She looked back at Hal and Clementine and then glared at Grant. "Grant, you're not seriously planning to stand there and meet that thing head-on with a fuckin' spray bottle."

"If not, then what did we come here for?" he asked.

He barely finished his sentence when hands shot out from the next shelf over, swiping all its contents off as one of the creatures, a skinny man wearing overalls, with scraggly hair encircling the bald crown of his head, emerged and headed toward them. Barbecue grill spatulas and tongs clattered to the ground. Bottles of lighter fluid toppled over next. Grant held the spray bottle out and his eyes went wide as he waited for the limping creature to finally reach him.

"Grant, come on!" Sally yelled.

Clementine stepped away from Grant and moved to Hal's side with her shotguns raised and ready. "I *think* it'll work," she said to Hal, "but I'm not *sure* it'll work."

The scrawny man, furious with infected rage, held his fingers out in front of him like claws and snarled as he grew closer. He was only about ten feet away when Grant pulled the trigger on his spray bottle. A stream of liquid flew about six feet away and was showering down generously when the creature stepped right into it.

"Take that, motherfucker!" Grant yelled, holding that spray bottle out in front of him like a kid with a super soaker water gun.

The infected man stopped in the stream and howled. Grant laughed and kept squirting.

Other infected came from around nearby shelves. Back in the makeup area, lipsticks and eyeliners fell to the ground. Boxed hairdryers toppled over and smacked against the tile floor. In the pool supplies, the entire shelf moved. It rocked as if being pushed from the other side. A pool pump fell from the shelf. Several boxes of floaties and innertubes came down next.

Grant's eyes went wide as he realized other creatures were coming. The one he was squirting with the permethrin growled and leaped through the stream. Grant stepped back and his boot heel touched the puddle at his feet. He slipped and fell on his ass hard. He scrambled backward as the skinny man hit the ground and started crawling after him. The permethrin had done nothing. It didn't even faze the man other than to make him pause for a second. Now, he was crawling forward while the others were coming from the left and right.

"Look out!" Clementine hollered.

The creature was about to grab Grant's boot when Grant rolled out of the way and Clementine sent a shotgun blast that took the insect-infested man's head clean off his body.

Sally was at Grant's side quickly, pulling him to his feet as the other creatures came from behind their shelves.

The pool supply shelf rocked one final time and then fell forward slowly. The rest of its contents showered the floor before the metal structure struck the ground with a loud clatter sure to bring any other creatures in the store their way. On the other side of the shelf, now crawling over it, were two more of the infected creatures, each wearing the blue smock that read: *How can I help you?*

"Go!" Grant yelled.

Clementine threw the duffle bag full of spray bottles to the ground and turned to run with them. She was the slowest in the bunch but hefting that heavy bag would have made it nearly impossible for her to escape. She spun and caught the closest creature right in the chest, shredding him with a burst of her shotgun.

Hal caught the next creature right in the middle of his forehead.

He'd always been a good shot. Guns seemed to like him, even if he couldn't stand the things. Right now, he appreciated the ones he had and was happy he'd decided to work as a park ranger. If he hadn't, he would be unarmed right now.

Rushed footsteps echoed throughout the store. *They* were coming from all directions.

Hal and Clementine had started falling back the second they heard the *things* coming, but Sally and Grant were too far from the exit, and Hal couldn't leave them behind. Clementine had given up shooting.

"Get to the truck!" she screamed. "They're fuckin' everywhere!"

Like ants shooting out of an anthill, hellbent on spreading their infectious disease, the creatures rushed through the aisles, leaped over cash registers, shoved through spinning sunglass racks, toppled towers of towels, and pushed over piled-up plastic storage bins. It was like a tidal wave of hissing, gnashing, howling beasts storming through the store, and headed right for them.

"Come on!" Hal yelled over the sound of clicking that arose from the oncoming horde.

It was so loud. Like they'd stepped into the loudest forest known to man. Like all the insects in the world were about to rain down on them.

Grant and Sally ran toward the back exit, narrowly missing the clawed hands of one creature. Hal stopped her with a bullet in the throat. The beast fell to the ground, clutching its neck, and still trying to attack.

Hal fell back, his gun still pointed at the swarm. If he didn't turn and run now, he'd never get the chance. There was no way he could shoot them all.

He spun and saw Sally and Grant ahead of him, running through the automatic doors. Hal wondered if there was a way to stop those doors from opening but quickly realized it didn't matter. The time it would take to figure it out was too much time. They'd charge him before he had the chance to lock it, and even if he could get the doors jammed shut, with so many bodies coming so quickly, they'd probably smash right through that glass.

The clicking and hissing seemed like it was only feet away from him, threatening to leap on top of his head, and for a moment, he thought this was the end. Those things could leap, and he wouldn't be far enough away to dodge them. If they wanted him, he was done for.

He'd just made it through the automatic doors when Grant yelled, "Duck!"

Clementine was behind the wheel of the pickup. Sally was in the passenger seat and Grant was in the bed, his rifle pointed right at Hal's head. Hal did his best to duck and keep running. There was no way he was going to stop his forward momentum. His head came down only about a foot when Grant pulled the trigger. Hal heard the grunt of one of the creatures, probably no more than six feet behind him. Then a second blast and a splatter. There'd been two right behind him.

"Get in!" Sally yelled.

Clementine was already flooring it before Hal made it to the truck. Grant leaned over the side and reached out a hand to him. Hal grabbed his hand and ran alongside the truck. He had only one chance to leap into the bed. If he missed this, he would fall, he would get dragged, and the creatures behind him would swarm all over him.

Hal yelled with all the fury he had inside and leaped at the truck. Grant yanked his arm at the same time, and Hal landed with his belly on the side of the truck. His feet swung on the outside. One of the creatures grabbed his foot and pulled, howling like a banshee, close to jerking Hal right out of the truck.

"Hey, you!" Sally yelled from the passenger side window. "Get the fuck off him!"

She pulled the trigger on one of Clementine's shotguns and tore the face right off the creature, like taking a giant ice cream scooper across his forehead and down to his chin.

Grant pulled Hal into the truck.

Sally screamed, "Oh my God, that was Danny Roy! I shot Danny!"

Hal didn't know Danny Roy, and he was having a hard time feeling sorry for the fucker who'd tried to rip him out of the truck. He looked out at the parking lot and watched as a sea of the monsters chased after them. They'd never catch the truck, but there were so many. They came from other areas of the parking lot too, and Hal wondered if the entire town was infected.

"My God," Grant said next to him.

"Thank you," Hal whispered.

"Look at them. They're everywhere."

"They've taken over the whole damn town."

23

"I don't care what you say. That was wrong, Lance." Bradley lowered his gaze and left his eyes focused on his feet. "It was wrong on so many levels."

He knew what would come next. As soon as he let his words leave his mouth, he knew what Lance's rebuttal would be. Of course, the bully in the room didn't disappoint.

"If you don't like it, you can leave too," Lance replied.

"If I don't like it, I can leave too," Bradley whispered. "Nice."

Bradley was a video game junkie. He played every new game the moment it came out and was working on a YouTube channel to show the world his skills. His only problem was his lack of personality. He could play like a champ, but he didn't have the humor it took to grab the audience's attention. He also didn't have the balls to stand up to Lance.

What he found most interesting about this situation was how true the games were. He'd played *The Walking Dead* and he'd played other post-apocalyptic survival games. In most of them, man was the real enemy. It wasn't the monsters, the creatures, or the beasts. It wasn't the hordes of the undead. It was the human beings that ravaged and killed anyone they deemed a threat. It was kill or be killed. It was survival of the fittest. All those other cliché terms to express the need for one man to dominate the other.

Only this wasn't a game.

And Lance was everyman.

He was the villain in all the TV shows, movies, and video games.

Bradley had no doubt if most of the world's population died tonight, Lance would be happy to stand strong. He'd go someplace with high walls and lead from atop a tower. His world would be for the strong only, and everyone else would exist only to serve or become monster fodder.

Just like in the real world, the assholes never died. Nearly every kid on campus was gone. Either dead or had become one of those *things* out there hunting them. Not Lance though. He'd run like the rest of them and now he was alive to torment the others.

Bradley hated knowing Nitsy and Robbie were out there right now probably searching for a new place to hide with danger lurking around every corner. He wanted to go out there and join them, to let them know he had no part in the decision to lock them out of the music room.

He was debating on whether or not to speak up and get himself ousted from the room when he felt fingers intertwine through his. His eyes moved up to his right hand where he saw the dainty hand of Phyllis holding his. His eyes traced her arm until he found her face. She smiled.

"If you go, I go," she said.

This was the first time she'd shown him any real attention. He'd had a small crush on her since yesterday when he walked her back to her room after their workshop. But he'd been afraid to take it any further. He always shot for the stars and fell flat on his ass. The girls he liked never liked him back and most of the time they never knew he liked them in the first place.

But Phyllis was here holding his hand now, and he saw there was a slight sparkle in her eyes. Moonlight shone in ever so slightly through the rectangular window set high in the wall. Bradley was focused on her pupils and her smile when he saw a shadow pass her face.

Yasmin screamed. "Oh, my God. Oh, my God. Oh, my God."

"What the fuck is it?" Lance asked, backing toward the door.

Bradley heard the tiny squeak of the mouse before Yasmin yelled, "Rat! I saw a rat! Right over there!"

"It's only a mouse," Beau argued, wrapping Yasmin up in a hug. "It's only a mouse."

Lance laughed. "A fuckin' mouse? You damn near gave me a heart attack."

"Keep it away from me," Phyllis added.

"A fuckin' mouse," Lance agreed. "How did I get stranded with such a group of pussies?"

"Excuse me?" Beau asked, pulling away from Yasmin.

Bradley cupped a hand over his mouth to hide his smile. Finally, someone was going to stand up to Lance, and it wasn't going to have to be *him*. He wanted to, but he knew Lance would pummel him. Beau was tall and he wasn't as wide as Lance, but he didn't look like a pushover.

"Nothing," Lance replied.

"Nah, man," Beau said. "Repeat what you said."

Lance was quiet.

"Yeah, keep your mouth shut from now on," Beau said. "You don't need to be saying shit about my girl."

"Oh yeah?" Lance asked, suddenly getting up enough bravery to stand his ground. "Or what, tough guy?"

"Or maybe you'll find yourself locked out there," Beau said, pointing toward the door. "With those things."

"Fuckin' try it," Lance said.

"There it is," Phyllis shouted, pointing at the corner of the room.

"There what is?" Lance asked, turning around to look, arms out at his sides like he was a bodybuilder on his way to do a few more reps at the gym.

The mouse squeaked, and then it made a different sound. Bradley thought it sounded a little bit like crickets. Like a chirping but not as pleasant as the bugs that kept him up some nights. The crickets at home were so loud. This sound coming from the mouse was strange.

The only word he could think to describe it was skittering like something was moving on its fur.

"Wish I had a BB gun so I could blast—" Lance started but then stopped. "Hey! Whoa. What the fuck?"

Lance screamed, and it was too dark to see clearly, but Bradley swore he saw the small rodent run up Lance's pant leg and all the way to his face. The bully turned around and the mouse was there. It was big, plump, closer to the size of a rat. Its teeth were lodged in Lance's lip, and its fur moved.

"Holy shit," Bradley said.

Phyllis screamed.

Yasmin cried out, "Get it off him!"

"I'm not touching it," Beau insisted.

Bradley wasn't either. He wasn't going anywhere near that thing. "Don't touch it!" he yelled. "I think it's infected, like the other kids."

"Oh, shit," Beau said, backing up with Yasmin so there were some desks between them and Lance.

Lance continued to yell. He dropped to his knees and grabbed his hair, wincing and screaming through clenched teeth.

"Lance?" Phyllis asked.

"Go!" Bradley said, as he pushed Phyllis toward the door.

They went around a row of desks to make sure they stayed as far away from Lance as possible. Beau and Yasmin weren't as cautious as they should have been. Instead of following Bradley and Phyllis, they went the long way around, taking them behind Lance on their way to the door. Beau was fast and had already reached the door. Yasmin was right behind him when Lance threw his hand out and caught her by her hair, yanking her into his embrace.

Yasmin screamed.

Beau turned and ran at Lance, immediately swinging his fists at the bigger boy's face. Lance soaked up the punches and lashed out at Beau, grabbing hold of his shirt. The young lovers fought with everything they had, punching, kicking, and clawing at Lance, but they were too close.

Bradley heard a *poof* sound, like the sound the city buses back home made when they lowered to allow passengers easier access to the stairs.

Then Yasmin and Beau were screaming the same way Lance had been seconds before.

It didn't matter how dangerous it was outside. The threat was now inside. Bradley threw the lock and yanked open the door. Phyllis followed him out. Behind them, in the classroom, the three students cried out in pain until it seemed they were howling with rage.

The transformation took seconds.

Bradley knew they had to get far away. They needed to find a hiding space. At first, the hallways seemed quiet. The overhead lights popped on as soon as they stepped away from the music room.

"Where do we go?" Bradley asked, his voice quivering.

Phyllis shook her head. "I don't know."

"Psst, over here," came a soft voice Bradley thought he recognized.

He peered across the dimly lit courtyard and couldn't see anyone.

"The cafeteria," the voice whispered.

Bradley and Phyllis followed the voice blindly. The courtyard lights shone down faintly over them. Across from the Stonewall Jackson statue, in the shadows of the cafeteria building, Nitsy was crouched down with Robbie by her side. Someone else was behind them.

"Eggo?" Phyllis asked softly.

"I think that is Eggo," Bradley replied, "with Nitsy and Robbie."

The music room door crashed open and out ran Lance, Beau, and Yasmin, all roaring with anger. Bradley yelped, and the three infected students homed in on the sound. The chase was on. The creatures ran down the hall, the overhead lights popping on one by one the closer they got.

Bradley didn't need to look back to know they were gaining on them. Phyllis was faster than he was. She let go of his hand and sprinted toward the cafeteria. Bradley ran as hard as he could. He was past the statue when a dark, growling figure stepped out from behind Stonewall Jackson.

The creature clawed at the air, nearly reaching Bradley when he dove onto the ground and rolled. It wasn't a planned move, and it wasn't a perfected one. He didn't come around gracefully like the action superstars in the movies. His arms and legs flailed, and he found himself sliding across the ground.

He peered up at the cafeteria building and saw Eggo running toward him with what looked like a rake.

All four creatures were close to Bradley now. The one that had emerged from behind the statue was only a few feet away, and Bradley kicked out at it while at the same time bracing himself for the pain that would come at his scalp. He prepared himself mentally to scream the way Lance had. The way Beau and Yasmin had.

"Get back!" someone yelled.

It was a gruff, manly voice.

A gunshot rang through the air and the creature closest to Bradley flew past him. It went silent.

Bradley scrambled to get away from it, knowing how the insects jumped.

"It's in the hair!" came the gruff voice. "Get away from it!"

"Bradley, come on!" Nitsy yelled.

"Bradley!" Phyllis joined in.

Over his shoulder, he saw Lance, Beau, and Yasmin coming at him. They were close. Maybe ten feet away. On the other side, past the statue, was a big man in camouflage pants, a black long sleeve shirt, and a green, backwards ball cap. He had a beard, wore a wicked grin, and held what looked to Bradley like one of the sniper rifles from his video games.

The man was on one knee, holding his rifle steady, when he whispered, "Bang."

He pulled the trigger and Bradley heard the grunt before looking behind him to see Lance fall. The man calmly turned his rifle, ejected his cartridge, and fired again. This time he nailed Yasmin in the forehead. Beau went down just as easily.

Nitsy, Robbie, and Eggo stood outside the cafeteria door, in awe, watching the mysterious hero shoot down each of the infected students. For a second, and only for a second, Bradley felt a twinge of guilt.

These were kids, like him, who'd only come to the conference for the experience and to help them get into a good college. It was a bragging right. Now, they were dead.

And I was almost one of them. If not for…

"Come with me," the hero said as he stood and held out his hand to Bradley.

Bradley accepted it and climbed to his feet.

The man turned toward Nitsy and the others. "Y'all need to come with me. I can get you out of here. If you stay, I do believe y'all are fixin' to die."

"Go with you where?" Nitsy asked.

"I'll tell you about it on the way," the man said. "We need to get goin' now. Are there any more of you alive?"

"Not that I know of," Nitsy replied.

"Holy shit," Robbie said from behind her.

"What's your problem, boy?" the man asked.

"You're not planning on taking us out that way, are you?" Nitsy asked.

Bradley and the man turned toward the front gate. On the other side of it, standing in the tree line fifty feet or so beyond, was a long line of animals.

Side by side they stood.

Quiet.

Intense.

Unmoving and watching.

A variety of West Virginian mammals. Large animals like bears, wolves, mountain lions, stray dogs, and boars. Smaller ones were mixed in. Tomcats, foxes, beavers, possums, raccoons, and more.

Bradley had never seen some of the animals out there on the tree line. All with fur. Each taken over by these… these head lice.

"Well this ain't good," the man said.

"Slowly move back into the building," Nitsy said.

The man nodded his head, agreeing, and never taking his eyes off the beasts beyond the gate. If even one of them moved, all of them would. If one pounced, they'd all pounce.

Bradley and the man backed up into the cafeteria. Once they were inside, Eggo shoved the rake through the door handles and held his hand out to the man.

"Eggo," he said.

The cafeteria was dark, but Bradley could see the man had bandages on his head.

"Andre," the man said as he shook Eggo's hand. "Andre Pete."

24

Grant remembered the scene at the end of the original *Texas Chainsaw Massacre* when the woman made it into the bed of the truck and looked maniacally back at Leatherface swinging his chainsaw around in the middle of the street. He thought Hal wore the same expression as they both watched the crowd of asshole monsters running toward them, none of them standing a chance at actually reaching them. Clementine was driving too damn fast.

Sally. Wow. Sally pulled the trigger and saved his rump.

The spray bottle hadn't worked. They'd risked their lives for something so damn dumb.

It couldn't hurt to try.

It almost hurt, but it didn't. They'd all made it out of there alive.

No thanks to you, you jackass. You almost got Sally killed and yourself along with her.

Clementine drove around Clydesville with seemingly no purpose. She drove past the bingo hall, which Hal said was already infested. Sure enough, those things were bumbling around inside, smacking into the glass window.

"They sure are stupid," Grant said.

"Yeah, but they're vicious too," Hal replied. "Kind of like hair piranhas. They don't know what to do until they find somebody to chase."

"Think they're aliens?"

"I don't know, man."

"Think that's what got Andre Pete?"

Hal thought about it for a second and nodded. "I suppose so."

Grant hadn't known Andre, but he'd seen the news, and he knew the story of the man whose truck flipped off the side of the highway, and his body had gone missing.

"I guess he could have been wandering out in the woods and nobody would have found him," Grant said. "If they did... they would have wished they didn't. He might have been one of the first infected."

Clementine pulled into the police station parking lot. The window was shattered and inside looked to be void of life.

"They got the cops too?" Clementine called out from the front seat. "That's impossible."

"Not in a town where the cops aren't used to anything but drunk drivers," Hal replied.

That was true, he supposed, but then again, who would be prepared for something of this magnitude? Grant was never much of a conspiracy theorist, but he'd heard a few things on the news and on some of the YouTube videos he saw on his phone.

"It's the chemtrails," Grant declared. "It has to be. Those bastards flying overhead, spraying God-knows-what down over us. They could have been dropping these parasitic head lice bastards all along. Maybe it only took this long for it to reach people."

"And animals," Hal told him. "I've seen dogs with it too."

"The damn chemtrails," Grant repeated.

"You think the government did this?"

"Don't you? They do all kinds of other shady shit."

"Nah, Grant. Not the U.S., man. We take care of ours."

"Population control, Hal."

"No. We didn't do this. I'd say it's either alien, or this is something that's been around for a long time, maybe buried in the soil, and someone dug it up. Someone or some*thing*. Could be a damn animal was digging a hole in the ground out in the woods and stumbled on a nest of these things."

"That would be one hell of a find. Can you imagine? Sitting there, maybe having a picnic out in the woods. Your family's enjoying their food, but the damn dog won't stop barking at something it found. It keeps yapping until you get up to take a look. There's a hole in the ground. The dog's been picking at it. You lean over to see what's in it and BAM!"

Hal jumped, shook his head, and closed his eyes. Grant had spooked him, and he knew Hal was ready to slap the hell out of him.

"Sorry, bud," Grant said, "but can't you imagine it?"

Hal was quiet for a moment. Grant realized Hal was quiet most of the time. He was too, he supposed, in regular day to day life. It hadn't occurred to him until now that he talked quite a bit when he was nervous. He wondered how Sally was doing with all this. A quick glance through the small window between the bed and the cab of the truck showed Sally was focused on the road ahead of them. She was quiet. After tonight, she would never be the same. None of them would. Nightmares were sure to come.

Sally glanced back at him and smiled.

God, she's an angel.

He vowed to himself to do anything it took to keep her safe. With a nod of his head, he returned her smile, and she turned around in her seat to face the windshield once again.

Clementine drove slowly, and for the first time since leaving the store, Grant was calm. In truth, the town was always quiet, but knowing those creatures were everywhere made things different. The silence wasn't peaceful like it once was. Now, it was eerie.

The truck rolled slowly through the hospital parking lot. The infection couldn't have spread to here. Surely, the hospital would be a safe place with doctors ready to wipe out this head lice virus tearing through Clydesville.

They didn't need to get out of the vehicle to realize something was wrong. The hospital's large, automatic doors were wedged open. A wheelchair blocked the door to the left and a prone body caused the right door to bounce open every time it bumped against the man's thigh. He was dead, in a pool of his own blood, and beyond him, the lights were on, but nobody was at the reception desk. Someone was always at that desk.

Grant thought the night secretary's name was Brenda. He'd come in once complaining of chest pains, and it had been Brenda in that seat. He was sure of it now. She was a sweet woman who spent the quiet evening hours weaving at that desk. That or reading one of her romance novels. He'd had to spend a couple of nights here while the doctor ran tests and returned him to normal.

Clementine stepped on the gas, and the truck lurched forward and picked up speed. She drove them up onto Maker's Hill, a spot that was usually used by teenagers as a make-out point. Tonight, it was empty. No cars filled the bald spot where the grass had been rubbed free from constant tires rolling over it.

Grant hopped out of the truck and moved to Sally's side, taking her hand and intertwining his fingers through hers. Hal stood to his right and Clementine off to their left. They all stood staring down at the town they knew so well. From here, they could see the entire shopping area. Downtown was too far away, but the bingo hall, the restaurants, the car dealership, and across the street were quite clear.

The dental clinic was dark and quiet, but across the parking lot the two-story, ten-screen movie theater was on fire. Grant wondered how it had happened. Were there people in there when it went up in flames? Or had it happened during some kind of battle with the creatures? He imagined people inside watching whatever movie was hot right now when one of the creatures walked into the auditorium. That's all it would take. One of them. Only one and then the entire theater would be stark raving mad.

You're one of the lucky ones, Grant.

As unlucky as he felt, he had to admit things could have been worse. If he hadn't gone to the diner that morning at that exact time and sat at the counter, who knew how things would have turned out. Sally could be dead too.

He probably would have been at home, but that didn't mean he was safe. All it would take was for one of those things to come marching up to his doorstep. He would have probably assumed it was someone trying to sell him something or one of the people from the church there to convert him. If he'd even opened the front door, he would be one of *them*.

Things definitely could have been worse.

Down in the parking lot near the movie theater, figures moved around. Wanderers in search of something. They could have been humans searching for a safe place, but he doubted it. The slow pace at which they walked and the mindless roaming told him they were probably the infected, searching for another scalp to jump to.

"How do you suppose it works?" Sally asked.

Nobody answered. Hal shrugged his shoulders.

"I mean," she continued, "if those things jump to somebody's head and then they jump off, wouldn't they take the infection with them?"

"I suppose some stay behind," Hal said, "or there wouldn't be any to jump on somebody else."

"Lice lay lots of eggs," Clementine said.

"My daughter got them once," Hal said. "Or twice. Twice, I think. Those damn things wouldn't come out. Thank God her mama took care of it."

Nobody replied to that. Everyone in Clydesville knew everyone else's story and plenty had heard about what happened to Hal's little girl. It was a damn shame. Grant didn't know how he could survive after something like that. A daughter and a wife taken from him? That had to be hell.

Grant thought back to the way Hal stood there in the Walmart greeting card aisle, watching one of those things rush at him, completely unmoving. Hal didn't even budge. Maybe the man had a death wish.

Keep Sally away from him. She don't need to be near anybody wishing to die.

"So, you think they're laying eggs," Sally said softly. "Makes sense I guess."

It didn't matter if it made sense or not. None of them would ever get close enough to find out without turning into one of the creatures themselves. Grant wondered if there were scientists somewhere in a lab tinkering with these tiny but so deadly creatures. Were they picking at them with scalpels? Had some of them escaped and started this whole thing?

There wasn't a lab for many miles. He supposed it was possible researchers at West Virginia University could be involved, but he doubted it. Once again, his mind went to the government. Hal thought they were aliens. Could be. He supposed they could have come crashing down on some shooting star or small meteor. He couldn't remember one hitting the area.

"God, that thing is burnin'," Hal said.

The movie theater was roaring. Flames licked at the night air. No fire department was coming to its rescue and if anyone was trapped inside, they were dead by now.

"They done got the police station," Grant said, "the hospital, the movie theater, the damn bingo hall. There ain't nothin' left to destroy."

Hal whipped his head to the left. "Shit. The kids."

"What kids?" Clementine asked.

"There is somethin' left to burn," Hal said. "Stonewall Forge is packed with teenagers for some kind of conference."

"Grant," Sally said.

"Oh, hell," Grant replied. "You've got to be kiddin' me. They had to come this weekend."

"Come on," Hal said as he headed back to the bed of the truck, "if there was ever a reason for the four of us to make it this far, it's this. We gotta save those kids."

He was right. Nobody said a word as they piled back into the truck. Grant and Hal worked together loading all the weapons. They had a rescue mission ahead of them.

25

"What do you think, Mr. Andre?" Phyllis asked, as the stern, lumber-jack of a man peered out the cafeteria window and watched the line of unmoving animals. Nitsy glanced over his shoulder and saw one of the motion lights pop on outside. Beneath it, an infected student wandered aimlessly, searching for its next victim. The animals stared straight ahead, their eyeballs reflecting the lamp's light, giving their pupils an amber glow.

Andre turned toward Phyllis and said, "Just Andre, please. I ain't ever been a mister."

"Sorry," Phyllis replied.

"They're still watching us, not moving."

"I think they're listening," Robbie said.

Andre turned toward him and waited to hear more.

"We bumped into a bunch of them outside," Nitsy said. "When we were still, it almost seemed like they couldn't see us. The moment we made a noise, they came running."

"They hear us," Andre said to himself. "Listen, I want to get y'all out of here. I have a bit of a plan. Something I've been cooking up since my cousin Carl turned into one of them things. Since my truck flipped and I—"

"You're the guy that park ranger was looking for," Nitsy said. "Remember, Phyllis?"

Phyllis nodded.

"What park ranger?" Andre asked.

Nitsy shrugged. "I don't know. He was here asking Mr. Hayes about you. Said a guy flipped his truck and went missing. He was asking if anyone had seen you."

"I… I didn't know anybody was lookin' for me. I went to see if my wife was okay, but she… the whole trailer park… it was gone. I thought maybe they'd been relocated or somethin'."

"Or something," Bradley said.

Everyone remained silent for a moment. Andre stared at the floor for at least a full minute before tearing his eyes away and going back to the window.

"They're still not moving," he said.

Thomas was starving. He'd just sat down to eat a bowl of Ma's chili when Moses went silent. That in itself was weird. The dog never stopped barking unless someone went out and shot whatever animal was giving him hell. Pa was out there smoking, but Thomas hadn't heard his father's shotgun. It was strange, but not alarming, so he'd raised his spoon and smiled in anticipation of the big bite of Ma's best making its way into his belly. He'd worked hard all day and couldn't wait to dig in.

That was when Pa crashed through the door. He was different. His eyes were bloodshot, and drool ran down his mouth. He swung out with his hands frantically, like he desperately needed to grab hold of something. Pa's fingers found a handful of Ma's hair, and Thomas fell out of his seat and landed on the floor in time to see something leap from his father's head onto his mother's.

Then she changed too.

His first instinct had been to protect his mom. Thomas grabbed the fireplace poker with every intention of swinging it at his dad, but then

Ma howled, raked fingernails at her scalp, and Thomas knew he needed to get out of the house before whatever was happening to them reached him too.

Using the pile of firewood alongside the house as a step stool, Thomas climbed up onto the roof, like he did so many other nights when Pa took to drinking and showed his angry side. It was his private place to lie beneath the stars and wonder what it would be like to run away with the kids who often came to Stonewall Forge for the many conferences held there. He often thought about what life would be like in other places like Florida, California, or even Hawaii.

This time, he lay there because he had no other choice. He was afraid to climb down. With his ear to the tin roof, he heard his parents thrashing around in the house below. Moses was gone. At least he thought he was. He hadn't seen the dog since earlier that evening.

Even when he heard his parents leave the house and wander out into the woods, he remained on that roof. He stayed there all through the next day, baking beneath the slivers of sun that pushed through the forest ceiling. He imagined himself looking like a zebra now, striped with sunburn and the pale skin that avoided the rays.

By the time Thomas was brave enough to leave the roof, the chili was dry, crusted over, and covered with flies. Ma had prepared broccoli too, as she claimed a growing boy always needed a green vegetable with supper. Every day. No exceptions. Nothing reeked like old broccoli. It was one of the reasons he hated the stuff. It tasted fine, but he couldn't help thinking his insides would stink like the garbage always did when he took it out the day after eating it.

His stomach growled with hunger, but he gagged from the stench.

Thomas was standing next to the dining room table when Moses came back. The dog walked into the house and stood by the door, staring up at Thomas the way he always did when he was expecting a treat.

"Moses?" Thomas asked.

The dog was filthy like it'd had a hell of a night. Its tongue lolled out and its eyes were bloodshot. It was the animal version of Pa, only the dog wasn't thrashing around and chasing after him the way his father had the night before.

"Moses," Thomas repeated. "You okay, boy?"

He knew the dog wasn't but standing there in silence didn't seem right. Moses didn't respond, but something on its fur did. Thomas realized each time he spoke, Moses's fur twitched. It shifted. Moved as if its fur were a forest full of birds about to take flight. Thomas had spent many of his days up on the roof watching birds and wishing he could hit the sky and never come back. He knew a dog's fur should never move that way.

When he backed up a few steps, the dog didn't follow. He retreated slowly, quietly, making every effort not to spook the dog. This strategy seemed to work. Moses didn't budge. He stood by the door, his chest heaving with heavy breath, and his tongue twitched every few seconds. It was the fur holding Thomas's attention. It reminded Thomas of snakes now, the hair slithering and searching, trying to locate him.

If he could reach the bathroom, he could lock himself inside and use the window to climb out and directly onto the roof. He'd done it before. With his boot in the window frame, he could launch himself up. Moses could never follow him up there.

Closing his eyes for only a second, he fought with the realization he'd be back up there, starving and dying of thirst, safe from whatever was happening below but suffering the elements. He needed food and water. Realizing he'd have to deal with the immediate threat first, he decided it was better on the roof.

He continued to move back slowly, and he was getting closer to the bathroom door when his boot touched a floor panel that always squeaked. The sound might as well have been a scream because Moses turned his head toward him, and as he did, his fur shifted that way too.

With only one bark to serve as a warning, Moses leaped onto the table and bolted toward Thomas.

Thomas turned, ran, and dove into the bathroom, kicking the door shut behind him. The dog hit the door so hard Thomas thought it would explode inward. It cracked but didn't shatter, but Moses wasn't about to give up. Whatever had driven the dog mad wanted inside the room, and Thomas knew each strike against the wooden entryway was one closer to the dog reaching him.

The boy climbed through the window and was halfway through the frame when he noticed the other animals in the woods surrounding the house.

They watched.

They waited.

They listened.

Moses continued to ram the door behind him. Thomas ignored the other animals and reached for the roof. His hands gripped the gutter, and it threatened to come apart in his hands. He'd never had to make this climb in such a hurry. The flimsy metal bent in his hand and broke apart.

A piece of the gutter clattered against the ground, its tinny material making a hollow clack as it struck the dirt.

It was like a gun blast to start the race. The animals in the woods shot forward.

Thomas had no time to look at them, but he could hear their paws pummeling the forest floor, pitter-pattering as they scurried toward the house, hellbent on reaching their prey.

Him.

Thomas dug into the roof and hoisted his body up and over the lip at the side of the house. His body rolled across the flat surface as what might have been a wolf leaped and snapped its jaw only a foot away from his leg. Remembering the sight of the dog's fur, he dragged himself farther from the edge, making sure nothing could leap high enough to reach him.

That had been earlier in the day, and he'd lain there on that roof for hours, wondering what would kill him first. Would it be the hunger and thirst? Or would he become desperate enough to leave his hiding spot and venture down into the house again only to be attacked by one of the rabid beasts?

He'd decided on the hunger and thirst because nothing was going to make him leave this roof.

That was until he heard the gunshot. Then another and another. It sounded like it was coming from Stonewall Forge, or at least from that direction. Someone was fighting back, and that gave him a moment of bravery, long enough to crawl to the edge of the roof and look down to see if the animals were still surrounding his house.

It was pitch black out there, but he knew they were gone. He could see the tree line bathed in soft blue moonlight, and there was nothing out there. He fell forward onto his chest and let his arm dangle over the edge of the roof.

With a quick jerk, he pulled his arm away, remembering the wolf that had leaped at him and the fury with which Moses had bounded over the dining room table. Like the time he got to go out on his uncle's boat down in Fort Lauderdale, and he let his hand dangle off the edge until his uncle warned him sharks can jump, he thought twice about being so daring.

Then he thought about the pretty girl he'd seen the other day at Stonewall. She'd had beautiful red hair, long and flowing, and skin so pale it reminded him of *Snow White*, one of the few VHS tapes Ma still owned.

Ma and Pa. They're gone now. You're all alone.

He didn't have to be alone though. Thomas knew he could go to Stonewall Forge and rescue those other kids. He wasn't sure how he'd do it, but he could. He could show that pretty girl how manly he was.

Thomas sat up and breathed in the forest air. He wasn't afraid of animals. He never had been. He'd gotten bitten by a copperhead once and barely flinched. Leaning over the edge of the house once more, he saw Pa's truck in the driveway. It was still loaded with all their work equipment. Once inside that old rusty truck, Thomas wouldn't be afraid of anything.

Carefully, he climbed down from the roof and peeked through the bathroom window. It was empty.

"Moses," he called out, to make sure the dog wasn't around.

All was silent. No sound of the dog's paws racing through the house to take a giant chunk out of his neck. No sound at all.

"Moses," he called once more.

When he was certain the dog was gone, he climbed through the bathroom window and into the house. The bathroom door was completely destroyed. The dog had chewed its way through the wood. Blood and saliva were all over the floor along with random clutter the dog had knocked over as it searched for the boy.

Thomas took his time moving through the house, always ready to run for that bathroom window if need be.

Nothing attacked him. All the animals had run toward the gunshots.

It wasn't until Thomas entered his parents' bedroom that he was struck with the realization he'd never see them again. They were both gone. They'd left the house and were out there somewhere searching for other people to infect. They were like zombies.

Pa was an asshole a lot of the time and Ma was much too overbearing, but they were his parents, and they were gone.

Thomas shook himself out of his stupor. He'd have plenty of time to think about his parents later. Right now, he needed to find Pa's shotgun, which was always under his bed, and get to that campus. Once he'd retrieved the gun and the box of shells from the nightstand, he ran to the truck, took the keys out of the visor, and fired up the engine.

Scrambling to roll up the windows, Thomas sat in the driveway for a few seconds and waited. The headlights shined over the trees and he thought any second a giant crowd of animals might come rushing at him. Then he thought about the bats that often swooped down over his house. What if they could be infected? He could fight off land creatures, but what if the ones in the sky came after him?

He hoped they'd had enough sense to stay far away from the madness down below. Land mammals had no way of escaping getting too close to other creatures, but bats and birds... they could stick to the treetops and watch the animals down below battle it out for supremacy.

Vultures. They would be the ones to spread it to the sky if whatever was infecting people and animals liked feathers too. He could imagine one of those sick, nasty birds picking at the flesh of an infected, dead animal.

As soon as the thought came to him, he pushed it away and stepped on the gas, throwing the old truck forward. He hopped up and down in his seat as he drove toward Stonewall Forge.

"I'm coming for you, you bastards!" he shouted. "I'm coming to get revenge for what you did to Ma and Pa."

Andre Pete stared through the window and waited. He didn't know what he was waiting for, but he supposed the animals would get tired of sitting there and either decide to attack or flee.

"What if we go out there and you start shooting them?" Eggo asked.

Andre turned and looked at the young man like he'd lost his mind. Robbie thought he might reach out and slap Eggo for asking such a dumb question. After a moment of silence, Eggo shrugged as if to say, "It was only a suggestion."

"I'd never be able to hit enough of them," Andre replied. "I might get a couple of the larger animals, like them black bears right there, but those small sonsabitches would be on me in a matter of seconds."

"What if you got to higher ground?" Nitsy asked. "Like up on the school's roof."

"It's not a bad idea," Robbie said. Andre seemed to be thinking about it, so Robbie continued, "If we go out the door, real fast, before any of those things have a chance to attack us, maybe Eggo and I could boost you up onto the roof and then run back in here and lock the door."

"It's risky," Andre said.

"So is sitting here," Robbie replied. "How long do you think it's gonna be before one of those things, or all of them, find a way in here. If they all started attacking the door, we'd be fucked."

"How many bullets do you have?" Eggo asked.

"I don't know," Andre said. "Quite a few. That ain't the problem. It's making sure I don't piss them off enough to come barreling through this door. You think this rake lodged between the handles is going to keep you safe for long?"

"That's exactly what I'm saying," Robbie replied.

"Right now, they're not interested in you," Andre reminded him. "And you're in a damn cafeteria so at least you have food."

"That'll run out," Nitsy said.

"It was a mouse!" Bradley announced. Usually, he was quiet, so when he spoke, the others listened. Everyone turned to look at him. "None of you asked what happened in the music room. It was a mouse. Phyllis saw it too. Somehow, it got into that room, and it jumped on Lance. He changed instantly. He became one of *them*. How long do you think it'll take for a mouse to make its way in here?"

Everyone was quiet.

"A mouse," Andre repeated under his breath. "A goddamn mouse. All right, I'll do it, but we need to be smart about this. And fast."

When Andre said they needed to be smart about it, apparently he meant smart was using Robbie's idea of boosting him up on the roof. Now that they were standing at the door with every intention of putting the plan into place, it seemed stupid. He and Eggo would interlace their fingers, the way young kids did when trying to help a friend reach the cookies on the top shelf in the kitchen, Andre would step into their hands, and they would shove upward. That was supposed to launch Andre onto the roof.

"I don't know about this," Robbie said as they were about to open the door.

"What do you mean?" Andre asked.

"Dude, you're like two hundred and something pounds," Robbie said.

"Two-twenty," Andre informed him.

"We've got this," Eggo assured them. "If we work together, we'll get him up there."

"I'm just saying maybe we should find something here in the cafeteria that he could, I don't know, climb."

"There's no time for that," Nitsy said as she put her hands on Robbie's cheeks and pulled him in close for a kiss. He looked at her in the dark cafeteria, her hair gone and the cap she'd worn below the wig keeping whatever real hair she had hidden, and he still thought she was beautiful. She had the face of an angel. If angel's wielded fiery swords.

This chick was braver than he could ever be, and he knew if she were strong enough to lift Andre, she would be out there instead of him. That gave him the strength to do it. "Hurry back to me," she added with another kiss.

Andre Pete considered telling the kids they didn't have time for all that lovey-dovey nonsense. They were at war, and the enemy was head lice that liked to chew their way into their host's brain. At least that's what it seemed like they did. Yet, as ridiculous as it seemed to be kissing at a time like this, he couldn't bring himself to break the two apart. He wasn't sure he'd ever been in real love.

Sure, he loved his wife. He loved her, much the way someone would love seconds on a good plate of meatloaf and mashed potatoes. Or the way he loved marching through the woods first thing in the morning on a hunting trip he'd waited all year for. He appreciated the pleasure of her company. That was all. But he didn't look at her the way this Robbie kid was staring at Nitsy.

Finally, the two broke apart and Robbie seemed to be ready to get their task underway. This wasn't going to be easy. Andre was a big man, much too large to be trying to climb up onto the roof, but what else was there to do? They were right. He might not be able to shoot and kill all of these lousy bastards, but from a higher vantage point, he could nail quite a few.

All he needed to do was free up a little time so he could lead them to his truck. It wasn't the best vehicle – not quite as good as the truck he rolled off the highway the night his cousin Carl went apeshit – but it would do. It was the work pickup he always kept parked at the farm. It would do fine hauling these kids away from here… if they could get to the damn thing.

Bradley, the young looking kid with the glasses, pulled the rake out of the door handles, and Andre pushed open the door. Its rubber seal brushed the concrete ground outside, and its whoosh sound was louder than expected. Robbie hesitated inside the cafeteria door, and it took all of Andre's power not to reach back and slap him. They had a job to do. This wasn't the time to be cowering in fear.

This was what separated soldiers from saints. Soldiers went out and got their hands dirty, they made shit happen, they stood in the face of danger. Saints waited on miracles.

No miracle was coming their way.

Andre stood with his hands on his hips, waiting for the other boys. His rifle was slung over his shoulder. The animals were at his back, still calmly watching. Somewhere far off in the distance, on campus grounds, a moan echoed off the hallway walls. It came from one of the infected students. The lights in the hallways on this side remained off though, which meant none of those *things* was nearby. If they were, they would set off the motion sensors.

Robbie looked toward the cafeteria doors and saw Nitsy peering out at him through the window. He blew her a kiss and she smiled.

Andre considered telling the two boys, "You know what, take your time. I can wait here all day."

He was grumpy, which he knew came from a lack of sleep and hating the position he found himself in. He liked being in control. He wished he could fly an Apache helicopter over the forest and blow all those animals to high hell. Then he'd turn it toward Stonewall Forge and blow these buildings to kingdom come.

Where the hell is the Army when you need 'em?

He hated all this standing around, and he was about to ask the boys if they were ready when he saw the two look at each other and nod. Eggo and Robbie bent down and interlaced their fingers together. Andre stood behind them and gripped each boy at one shoulder. He put one of his boots inside the boys' locked fingers and prepared to be hoisted up.

They had a good, firm grip. For the first time, he thought this might actually work. If these two really gave it their all and threw him up there, he could easily get onto the roof.

One...

The boys provided a little give so Andre could feel the countdown begin.

Two...

A second bounce. It was almost time.

Three...

They stood up and shoved. Andre pushed down against their hands with a straight, strong leg. He felt himself shoot upward, but he also felt the boys go down. He'd pushed too hard against them, and with his heavy frame, they didn't stand a chance. They hit the ground hard but did a good job of keeping quiet in the process. At the same time they fell onto the sidewalk, Andre grabbed the roof's edge with both hands, and threw himself up to his elbows. His feet dangled down, but he'd made it.

Until his rifle slid down his arm and banged against the side of the building.

The clack was loud, and suddenly Andre realized it would be his own damn fault those *things* attacked. The boys had done well. It was *his* dumb ass who'd allowed his rifle to slip.

A motion sensor popped on to their right. Then more. At several places along the campus corridors, lights shone down on students hunched forward and searching for someone or something to attack. If they'd been there all along, the shadows had concealed them. Not anymore though. Now, they were hissing and clicking. One of them let out a screech as she howled at the moon.

Andre's eyes went wide and he scrambled, walking forward with his elbows, trying to swing his right leg up and set it on the edge of the roof, but he'd fallen down a little too much when he heard the howling sound. At this point, he wasn't sure he was going to be able to make it up there.

"Oh, shit," Eggo said.

"Get inside!" Andre yelled as he continued his awkward climb onto the roof.

It wasn't going to happen. He'd slipped too far from the roof, and he didn't have the strength he once had. Not with his bum leg. One of the *things* was close, no more than thirty feet or so, and it was coming at them quickly. Andre gave up on the climb and fell to the ground. He dropped to a knee, aimed his rifle, and shot the girl in her forehead. She fell backward onto the ground.

"Go inside!" Andre repeated.

"Come with us!" Robbie replied.

Andre aimed at a male figure headed their way. He pulled the trigger and shot it right through the heart.

"Come with us," Eggo said. "You can't kill them all."

"No, but I can kill some," Andre argued. "Now go on! Git!"

Robbie grabbed Eggo's shirt sleeve and pulled him toward the door to the cafeteria. Nitsy opened it for them and they ran inside.

Andre took aim at what looked like a male staff member. He was larger and older than the others. This one strode through the courtyard, passing the statue of Stonewall Jackson, and looked like he was about to charge. Andre aimed his weapon at him, but two more creatures came running at him more quickly. He would only be able to kill one, maybe two of them before being taken out himself.

The big man was the most crucial. He was closest and would definitely be the most difficult to handle if he got any closer. Andre aimed for his head, but the big guy was running too hard, his head shaking too much. The bullet grazed his cheek, but he kept coming. Now, Andre was certain he would only get this one last shot before the next two creatures, one male and one female – both students, reached him.

Andre pulled his trigger and lodged a bullet right in the big man's skull. He hit the ground hard, sliding to a stop about ten feet away. Any closer and Andre would have been a dead man. The other two were now about the same distance as the dead creature.

Worst of all, the animals at the tree line were no longer sitting still. The gunshots had awakened them, and they were now coming toward him too, not running but walking side by side like no animal had any right to do. He'd never seen anything like it. They were calmly moving forward like they had all the time in the world to pick the meat from Andre's bones.

The two infected humans roared and shrieked as they sought Andre like heat-seeking missiles, using the sound of his gunshots to home in on. Andre raised his rifle and shot the female student in the chest. It was the best shot he could get off in time. She stumbled back but didn't die.

This is it. Go out with a bang.

Andre would fight to the finish, even if that meant putting a bullet in his own head at the last second. Both of the infected students were coming fast, and Andre wasn't going to be able to get off another shot before they reached him. This was the end, but he'd take at least one of them with him. Andre was preparing his final shot when the cafeteria door crashed open behind him.

Robbie stepped out with the rake in his hand. Eggo was right behind him with a large kitchen knife. Nitsy wielded a broomstick, Bradley held a lunch tray out like a shield, and Phyllis clutched a rolling pin. Andre would have laughed if the situation weren't so dire. It was like his backup had arrived, and it was the *Scooby-Doo* gang.

But this wasn't funny. They were all putting themselves in grave danger. The monsters kept coming at them until a horn blared from somewhere in the distance. It came from a car or a truck, and it was loud enough that it caused the creatures coming toward them to stop and look at the gate and the land beyond.

Andre would look for its source in a second, but first, he used the distraction to plug a hole in the male infected student, right between his eyebrows, and then put one more bullet in the female whose shot to the chest had only delayed her attack.

With the immediate threat eliminated, Andre looked out at the field in front of the campus and saw the animals had stopped moving. Whoever was blowing that horn was going crazy, honking it like a madman.

The lights on campus flickered, turning on and off like a lightning storm on earth. Thomas was well aware of the system in place at Stonewall Forge, and he also knew students weren't allowed to roam the grounds this late at night. That meant something was definitely going on there. The infected people and animals had made their way over there. He only hoped he wasn't too late.

In Pa's pickup, he felt like he was driving a tank. With its giant grill out front and the bed of the truck weighed down with heavy equipment, he was going to destroy everything in his path, and he had his sights on the glowing orbs of the animals' eyes reflecting his headlights.

They stared directly at him, and for a moment, he hesitated. Only because he'd never seen so many animals in all his life. He'd seen black bears and he'd come across plenty of possums, but this was the craziest thing he'd ever encountered. It was a sea of sickness. Four-legged creatures with fur that moved on its own, and they were all watching him, wondering if he would have the balls to go through with this. He'd show them.

"Come on, motherfuckers!" he yelled, ignoring Ma's constant pleas to watch his language and be a respectable young man.

There was a time and place for respectable, and it wasn't right now.

Thomas blew the horn again and stepped harder on the gas. He had no intention of slowing down. He wanted every bear, every wolf, every fox, every raccoon, every dog, and every other beast to step right up and see what he had to offer.

Let them come. Let them turn toward him and try chasing him back up onto that roof. No, he'd cowered enough for one day. Now, it was time to take action. He would get his revenge. As Pa always said, "It's time to man-up and take what's coming to you." Pa always said it with his belt wrapped around his fist, but the words meant the same no matter what weapon you were wielding, and right now he was wielding a hammer on four wheels.

"Come on, baby," Thomas said aloud as he grew closer and closer to the animals.

They didn't move like he expected them to. They didn't run when they heard the blaring of the horn. They didn't flinch with the revving of the engine. They stood their ground, and Thomas smiled insanely in his adrenaline-induced heroism.

The campus was coming up quickly with its wrought-iron gate.

Thomas had no intention of trying to drive through that thing. No, he'd stick with killing whatever person or animal was out here in the yard.

A yard he'd mowed and weed-whacked nearly every single day since he was ten years old. He remembered Pa finally letting him work the push mower while Pa sat on the riding one. The push mower was always good at getting the areas around the trees.

Two tears fell from Thomas's eyes at the thought of never seeing that mean old bastard again. The old man might have handed out a good ass-whoopin' from time to time, and he might have had very few kind words, but he was Thomas's father, and he knew he'd miss him. Same with Ma.

Through clenched teeth, Thomas yelled, "Yes! Stay right there in front of me you sorry sacks of shit. Take what's coming to you!"

It was an elk out front of the rest. Large and with big antlers, it stood its ground, puffing out its chest and glaring back at the headlights like it couldn't believe Thomas had the balls to approach it head-on.

"You want some of this?" Thomas called out, noticing there was a skunk right behind the elk. He hated skunks.

The elk seemed to want some of this because it didn't budge.

Thomas pointed the truck right at the long line of animals, gripped the steering wheel, and held on for dear life as he smashed the front grill right into the elk. The thud was loud, and Thomas jerked in his seat, but he didn't take his foot off the gas. There were so many more animals to mow down.

The skunk was small, and Thomas wasn't even sure if the truck hit it. The small black bear he definitely ran into. His truck was a bowling ball cracking pins as it drove through every animal in that line. He crushed skulls, penetrated bodies, and mowed down everything in his way. None of these four-legged creatures stood a chance against Thomas's battle tank.

In his headlights, he saw each animal fly to the left, to the right, and right down the center, and he never stopped. He kept going. Until he reached the end of the animals and his headlights shone on the small group of people headed to the campus.

There, in front of him, was Pa and Ma, both mindless zombies looking back at him. He should have continued forward and taken them out, but he couldn't. At the last second, he chickened out and jerked the wheel to the right. The truck was moving too fast, and that sudden turn caused it to hit clumps of dry grass. The vehicle skidded sideways until the tires caught the earth hard and the truck flipped over on its side.

Thomas bounced around the cab. Random items took flight with him. He saw an old cheeseburger wrapper, a ballpoint pen, a red lighter, and a cardboard cup used to catch his father's tobacco spit. The cup hit the seat as the truck flipped and brown, wet, muddy filth coated the seat and Thomas's arm and leg.

When the truck finally came to a rest, Thomas sat up and gagged. He fought the urge to vomit and climbed out of the cab. His head was pretty banged up. Blood trickled down from his forehead, ran over his cheek, and dripped on the grass.

"Hey, you all right?" came a loud, barking voice.

"Pa?" he asked.

Deep down, he knew it wasn't his father's voice, but it sure sounded like him. The disgruntled way he always spoke. Thomas stood there next to the truck and stared at the grassy lawn around him. Dead animals lay on the ground behind the truck. A few that weren't dead were mewing and whining, dragging themselves across the ground.

It took him a second to remember what happened.

The sound of a gunshot brought him back to his senses. His ringing ears began to clear some and he heard random voices behind him. Thomas turned to see a big man with a rifle walking toward him with a group of teenagers right behind him.

"He looks stunned," one of the teenagers said.

"I recognize him. He was with the caretaker." This girl was bald. Her face seemed familiar.

"Hey," the big man with the rifle said as he grabbed Thomas by both shoulders and shook him gently. "You need to snap out of it. Those things will be on us soon."

"Ma?" Thomas asked. "Pa?"

He pushed past the big man and looked at the bodies lying on the ground behind the truck. His mother and father were both there. They were crushed and almost unrecognizable. When the truck flipped, it had whipped right over the crowd of infected people.

"Holy shit!" one of the teenage boys said. "He took out all the animals."

"Not all of them," the big man said, and finally Thomas felt his head clear completely. He remembered what he'd seen. What he'd done. This was his handy work. He'd taken out most of the animals, but some had gotten out of the way.

"Andre, we need to go," one of the teenagers said to the big man.

Andre nodded and replied, "We need to get to my truck. It's right over there."

He pointed to a red pickup truck parked not far away.

"Go ahead," Andre commanded. "I'll stay here and watch your back. Take this guy with you."

Thomas didn't argue when Andre pointed at him. He didn't have it in him to fight. His entire right side was drenched in his father's tobacco spit and blood was dripping from other places. He'd snapped out of his haze, but he still didn't feel entirely right.

"The gas can," Thomas managed, talking to Andre.

"What?" Andre asked.

By now, infected teenagers were making their way through the heavy front gate at Stonewall Forge. They'd be on them soon.

Thomas looked at the contents that had fallen from the bed of the truck. The riding lawnmower lay on its side. The push mower had gotten flung pretty far away. It was a red metal gas can he was pointing at.

"Set them on fire," Thomas said.

Andre smiled and nodded. "That's a damn fine idea, ain't it?"

Thomas returned his smile and followed the other teenagers while Andre slowly backed toward them, keeping his gun trained on the fallen pickup truck and its contents littered all over the ground. He kept his aim on that gas can and waited for the infected teenagers to stumble out of the Stonewall Forge gates and toward the truck.

Many of the animals were still making noises, still crying, still whining, and that was loud enough to draw the students from inside the campus. Soon, five, ten, twenty, thirty students were making their way to all that ruckus.

And Andre kept his aim on the gas can.

When it was clear no more students were going to leave the campus gates, Andre dropped to a knee, steadied his rifle, and pretended that gas can was the head of a deer. He relaxed and focused on his breathing like he always did on a hunt. After closing his eyes for only a few seconds to calm his nerves, Andre held his breath, and he pulled the trigger.

The bullet struck the gas can dead center, and the can exploded, catching every teenager and animal in its vicinity on fire. The infected students screamed, and a God-awful sound followed. Those tiny head lice screeched. They wailed as they were consumed by the flames.

26

Hal and Grant sat in the rear of Clementine's truck, weapons ready, waiting on the chance to shoot anything that moved. The road out to Stonewall Forge was a long, dirt-covered path for the most part. Dust clouds swarmed the truck, making it nearly impossible to see. Hal was exhausted. He had to wipe the dirt from his eyes and blink constantly to keep them open.

So far, they'd encountered nothing. The woods were eerily quiet. Only the drone of the truck engine broke the silence.

Hal hated facing the rear of the truck. He wanted to turn around and face the front but knew if he lost his balance, he'd end up on the forest floor with a broken leg or worse.

"Does this seem dumb to you?" he finally said aloud.

Grant shrugged. "What do you mean?"

"The bad guys will be up there."

"Bad guys? These are parasitic head lice, man."

"You know what I mean. If we're pointed to the rear, we ain't gonna be able to shoot the things Clementine passes."

Grant nodded, seeming to finally understand what Hal meant.

"But unless we're going to ask her to drive in reverse," Hal added, "I guess there ain't much more we can do about it."

This left him feeling like an asshole, presenting problems with no potential solutions. He realized he'd probably only voiced his frustration out of a need to bring some life into the situation. Or, quite possibly, to ease his nerves. Sitting in silence was enough to drive him mad.

"You could always lay over the cab of the truck," Grant joked.

"Or *you* could!"

"With her driving, we'd get bucked right off!"

Both men were laughing when the first sign of trouble hit. Clementine slowed down and yelled through the window back at them, "There's something on the road up ahead."

"Run it over!" Grant yelled.

"And fuck up my truck?" Clementine asked. "If you boys want to walk the rest of the way there, I'll go ahead and run it over."

"Nah," Hal replied, "don't you be fuckin' up this truck. Not yet."

He turned and stood slowly. Grant did the same so that both men were looking out at the road over the roof of the cab. Hal squinted his eyes and could barely make out a shadowy figure sitting in the center of the road. It was wide, short, and had no interest in moving out of their way.

"Is it a person?" Grant asked, pointing his gun at it.

"Don't look like any person I've ever seen," Hal replied.

He supposed it could've been a small man sitting naked on the ground if he were curled up in a ball and looking away from them.

Clementine stopped the truck.

Hal didn't like this.

They were out here in the open now, trees to both sides, in total darkness. The forest was too quiet. None of the usual insect sounds brought the night to life. Hal didn't like sitting here one bit. Every second that passed seemed to bring the trees and all the blackness behind it closer to them.

Hal slapped the roof with an open palm and called out, "Drive closer to it. If you have to, run that sumbitch over."

Clementine inched forward, and the thing in the road didn't budge.

From Hal's estimate, they were only about halfway to the

Stonewall Forge campus. If Clementine gunned it and swerved right, it was possible they'd be able to drive around it, but it would be awfully close. Trees hugged both sides of the road. The risk of swiping one was too great.

"Hey!" Hal yelled at the thing in the road. "Get the fuck outta the way!"

If he wasn't worried about waking up everything in the forest, he would have told Clementine to lean on her horn.

She moved the truck closer. The thing in the road twitched a few times and then it unraveled and stood upright. A huge man wearing a bear-skin coat stood up, and as he did, the front of his body came into view. He stood over six feet tall and was completely naked beneath his fur.

His mouth was twisted in a toothy, wicked grin.

One eye looked toward the sky. The other was missing from its socket altogether and dangled down over his cheek with what looked like fleshy yarn.

At his stomach was a giant gash that seeped blood. The wound pulsated with his heartbeat and crimson fluid pumped out with each jerk of his chest.

His flaccid cock dangled and seemed to dance with the same rhythm while one hand went to his scalp and scratched. The other reached out to them with one finger raised as if to say, "Hang on a minute. Wait for it."

"He ain't right," Grant whispered.

"Clementine, drive around him," Sally called out from the passenger seat.

Hal didn't want to go around him. He didn't want to get close to him at all.

The man in the middle of the road grumbled and opened his mouth wide. The sound coming from his throat rivaled that of the truck's engine. Hal could imagine the guy's throat ripping with the sound, his flesh stretching and tearing as he pushed that God-awful noise past his lips.

"Clementine, you drive around him," Grant recommended. "Sally, you slide toward the center of the seat. Stay away from the window in case this fella gets grabby."

"Just shoot him, Grant!" Sally replied.

Grant looked to Hal for an answer.

Hal shrugged. "It's what we came out here for, ain't it?"

Grant agreed with him and then leaned down to speak through the window into the cab. "We're gonna shoot him. As soon as he falls, you barrel right over him."

"You got it," Clementine said.

It occurred to Hal that there was no concern for what they were about to do. None as far as killing the poor bastard went. If there was any worry at all, it was for the wellbeing of the truck and its passengers. Of course, their safety was the most important thing, but for the first time since this all started, Hal wondered if this would be considered murder. At some point, if the government sorted this out and came up with a cure that brought everyone back to normal, would he and this ragtag mob be guilty of slaughtering these *things*?

He doubted it. That would be absurd.

His thoughts were interrupted by Clementine yelling, "Well, if you're fixin' to do it, do it!"

Hal aimed his rifle sight at the crazy man's forehead, and as he did, the man lurched forward, causing Hal to hold off on his shot and re-aim.

"He's coming right at us!" Sally yelled.

"Shh," Grant warned them.

"Shh? You're about to shoot a rifle," Clementine reminded him.

Hal wished they'd all shut up. He readjusted his aim and pulled the trigger. A jet of red mist popped out of the back of the man's head, and he crumpled to the ground. If there had been birds in the trees, they would have taken flight, but nothing living was in the nearby vicinity. Any soul not already hijacked by these creatures had long since fled the scene. Still, the boom echoed off the trees and caused Hal to wince.

For at least a full ten seconds, nobody moved.

They only listened to the crack of the rifle repeat itself. The wind blew and ruffled the trees. Branches waved at Hal as he waited.

Was anything going to come at them? He expected to hear the growling of monsters, the stomping of feet, or at least heavy panting headed their way. Yet, there was nothing.

There's nothing because everything in these woods is probably at Stonewall Forge by now.

He remembered visiting the campus and seeing the kids walk the halls, headed toward meetings, or going to lunch, whatever they had going on that day. Those children, barely teenagers, should have chosen some other weekend to come visit. A week ago would have been fine. Perhaps a month from now and this would all be over, but this was bad timing all around.

"Holy shit," Grant said. "You nailed that asshole."

"We have to get to the campus," Hal demanded.

"Did you see that?" Clementine asked, slapping the steering wheel as she hopped up and down in her seat. "Took him out quick."

"It ain't the first one we killed," Grant reminded her.

"I know, but that was a perfect shot!" she called out. "Did you see the way the blood flew out the back of his daggone head?"

Hal's gaze was fixed on the body he'd just sent to the soil. He heard a strange growl that at first seemed to be coming from the man. By the time he realized it wasn't coming from him at all, it was too late. The pitter-patter of feet racing toward them was coming too quickly, and Hal couldn't gauge its location. It seemed to be on the left, but he wasn't sure if it was approaching from behind them or up ahead.

Clementine wasn't paying attention. She'd turned in her seat to peer out the rear window at Hal and Grant. The beast tearing through the trees seemed to sense her lack of alertness. The big, grey wolf charged at her on all fours. The fur near its ears was matted with what looked like mucus and blood. Its snout seemed to have lifted up as if trying to peel off its face. The shrieking, furious monster hit the glass face first and smashed through the driver's side window, landing on Clementine and clamping its large jaws down over her forearm. Sally screamed and kicked her feet at the wolf.

"Sally!" Grant yelled. "Get out of there!"

"Clementine!" Sally screamed.

"Get it off me!" the older woman hollered.

In her terrified craze, Clementine mashed her foot down on the gas pedal. The truck shot forward, veered left, and slammed into a tree. Hal and Grant both flew forward in the bed of the truck, hitting the cab with their bodies before falling back into the bed.

Hal climbed to one knee and saw the entire front end of the truck was crushed. Smoke billowed from under the hood and the engine hissed. They wouldn't be driving it anywhere now.

Through the rear window, Hal saw that Clementine's head was at an odd angle. She was in bad shape, and the wolf was still hanging on, dangling out the window, growling as it shook its mouth back and forth.

For a second, the older woman seemed to be out cold. Oblivious to what was taking place around her and what was happening *to* her.

The skin on Clementine's arm came apart in the beast's mouth. It stretched and tore. The woman regained consciousness with a screech of pain like nothing Hal had ever heard before. She screamed in agony as the wolf's teeth ripped through her muscle and bore down on bone. Its entire snout was painted red now.

Sally went crazy when she saw the blood. Her flight instinct took over and she shoved herself backward out of her seat, tossing herself through the passenger side door and onto the hard ground outside.

The wolf gnawed on Clementine, and even when Hal pointed his rifle at it and blew a hole through its center, the beast kept its clench on her.

Clementine, her face a mask of pain, yanked and pulled, trying to shake her arm loose.

Through the smoky screen obstructing his view, Hal swore he saw the wolf's hair move.

"No!" he yelled, fully aware of what was about to happen.

He pointed his rifle at the wolf and shot it again. This time it fell from her arm, its teeth momentarily stuck in her flesh before its body plopped to the muddy ground.

But Hal was too late. He knew it the second he saw her suddenly go rigid. Like every muscle in her body spasmed at the same time. Her back snapped into a perfect posture. Her jaw fell open and the only sound that came out was, "Ohh... ugggg." These weren't moans of pleasure or even pain. They were the body's inability to rationalize what was happening. She was in total shock. In awe. Then it was like realization suddenly came over her. "Sally?"

Sally had risen to her feet and was terrified standing outside the door, and she had every right to be, as Clementine's short-lived clarity became all-out madness. With an agonizing cry, the older woman threw her fingers to her scalp and clawed at herself.

"It hurts!" she cried.

"Get away from her!" Grant yelled at Sally as he leaped out of the bed, grabbed hold of Sally's arm, and pulled her away from the truck.

Sally, who wasn't ready to be yanked off-balance, tripped and fell on her ass. She frantically swatted at herself, slapping her own arms and legs, driving her fingers through her hair and scratching at herself.

"Did they get on you?" Grant asked.

His gun was pointed at Sally, and he shook with his finger an inch from the trigger.

Hal didn't know what to do. These were his friends, and all he could do was stand there and watch them while he contemplated whether or not he needed to kill them.

Clementine screamed from inside the truck. Hal needed to do something, so he climbed out on the passenger side. Grant moved out of his way, giving him space to reach the truck's cab.

"Did they get on you?" Grant repeated.

Sally glanced up at him, snarled, and said, "Grant, get that fucking gun out of my face!"

Grant lowered his gun. Sally climbed to her feet.

"Did they—" he started to ask again.

"No," Sally replied. "I don't think so."

"Grant, watch your backs," Hal reminded him. "Where there's one wolf..."

"Yeah," Grant agreed as he turned toward the trees.

"Clementine," Hal called out to the older woman still seated in the driver's seat.

Clementine stared back at Hal with bloodshot eyes. She reached to her head and dug into her scalp. Her nails broke the skin, sending rivulets of blood down from her hairline. She pulled so hard one nail lodged in her flesh and broke in half. The others raked the skin down, ripping it and causing more blood to soak her temples, cheeks, and on down to her neck.

Hal kept his eyes on her as he leaned back and called out to the others. "They got her. She's turnin' into one of them things."

"Get away from her, Hal!" Sally yelled.

He couldn't believe his eyes when Clementine grinned at him through gritted teeth covered in blood. It seemed like she was trying to speak to him, but red spit dribbled out of her mouth with each unintelligible grunt. He backed up a step when she began to slide along the seat, dragging her ass along it as she swiped her arms out at him in a desperate attempt to bring him closer.

"I'm sorry," he whispered to her as he lifted his rifle, aimed it at her head, and pulled the trigger.

The bullet tore through her skull, exploded the back of it, and shattered what was left of the driver's side window. Clementine went slack. Her face was destroyed.

A growl came from the woods behind him to Grant and Sally's right, and before any of them had the chance to react, a rabid fox leaped from the trees and bit down on Grant's leg. It was small but fierce as it tried to climb his leg. Grant, unable to keep his balance, fell to the ground and used his free leg to try and pry the animal off him.

Hal aimed his gun at the fox, but he couldn't take the shot without destroying his friend's leg.

Sally backed away and turned to find she was face to face with a small black bear. It was only about six feet away from her. She screamed, "Hal!"

"Fuck!" Grant yelled as he kicked his leg and threw his head back against the ground, trying to keep his hair as far away from the fox as possible. His gun was useless with the creature wrapped around his leg. It was clear he was as afraid to take the shot as Hal was.

The fox's fur shifted. The lice were about to pounce.

The bear in front of Sally lifted up on its hind legs, putting itself too close to her hair. Hal sensed she was in the most danger, so he turned toward the bear and shot it in the neck. It fell to the ground and whimpered, but it didn't stop coming.

"Sally, run!" Hal yelled. "Get in the bed of the truck!"

He turned his attention back to Grant but still couldn't take the shot. So, he did the next best thing. In high school, he played a little bit of football. He wasn't the best field goal kicker, but he had a hell of a punt. So, he ran at the fox, lined it up perfectly, and blasted it with his boot. He wasn't expecting the fucked-up furball to take flight, but it did.

Hal waited a second to make sure Grant wasn't infected. He'd seen how quickly the transformation happened. Grant scooted his ass against the ground, staring at the forest with fear in his eyes, but he didn't scream, he didn't howl, and he didn't try digging to his brain with clawed hands. He was okay.

Sally's scream brought him back to her situation. She was in the bed of the truck now, but the bear was tall on its hind legs and was swatting at her, growling, and trying to climb into the truck.

"Get it, Hal!" she yelled.

Hal rolled into the bed of the truck, stood up, and aimed at the bear. It looked back at him with eyes that seemed possessed. Blood seeped from its jaws and it swung its paw out with a deadly fury. If this were an action movie, it would have been the perfect time for a one-liner, but he couldn't think of anything witty to say. Then it came to him. Before pulling the trigger, he looked straight in that bear's eyes and said, "Hey, bear. You *bear*-ly stood a chance." Then he shot it in the face and the beast fell to the ground, dead.

Grant backed toward the truck and climbed into the bed, meeting Sally in the middle. The two hugged each other and Hal couldn't believe his eyes when Grant pulled her into his arms and kissed her hard. She struggled for a second and then relaxed in his arms and went with it.

"I'm sorry," Grant said as they finally broke from their embrace. "I needed to do that."

"Maybe you should've done that a long time ago," she replied.

"Maybe you shouldn't have done it at all," Hal joked with a roll of his eyes.

He had nothing against love, but now wasn't the damn time for these two to be acting like horny teenagers. They needed to get to Stonewall Forge.

"How high do you think these things can jump?" Hal asked as he stared down at the dead wolf and the bear lying only a few feet away from it. He moved closer to Grant and Sally.

"I hope it's not that damn far," Grant replied.

The fox that had attacked Grant's legs came darting out of the woods, aimed right at the truck. It snarled and leaped into the air. This time Grant pointed his pistol and caught it with a bullet in midair. Hal didn't get to see where the shot landed as the tiny animal was flung by the force right back into the forest.

"Damn that thing is angry!" Grant yelled. "It almost took my damn leg off earlier."

"*Was* angry," Hal agreed. "Ain't much of anything now." He looked down to see Grant bleeding through his jeans and added, "If it got any closer to you, you would have ended up like Clementine."

Sally wiped tears from her eyes, and Hal felt insensitive for talking about Clementine like that.

"Hell, I'm sorry," he said. "I didn't realize y'all were that good of friends."

"All these poor animals," Sally said through her tears.

"Poor animals?" Hal replied.

"They're fucking victims, Hal," she shot back.

Hal rubbed his temples, trying to force away the headache coming on. "All right, don't get all snippy."

"What do you think?" Grant asked.

"Truck ain't worth a damn now," Hal replied.

Grant nodded. "So we walk."

It seemed their only option but marching down this dirt road with rabid raccoons and other ferocious furballs more than eager to take a bite out of them didn't seem like a good idea. The truck had been the plan. Now, they had no plan at all.

27

It was a bonfire made of blood and bone. The shrieks emitting from the infected teenagers would haunt Nitsy for the rest of her life. They had been people once. They'd sat with her in the auditorium, each with his or her own reason for coming to the conference.

Now, seated in the bed of Andre's truck, with Robbie's arm around her, she watched them burn. She heard the monsters inside them scream in their suffering and that was the only part for which she was grateful. She couldn't help wondering if, deep inside their minds, the teachers and students were in there somewhere. Did they feel the pain of the fire's flames?

Phyllis and Bradley were both seated up front with Andre. Robbie had tried to talk Nitsy into riding in there with them, but she'd refused. She wanted to stay with him. She trusted him. Looking at him now, she watched as his hair blew in the wind, and it was the first time since leaving the cafeteria that she'd thought about her wig being gone. He was seeing her right now, the real her, without being glammed up. Robbie didn't seem to care. Maybe he was *the one*.

"They're all gone," Eggo said softly, barely audible over the sound of the truck's engine and the wind whipping by. "Every fucking one of 'em is gone."

The nightmare was over. At least Nitsy was fairly certain it was. This couldn't have been taking place outside of the Stonewall Forge campus, right? This was a bad dream they were finally driving away from.

"At least y'all got your families to go back to," the caretaker's son said, his eyes looking glossy as he stared at the fire.

Nitsy didn't know the boy, but she sensed his pain, and she wished she could hold him. His bravery had saved them all.

"They got Pa... and Ma... I ain't got nobody no more."

"You were very brave back there," Nitsy said. "That was a really heroic thing you did."

He turned his head toward her and was silent for a moment before he said, "I saw you the other day. But... but you had hair."

Nitsy wasn't expecting to laugh, but the statement caught her off guard and caused her to. It felt good, so she laughed some more. Soon, Robbie was laughing too.

"What... what is it?" the boy asked.

"What's your name?" she replied.

"Thomas," he said.

"Thank you, Thomas. I'm Nitsy. I needed that laugh."

"I didn't mean to be funny," he said.

"I know. And it wasn't you. You see, that was a wig. It's a long story, but that wasn't my real hair."

"Thank God," Thomas replied, "Because I was gonna ask you what happened to it. Thought maybe you'd lost it in the fire."

The way the boy said the word *fire* made her laugh again. He pronounced it *far*.

"I lost my hair before the fire," she informed him, "but it'll grow back."

Robbie pulled her to him and squeezed her tight.

"So, what happens now?" Eggo asked.

Nitsy looked up at the moon shining its bluish glow down over them. "I hope we can go home."

The truck, which had been bumbling its way over the uneven dirt road, swerved sharply, throwing them all off balance. Nitsy's head bounced off Robbie's and they both cried out in pain.

"What's happening—" Eggo began, when a loud snarl filled the air, cutting him off.

To their right, a large dog dove at them, but the truck was moving too quickly, and its snout hit the side panel. It yowled and for a moment, only for a second, Nitsy felt bad for it. It was infected right now, but yesterday it might have been someone's pet.

"Ah hell!" Andre yelled from the driver's seat.

Nitsy peered through the truck's back window and saw a giant buck standing in the center of the road. Its antlers were tall and wide. It was an impressive creature. Any hunter would dream of seeing one like it out in the woods, but standing in the middle of the road, with its chest puffed out the way it was, it seemed to be daring Andre to hit it.

"There's a deer in the road," Nitsy informed the others.

"An infected one?" Eggo asked.

Thomas looked through the window. "It's hard to tell. Sometimes they're just dumb like that."

Andre slowed the truck down, and as he did, other animals came out of the forest, behind the truck, and moved toward them. This flock of random beasts walked slowly toward the bed of the truck.

"Andre," Eggo called out. "Look behind us, man."

To Nitsy, the animals looked possessed, like it wasn't only some kind of worm or bug inside them, but more like a demon had crawled inside their souls. Their eyes glowed in the moonlight, but there was no life there. A bear's head hung to the side like it was broken. A wolf's pelt was soaked with its own blood and it walked forward weakly. A gash at its side opened and closed with each step like a red, dripping mouth gasping for air each time its paw touched the earth.

A woman moved out of the trees, walking slowly like she'd been given new legs. Her hair was pulled up from the scalp. Chunks of flesh clung to it and kept it glued to the skull, but it was clear she'd tried to pull her hair out in one big handful.

"Grace," Thomas whispered.

"What?" Robbie asked.

"Grace Connor," Thomas said. "She leads the choir at my church."

The woman trampling through the grass and following the animals didn't seem like the churchgoing type. Her shirt was ripped, and one boob hung freely. Every part of her was doused in blood except that boob.

"She don't have her tittie out like that in church," Thomas said, his eyes still glued on the woman.

"Brace yourselves," Andre yelled. "If this motherfucker don't wanna move outta my way, I'm fixin' to move him."

With that, he stepped on the gas and the truck leaped forward. As it did, the animals took off at a sprint, chasing after their trail of dust. Eyes glowed through the dirt cloud and they were coming fast. Nitsy closed her eyes, clutched Robbie's hand, and prayed they'd blow right past that deer. If they didn't, if the truck slowed down even a smidgen, the wolves nipping at their heels would leap right over the tailgate and it would all be over.

Andre didn't slow down.

He drove faster.

Nitsy didn't have to look to know they were about to hit the buck.

"Come on, you fucker!" Andre yelled.

That was the signal.

"Hold on!" she yelled.

Nitsy leaned forward and tucked her head between her knees, covering her head with her hands the way she'd been taught to do in kindergarten whenever their teacher made them practice for a tornado drill. It was the only thing that came to mind.

The moment of impact felt like they'd hit a brick wall. The truck slammed into the weight of the animal, bashed through its meaty hide, and must have knocked it to the side because only the left tires seemed to hobble over it.

Eggo was nearly thrown out of the truck bed as it bounced over it. "Holy shit!" he yelled. "We nailed that sucker!"

He leaned over the side of the truck to get a closer look at the deer, and it happened in a split second.

Eggo was in mid-sentence with, "Damn, we fucked that thing—" when he switched to, "Wha... ah... no..."

His hands went to his face and he thrashed around, scratching at his eyebrows, and swatting at his head and cheeks. Robbie and Nitsy threw themselves to the opposite side of the truck, closer to Thomas, and watched as their friend panicked. Eggo's eyes went wide as he realized what was happening to him.

Their theory earlier about shaving their heads was wrong. The lice had latched onto Eggo's eyebrows. The young man screamed in pain and scratched so hard at his face that his forehead and cheeks began to bleed.

"Eggo, no," Nitsy whimpered with her hand over her mouth. "No. Don't do that to yourself."

"It hurts so bad!" Eggo yelled.

His fingernails had made their way beneath his eyebrows, and he pulled, peeling his upper brow off his face. Blood ran down over his eyes, across his cheeks, and into his mouth where it bubbled with each gasp and grunt the boy made.

"He's infected!" Robbie yelled. "Stay back!"

"Fuck this," Thomas announced as he slid a little closer and kicked Eggo hard in his chest. The thump was loud, and the force was enough to knock Eggo over the side of the truck.

Inside the cab, Phyllis screamed.

Andre slowed the truck down to see what was happening and the animals grew dangerously close.

"Don't stop!" Nitsy yelled as she slapped the roof of the truck.

Robbie joined her. "Go! Go! Go!"

Nitsy turned toward Thomas whose eyes were in his lap. The boy clearly wasn't proud of his decision, but he'd saved them. She knew that. Robbie would have never done that to Eggo, and she doubted she would be able to either. Thomas had saved their lives a second time tonight.

The road seemed to smooth out some after passing the deer.

They drove on in silence. She couldn't believe Eggo was gone. One second he'd been fine. He'd been with them, safe in the back of the truck, and all it took was for him to lean closer to one of the animals. The lice had jumped on him.

"He was bald," Robbie mumbled. "He didn't even have hair."

"It looked like they got into his eyebrows," Nitsy said.

She touched her own and realized how lucky she was. It dawned on her how close she'd come to death herself. If she hadn't been face down, buried in a pile of infected teenagers in that auditorium, if the lice hadn't thought they could get in through her hair, they could have burrowed into her eyebrows as well.

Even now, she was lucky. If Thomas waited even a few seconds longer to kick him out of the truck, they might have dove at her and even though she was missing her wig, she still had strands of hair here and there, some of it constantly coming out of her cap. Then there was Robbie. They could have easily gotten to him.

She leaned her head against Robbie. "We're going to shave your head."

"Gladly," he replied. "My eyebrows too. Maybe even my – can you shave lashes? If you can, I'm shaving them too. My arms and legs too."

Nitsy noticed Thomas was looking at her boyfriend funny.

"What?" she asked.

"I'll shave my head, but I ain't shavin' anything else."

Robbie laughed and she started to before remembering the sight of Eggo with panic written all over his face. How could she make jokes at a time like this?

"Eggo would be laughing too, you know," Robbie said. He'd known exactly what she was thinking.

"He's going to be out there, walking through the woods, like all the others." It saddened her, even more, to know his smile would be gone. Her team leader would be wandering around aimlessly, attacking any living thing he came across.

"Hey!" came a voice over the truck's engine.

At first, Nitsy thought it was Andre trying to get their attention again, but she looked through the rear window and past the front windshield to see two men and a woman standing in the center of the road.

"There's people out there," Nitsy said.

"Run 'em over!" Thomas yelled.

"Are they infected?" Robbie asked.

"I don't think so," Andre replied. "They're waving their arms around like they want to be picked up, not like they want to eat my brains or whatever." Andre leaned closer to the windshield and said, "Hal?"

28

They were stranded, weighed down with bags full of guns, and they were walking. Hal didn't like the idea, but what else were they going to do? They'd set out to save the kids at Stonewall Forge, and he couldn't think of anything better to do now that they were on foot. Walking in the opposite direction would only mean walking toward town, and they already knew what the town looked like. Those things were everywhere. At least out here, they might not be up against many of them.

As long as the damn animals stop coming at us.

Luckily for them, they hadn't come in contact with any other four-legged bastards since they'd started their stroll.

They'd walked for at least thirty minutes when headlights shone from down the road. As far as he knew, these creatures couldn't drive. That was good news. Somebody was headed toward them.

Hal was still surprised to see the oncoming vehicle when Grant and Sally threw their hands in the air and waved. They weren't quiet about it either.

"Hey!" Grant yelled.

Sally was right beside him. "Stop the truck!"

The truck didn't stop though. It kept coming, and it seemed like the driver was going to roll right over them.

"Get out of the road," Hal warned.

"He'll stop," Grant argued.

"He's not slowing down," Sally said.

When the truck was so close Hal could taste the dust coming off it, the driver slammed his foot on the brake and the truck slid to a stop about two feet in front of them. The driver rolled down his window and called out, "Hal?"

Somebody knew his name, but he wasn't familiar with the voice. It was too damn dark in the cab to get a good look at the driver, so he cautiously made his way around to the driver's side.

"Get in the back, kid," the driver said to somebody else in the cab with him.

Two kids climbed out. A teenage boy and girl. They jumped into the bed of the truck and finally, Hal was close enough to see the driver's face.

"Andre?" he asked.

"Andre," Sally whispered behind him. It took a few seconds to sink in. "Wait, *Andre* Andre? The Andre that went missing?"

"Andre, go!" a girl screamed from the back of the truck.

"They're coming! Go!" another teenager yelled.

"Come on!" Hal yelled at his friends, and they piled into the cab of the truck.

It was a tight squeeze. Hal had to throw a leg over the gear shifter. Sally climbed onto Grant's lap.

"Please! Go!" the young girl in the back yelled.

Dogs barked behind the truck, and Hal suddenly sensed what all the yelling was about. More of the damn animals were on their way.

Grant slid the rear window open and asked, "Any of you kids know how to shoot?"

"Yessir," a big country boy replied.

"Take it," Grant said as he handed the boy a pistol.

"Thank you kindly," the boy said as he turned around and shot a big black dog that was too close to the tailgate. Any closer and it might have leaped right in the truck.

"Come on, come on, come on," Andre slapped the steering wheel anxiously, begging the truck to drive faster.

The animals didn't reach them, but then it looked like Andre was easing up on the gas. The driver checked the rearview mirror, saw the animals getting closer again, and then gunned it.

"What are you doing?" Hal asked.

"I need these sonsabitches to follow us. We need them all close behind."

"Why would you want to do that?" Sally asked with a whine in her voice.

"So I can kill 'em," he said.

Hal looked at the guy he used to go to sobriety meetings with and wondered what he'd been through over the past couple of days. He looked like shit.

"Andre," Hal said. "Everybody's been looking for you, man. Where have you been?"

"Workin'," Andre said as if it were the most reasonable explanation possible.

"Workin'," Hal repeated and then chuckled. "Workin' on what, man?"

"My cousin Carl got the infection first," Andre said. "I saw it happen. Jumped all over his head. He changed. Like how you seen 'em. And I knew it was some kinda bug that got in the hair. Like little flies or worms or—"

"Lice," Sally interrupted.

Andre took his eyes off the road for a moment and looked at her. "Hey, Sally."

"Hi, Andre," she replied.

"Yeah, like lice," Andre returned to his thoughts.

He paused and there was a moment of silence.

"Hal, you remember when I told you about my farm?" Andre started right back up again.

Hal had the feeling he should know what Andre was talking about, but he didn't. Andre, from what he'd heard, was always trying some way to make money. At one point he was trying to burn images of American flags into wood so he could try and sell them to patriotic folks on Facebook. When that didn't work, he inquired about opening his own gun range. Hal had even heard he was a moonshiner at one point.

"No," he admitted. "I don't."

"It's fuckin' beautiful," Andre assured him, then turned quickly to Sally and said, "I apologize for the language, Sally."

She only smiled back at him. He was making himself sound like a lunatic.

"What's beautiful?" Grant asked, speaking up for the first time.

A flash of recognition came over Andre's face and then he said, "Hey, you're that dude who makes furniture, ain'tcha?"

Grant nodded.

"We need to talk," Andre said. "Might be some good business we can go into together."

"Tell us about the farm," Hal interrupted, trying to bring the man back to the present. They didn't have time to chat about business.

"Ladybugs," Andre said.

"Ladybugs?" Hal asked.

"Ladybugs?" Sally and Grant both said at the same time.

Hal did recall Andre mentioning something about ladybugs and organic farming.

"Ladybugs," Andre repeated. "Those vicious little bastards are gonna help us."

If Hal were a balloon, Andre had just stuck the pin in that would deflate him. All his hopes went right out the window. The excitement, that anxious, nervous energy Andre had that was driving him onward toward their destination was all based on pretty insects kids played with. He glanced into the bed of the truck and thought about these teenagers hoping the adults they'd stumbled upon would save the day.

And he's got fuckin' ladybugs.

"You... you were coming from the school?" Hal asked, trying to take the conversation as far away from insects as possible.

Andre nodded. "I was hiding out at my farm when I got the idea, but then I remembered what I'd heard about a school conference or something like that taking place out at Stonewall. Couldn't leave these kids to fend for themselves."

Hal admired Andre's bravery. They'd had the same thought. Someone had to save the kids.

"I was too late though," Andre went on. "The place was infested. Only these kids in my truck survived."

"My God," Hal replied.

"How many kids were there?" Sally asked.

"A lot," Hal answered. He'd seen so many of them when he'd visited the campus. "A whole lot."

Hal closed his eyes and leaned his head back against the seat. They were too late. How many kids had been at Stonewall Forge? Hundreds? Again, he thought about his daughter. Sweet Susanna. She would have grown to be one of the smart kids. She would have been a leader. She might have been at Stonewall Forge when all this started. He wouldn't have been able to save her any more than he'd been able to save the others.

Get out of your head. Focus on saving the ones you can save now.

Would he be able to save them? With a plan like *ladybugs,* he wasn't sure. He wished it were some kind of code word like in all the 007 movies. *Goldeneye... Octopussy... Ladybugs.* He doubted Andre was hiding a bomb in a shed though.

When they pulled off the dirt road and onto the main highway, Andre said, "We're almost there. Only gotta go up the mountain a couple of miles. They still behind me?"

Hal slid open the window to the back of the truck. "They still hunting us?"

"It's hard to see," Nitsy said as she leaned forward and peered into the darkness behind them. The cloud of dust enveloped the truck like a thick blanket.

"I need them to be followin' me," Andre said.

He stopped the truck completely.

"Maybe that ain't a good idea," Grant said. "You know, stoppin' the truck like that."

"They need to catch up to us," Andre replied.

Grant shook his head. "Yeah, but damn. We don't want 'em jumpin' into the truck."

"See anything?" Hal asked Nitsy.

Nitsy shook her head. A few feet beyond the tailgate, the dust dissipated, and a mountain lion shot through the remaining dirt. Its front paws landed on the tailgate. Its large teeth were razor-sharp, and its bloodshot eyes were wild with rage. It was halfway into the bed of the truck when Nitsy screamed and Andre stepped on the gas.

The truck leaped forward, and Andre turned right onto the highway. The force yanked the mountain lion to the side. It slid along the tailgate, scrambling to find purchase, and crying out in a banshee-like wail.

Thomas pointed his pistol at the big cat and pulled the trigger just as Andre put his foot on the gas again. The truck bucked, Thomas rocked, and the bullet flew into the beast's ear. It screamed in pain, but it didn't let go of the truck. Its fur shifted and Hal's eyes went wide. He knew what that meant.

"Shoot it, kid!" Hal yelled. "Shoot it before it's too late."

Thomas took aim again and pulled the trigger. The slug slammed right into the cat's forehead. This time it went down. Hal looked in the side mirror to see its body bounce off the street. It was only on the ground a second or two when the remaining horde of animals trampled it and kept coming.

Andre continued his back and forth pace all the way up the mountain. Hal'd been all over Clydesville, but he'd never been up this mountain. He hadn't even known there was a road up this way. The bushes were thick, the road was rough, and he figured that was exactly what Andre liked about it. The more unforgiving the terrain, the less likely cops would choose to travel that way.

Before long, they came to a dead end, and there in front of them was a tall, white, square building with an antenna on top. It looked like it might've once been a radio station.

"What the hell is this?" Hal asked.

"I told you," Andre replied. "It's my farm."

Sally scratched her head. "This don't look like a farm."

Hal had only seen one farm like this one. It was during a trip with Sheila down to Nicaragua one summer. It was before Susanna was born. Back when they loved each other dearly. Back when they found time to do things together. They'd asked a local man, a friend of the hotel owner where they were staying, to drive them around and show them around the small town. He took them to a shrimp farm. It was all indoor, and it looked a lot like Andre's place.

"All right, hurry inside," Hal yelled at the kids in the back of the truck.

Andre had sped up as they ascended the mountain, probably giving them a good five minutes lead time. Five minutes wasn't much time at all.

The kids were barely out of the truck when a siren shrieked from above. Hal glanced toward the roof and saw Andre up there cranking an old-fashioned tornado siren.

"What the hell are you doin?" Hal shouted up at him. "And how'd you get up there?"

"Is he fuckin' crazy?" Grant asked.

The kids all ran inside.

"You should see it from up here," Andre yelled. "I can see clear to Walmart! And they're hearin' me all right. You should see 'em go. A whole crowd of 'em is searching for the source of this sound. They're comin', boy!"

In the distance was the sound of dogs barking and other random animals growling.

"You're getting the attention of a lot of unsavory things!" Hal yelled up at him.

"What?" Andre asked.

The siren was going strong. He wasn't going to hear him.

Andre finished cranking the siren and hopped down from the roof. The machine continued to wail.

"That oughtta blow for a little while," Andre said.

"The fuck's wrong with you, man?" Hal asked.

"What?"

"I said—"

"I know what you said. I told you. We need them all to come this way!"

"You're crazy!"

Coming up the driveway was the crowd of animals. Grant and Sally raced into the building.

"Shit," Andre said. "We better get inside."

"You're crazy," Hal repeated as he followed Andre to the door.

Andre went in first. Hal looked once more at the monsters headed their way. Not only were there every form of wildlife the area had to offer, but two-legged beasts had come up the mountain too. People, most of whom he would probably recognize on a normal day but now looked like shit, walked beside the animals. All infected. All eager to spread their disease.

"Lord help us," Hal said as he pulled the heavy metal door shut behind him.

Andre barred it. "Don't worry, friends. They ain't gettin' in here 'til we want 'em to."

The scent of the farm hit Hal first. It was earthy, a lot like the woods he patrolled. The light scents of flowers came to him first and then cilantro. He knew that smell very well because his favorite Mexican restaurant loved to cook with cilantro, and he had to ask them to tone it down a notch every time he ordered from them.

When he finally turned around, he saw all the kids, Grant, and Sally staring slack-jawed at the center of the room. His eyes hadn't made it that far, but once they did, he understood what had captured their attention. Behind him, the creatures banged against the door and the walls, providing a drumroll for the magic there in front of him.

At the center of the room was a giant, plastic, transparent tent. Inside it stood three humungous trees that reached the ceiling. Their gigantic trunks and branches were swarming with thousands... quite possibly millions of ladybugs. The miniature, living friends of so many of the world's children looked like soldiers in a red and black army climbing over each other at the lower parts of the trees.

Between the trees and the tent's door was a blanket of grass with flowers and other shrubbery. The ladybugs were everywhere. It was like an island right in the center of Clydesville where all the planet's ladybugs had decided to call home. Some of them took flight, making their way from branch to branch or from flower to flower.

"My God," Hal said.

"Told ya," Andre said. "Ain't they beautiful?"

"What is this?" Sally asked.

"My farm," Andre said proudly. "It's not really legal right now, but this here's for all them organic farmers out there who don't like using chemicals on their fruits and vegetables. So they use ladybugs. They buy 'em in bulk and let them roam around the farm, eating all the little parasites and pesky bugs."

"And you think they'll eat," Grant started and then paused and pointed at the door with all its knocking and pounding coming from the other side, "those things?"

"They will," Andre assured them. "I seen 'em do it."

"This is unbelievable," Hal said. "Smells like cilantro."

"Yeah, they love that shit," Andre replied.

"It's so cool," the young girl with no hair agreed. "I've loved ladybugs since I was a kid, and this... this is fantastic."

"I've never seen anything like it," the other young girl added.

"Badass, evil parasite eating ladybugs," the boy with the glasses said.

The big country boy only stood there with his mouth agape.

"What are y'all's names?" Hal asked.

Nitsy was the cute bald one. It seemed Robbie was her fella. The big ol' boy with the gun was Thomas. The boy with the glasses was Bradley and the other girl was Phyllis. He'd more than likely forget the names, but at least, for now, he knew what names to shout out if shit got bad.

The pounding outside grew louder, and even though Hal heard it, he was more focused on the silent world in front of him where these pint-size beetles couldn't care less about what was going on around them. It was like watching fish in a tank. They would move around and go about their business freely until something deemed a hazard was introduced into their world.

Hal understood. They needed to introduce the infected.

Yet, even though Andre swore the ladybugs would attack the head lice, Hal found it too difficult to believe.

"In the daytime, I open up that panel there so their world can get some light," Andre said, pointing up at the ceiling. "I'll climb up there in a bit and make sure the siren keeps goin'."

"And then what?" Hal asked.

"And then we see what my little friends here can do," Andre said.

29

The siren blared. Then it died.

They'd all been sitting outside the tent, watching through the transparent fabric as the ladybugs fluttered around the room. Hal kept asking about the plan, but all Andre would tell him was, "We have to wait until they all get here."

When the shout of the siren ceased, Andre looked up at the ceiling and cursed, "Damn. That was sooner than expected."

"Now what?" Hal asked.

Hal looked exhausted, like he hadn't slept in days, and Andre had to wonder about his own appearance. The cuts and bruises from the night his other truck flipped still ached like a motherfucker. His body was stiff, and he knew the climb up to the roof would be an agonizing one. It hurt earlier when he did it, and he wasn't looking forward to feeling that pain again, but it had to be done.

"Look," Andre said as he stood and spoke to them all, "I have a plan… of sorts."

"A plan of sorts?" Bradley asked. "That doesn't sound like a very good plan."

Andre had only recently learned all their names and he had a feeling this kid would be one of the ones to challenge him. He had that class nerd vibe. Like he probably already knew everything there was to know about ladybugs and was going to suggest shit the whole night. Andre didn't have time for any snot-nosed brats. He'd only wanted to save them. Now, he was stuck babysitting.

"It's a damn plan," Andre assured him, "which is better than what I hear you proposin'!"

Bradley looked down at his lap. His little girlfriend gave his hand a squeeze. Andre waited to see if Phyllis would give him any lip. She didn't.

"Let's hear it," Grant said.

Andre cleared his throat. "I'm gonna climb up there and get that siren going again. I'll also look out to see how many of those *things* are headed this way. If it looks like we got 'em all, we'll get started."

He paused long enough for Hal to raise his eyebrows and say, "That's the whole plan?"

"No, that ain't the whole plan," Andre replied. "Then we're going to let 'em in here."

"Are you out of your fucking mind?" Hal challenged him.

"The ladybugs," Andre said as he pointed toward the tent. "We let them in here and then we hide in the other room while the ladybugs go to work."

Everyone started to argue. It was really pissing Andre off. He regretted bringing them all here. He really didn't need them around for this to go down, but they hadn't had much time, and he needed to get on with his plan. Andre rubbed his temples while the others argued with him. Or, not with him since he wasn't really a part of the argument anymore. He'd backed off and was now a spectator as the rest of them discussed the situation.

Finally, Nitsy spoke up above the rest, "Excuse me, Mr. Andre, but what is it the ladybugs are supposed to do?"

"Just Andre, honey," he replied. "And what they're supposed to do is eat those goddamn lice right off their goddamn heads."

"And if they don't?" Hal asked.

"Then we run like hell," Andre said.

Sally scoffed. Grant rolled his eyes. The kids made those stupid sounds kids make with their mouths whenever they're told to put away their phone at the dinner table or turn off their video game. Every time he saw that disgusted look on a kid's face or heard that noise, it reminded him how happy he was that he never had kids.

"You said the ladybugs are supposed to kill the creatures," Nitsy said, "but what about the hosts? All those people out there?"

"Yeah," Bradley chimed in. "Even if you kill all the microscopic ones... even if the ladybugs eat all the eggs growing on their heads, the people—"

"I like Nitsy's word, the hosts," Andre interrupted.

People sounded too personal. His wife, Lizzie, was probably out there somewhere, and he couldn't afford to think of her as a person anymore. Sure, they hadn't had the most romantic of relationships, but they were hitched, and that meant something to Andre. For all the bitching and complaining she did, there were a hundred good things about her.

Andre shook off the image of his wife cuddling up close to him on the couch to watch TV. Like an asshole, he'd started sitting in his personal reclining chair. That was a little bit fucked-up. He realized that now, and it was too late.

"They're hosts," Andre repeated.

"Sure," Bradley said, "whatever. The ladybugs can't eat the ones already inside the hosts, right?"

"Probably not," Andre said. "Sadly, I think we'll have to use the guns on them. But at least the little ones can't jump on anybody else, you know what I mean?"

"Have to expect *some* casualties in a war," Thomas said.

Andre liked that kid. It was a shame what happened to his parents, but he seemed like a smart boy.

It wasn't a perfect plan, Andre knew that, but it was the only reasonable one he'd come up with, and like Thomas said, there were always casualties in war. This was definitely a war, and he was lucky to have a weapon that might turn the tide. It just so happened he'd started this farm a while back and had made a shit ton of money selling plastic containers of these ladybugs to farmers growing organic vegetables. It also just so happened ladybugs ate pesky insects... like lice.

Hal chewed his inner cheek and then finally said, "So, your plan is to have the ladybugs kill all the eggs and lice *without hosts* and then open fire on all the hosts?"

Andre shrugged, and even as he did so, he knew he hated his plan, but if it helped prevent the spread, it was something. The pounding on the door was starting to worry him a bit. He'd thought that solid barrier would have no problem keeping *them* out until he was ready to let them in, but they wanted in here something fierce. The door might not be able to hold them much longer. He needed to get the rest of them up here before he ran out of time.

When nobody asked any other questions, Andre nodded and walked into the tent. He was careful not to step on any of the ladybugs, which was hard to do with them everywhere. They moved around his feet, flew between his legs, and one landed on his arm. Picking it up gently and putting it on a leaf, Andre whispered to the bug, "Stay right here, buddy. I need all the soldiers I can get."

At the back of the room, behind the large tree, was a Velcro flap that let him exit the tent. On the other side was a steel ladder that led up to the roof. He climbed it quickly, feeling his muscles wince and his wounds ache with each step. At the top, he unlocked a heavy hatch and shoved it open.

Next to the open hatch, he sat on the tar roof for a second. The siren was bolted to the edge, over near the front of the building, but he took a moment to appreciate the fresh, clean air outside. Inside felt stuffy to him. He'd spent so much time in the farm that he could barely appreciate the garden-like scent in there. Everyone else seemed to enjoy it. To him, it reminded him of the war and being underground and in the trenches. He felt claustrophobic in there.

If Carl had been around longer, he'd planned on bringing him into the business, mostly to help him run things in the farm while he was out handling most of the logistics. A ladybug farm required acquiring the bugs, which he did from a few spots in the country, bringing them here to the farm, and then finding buyers. All without drawing law enforcement. That was the best thing about Clydesville. The cops here were local. They lived in the same neighborhoods as the residents. They were friends. They didn't pry unless they had good reason to. The state cops were a different matter.

The moans, grunts, and growls of the creatures, or hosts as he now thought of them, were loud from down below. They were still banging on the front door and the walls. They'd tear their way in eventually.

What is their plan?

What were they hoping to do? Andre had seen enough old Sci-Fi movies to know aliens often came to earth in search of things their planet lacked like water and oxygen. Maybe cows or anuses to probe. But these fuckers, if they were even aliens, seemed to want nothing more than to drive everybody mad. What was the point of that?

He thought back to the moment he shot the deer, and he couldn't help feeling that was the start of it all. Before then, everything seemed normal. He'd gone on about his day the same way he had every other. Sure, he'd taken a few swigs of the sauce, which he wasn't proud about since he'd vowed to kick the habit, but things were pretty good. With the farm going strong, he stood to make a substantial income.

Now, this shit.

"All right, you loud pricks! Keep it down! We'll be gettin' to you shortly."

He teased them, but in reality, he wanted them to be as loud as they could be, so they'd attract more of their kind. Stepping to the edge of the roof, he looked down the mountain and saw the shopping center parking lot was now empty. He could see the majority of the road from here and he didn't notice any of them walking, which meant most of them were already here or close.

"Good. Come on, you fuckers. Come to the dinner bell."

Speaking of the bell, it was time to get the siren going again.

At the roof's edge, Andre squatted down and cranked the handle. The blast was so loud it damn near deafened him. He knew he should have worn earplugs, but he'd forgotten them. After all, he'd been busy killing fuckin' zombies for cryin' out loud.

Hosts. They're human. Remember that. They're only hosts for these lousy pieces of shit.

With his ears ringing, Andre backed up while still in the seated position.

His ass bumped into something. His elbow felt it too, and it was furry. The siren was so loud he barely heard the skittering of what was clinging to the animal's pelt, but it came to him loud enough to make his teeth clatter.

Something was behind him.

Something infected.

Andre was unarmed except for the knife at his belt. He hadn't felt the need to carry his gun up here. He was supposed to be alone, at a higher elevation, where these things couldn't get him.

From his peripheral vision, he spotted the nearby tree, and he knew. Whatever it was, it had climbed up onto the roof using that tree. Before he'd taunted them, they would have had no reason to come up to the roof, but he'd been a dumbass, and because of that, he was as good as dead.

He knew he was a goner, but at least he might have time to warn the others.

"Hal!" he yelled.

But as soon as that one word left his mouth, he felt the shower of blades hit his scalp. Like broken glass falling from fifty feet up, the tiny sharp pieces bit into him hard and his entire head felt like it was on fire. Bullets hit his skull, or at least that's how it felt to him. For a second, he remembered the pain that had come with his leg being shot up in the war, and he thought, *It feels like that... all over my head.*

Then the ringing set in, the high-pitched scream that ran through his cranium and settled somewhere in his brain. He thought his eardrums might explode. Like a syringe had been shoved through one temple and out the other, his mind felt as if it had been skewered. Andre's eyes watered and an odd numbness came over him.

With his last ounce of sanity, Andre pulled out his knife and shoved it through the throat of the mountain lion crouched behind him.

He tried to speak again, but his voice caught in his throat. He wasn't in control anymore, but the searing coals atop his head kept burning. Like his head had been dipped in acid, the pain was excruciating. And his fingers tearing through his flesh didn't help.

30

"Hal!"

"Did you hear that?" Sally asked.

Nitsy had been sitting next to Robbie on the floor. He squeezed her hand from time to time to assure her she wasn't alone, but other than that, they sat in silence. Silence meaning they didn't speak much between them, because silence definitely wasn't in the building. The *things* outside wouldn't stop banging on the door and walls. Phyllis and Bradley sat across from her, both with their hands over their ears.

She was so tired, and her eyelids kept bouncing like miniature basketballs. Even though she was terrified, her body was forcing her to sleep. Thomas seemed to have no problem resting. He was even drooling. Seeing him out cold only fueled her desire to sleep. Nitsy's eyes were dancing lazily when she heard the cry for Hal. She pulled free from Robbie and stood up.

"I heard it," she said.

She stepped toward the tent and peered through it to the other side. The hatch at the top of the ladder was still open.

"It sounded like Andre," she added, "yelling for Hal."

"The siren's going strong," Hal replied, "what could be the problem?"

"Maybe he needs your help with something," Sally suggested.

Nitsy felt a cold chill down her back. That wasn't how it sounded at all. She thought it sounded more like a painful cry or screaming for help. Not the kind of help Sally was talking about. He didn't need somebody to hand him a wrench so he could tighten a bolt. Something bad had happened to him.

When Hal moved toward the tent, Nitsy put a hand on his arm. "Wait. Don't go."

"What is it?" he asked.

"I think something's wrong."

"Wrong how? This whole situation's wrong."

"I mean wrong with Andre. When he yelled your name... it sounded like he was scared."

Hal thought about it for a second. "I don't imagine Andre being scared of much."

"Exactly."

"Want me to go with you?" Grant asked.

Hal nodded. "Might be a good idea. We don't know what's up there."

Sally covered her ears with her hands. "I wish he'd kept that damn siren off."

The siren was so loud. It set Nitsy's nerves on edge. Between that and the insistent pounding coming from outside the building, she thought she was going to lose her mind. She didn't know much about structures like this, but she couldn't imagine it would withstand much more force. The door was going to come off the hinges soon. She thought she heard debris falling on the inside of the building, like the doorframe might be giving in.

"Sally," she said. "Look."

Sally glanced over at the door and shrugged.

"It sounds like it's crumbling," Nitsy informed her. "I don't think we have much time."

"Grant?" Sally said.

By the time Nitsy looked back at the men, they were already inside the tent, making their way to the other side.

"They'll be back soon," Sally said.

Nitsy hoped she was right. She and Robbie both watched with the pads of their fingers touching the transparent material of the tent. Hal and Grant moved slowly past the bugs, careful not to squash any. There were so many. For a second, Nitsy was reminded of that game in school where her teacher filled the jar with jellybeans, and everyone had to guess how many were in there. The person who guessed closest to the correct number won the entire jar. She never got close. As she counted a few of the ladybugs and tried to come up with an estimate of how many were in there, she realized it was a waste of time. She would be wrong. She would guess nowhere close to the correct number.

"How many do you think are in there?" she asked Robbie.

"A million," he said, and he wasn't joking.

"There can't be that many, right?"

"I've lost count eight times already. I counted well over a thousand and I was still at that bush over there."

"I'd say there are about seven hundred fifty-five thousand of them," Thomas said from behind, making them both jump. Nitsy hadn't even seen him there.

"Damn, that's a random ass number," Robbie said.

Thomas only shrugged.

Hal and Grant made it to the other side of the tent and carefully crept through the Velcro seal. Nitsy could see them move to the ladder. Hal was out front. He seemed like a brave man.

"Andre!" Hal yelled. "You okay, buddy?"

At least that's what it looked like he was yelling. Nitsy couldn't hear him over the sound of the siren. It really didn't matter what he yelled. Nitsy knew he wouldn't get an answer. If Andre were still alive, he would have returned by now. The siren had been going on for several minutes already.

"I don't like this," she said, turning toward Sally.

"Me neither," she said.

"If something's wrong, I mean if he's alive, they can't leave him," Robbie argued.

"I don't know," Nitsy said.

"He could have slipped or tripped. What if he broke his leg? It could have nothing to do with what's going on out there? It sounds unlikely but people still get hurt."

She knew he was right, but she doubted it was a slip and fall or a sprained ankle. Andre was dead. Or worse.

Hal yelled something else up the ladder. It was clear there was no reply because he turned toward Grant and they discussed it. Grant shrugged his shoulders. Hal took a deep breath then gripped the ladder, clutching a pistol in his hand as he started to climb.

"Don't!" Nitsy yelled through the tent.

Hal turned toward her and stepped off the ladder. He motioned with his hand over his ear to say he couldn't hear her.

"Don't climb the ladder!" she yelled.

He still couldn't hear her. Nitsy opened the tent and stepped inside. Right away, a ladybug landed on her arm. Another touched down on her nose and another on her head.

Hal and Grant stepped through the other side.

"What did you say?" Hal asked her.

The ladybug on her nose walked around and it tickled. She giggled.

"I said don't go up there," Nitsy said. "Please."

"We have to check on Andre," Hal said.

"And close that hatch," Grant added.

Both men were barely inside the tent when something fell through the hatch behind them. It was heavy and hit the ground with a thud. Nitsy watched in horror as Hal and Grant both turned to see Andre rising on the other side of the tent flap.

There, they stared face to face with what remained of their friend. His scalp hung loosely from the top of his head, like tattered clothes ripped apart by razorblades. Blood ran down his face. His eyes were beet red and drool dripped from his lips. His left leg was broken, most likely from the fall, and he dragged it as he stepped closer to the tent.

"Nitsy, get to the other side," Hal ordered.

She was frozen in fear, and she could only watch as Andre, with one quick jerk, reached through the tent, grabbed hold of Grant's shirt, and yanked him out through the other side. Grant screamed and thrashed around wildly, but Andre bit down on Grant's neck and ripped his head to the side, tearing off a huge chunk of flesh.

Andre's hair shifted, and Grant cried out in terror and pain.

Sally screamed. So did the others behind Nitsy.

The flap was open slightly, and the ladybugs didn't react.

"Why aren't they doing anything?" Nitsy asked.

Before she got an answer, Robbie was pulling her out of the tent by her arm.

Hal took aim and fired at Andre, shooting him through the plastic wall and hitting him in the middle of the forehead. Grant was flipping around on the ground, writhing in pain, and Hal went to work quickly. He pulled on his friend's feet, yanking him into the tent. Then he backed away and watched. Still, the ladybugs didn't react.

A few moved closer to his body, seeming to be interested in him, but they didn't jump on him the way Andre seemed to think they would.

"Grant!" Sally screamed from behind.

"Shoot him, Hal!" Nitsy begged. "Put him out of his misery."

Hal pointed at him and pulled the trigger.

31

They didn't react. They didn't do *shit*. Andre had brought them all the way up here to this building, and now they were going to be stuck here. Hal covered his ears for a second to block out the sounds of the siren and the creatures trying to burst through the door. He thought he was going to lose his mind.

We're fucking trapped!

"It won't work," Nitsy said as she slid back down to her ass on the floor.

Hal didn't want to hear any of them. Andre was dead, Grant was dead, and they were trapped.

"Fuck, fuck, fuck, fuck, fuck," he repeated under his breath.

"Grant," Sally cried into Phyllis's shoulder.

"It's not going to work," Nitsy repeated.

"We need to close that hatch," Thomas, the big ol' country boy said.

"Everybody shut up," Hal begged. "Please, be quiet for a second."

They didn't get any quieter. The siren wailed, the creatures pounded and shrieked, Nitsy said things that were blatantly obvious, her boyfriend reassured her of things he couldn't be sure of, Sally cried for a man Hal was sure she didn't love, the caretaker's boy kept volunteering to close the hatch when he had no business with it, and the other two whispered encouraging words to whoever would listen. Hal was going to lose his damn mind.

"Maybe the ladybugs couldn't see them," Robbie said. "I mean… look at them now."

"They're chowing down, now," Thomas agreed.

Hal lifted his gaze and turned to stare through the tent. The boys were right. The ladybugs were practically covering Grant's head now. Hal, who'd been sitting on the ground, slid closer to the tent flap, and stuck his head in.

He couldn't fucking believe it.

"Do you hear that?" he asked.

Nitsy looked at him like he'd lost his mind. He wasn't crazy. He knew what he was hearing.

"Hear what?" Nitsy asked.

"Squealing," Hal said with a soft chuckle. "They're fucking squeal-ing. I think the ladybugs are eating them right off his fucking head."

Robbie moved closer and soon after Nitsy, Phyllis, Bradley, Thomas, and Sally too. They all heard it.

"It's because they didn't jump," Hal suggested. He wasn't sure about it, but it seemed to make sense. "When Andre pulled Grant out of the tent, they didn't see the things jump from Andre to Grant. They were already on Grant when I pulled him into the tent. So, maybe it only took the bugs a minute to sense out the little fuckers."

"That's not great," Robbie said. "These things are going to come through that door any second, and when they do, we won't have a minute for the ladybugs to *sense them out* as you put it."

He was right. They'd all be dead if it took that long.

And they kept on pounding from outside. Hal stood and moved closer to the door. The frame was starting to crack. They were pushing right through the damn wall. If he had to guess, they had maybe ten minutes, tops, before these creatures shoved the door right through the frame. If that didn't happen first, the walls would come tumbling down.

They were in a death trap. They could risk climbing up to the roof and trying to get down that way. Maybe most of the creatures were over here by the door and they could hop down on the other side. It was a tall building though and the chances of them getting hurt on the way down were high. That was if whatever had gotten to Andre wasn't still up there waiting for them.

"We need those things to jump," Hal said. "Or at least to be active enough for the ladybugs to see."

"Got any ideas?" Phyllis asked.

It was clear her boyfriend, Bradley, was trying to come up with something. For a second, it seemed like he might figure this out. Then he lowered his gaze and Hal knew he'd given up.

"I've got one," Hal said, "but it means I probably won't be joining you all on the rest of this journey."

"What?" Sally asked. "What the hell does that mean?"

"It means it's a suicide note," Nitsy said.

Everyone was quiet.

"Look, I don't have a whole lot to live for," Hal told them. "When Susanna, my daughter, was taken from me, my whole life fell apart. When my wife Sheila went to be with her, I knew I needed to be close behind, but I haven't been brave enough to do it. Maybe this is my way out."

"Hal," Sally said, "no, we'll find another way."

"There is no other way," he insisted.

"Why don't we burn this place to the ground?" Thomas suggested. "Fire seemed to work back at the campus."

It wasn't a bad idea. Hal had considered that option himself. Fire killed most things, and he was sure it would kill these too. If the U.S. Army showed up and took care of it, that might work, but he had no flame thrower to aim directly at them. If he set the building ablaze, they'd simply run off into the woods and wreak havoc someplace else. That would be a temporary fix and definitely wouldn't save them. The second they stepped outside the fiery building they'd be surrounded again.

No, his idea was the only one he could think of that might work.

"It's a good idea," Hal said, "but they'd only run away."

Pieces of the wall came down on the floor around the door. They didn't have much time.

"Trust me," Hal said. "I'll do everything I can to get back to you guys, but I need to do this. We have no time. Come with me."

They all argued with him as he ushered them to a back room that was clearly used as an office and bedroom. It didn't surprise him that Andre slept here. It was where he'd hid since his truck crashed.

"Tell us what you're going to do," Nitsy demanded. "It's kind of important. What if it fails?"

"Then you all can climb out that tiny window and take your chances," he said as he pointed at a narrow window above Andre's desk. "Maybe if enough of them are in here, none of them will be out there."

Hal stepped back out into the main room and retrieved his duffle bag. When he returned to the office, he reached into his bag and handed them each a gun. "My friend Clementine gave me these guns," he told them. "She was one hell of a lady. You take care of these. They'll just be a precautionary measure. Now, lock this door behind me. If I start barking out orders, follow them. If you hear nothing but yelling and screaming and they come to this door, then climb out that window and run like hell."

Thomas raised both eyebrows. "I don't think I can fit through that window."

"Hal, no," Sally said as she wrapped her arms around him.

"For Grant," he replied. "He didn't deserve to go out like that. Neither did Andre or Clementine or any of those kids back at Stonewall."

She closed her eyes. God, she was a pretty woman. Hal had never looked at a woman and found her truly attractive. Not since his Sheila had died. But he thought Sally was a pretty girl. She kissed him on the forehead and said, "For Grant. For the others."

"Mr. Hal," Nitsy said.

"Hal," he corrected her.

"Hal," she replied. "I don't imagine you'd remember this if you were turned into one of those things, but if you decide you need our help, use the code word..." She looked around the room and saw a music CD cover on Andre's desk. It was Hank Williams Jr.'s 'Family Tradition.' She picked it up and showed it to him, pointing at the first word in the album title. "You yell out the word 'family' and we'll come running. Guns blazing. You might not have a daughter or a wife, but we're family now. Use that word. Family."

Hal nodded. "Family."

When he closed the door behind him, he felt his eyes welling up. Nitsy reminded him a bit of Susanna if Susanna had grown to her age. He needed to do this for the kids in that office. He wouldn't yell out that word, *family*, unless he really thought there was a chance for them to help.

The door was so close to caving in. He doubted he had even a few minutes left. They'd come bursting in here, all manners of beast, ready to take his head off. He'd be waiting for them. He had a pistol in each hand, fully loaded.

He walked into the tent and looked around at the ladybugs. They were everywhere. He knew he was crazy for talking to them, but it felt wrong not to. "Hey little buddies. Listen up. I need your help. There are going to be some real bad things coming in here to get me. I need you to protect me. Can you do that? If we work together, I think we can end this here."

Of course, there was no answer, but one of the ladybugs landed on his nose. He'd seen one do it to Nitsy earlier and he couldn't help thinking maybe this was the leader of all these bugs. Maybe this was his or her way of saying, "Don't worry. We've got your back."

He laughed. It was a dumb thought.

To complete his plan, he only needed one thing from this room. He set his guns down on the grass, walked over to the one plant in the room he was familiar with, and started picking off its leaves. He held one up to his nose to make sure he was taking the right plant, and its scent was undeniable. It was definitely cilantro. The ladybugs were all over the leaves. He carried as much of the plant with him as he could when he made his way back to the biggest tree at the center of the room.

The ladybugs swarmed over the tree. It was definitely their home base. They looked like a blanket of red and black draped over the tree's trunk. Only this blanket moved. It was truly a sight to see. The sheer number of them seemed impossible.

Hal was afraid of squishing them. He needed as many of them alive as possible, and he needed them on his side. So, he carefully pushed them away from the ground in front of the tree, and when he'd cleared a large enough spot, he sat down. He reached for his guns and brought them closer to him, so they'd lie on the ground at his sides. The lady-bugs were already crawling on him.

If these had been any other kind of bug, he wasn't sure he could handle it. If they'd been cockroaches, he would have been in that office with Sally and the kids. But these were the child-friendly bug from his youth. He was pretty sure they were supposed to bring good luck.

To make sure as many of them came to him as possible, he placed the cilantro leaves on top of him. Some on his lap, some on his shoulders, and the rest right on top of his head. The ladybugs responded as he hoped they would. They loved the stuff. If they didn't, Andre wouldn't have had it in here.

As Hal sat and waited, the overhead heat lamps caused him to sweat. It was either that or nerves. Quite possibly both.

The pounding outside continued. From where he sat, Hal could watch the door and would see if any of them entered.

Any second now.

He wasn't sure if he was imagining it or not, but he could have sworn the door was starting to buckle. It almost looked like it was starting to dent inward. The shrieks grew louder in anticipation. They knew they were about to burst in here.

Hal could barely sit still. His heart threatened to rip through his chest and run away.

The sounds were the worst part.

It was like an entire zoo was outside that door waiting to kill him. Humans included. The ceiling crumbled in front of the door. Debris fell on the ground. It sounded like the horde of infected creatures outside had found a battering ram and were working in unison. Of course, that wasn't the case, but the force with which they hit the door was so powerful it vibrated the floor beneath him.

When the door finally caved inward, it was like an ant hill bursting. He'd once seen a crowd of cockroaches fall out of a cabinet in a filthy apartment in Nashville. They seemed to stumble over each other as the door was pulled open. The creatures outside fell the same way, like a black tidal wave of death scattering through the small space.

Then the door fell all the way to the ground, and whatever was outside got so excited to enter, chunks of the cinderblock wall came down too. The clicking and skittering sounds fell toward Hal like an avalanche coming to decimate him.

Hal's first instinct was to run, but he gripped his gun handles instead, and he waited. The smart thing to do would be to close his eyes, but he couldn't do that either. Not seeing was worse than seeing.

And what he saw was terrifying.

A bear with its entire snout ripped to shreds pushed through the opening. It let out a growl that made Hal piss himself. His bladder actually let loose and filled his pants. The teeth on the thing were huge.

Climbing over it, as if it weren't a bear at all, was a woman with long, stringy hair. One eyeball oozed out of its socket and one cheek was ripped open, quite possibly by the bear, so now her muscle and teeth showed through the side of her face.

A wolf came through the opening and was missing a leg. It dragged itself through the bottom of the crushed wall.

Were they out there fighting each other?

It seemed entirely possible. Everything coming through the wall seemed totally destroyed but still hellbent on finding victims or... new hosts.

None of them had seen him yet. As all these monsters came piling into the building, they were lost. They didn't know which way to go. Some of them were headed toward the office where Sally and the kids were hiding. It was time to be a hero.

God, if it's my time to go, please make this as painless as possible and please bring me home to see my wife and my baby girl.

Hal closed his eyes and yelled, "Over here! You want some fresh meat? Come in here and get it."

The room went silent for a second. Almost like the creatures couldn't believe their ears, like they couldn't believe the audacity of this man.

A cow pushed its way into the room. It almost got stuck in the entrance, but it fought its way through, and one of the door hinges cut into its side and ripped along the length of its body. The cow mooed, breaking the silence. The long gash that now ran along its side barely leaked blood, and the cow hardly seemed to register the incision.

It was the human woman with the stringy hair that approached him first.

Behind her was the bear. Then the wolf and two other humans. Hal couldn't quite tell what sex the first one was. His face was so badly mangled, and the front of his body was covered in blood. He thought it must be a man. The other one was definitely a guy. A tall, skinny man with his left arm nearly ripped all the way off.

"I said I'm in here, you pieces of shit! I'm right in here! You want some fresh meat? Here's your chance."

Behind him came a new sound. It was the purr of a cat. Only, it didn't sound like a small feline. This wasn't the house pet kind. Hal turned his head slowly and watched as a mountain lion pushed through the Velcro strip. The mountain lion was big, with fur that should have been tan, nearly white, if not for the knife protruding from its throat and the growing bloodstain at the front of it.

Andre.

This must have been the beast that turned him. Hal smiled, knowing his brave buddy had gotten one last lick in.

But he also knew this was the end.

The other monsters were in front of him, making their way slowly into the tent, but it would be this one behind him that did him in. Any second now, those lice would leap, and then he'd be like all the others.

He wasn't ready to go out yet. He needed to go out fighting. Slowly, he lifted the pistol in his left hand and pointed it up at the mountain lion's chin.

Its fur shifted and he heard the noise the lice made. Their cricket-like calling. They were going to jump.

He pulled the trigger and the boom was deafening in the small room. The mountain lion screamed and fell down dead, but not before its lice made their leap. Their final attempt at survival before their host hit the ground.

Hal watched in terror, knowing his head was their destination. This was the end.

Then something incredible happened. The ladybugs around him went crazy. The ones on his head flew to meet the cloud of lice head-on. The squeal of the lice was definite this time. He knew he'd heard it earlier. Now, they squealed for their lives as the ladybugs flew right into the black mist and found dinner.

Still, Hal waited to see if he was going to be infected. Surely, at least one of them had hit his head. He felt the movement there in his hair and he knew the pain would hit any second. He'd heard others scream as they transformed, but then it dawned on him that his head was covered with ladybugs. It was the bugs walking around, eating the cilantro, and now waiting to chomp down on any lice that might make it through their flying brethren.

Hal slid back toward the tree, closer to the ladybugs.

What must have been a hundred of the creatures now swarmed the inside of the farm, searching for fresh hosts, and the ladybugs had homed in on them now.

The ladybugs went crazy. They took to the air, all at the same time. They were so thick Hal couldn't see. The air above him was black. Like a cartoon bunch of bees chasing after prey, this thick black shape soared through the air. Pieces of it broke off and landed on the heads, fur, and hides of all the animals and humans in the room.

Some of the creatures tumbled over each other at the tent's entrance, propping the flap open, and allowing the ladybugs to fly out in search of more food.

Squeals went up around him as the ladybugs feasted on the lice.

The bear roared and swiped at the space all around him. Its claws swept the air, but it was too late. The ladybugs were all over him, and the lice screamed.

Dragging itself along the ground, the wolf howled and chomped at the air, but again, the ladybugs had already identified it as a target and were slamming into its fur.

The woman with the stringy hair hit her knees and cried out. Her head was covered in a helmet of red and black.

It was the most amazing thing Hal had ever seen or would ever see in his entire life. They protected him. They were fighting with him. They were hungry, and they'd found their cuisine.

Hal could do nothing but sit and watch the beautiful insects devour the monsters that had tormented them all night and had killed so many people in Clydesville. Andre was a fucking genius. If he hadn't brought them up here, this may have never ended.

Thank you, God.

For a second, he was sad. As he watched the human hosts fall to the floor and the animal ones fight for their lives, he thought of all they'd lost tonight. There was only one way this would end for them. He'd have to kill them all.

He also thought of Susanna and Sheila. He'd been happy at the thought of finally leaving this planet and seeing them again. He hadn't been thrilled to die, and he was afraid of the pain he knew he would feel, but he'd been ready to see them again.

Now, that would have to wait.

It took what Hal guessed was about thirty minutes for the ladybugs to eat all of the lice and their eggs. When they flew back to the tree, he knew they were done. Unfortunately for him, each body in the building was still infected. Whatever had infiltrated their bodies was still in there, and they were coming for him.

The girl with the stringy hair raised her head and lifted her chest up with her arms. She stared right at him and grinned.

It was his time to finish what his tiny buddies had started.

"Let's do this," he said as he put a bullet in the girl with the stringy hair's head. She fell back to the floor.

This was the part he couldn't handle alone.

As much as he didn't want to do it, he was hit with the realization that he could quite possibly make it out of here alive if he had help. He shot the wolf and then the bear five times. He would run out of bullets before he could kill all hundred or so of these bastards.

He thought of Nitsy and her code word. He'd originally had no plan to use it, but those kids could help him stop these things from escaping. Hal smiled as he leaned his head back against the tree and yelled, "Family!"

In no longer than ten seconds, the office door burst open, and the sweet sound of gunfire filled his ears.

"It worked!" he yelled over the sound of the blasts. "The bugs ate the lice! Kill the hosts!"

And they did.

Like a video game come to life, these kids blazed their way through the farm and shot everything that was no longer human. Hal did his part and watched as the bodies hit the ground.

These kids might never forget this, but at least they'll live to know they might have saved the world tonight.

The air smelled of gunpowder, the kids' maniacal laughter filled his ears, and Hal smiled knowing he would finally rest tonight. The hosts would all die. Hal and his ragtag team of teenagers, plus Sally, had won.

32

The side of the bus read Carnal Cavity and Cyanide Super Soaker –
Two Bands, One Nationwide Tour.

Nobody would be excited to see it. Not unless they were diehard
heavy metal fans who kept up with the scene. It was a nice bus though.
It was once owned by Greyhound, so it had the old fabric seats that
now smelled like pot and karate dojo. Marijuana and sweaty feet.

Carlisle drove the bands around because his kids were all adults
now, their kids were in high school, and his wife left him ten years ago
for a younger man. He used to be in a band himself back in his twenties and he smoked medical marijuana now, so he figured why the hell
not. Driving this bus wasn't much more difficult than driving the
camper he used to take his family up into the mountains in.

In fact, his family might have been a lot louder. These guys usually
stayed up late either working on music or playing video games, but
they only got really wild when they let groupies into the bus after a
show. Carlisle had to admit, some of the women they picked up were
even able to get him aroused, and that wasn't easy to do nowadays.
Then, some of the others were so skanky he was afraid he'd get an
STD when they blew him a kiss on the way out.

"What a sweet old man."

"Look at the old pervert watching."

"He reminds me of my grandpa."

The things these women said to him or about him should have infuriated him. They would have a few years earlier. He couldn't remember when it happened, but at some point it was like a switch was flipped, and he stopped giving a damn. They could have said just about anything to him now and he would have shrugged it off. As long as he got paid and was able to think of things other than Angela and the young Russian stud she'd left him for, he was okay.

"Hey, Mitch, I need to stop for gas," Carlisle called over his shoulder.

Mitch Hedrum was the lead singer for Carnal Cavity, if you could call it singing. He'd heard the boy sing a few times and when he wasn't busy trying to impress his hardcore fans, he actually had a nice set of pipes on him. Only yesterday he'd heard him singing Journey's 'Faithfully' almost as perfect as Steve Perry. That was when nobody else was around, of course, and Carlisle would tell no one about it.

Like the 80s bands these guys based themselves on, Mitch had long, messy black hair that hung down past his shoulders. He wore makeup on stage. Carlisle didn't understand that, but he didn't challenge it. He wouldn't have been caught dead wearing makeup back when he played guitar for Herbal Hiatus. None of the guys would have. They sent messages through their music back then, and the message wasn't that it was ok to glamour up. No, they were badasses back then. They worked construction sites and patrolled the mean streets of Pittsburgh during the day, took to the stage at night, and fucked groupies in the early morning hours. That was how he met Angela.

Angela. My queen.

"Mitch," he said again, "I need to stop for gas."

Mitch finally lifted his heavy eyes from the notepad he was scribbling in. Carlisle imagined it was either song lyrics or he was doodling ideas for the band's new logo.

"Okay, mate," Mitch said.

He threw the word "mate" around like he was from England or Australia. He was from Houston.

"Where are we anyway?" Mitch asked.

"Fifteen... twenty miles from Clydesville I suppose," Carlisle replied. That was what the last sign he passed said anyway. Wherever the hell Clydesville was. Somewhere in West Virginia.

The bands had a party they were going to in Myrtle Beach, then they were headed down to Georgia for the Battle of the Broke Bands. It was a small band, indie rock, competition that from what Carlisle witnessed last year, was less about the music and more about the dope. It was the Woodstock of his day only with lesser known bands. Naked people sliding through mud, people fucking all over the place, and clouds of smoke that threatened to rain bongwater.

"Good," Mitch said, "I need to stretch my legs anyway."

Carlisle pulled the big bus into a gas station parking lot. It was the only place in sight. One of those quick stop joints. Get in, fill up, take a piss, grab a snack, and get the hell out of our state kind of places.

"If anybody wants to step off the bus for a few minutes, now's your chance," Mitch said. "I know some of y'all wanna fill your lungs with cancer."

For all the marijuana Mitch smoked, he wouldn't let anyone light up a cigarette on the bus. Not even those vape things everyone was smoking.

"Yeah, I need a smoke," lead guitarist for Carnal Cavity, Vick Timms, announced.

"Me too," went up around the bus.

The rest of the band: Charlie Morris, Jordan Long, and Opie Sanders stepped out followed by all the members of Cyanide Super Soaker: Cliff Downs, Roger Rickshaw, Leanne Main, Cynthia Kitt, and Harry St. James.

Pete Barrett was the manager of both bands. He and Carlisle got along fairly well. They were both outsiders as far as the bands were concerned. They often shared conversation over whiskey and cigars.

"I'm starved," Pete said as he brought up the rear. "I'm gonna go inside and see if they have any chips or donuts. Maybe a honeybun or something."

"If you find any kind of pastry, buy me one, would ya?" Carlisle asked. "I need to fill this sucker up with fuel."

"Sure thing."

By the time Carlisle made it off the bus, all the metal heads were already crowded out by the highway with a cloud of smoke around them. Mitch was inside the gas station with Pete.

Removing the nozzle from the gas tank, Carlisle started filling up the big beast of a bus. It took forever and this was clearly going to be one of those tanks that pumped fuel at a snail's pace. He had his head down and was close to nodding off when he heard the rumble of engines and the band members excited about something.

"Holy shit, man," Leanne Main called out, her pink pigtails blowing in the wind.

"The fuckin' Army's here, bro," Jordan added.

He had his arm around Leanne. The two had been having sex since the start of the tour. They were the glue holding these two bands together. With all the bands' bickering and arguing, they were close to traveling in separate buses.

Carlisle looked past the band mates and toward the highway they'd exited to get to the gas station. From where he now stood, he could see the overpass where forest green, armored vehicle after armored vehicle sped by.

"Go get 'em, boys!" Roger Rickshaw, the class clown of the bunch who was always drunk, yelled.

"It's not like they're driving to war," Carlisle said under his breath, "you stupid son of a bitch."

"Where do you think they're going?" Mitch asked, causing Carlisle to flinch.

He hadn't heard the man approaching.

"Got you some of those pecan swirl cinnamon roll things," Pete said as he held up a small paper bag. "I'll put it in your seat." He noticed the line of army trucks flying by and said, "Must be a base in Clydesville."

That was probably it. That made the most sense.

"Yeah," Carlisle agreed. "Maybe they're headed back from a training exercise."

"Plenty of wooded areas around here for that kind of thing," Mitch said. "We used to do our training exercises at Camp Bullis."

"I didn't know you were in the army," Carlisle said, suddenly having a whole new respect for the boy.

"Air Force," Mitch informed him, "was only in for about a year though before they found…" he shrugged his shoulders for the next part as if to say you should know this part already, "… weed in my system."

"Of course," Carlisle replied.

Mitch laughed. "Hmm. Guess we're not the only ones up this hour."

Carlisle followed Mitch's nod and saw a man walking out of the tree line about thirty yards or so away from where the band members were gathered. He had short blond hair, raggedy clothes, and walked with a limp. Carlisle couldn't be sure, but it looked like he had a long scar on his face. He was definitely a local boy who'd seen a brawl or two.

"Probably on his way to work," Pete said.

The interesting thing about the man was it didn't seem like he was headed toward the gas station at all. In fact, it seemed like he was interested in the band members themselves. Carlisle wondered if he was a fan. Did he see the names on the side of the bus and get excited? He sure looked enthusiastic about reaching them.

"Looks like he's headed our way," Mitch said, "I better get over there and make sure Roger doesn't say anything to piss off a local."

"Good idea," Pete said.

They both walked over to the other band members. Carlisle was stuck to this damn gas pump while it slowly did its job. He might be here all damn day trying to fill up this bus. The cost of gas had risen, and it seemed each time they filled up was more expensive than the last.

"Whoa," Carlisle heard Roger say.

Leave it to Roger to be the first to say something.

That guy was going to be the reason they all ended up in jail someday. He was always pissing somebody off. This time, it seemed he'd
set his sights on the local boy limping toward him. Now that he was
closer, Carlisle could definitely see he had a scar and his eyes were
wide open, crazed looking.

Wind blew through all the band members' hair and Carlisle chuckled. It reminded him of a shampoo commercial.

"Hey, pal, good morning," Roger called out to the local man.

"Roger," Mitch said with a warning tone.

"What? I'm just saying good morning."

"Watch it."

"Whatever, man."

The local man limped closer. He was only ten feet away when
Carlisle swore he heard a growl.

"What's wrong with him?" Leanne asked.

"Hey, stay back, man," Jorden warned him.

The local man didn't listen to the warnings. He kept coming.

"He's bleeding," somebody in the group said.

"Nah, he's really fucked up," somebody else said.

"I'm going to need you to back up," Pete ordered.

But the local man kept coming. His growl grew louder.

"What's wrong with his hair?" somebody asked.

That was the last thing Carlisle heard before the PFFT sound. What
appeared to be a black cloud burst forth from the local man's head and
spread out over the entire crowd of band members.

"What the fuck!" Mitch yelled.

Everyone was swatting at the air. Then they were smacking their
own heads, then clawing at them. Roger was the first one to scream.
He shrieked like he was mad. Then the others followed. Everyone was
screaming and scratching at their own heads. Some of them fell over,
some dropped to their knees, and some clawed at the others.

And there was blood.

So much blood.

Carlisle replaced the nozzle on the gas pump, closed the gas valve
on the bus, and then backstepped slowly toward the bus door. It was

either get on the bus or run toward the gas station. He chose the bus. The gas station attendant was on his own.

Mitch was the first to slam into the bus door. He slapped at it and growled, foam oozing from his mouth. His hair had been torn back from the front of his head, revealing a bloody mess beneath. Carlisle looked at him for a second and couldn't believe that only a couple minutes before he'd been talking to him, having a normal conversation, and now this.

The other band members reached the bus and banged against it. They slapped the windows, clawed at the siding, and tried climbing onto the bus. Carlisle had no other option but to leave them here. He started the engine, he put the bus into drive, and he gunned it. He left the gas station in his rearview mirror and pulled onto the highway while the crazed band members walked slowly after him in the direction of Virginia.

It finally occurred to him why they'd seen the Army vehicles, but if the Army was headed toward Clydesville, they were going in the wrong direction.

The End.

Thank you so much for reading Scalp. I hope that ladybug ending helped relieve some of that head itching. I hope you liked the story enough to take a look at my other work. You'll find a list on the About the Author page coming up.

If you haven't already, you should definitely check out A Foreign Evil: Diablo Snuff 1, Passion & Pain: A Diablo Snuff Side Story (where you first meet Kong), The Grindhouse: Diablo Snuff 2, and keep your eyes open for The Maddening: Diablo Snuff 3. That one will be on its way soon if it's not already published by the time you're reading this. You might also want to check out my full-length novel, Grad Night, which loosely mentions Diablo Snuff.

Thank you again for reading, and if you have a chance to review this book, every review is always so appreciated.

ABOUT THE AUTHOR

My name is Carver Pike. Since as far back as I can remember, I've been fascinated by everything horror. I'd sit cross-legged in front of the TV and watch The Texas Chainsaw Massacre while devouring a bowl of Kaboom cereal. I always wished the ghost at the end of each episode of Scooby-Doo wouldn't be just another man behind the mask. I wanted real ghastly ghouls, dastardly demons, and malevolent monsters.

At some point, I knew I couldn't sit back and keep watching this horror world from the stands. I wanted to be in the game. So, now I wield this virtual pen and sling ink onto this page with the hopes of someday being a major player. I want to create those worlds you visit, feed that fear that keeps you up late at night, and entertain you in ways only the greatest storytellers can.

I'm currently living in West Virginia where there is plenty of spooky stuff to write about. When I'm not writing, I'm usually watching horror movies, reading a good book, or interacting with readers on social media.

Hopefully, we'll form a great author-reader relationship and you'll come to trust that Carver Pike will always keep you entertained.

Check out http://www.CarverPike.com for more info.

ALSO BY CARVER PIKE

Be advised, some of the other works by Carver Pike are graphic in nature and should only be read by a mature audience. Make sure you read the blurb first to see if a book is for you.

The Edge of Reflection Series

Twisted Mirrors

Figments of Fear

Seed of Sin

The Fractured Fallen

Diablo Snuff Series

A Foreign Evil

Passion & Pain: A Diablo Snuff Side Story

The Grindhouse

Slaughter Box: A Diablo Snuff Story

Grad Night

Redgrave

Shadow Puppets: Scarecrows of Minnow Ranch

Scalp

The Collective Series (a 10-episode multi-author series)

We All Fall Down: Quills and Daggers 2 (Episode 10)

Discovering Ivory in a Charcoal Cave: A Journey to Beat Depression

www.ingramcontent.com/pod-product-compliance
Lightning Source LLC
Chambersburg PA
CBHW020941260626
47169CB00006B/1768